Nightmare Voyage

From Collision to Redemption

Capt. Marlena Brackebusch

Island Sailing Publishing
Naples

This book is a work of fiction. Any names, characters, places, and incidents are purely the imagination of the author. Any resemblance to actual locations, business establishments, people living or dead, or events is coincidental.

Island Sailing of SW Florida, inc Publishing
PO Box 472
Naples, Fl 34106

Please visit our website at www.sailnaples.com and www.islandsailingpublisher.com

Printed in the United States of America

ISBN: 0-6154-4591-8
ISBN-13: 9780615445915

Dedication

For my dear brother, Warren, who is always the wind beneath my wings.

Acknowledgments

Capt. Kris Baker, my wonderful sister. Thanks for all you support in this endeavor and throughout my life. And thanks for putting up with all the revisions and for supplying some great characters, especially Eva.

Capt. Toby Castellarin. Thanks for you endless hours of listening to me try to write this thing. Thanks for all the proof reading.

Capt. Vic Farmer. Thanks for the initial proof-reading and all your encouragement and making me realize there was a better way to structure my writing. I hope I got it right!

Other Novels
by Capt. Marlena Brackebusch

Treacherous Voyage

The Ultimate Voyage

Chapter 1. Alone at Sea

It was a dark, dirty night, like many nights before. The waves calmed down. Even though a chill crept through me, the smooth water was a welcome relief. Only hours before, Joey and I were coasting on the waves, driven southwest by a warm fifteen-knot wind behind us. The sailing yacht, a thirty-eight footer named *Wind Rose,* was chewing up the miles from Boston to Ft. Lauderdale, Florida.

Now everything had changed. The long, undulating swells of the ocean passed beneath me. I drifted completely alone, wearing nothing but my life jacket, T-shirt, and shorts. The strobe light on the floatation device blinked away as I kicked in the bigger swells. It was a great effort to keep my head above the surface of the cold ocean.

"How the hell did this happen?" I yelled at the impersonal sea.

There were many more hours until dawn.

"Hang on, Linda." The sound of my own voice was reassuring. Someone would find me soon, right?

It took great effort focusing my eyes on the green glow of the watch dial which read two A.M. Fortunately, the rain squalls which pummeled me earlier moved off to the west. Wow, what a big swell. The breaking crest nearly crashed over me. I turned my head quickly, thrashing with my hands and feet. The foam slapped the back of my head.

"Joey, where the heck are you?" Dammit, Linda, you will not cry. For the past two hours, I've hollered for my lost partner every fifteen minutes, since the dim outline of the sailing yacht was thrust away by the sea.

Joey and I were inseparable for the fifteen years since his divorce. Was his wife sick and tired of the traveling which separated him from his family? My partner owned a trucking company, driving his big rig stuffed with all kinds of freight around the U.S.

A cold wave slammed into my face, bringing me back to the present. There was no relief from the abrasive salt stinging my eyes. The rough plastic of the inflatable life jacket chafed my neck. The skin was rubbed raw. A sliver of moon added faint light to the slick, dark ocean.

"Dammit, Linda, you're such an idiot. Why the hell didn't you hook the tether to your safety harness on to something?" When I made the Mayday call from the cockpit, I should have latched the strap. One minute of inattention may cost me my life.

Tears formed for the hundredth time in only a few short hours. Even though the boat was sinking, there was a better shot at survival if I was with Joey. Did he manage to launch the liferaft?

The blink from the strobe light allowed my eyes to catch movement to the right. A streak of light shimmered below. Water erupted in front of me as the shadow of a fin zigzagged back and forth. A moment later, the apparition disappeared into the sea.

"Don't panic, girlfriend. It was probably nothing."

There was only silence. I stared into the pitch-black water, seeing nothing. My eyes rose to scan the horizon. It would be great to find the liferaft or a cushion from the boat. Something to hang onto would make my life easier. There was only water.

"OK, so I need a plan." Even though my life seemed like a chaotic trip around this planet with a lover fifteen years my senior, I was always very organized and self-sufficient. Joey's egocentric mentality only contributed to my capabilities. I had to excel at everything to survive.

Splash. Something broke the surface of the water behind me. I swiveled around to see the tip of a triangular fin submerge.

"I guess I don't need my degree in marine mammal biology to figure out who you are, now do I?"

The water all around was the fabled Gulf Stream, one of the world's most prolific fishing zones. It was also home to one of the planet's largest apex predators of the sea—sharks.

Panic flooded my senses.

"Dammit, Linda, you need to stay calm." My shout didn't help the situation. OK, I thought. What did I have to fight with?

I realized there was no dive knife strapped to the usual spot on my leg. It was always there when I went scuba diving. I could count on no weapons, only my two fists, which were clenched as tightly as my teeth.

The pink beginnings of a new day were hardly noticed. My focus on the shark intensified. As I sensed movement off to the right, my pulse raced. The sea erupted to my left. Fins slashed toward me, boiling the water.

A firm blow to my ribs thrust me aside. The ragged breaths struggled out while my body tensed for the inevitable pain from the shark's bite.

The swirling ocean subsided to the unmistakable breaths of dolphins. Gentle curved fins slowly circled me. Having swum with wild marine mammals before, I had no fear of them. These gentle guardians of the seas dealt with the shark, for now. The first rays of dawn caressed the ocean, giving me a glimmer of hope. My attention diverted to the searing dryness in my throat.

A few rays of sunlight stretched over the horizon. It was great to see the dawn of another day. Eagerly, my eyes scanned the vast world around me. With the growing daylight, I should be able to find something to hang on to. Any minute now, a Coast Guard or fishing boat will pop over the horizon. With the burgeoning glow, the rescuers should locate me easily.

As morning neared noon, my stomach growled in protest of the many hours without food. Hunger was the least of my problems. The sun rose high overhead, scorching me. There was a gritty, salty desert in my throat.

"Where are you, Coast Guard?" Morehead City, North Carolina and its Coast Guard base were only a short ride away by a fast patrol boat. Many hours had passed since I set off the EPIRB emergency beacon. Now, as cat's paws flickered on the surface, the wind picked up. No rescue boats broke the solid line of the horizon.

"Where are all the fishing boats?"

A couple of hours passed with the sea still empty. The waves bounced me around like a beach ball. In my past sailing adventures, the Gulf Stream had always amazed me with its azure waters sparkling. Normally this electric blue area was really beautiful to see. Now it was a daunting wasteland.

OK, so they were taking a long time to find me, but it should be soon, right?

Tears threatened again.

"Linda, don't cry. Be tough. You can do this."

I steeled myself.

"Why are the damn waves picking up? Do you really have to make this harder on me?"

The inflatable PFD did a pretty good job of keeping my head above water, but I still had to paddle in the bigger swells. The baby blue sky above would normally make me smile. Now it only helped the sun to scorch me.

Gee, it was getting hot. My face already stung and burned. I tried to turn away from the blinding sun, but the reflection off the water was just as intense. There was no escaping the dazzling rays. At least it beat the bone-chilling cold of last night.

As the day dragged on, black, rolling clouds began to form on the horizon. What was the Jimmy Buffett song about "squalls out on the Gulf Stream"? As darkened clouds approached, lightning streaked from the sky, splitting into long, glowing white tendrils. The booms of the thunder were deafening.

"Oh great, now I could get electrocuted." Joey and I had been through our share of electrical storms aboard many boats.

"Linda, don't be such a wimp." My partner would chastise me. "If you get zapped, you get zapped. Get up here on deck. Shut off the electronics while I reef the sail." Cautiously, I would poke my head out of the cabin. A bolt of lightning would always strike at that exact moment.

"Damn you, Joey, where the hell are you?" A couple of tears mixed with the first sprinkles of rain. My thoughts concentrated on getting drinking water, though I had nothing to catch the precious liquid in, no cup or bottle.

Survival was one aspect of sailing which I always stressed to my students. Throughout my twenty-five years of teaching sailing and delivering boats, safety had always been my number-one priority. It's not so easy when you're thrown into it.

Maybe I could pull my life jacket off for a minute or two. My shirt could be held over my head to rinse the salt out of it. When it absorbed water again, I would have a cool, clean drink. With a squeeze of my shirt, the liquid would drip into my mouth.

The only problem with this plan was the rising waves. Removing my life jacket in these conditions would have been suicide.

In a flash the squall was on me, surrounding me with towering ebony clouds and blinding showers. Flashes of light blasted the wave tops. The wind whipped the sea into a frenzy. Tipping my head back, I tried to catch a few precious drops to ease the thirst. A salty wave rushed in, choking me.

My attempted snagging of rain water was too exhausting. I closed my mouth.

"Stay afloat, Linda. The squall's almost gone." Bright spots peeked through the charcoal cumulus towering overhead. A chilling cold crept in. Darkness was a mere couple of hours away. A rescue boat had to be here by then. When they picked me up I would be sipping a nice cup of hot tea, bundled up in dry blankets.

The hours dragged by. My thoughts turned to Joey again. How great would it be to see his Robert Redford smile? Was he OK? Staring at my watch, I realized eighteen hours elapsed since we were separated.

"Joey, come on already. Get your ass over here and help me." I had no idea why I thought he would be my savior. To say he treated me with indifference wasn't fair. He could be such a sweetheart as long as he got what he wanted.

A big wave slammed cold water into my face and up my nose. Coughing out salt, I decided to concentrate on swimming.

The sky cleared. Wow! How did the sun get so low on the horizon?

"Damn, it's six o'clock. Sunset it only an hour away. Come on, Coast Guard. You had to receive my emergency signal."

Capt. Marlena Brackebusch

As twilight slipped into night, the darkness was complete. The sky was very black with no moon. After the pounding thunderstorms and blinding rain passed a few short hours ago, the struggle to stay above the waves and keep warm was a difficult battle.

Painful cramps constricted the muscles in my arms and legs. The confused swells peaked at five feet. Cold water swirled around in the black sea, depleting the last of my strength.

"What was that?" There was a faint red light in the distance. It looked like a big ship steaming southwest, probably headed for Charleston. The Coast Guard must have radioed a "Pan Pan" alert to all vessels, asking them to look for us.

The ship's lights grew brighter as it headed closer. The thought of rescue almost made me leap out of the water with joy.

Suddenly the black hull loomed, as the red and green lights were nearly overhead. I thought the ship had seen me. The big uncaring steel Goliath appeared to slow down. Now it looked like it would run over me.

My quick, frantic arm strokes didn't widen the distance much. The bow wave engulfed me. My lungs burned with flooding salt water. The whoosh of the propellers was deafening.

I spun and tumbled alongside the freighter, popping up astern in the bubbling wake. Sobs racked my uninjured body. The near disaster further sapped my strength, adding to my already long list of problems.

"Damn you guys on watch. You should have seen me." I shook my fist at the departing ship.

The night dragged on. Another glance at my watch told me it was only eleven P.M. This was shaping up to be a long night. The cold and shivering and desolation only became worse. Where were all the fishing boats that usually plied these waters in search of a good catch of mahi mahi or tuna?

A streak of light in the bio-luminescence below reminded me I was not alone. The sharp bump announced the arrival of another shark. The predator didn't attack. Rather it played a sort of cat and mouse game.

"How much more of this do you expect me to withstand? Come on, Neptune, give me a break," I said in the toughest voice I could muster. "Either kill me or let me out of this hell."

Despair crept in. It was difficult to stay awake. The biting cold cut to my very core. Arms and legs refused to work as the cramping worsened. Again I thought of Joey. How could this delivery have gone so wrong?

Looking up at the sky and watching the stars twinkle, I realized there was no more fight. Numbness and tingling made my arms and legs useless. The energy reserves were spent. A little nap would have been great.

"Lie back, Linda. Get a little sleep. It doesn't matter anymore."

The back of my head sank into the water. The ocean didn't feel cold. A small wave caressed my face, allowing a few drops of water to sluice into my nostrils. Brine slid down the sinuses.

Stars twinkled brilliantly overhead. It was such a pretty night. Let the sea take me. I could only hope the end would be painless.

Chapter 2. The Delivery

"Are you finished packing?" Joey's voice drifted down below as I stuffed my foul weather gear into the green duffel bag. How many times had this scene repeated itself over the past ten years?

"Just a minute. I'm going to recheck my list again. I don't want to forget anything," I said while grabbing my notebook.

"Hurry up. I don't want to miss the flight."

"Yeah, yeah." Spare hand-held radio, check. GPS, check. Tools, check. Safety harness, check. Everything seemed in order. The pad of paper was placed into the zip lock bag along with my keys to the boat. The heavy luggage was thrust through the companionway.

"Joey, can you grab this?"

"I got it, hon." The six-foot tall delivery captain who doubled as my lover easily hefted the bag to the dock. As I stepped on deck to lock the doors, my eyes scanned the yacht which we've called home for over fifteen years. *Dark & Stormy*. Our yacht's name was also analogous to our relationship of late.

Before leaping onto the dock, I climbed to the mast. A gentle pat on the warm steel was my ritual every time I left her for a yacht delivery.

"I'll be back."

"Oh for goodness sakes, you always act like you're not coming back." Joey glowered at me from the cement walkway behind the Cove Inn hotel. "We're going to be late for the flight."

"I'm coming."

The big jet rumbled down the runway. My hand gripped the armrest between us.

"Geez, Linda. The plane isn't going to crash. Don't be such a baby."

"Thanks, Joey. I can also count on your support. You know I hate flying." Without another word, he reclined the seat back and was soon quietly snoring. I fidgeted, taking deep breaths. Returning to Boston would be nice, even though our stay would be short.

There was a thirty-eight foot sailing yacht named *Wind Rose* which awaited our arrival. We needed to sail the boat to her new home in Ft. Lauderdale. As usual, the boss was in a hurry.

"He wants her in two weeks." Joey informed me two nights ago after terminating the call with the owner. "They are always in a damn hurry."

"It would be nice to spend a couple of days in Beaufort."

"That's not going to happen. We'll be lucky to get an afternoon there, barely enough time to refuel and wash up the boat."

The plane touched down about three o'clock, locating the yacht was on my mind. We grabbed a cab to the Constitution Marina on the Charlestown side of Boston.

"Where do you think "D" dock is?" Joey asked. We hunted around for the pier.

"It's over here." He wheeled our bags to the boat in a dock cart. "Yep, it says *Wind Rose* right here on the transom."

After hopping aboard, we found the keys stashed under the compass cover, right where the boss promised they would be.

The afternoon sped by as all the on-board systems were checked. *Wind Rose* featured a new GPS-chart plotter, good bilge pumps, and by the look of it, a well-maintained engine. The fuel tank read full. The refrigerator looked clean enough, so on it went.

My nose wrinkled at a slight musty smell from the boat having been closed up. The hatches were soon propped open.

"Linda, can you fire up the engine?" Joey called from below.

"Got it." My index finger pushed the start button on the engine panel. The motor roared to life with a puff of grayish smoke venting out from the exhaust along with the cooling water.

Joey poked his head out of the companionway, wiping the sweat from his brow. Though he recently celebrated his sixtieth birthday, he was still a handsome man. At six feet, with a moderate build topped by a hint of gray around his temples, he still received admiring glances from women.

The sun sank behind the Boston skyline.

"Why don't we knock off the work for today? We should get dinner then provision the boat," Joey said.

"Sounds good to me." I returned his smile. After a refreshing shower, we walked hand in hand to the marina's busy bar-restaurant, The Crow's Nest.

Most of the seats were taken by trendy business people, overdressed for this casual setting, with a sprinkling of sailors among them. A table opened up near the water, so we grabbed it.

"Two Dark and Stormy's," Joey ordered from the waitress. The concoction of Gosling's rum and ginger beer was our favorite drink. A glance at the menu showed many tempting seafood dishes, including Maine Lobsta, done ten different ways.

Oh, what the heck, we were heading offshore for a couple of weeks. A little extra indulgence in boiled lobster dripping with butter wouldn't hurt me.

"I'll have the broiled flounder." Joey was always so predictable.

We clinked our glasses, toasting a safe voyage.

After dinner, we caught a cab to a nearby grocery store. The boat needed to be provisioned for the long sea voyage. The cart was piled high with bottled water, lots of paper towels, along with both fresh and packaged foods.

"Joey, what kind of beer do you want?"

"Bud Light." The case of canned beer was shoved to the bottom shelf of the shopping cart.

Back at the boat, my mate passed plastic shopping bags full of food to me in the cockpit. Soon the area was piled high with provisions. This process was repeated to get everything below. Bag after bag, I reached up to grab the food.

"Gee, where are we going to put all this stuff?" I asked him.

He grinned at me. "I don't know, but you always find cubbyholes for everything. Let's put away the cold food then call it a night. It's almost ten o'clock." We were beat. The V-berth beckoned.

"Rise and shine lady. We'd better get this boat underway." During the motor ride out through Boston Harbor, I took the time to stow the last of the provisions and gear.

"Linda, come out here. We're going by Boston Light." Three steps launched me on deck.

"She's so pretty. It's been a while since we've seen her." Seagulls squawked while circling the picturesque landmark. A strong current drove us to sea by the bobbing lobster pots.

"Take the wheel. I'll raise the main." A gentle west wind stirred from the direction of Nantasket Beach. By the time the sloop reached Minot's Light, the sails were drawing nicely.

"I'm going to change course for the canal and shut off the motor." Joey didn't respond. He was already napping below.

The next twenty-four hours flew by as we motored through the Cape Cod Canal then slogged our way across Buzzard's Bay.

"There's Block Island Light." I pointed out the blinking white light to Joey during a watch change that night. Our ship ghosted along in the light westerly.

"I wish we could pull in."

"Sorry, Linda. We need to make time. With this light wind, the delivery schedule will be tough to keep. I don't want to waste fuel at this point in the trip."

"I know." Disappointed, I crawled into the V-berth. The light winds persisted down the coast of New Jersey. The following morning, conditions changed.

We jumped over the waves in a freshening westerly wind. The bow rose to meet the next wave. She slid off the back side, sending showers of salt spray over the bow. Crystals glistened in the noontime sunshine.

It was an awesome ride, coasting down the six footers with a great breeze. Joey and I settled in nicely to our four-hour watch schedule. He was napping below as I sat on the stern rail seat enjoying the day. Wispy clouds floated overhead. The day could not be more perfect.

"What's for lunch?" My partner asked while leaning out of the companionway hatch. He paused a moment to rub sleep from his eyes.

"How about a sandwich and a cold soda?"

"I'll get it. You look too comfortable there." My mate turned back below. I was shocked at his offer to make lunch, as he was usually too self-centered to offer.

A hand appeared out of the hatch holding a turkey sandwich with tomato on rye, wrapped in a paper towel. The cold Diet Coke followed. My feet returned to their propped up position on the sheet winch, as I leaned back, enjoying the meal.

The warm sunshine caressed my back throughout the afternoon. A new paperback novel provided entertainment when I was not marveling over the gently breaking waves. Joey hunched over the chart plotter, checking our position.

Wind Rose surfed down the waves, bobbing and weaving.

"It looks like the wind is trying to veer to the northwest."

"That's a great thing, Linda. Once around Hatteras, we need to change course more to the west to stay out of the Gulf Stream."

"How far are we from the light?"

"Only thirty miles to go. We'll swing around Diamond Shoals then it's home free to Beaufort." Joey's hand was pressed against his forehead as he tried to shield the afternoon glare from his eyes. He scanned the horizon. The only boat traffic seen for a couple of days was a container ship headed north, late last night.

"It's odd we haven't seen many fishing boats."

The afternoon slid into sunset. It was not long before our stomachs asked for food. Anyone who had ever sailed offshore knew the effort it took to cook dinner. Some had suggested it could be an Olympic event.

While I held up the refrigerator cover, my eyes settled on two pork chops just waiting to be devoured. The balancing act continued as the frying pan teetered on the gimballed stove.

Wind Rose gyrated and twisted in a big wave. The engine cover was in exactly the right place to support my left knee. The chops sautéed nicely with fresh ground pepper and a touch of salt. Served alongside a garden salad, the food chased away my captain's hunger.

"Linda, you never cease to amaze me. I guess that's why I keep you around because you're the only one who can cook with the boat bouncing like this." Joey gave me his most charming smile. The plate of chow was carefully balanced on his knees.

The food was washed down with a single glass of wine. White foam, which flung itself off the tops of the swells all day, disappeared, leaving gentle rollers.

Once the galley was tidied up, we enjoyed the last streaks of magenta in the western sky.

"What a beautiful day." Joey leaned back against the stern rail. The sea around us remained deserted as our little ship approached the offshore shoals of the Outer Banks. This area of the ocean had claimed many shipwrecks over the years. All sailors are humbled when the sea allows safe passage through this graveyard of the Atlantic.

Darkness descended. My watch ended at nine P.M. with the comfortable V-berth beckoning. It seemed as though my head only touched the pillow when a voice woke me.

"It's your watch." Joey gently shook me awake. The swells had died down to an easy roll. Did we round Cape Hatteras? The luminous dial on my watch told me the time–one A.M. It was a struggle to get on deck with my head still foggy from sleep.

The slight chill in the air was washed away by hot coffee. The chart plotter's screen displayed our position a few miles to the east of Hatteras.

A shift in the wind veered the zephyr more to the north. Our mainsail and jib were flying on the port side, filled by the gentle breeze. With the lessening wind, our boat speed dropped to a mere four knots.

The autopilot was tweaked ten more degrees to the right. The cold metal handle was inserted in the top gear of the big sheet winch. The rope groaned until pulled tight, allowing our sloop to reach across the wind.

Diamond Shoals light blinked off our starboard quarter. The quick red flashing light near the abandoned Texas tower was the only artificial beam reflecting off the water. Stars burst from the sky with the Milky Way streaming endlessly from horizon to horizon. The autopilot steered back and forth through another watch.

Wednesday was more of the same—just great sailing—as we lazily clicked off the miles. The wind was east as we approached Cape Lookout Shoals, North Carolina.

"We're making great time." I smiled at Joey, who was scheduled to go off watch at five P.M. "We should be in Beaufort by tomorrow morning."

Joey turned to look at me. "Always the optimist," he laughed, heading below for a nap.

Thoughts turned to our landfall in Beaufort. The boat needed to be washed down and refueled before we could enjoy a nice breakfast ashore. A long, cuddly nap might while away the afternoon. Refreshed, we would head out early the following morning for our final leg to Lauderdale.

Streaks of color burst from the horizon, with the magenta reds and oranges painted across the purple clouds. The wind picked up. I hoped the buttermilk sky to the west wouldn't bring too much weather, as some sleep tonight would be nice.

Our red and green running lights were switched on. The last half-hour of watch was spent behind the wheel, looking at the chart plotter, mentally calculating the time remaining to get to Beaufort. Joey slept through his entire watch and dinner. There were a couple of sandwiches in the fridge he could munch on later. Rest, so you could be alert while making landfall, was more important than food.

"Joey, it's your watch," I called to him while making a cup of coffee. He grabbed the mug while brushing my lips with a kiss. With one hand braced against the bulkhead, my guy climbed the companionway ladder one-handed.

"Don't forget your safety harness."

My head leaned on the cool pillow. It often took a long time to fall asleep offshore. A couple of spice bottles clinked against each other in the galley. Finally, relaxation won out. The creaks and groans of the rigging faded away.

CRUNCH!

A loud bang shocked me awake. It took a second for my head to clear the sleep as I leapt out of the V-berth. My feet stumbled, carrying me to the deck. Joey was standing on the cockpit seat, staring into the black sea off our port bow.

"What did we hit?"

"I didn't see anything." His reply was curt as he pushed past me, heading below.

A glance at the depth sounder showed 212 feet of water. Joey rushed to the V-berth to check for damage. A red light on the instrument panel below indicated the bilge pump was running.

"Linda, come give me a hand." I crowded behind him in the V-berth.

"Shit! The water's pouring in."

"No kidding. We've got to wedge something into this hole to slow it down. Give me those pillows."

My partner stuffed the breach. We tried to wedge extra bedding in, to hold the pillows in place. More cold ocean water streamed in. The makeshift repair was not working well. How the heck were we going to keep the ocean out?

"Get one of those floor boards from the dinghy out of the back cabin," Joey said calmly, despite the growing disaster around us.

Slipping and sliding on the wet cabin sole, I rushed to the aft cabin. The cold ocean was already overflowing the bilges.

With the floorboard securely in hand, I sloshed my way back to the bow. Joey wedged the floorboard over the hole, slowing the flow to a trickle. We turned to tackle the rising water in the cabin.

Joey grabbed my shoulders. "Linda, get on the radio. Call the Coast Guard to let them know our situation. Give them our position."

Grabbing the microphone of the VHF radio, my call went out to the Coast Guard. Joey vaulted into the cockpit and frantically operated the manual bilge pump.

There was no reply to the radio call. We were still too far offshore. I transmitted our position anyway, hoping another boat heard it.

I whispered to myself. "Get your life jacket, Linda." Back in the V-berth, water relentlessly streamed past the makeshift repair. After struggling into the inflatable life-saving device, I grabbed a nearby pail.

Bucket after bucket, my arms stretched overhead, lifting the heavy water from the floor of the cabin out into the cockpit. Adrenaline kicked in, allowing me to bail like a madwoman. My arms screamed from the exertion.

It didn't take much water streaming back down my arms to soak me. Even though the water was chilly, the cold didn't register in my panicky brain. Joey leaned in to see the level slowly rising.

Outside, the rollers were on the increase, rocking the boat heavily. This made standing nearly impossible, with little waves sloshing around the cabin. The level was almost to the height of the battery switch.

"Linda, we may have to abandon ship." Joey turned back into the cockpit. "Get the EPIRB." The EPIRB emergency beacon would send an encoded signal to a satellite, if need be.

My partner disappeared as he went on deck. Was he going to launch the liferaft? Geez. I blindly reached for the emergency beacon stowed next to the companionway.

It took a moment for numb fingers to manipulate the release. My left arm cradled this vital link to survival as the water in the cabin swirled around my knees. Struggling into the cockpit, I stretched for the radio microphone.

"Joey, I'm calling a Mayday."

A deep breath filled my lungs. I had never made a Mayday call before.

"Mayday, Mayday, Mayday, this is the sailing vessel *Wind Rose*." Was that my voice quivering?

"We are taking on water and sinking at position thirty-four degrees twenty-six minutes north, seventy-six degrees twenty-three minutes west. This is the *Wind Rose*, over."

The lights went out. All power on board the boat was lost. We were engulfed by the pitch black night.

Turning my attention to the EPIRB in my other hand, I flipped the switch to activate the beacon. The green light flashed, telling me it was sending out our emergency signal to the satellites. With any luck, the cavalry would arrive quickly.

Joey was struggling with the liferaft on the dark, pitching deck. A roaring wave crested over the transom. Our stern pitched skyward. Hundreds of gallons of white foam cascaded into the cockpit.

This rogue wave swamped the boat, ripping me from the cockpit. Over and over I tumbled. The cold water was shock. The realization hit me much too late. I forgot to clip my harness in.

Whoosh! The automatic life jacket inflated. In the wet blackness, there was no telling which way was up. The pressure in my chest was horrible.

The life jacket closed around my throat, dragging me upward. My head cleared the surface. A quick breath was allowed before a wave slammed into my face.

Choking out the seawater and kicking hard, I tried to orient myself. Where was the boat? Another breaker slammed into me.

A moment's lull in the upsurge allowed me to scan the horizon. *Wind Rose's* shadow loomed a hundred yards away.

"Swim, Linda, swim, dammit." Legs kicked, arms thrashed, but the sinking wreck drifted further away.

"Joey," I hollered into the deafening wind. My eyes strained to see the dim outline of the boat and mast.

He was nowhere to be seen. A huge swell cascaded, slamming me several feet underwater while rolling me over and over. When I broke the surface, the realization hit me. The EPIRB was gone.

Struggling with every stroke and not making much progress, my already exhausted arms and legs dragged me slowly toward the sinking boat.

Joey had to be somewhere nearby.

"Joey," I hollered again. Another wave crashed over me, spinning me underwater. As soon as I surfaced a few seconds later, the wind was knocked out of me. The boat was even further away.

Lungs expanded and contracted, trying to catch a breath in this maelstrom. The sound of my heartbeat banged away in my chest. There would be no further attempt to swim back to the boat. The sea would not allow it. My salt-filled eyes scanned the inky horizon. There was no sign of Joey.

Now twenty-four hours later, my resolve was gone. A bigger wave broke over my face, sending a rush of cold water blasting up my nose. I was shocked back to reality.

My arms pinwheeled. I sputtered and choked on the salt. Using both hands to push the soaking wet hair from my face, I squinted into the distance.

Was there a green light out there?

My eyes blinked again. Yes, there was definitely a small green light peeking above the swells. It was much dimmer than the lights of the ship seen earlier.

It headed this way. My hopes rose. I waved my heavy arms in an attempt to catch their attention. The strobe light flashed its anemic blink. Only a squeak came out of my throat.

There was a splash next to me. A man in a red survival suit grabbed my life vest. The boat motored away.

My water logged brain panicked. Swim for the boat, Linda. Why was it leaving?

The man tightened his grip on my life vest, dragging me against him. I struggled, not realizing his good intentions. His left arm wrapped around me while his other hand cradled my chin above water.

There was no more fight left in me.

"It's OK, take it easy. My name is Eric. I'm here to rescue you."

Chapter 3. The Rescue

The man tightened his grip on my life jacket. His hand reached under the water. Something tangled around my feet.

"No." The scream wouldn't come out of my frozen throat. The only recourse was to fight this man. Due to the hypothermia and overexertion, my brain was not making sense of the situation.

"Take it easy. I'm trying to put a survival suit on you to warm you up. Are you injured?"

"Sharks." The man leaned over to hear the weak words.

He smiled in the dim light. "There are no sharks. Don't worry. Try to relax. I'll take care of you."

As if on cue, something bumped our legs. I went ballistic. The man dragged me against him. My limp body hung in the water. Rough material from his survival suit abraded my cold cheek.

"Tom, get back over here. There are sharks in the water." His face went in and out of focus as he spoke into a hand-held radio. The grip on my life jacket tightened.

A wave bounced into us. A loud motor was heard close by.

"Get her on board." The man holding me shouted.

A hand from above closed around the back of my life jacket. The man in the water released me while pushing my legs upward.

Capt. Marlena Brackebusch

My right ribs exploded in pain as a wave slammed me against the side of the rolling boat. As the boat rocked back toward me, my body was jerked along the side of the hull. Another roll landed me face down on the deck.

The cold, slimy metal pressed against my cheek.

"We should roll her on her side." Several pairs of hands moved me to my left side. A rough hand supported my head.

Glimpses of the boat went in and out of focus. The harsh deck lights were blinding. A bearded face stared down at me. Fear ripped through me.

"Easy." The man whispered. Something was wrapped around my shoulders. My brain was too muddled to understand these men were trying to help. I struggled.

"It's all right. Don't fight me. We're going to warm you up with this blanket." Hands tugged at the survival suit wrapped around my legs. A soft cloth was placed between my head and the slimy deck.

The man who'd jumped into the water appeared over me, blocking out some of the harsh light.

"Relax, you are safe now." Another blanket was wrapped around me.

"Let's get her below." The two men picked me up. My head flopped against the man's arm still inside his red survival suit. They carried me through a steel door to the inside of the boat. After a short walk down a corridor, the men placed me on a bunk.

"Get some dry clothes on, bro." The man in the survival suit headed for the door. What was his name, Eric?

The other man removed the wet blankets from around me. He gently dried my face with a soft towel.

My disjointed brain was not making sense of this situation. Who were these men? Where was Joey? Fear crept into my frozen brain.

Kind eyes stared down at me. Longish, dark hair with a sprinkle of gray framed this bearded man's face. He must have seen the panic in my eyes.

"I'm Tom. What's your name?" His smile eased a little of the fear. What the heck was going on? Why couldn't I think straight?

"Easy, lady. You're really cold. Let's see if we can warm you up, OK?" He brushed the back of his hand against my numb cheek.

"These wet clothes need to come off of you." He tugged on my T-shirt. Why was this man trying to take my shirt off?

"No." I tried to push his hand away. His smile didn't calm me down.

"Don't fight me. I won't hurt you."

The other man returned. He frowned at the look on my face.

"What's the problem?" The blond fisherman sat on the edge of the bunk, next to me.

"Our mermaid is frightened. She's not too coherent right now. Her skin is very cold. It looks like we have a bad case of hypothermia to deal with."

The man who'd jumped into the water leaned over me. His sandy blond hair was still wet from the ocean. Ice-blue eyes searched mine.

"Lady, we are going to do whatever it takes to make you feel better." He reached down, pulling me against his chest. My body was so weak. I could no longer struggle as they replaced my sodden clothes with flannel pajamas.

"I'll use my body heat heat to warm her up. Let's see if we can get her temperature."

"Her temp's ninety-two degrees."

The man, now lying next to me, pulled my nearly limp body against his. A big comforter covered me. I felt the other man grab my wrist, feeling for my pulse.

"Her pulse is a little slow. We need to warm her up."

Another blanket was added, along with a towel draped around my head. The man next to me, drew me tightly against him. My head swam on the edge of consciousness. Salt water churned in my stomach.

"Sick." My arid throat barely allowed the sound to croak out. The men rolled me onto my right side. The man now lying behind me supported my head. The other fisherman placed a bucket under my face.

The salt water swallowed earlier erupted in spasms as I puked and puked. The room spun. My stomach burned and twisted. The man supported my head and kept my airway clear.

A thick stupor overwhelmed my mind. I was barely conscious.

The stomach cramps eased. The spasms stopped for now. A damp towel wiped over my face.

"Easy, lady. Try to relax." My head was drawn against the man's chest. Again, the blankets covered me. I fought to stay awake. Was I still on the sailboat? I didn't think so. Where the heck was I? Though barely conscious, I was aware of how awesome it was to be out of the water, warm and dry.

My brain struggled awake. Arms were wrapped tightly around me. My head was resting on his arm. Joey? Why was I shivering? Something abnormal had happened, but I had no idea what it was. For some reason, fear edged into my brain. I tried to roll onto my back. The pressure of the arms around me eased.

I lifted my eyes to see a blond man lying next to me in the dim glow from a cabin light. What the heck?

When I attempted to sit up, a raging pain stabbed at my right ribs.

"Take it easy, lady." A bearded man sat down on the bunk next to me. "You're all right."

Words tried to escape from my bone-dry throat. Why couldn't I talk? My head, swirling from a combination of nausea and pain, fell back onto the pillow. Shivers screamed at my brain, telling it just how cold I was.

"She's shivering again." The man lying next to me drew me against him. What the hell was going on?

I struggled, to no avail. Muscle cramps invaded my legs and back. It hurt terribly. The man sitting next to me ran his hand down my back, kneading away some of the agony.

"No."

"Calm down. Don't fight us. Your muscles are cramping from the cold." As my body warmed the muscle cramps worsened. My own moans resonated in my ears.

"Tell me where it hurts." The man sitting behind me whispered.

"My legs."

He reached under the comforter, feeling the severe cramping in my thighs. The long muscles were in spasm. Why the heck were my legs hurting so much? When the man reached down to massage my sore legs, I panicked. My body twisted in an attempt to get away from these guys. Pain stabbed at my ribs.

"Let me go."

"Stop fighting us!" The man lying next to me attempted to stem my struggles. "Listen to me. You were in a boating accident. We're trying to help you."

A boating accident? What the hell?

"I pulled you out of the water. You were very cold. Don't you remember?"

No, I didn't remember. Why did my ribs hurt so badly? The cramps in my legs eased due to the man's gentle massage. Damn, I felt so cold.

"Water." The words rasped out of my dry throat.

The man next to me held my head as the bearded man allowed a few tiny drops of water to flow between my lips.

"Not too much. I don't want you getting sick again."

The bearded man leaned over me. "I'm Tom. This is my brother, Eric. You're aboard a fishing boat. Everything's going to be OK."

Why did these men seem so familiar to me? I didn't know, but somehow I thought I could trust them. There didn't seem to be much choice.

"Are you in pain?" The man, Eric, lying next to me asked. I lied, shaking my head no. As long as I didn't move, my ribs only throbbed.

Over the next couple of hours, the muscle cramps and vomiting were miserable. After the last bout of sickness, I begged the men for more water.

"Only take a few sips." The man sitting next to me advised. My dry throat tried to take in the water but my stomach wouldn't allow it. I was sick again. Tom gently wiped my face with a damp towel.

My head flopped back on the pillow.

"Bro, we have to deal with this dehydration. I'll be right back."

Tom left the cabin soon returning with a plastic box full of stuff. Another fairly tall man was with him. Black hair matched his dark mustache. The T-shirt, jeans, and Yankees' ball cap he wore didn't disguise his commanding presence. Could he be the captain of this fishing boat?

"How's she doing?"

"Mark." Tom addressed him. "She was in stage three hypothermia. We've warmed her up, but she still can't keep any fluids down. I'm worried about the dehydration and electrolyte loss.

"We should start an intravenous line on her." My ears perked up at that. Did he say an intravenous line? Who did he think he was, Dr. Kildare? There was no way a fisherman was sticking me with a needle.

Tom settled down next to me. He reached under the comforter, pulling out my right hand. I jerked it away, reburying it beneath the blanket.

"Hey, I won't hurt you, lady." He attempted to withdraw my hand from under the blanket. His grasp was much tighter this time.

"No."

Tom held my wrist. I struggled to keep it under the comforter. He let go, with a grin.

"Do you think think you are stronger than me?"

My only answer was a stare.

"Listen to me." He leaned closer. I shrunk back, but Eric was right up against my left side. Tom looked me in the eye.

"I've had a bunch of medical training. You need some fluids. If you get too dehydrated your heart could stop working. You're not going to die on my watch. Why don't you relax and let me get some hydration into you."

He reached beneath the blanket only to meet with further resistance. He grinned again.

"Lady, it's three against one. We are going to put this intravenous line into your arm. We can do this the easy way or the hard way. It's your choice."

My confused brain wandered through my limited options. There was no doubt these men could easily overpower me. A tear of frustration slid down my face. How the heck did I get into this mess? Tom gently brushed the tear away.

A spark of recognition passed through my head, as I looked at his face. "*Denali*."

"That's right." The man grinned. He was Tom Iverson, the captain of the crab fishing boat *Denali* from the TV show. The man lying next to me was his brother and co-captain Eric.

From watching the show, I'd learned they both had extensive medical training. This gave them the ability to deal with any injury incurred, sometimes thousands of miles from shore on the frozen Bering Sea. They were not just any fishermen.

"Do I get the feeling we have a fan here?" Was he teasing me or trying to calm my frayed nerves. "Can I put the intravenous line in now?"

As there were no other options, I nodded my head. The fishing captain pulled my hand from under the blanket with no further resistance from me. A moment later, clear fluid ran into my arm.

Eric released me. He climbed off the bunk.

"Her body temperature is high enough for now. Let her get some rest." He tucked the comforter around me. Exhaustion took hold as I drifted off to sleep.

Chapter 4. The Coast Guard Airlift

While I was asleep, Mark radioed the Coast Guard to inform them of the rescue. He also told them Joey wasn't found. An update was given on my condition and the rapidly improving hypothermia. Mark and the Coasties decided an airlift from the boat would be the best way to get me ashore to a hospital, allowing the men to continue their fishing trip.

Due to high seas along with my stable condition, the Coast Guard decided to delay the airlift with the Jayhawk helicopter until later the next day.

As consciousness returned, my eyes opened to see Eric sitting right next to me. He was all of six feet tall and muscular, with dirty blond hair. His face was handsome yet rugged. Through the port-hole, I could detect only darkness. It was still nighttime.

"How are you feeling?" He lightly brushed the back of his hand across my forehead.

"Thirsty."

"How about a little water?" When I tried to push myself to a sitting position, my ribs twinged painfully. The man slipped his hand behind my head, while raising the bottle of water to my lips.

"Let me help you. Go easy on the water until we're sure your stomach can handle it."

"Thanks." Luckily, my stomach didn't revolt this time. He eased my head back to the pillow.

"Try to get some more sleep." The nausea had eased, but my body still felt weak. Sleep inundated me.

When I awoke next, Tom was standing over me with a coffee mug in hand. "I brought you some tea."

"That was nice of you." My throat was still raw, but I managed to croak out a few words. Once again, I tried to sit up, but my ribs raged with pain.

"Watch the intravenous line. Don't pull it out." Both men leaned over me. When Tom lifted me by my right arm, I yelped in pain.

"Hey, what's hurting you so badly?"

"Nothing," I panted through the pain.

"You're not going to tell me what hurts? Is it your stomach?"

"My stomach's fine. I'm all right."

"I don't want to play twenty questions with you. Are you always this stubborn?"

"Yes. I'm fine, Tom."

"Just one more question. It's not your chest?"

"No. I'm just sore."

His eyes narrowed at me. "You're also a lousy liar."

The little sips of tea tasted sweet while calming my stomach more. When the tall, dark fisherman took the nearly empty cup from me, he continued to stare.

"Brother, can you sit with her?" Eric asked Tom. "I'm going to take a nap." The elder brother nodded his assent. The blond man patted my arm.

"Get some rest, Linda. I'll be back later." Before sleep engulfed me again, I wondered how the fisherman knew my name. This nagged at me throughout the night.

Sunlight streamed in the porthole when I awoke next. Both Eric and Tom were at my side.

The other man entered. Was his name Mark?

"The Coasties have a helicopter coming to get our mermaid. They want to take her to a hospital in Morehead City."

"No!" My shout surprised the fishermen.

The captain of the boat studied me. "What's wrong?"

My still dry throat made it difficult to explain the fear of flying, especially helicopters. There was no way I was getting in one of those.

Tom sensed my distress. "Flying in helicopters is a piece of cake. Don't worry."

"I can't." A couple of tears dripped down my cheeks. I wiped them away before the guys saw them.

"The helicopter will be here in twenty minutes. They are sending a doctor on it. I don't think we can stop them from taking you off the boat, even if we wanted to."

"No. Please tell them no." I tried to push myself off the bunk. These men had to listen to me. Tom grabbed my shoulders. "Please don't make me go."

The elder brother must have seen the terror in my eyes. "Listen to me, lady. You need to lie down. Don't pull the intravenous line out."

"Please, Tom. You have to understand."

"I understand you need to lie back down. Now."

Eric came over. He sat on the side of the bunk, next to me.

"Linda, calm down. Maybe we can work something out." He pushed me back against the pillows. "Trust me. Why are you so afraid?"

"I'm terrified of flying," I said. "There is no way I can get into a helicopter. Please let me stay. I promise I won't be any trouble."

Tom grinned. "You're already a whole bunch of trouble."

Eric turned to Mark. "We only have a few days of the trip left. Why don't we let her stay, then bring her in with us."

Mark scratched his chin. "I don't know if the Coast Guard will agree since the helo is already airborne and almost here, but I'll try."

Loud vibrations from the chopper's motor could be heard through the deck of the fishing boat.

Mark left the room, presumably to meet the Coast Guard. He returned a few minutes later with a Coast Guardsman dressed in a red jumpsuit carrying a bag with a white cross one it.

"Linda, this is Dr. Bob Wilson. He wants to check you out to make sure you are all right." Tom stood up to make room for the doc. Eric squeezed my arm.

"Let him check you out."

"How are you feeling?" The doctor reached for my wrist, when he noticed the intravenous line.

He looked questioningly at Mark. "Who put this intravenous line in?"

"I did," Tom said.

"Where did you learn how to do that?"

"In Dutch Harbor, Alaska. From a Coast Guard doc. My brother and I own a crab fishing boat on the Bering Sea. We've had lots of medical training."

The doctor stared at Tom before turning his attention back to me, checking my heart and probing my abdomen.

"Does your stomach hurt?" I shook my head no. He noticed the soreness on my upper right side. Lifting the pajama top, he saw my bruised ribs. He reached over to check them when I intercepted his hand.

"How did you hurt your ribs?"

"First the dolphins pushed me out of the way of the shark." The explanation caused raised eyebrows on the Coast Guard doctor's face—he must have thought I was still delirious.

"When the fisherman pulled me on board, a wave hit. My ribs smacked the side of the boat."

"Oh, yeah. You're just sore." Tom crossed his arms while staring at me.

"Let me listen to your breathing. I promise not to touch your ribs too hard." He put the stethoscope to my chest, listening for a moment.

"Your breathing is fine, but I'm worried about the amount of pain you are in. We ought to take you off the boat to get x-rays. **If** a rib is broken, it could puncture your lung."

"Doc, so what you're saying is, other than the ribs, she's OK?" Tom asked.

"Yes. But I would still get the x-rays. I understand your fear of flying—I'm not all that comfortable with it myself. It's very safe. I will give you a sedative so you won't know what's happening." He reached into the medical bag, withdrawing a syringe.

"No, I don't want any drugs."

"It will be fine. Relax." The doctor reached for the intravenous line. The melee began. My feet managed to get enough purchase to spring me off the bunk, past the doctor. Eric was in my path. He grabbed a hold of me. The intravenous line pulled out of my arm, spraying blood on the floor.

Tom grabbed my right hand to stop the bleeding. Eric attempted to force me back toward the bunk. The Coast Guard doc grabbed my left hand, but I managed to push him away with what little strength was left in me. Mark shouted, stopping everyone in their tracks.

"Everybody stop! Eric, get her back on the bunk. Tom, stop that bleeding. Linda, chill out and lie down."

"You." Mark directed this at the Coast Guard doctor. "Back away from her. Leave her alone."

We all followed Mark's directions, but I only sat on the bunk, clutching my sore ribs while panting from the pain. I would not lie down. Tom managed to stop the bleeding.

Mark turned to the doctor. "It looks like that decides it—she's staying with us."

"I'm not signing her off with her ribs like that."

"Do whatever you need to do, but she's not getting into the helicopter. I won't put her through that."

"Thanks, Mark." The captain of the fishing boat glared at me. So did the doctor, who turned to leave the cabin.

He returned a few moments later. "My lieutenant is not too happy with this situation."

"I can't help that. The decision is made," Mark said.

"You...." the Coastie directed this to the boat's captain, "are officially ordered to go directly to Beaufort. Keep in radio contact with us. Upon your arrival, the marine safety officer in Morehead City will be waiting to talk to you."

The doctor turned to me before leaving.

"I've never had an injured person refuse to get into a rescue helicopter."

There was no reply from me because I didn't know what to say.

After the doctor and Mark left the cabin, a grin spread across Eric's face.

"Linda, you really fought the Coast Guard doc off. Remind me never to get into a tangle with you."

My head stopped spinning, allowing me to relax. It was only a few minutes until sleep took hold again.

When I awoke next, the late afternoon sun was streaming in the porthole. The boat bounced around. The waves must be building. Thank goodness I was not still adrift.

"How are you feeling?" Eric asked.

The room started spinning again.

"OK, but I feel dizzy."

"Drink water. It will take a day or two for your body to get caught up with the dehydration."

Capt. Marlena Brackebusch

The cool water felt great against my gritty throat. A few moments later, Tom came in carrying a bowl of soup. My stomach was still queasy, but I tried to force a few spoonfuls down.

"Where are we?"

Tom sat to my right. "We are southeast of Cape Lookout Shoals."

"Are we looking for Joey?"

"Yes, but we are steaming for Beaufort per the Coast Guard's orders. The guys on watch are keeping an eye out for him."

"We have to find him." My legs swung off the bunk. When I tried to stand up, dizziness inundated my brain. Eric grabbed my arm, steadying me.

"You need to lie down." The fisherman attempted to push me back down on the bunk.

"Eric, take me to the wheelhouse, please. I can help look for him."

The younger brother looked to Tom with a shrug. The elder brother turned toward the door.

"Let me check with Mark. I'll be back with warm clothes. Sit down until I get back."

Eric's eyes bored into me. "Sit. You really should lie down and rest."

My hands rubbed over the dry, salty skin on my face. A shower was really needed to get this crusty salt off.

"Where is the shower? This salt's got to go."

"There's a shower in the head." Eric motioned toward the bathroom adjoining this cabin. "I'll help you."

Struggling to stand up, my legs shook. Eric helped me to the bathroom. Pushing him away, I closed the door behind me.

Leaning against the wall, I shivered with joy as the warm water washed the salt and grime away. It felt great, but an uneasy feeling crept in.

The uneasiness of being in the water overwhelmed me. The shower curtain was brushed aside. I had to get out of the water.

In my haste, I lurched out of the shower, banging into the sink. I pulled a towel around me. My lungs drew in a breath.

"Linda, what the heck is going on?" Eric opened the door.

"I'm fine." My foot pushed the door closed.

"I have some clothes for you." Tom's voice came through the closed door. He opened it a crack, handing them through.

"Thanks." It was such a weird sensation to be at the mercy of these men I didn't even know. The realization hit me. Everything was lost with the sailboat. The scenarios of my immediate future bounced around my brain while I dressed.

It was difficult to slide the T-shirt and "North Carolina" sweatshirt over my head with the ribs hurting so much. Luckily, the clothes were a couple of sizes too big. The navy blue shorts were baggy, but would have to do. I ran my fingers through my knotted, wet hair.

Back in the cabin, Eric helped me to a chair. Though physically spent, I was determined to find Joey.

"Your hair looks pretty knotted."

"I don't think spending a day floating around the sea was good for it." When I reached up to brush the snarls out of the back of my locks, the pain in my ribs erupted.

"*Ow!*" I did not do a good job of hiding the pain.

"The ribs?" Eric asked. "Why don't you let me brush your hair."

"I can do it." The fisherman straddled a chair in front of me. The brush was between us, held by both of our hands. He grinned.

"Are we going to have a tug of war over this? I am a big brawny fisherman, you know. It wouldn't be too difficult to take this away. Why won't you let me help you?" He gently pried the brush out of my hand.

"Allow Monsieur Eric to style your hair." The horrible attempt at a French accent brought a smile to my face.

"Gotcha, Linda. I finally got a smile out of you."

Though this man was trying hard to be a sweetheart, I was not used to being so dependent on anyone, especially in my relationship with Joey. God forbid, he would lift a finger to help me.

"Do you want to go to the wheelhouse?"

"Yes, please."

We walked from the cabin to the wheelhouse. It was a struggle for me to climb the three steps to the door. Once I stood inside, my eyes examined all the equipment.

Mark was seated in the captain's chair to the right. The autopilot, in front of him, was steering. To his right were all the radios and communications gear. Directly in front of him were the engine gauges and controls. A GPS-chart plotter with radar were off to his left.

"Feeling better?" The captain asked.

"Yes, but we need to find Joey. Thanks for letting me stay."

Mark grunted a reply. He didn't appear too happy with the situation.

Scanning the GPS and chart plotter, my mind drifted back to the night of the accident. Reaching for the chart plotter to zoom in on the area, I glanced to Mark for approval. He nodded, watching my every move.

What were the coordinates when *Wind Rose* sank? Think, Linda. "He must be close by."

Eric leaned over. "What did you say?"

"Thirty-four degrees, twenty-five minutes north. We are within a mile of the location where *Wind Rose* went down." I looked up at Eric as Mark checked his log.

"That's right. I have thirty-four, twenty-six north from the Coast Guard." He seemed surprised.

It was obvious they thought I was simply a mermaid pulled from the ocean. They didn't know my extensive background with the sea included a master's of marine mammal sciences obtained from U-Mass, Boston, along with the Woods Hole Oceanographic Institute.

Top that off with my dive master's license and U.S. Coast Guard Master's license. Not a bad resume for a mermaid. I didn't mention any of this because, in the past, my accomplishments had tended to intimidate most men, though maybe not these tough fishermen.

"We have to search here. He may have gotten into the liferaft. It would tend to drift northeast with the Stream. We have to head that way."

"No," Mark said. "We've been ordered to Beaufort. That's where we are heading."

"Mark." My voice was a little too loud. "We have to search. We can't go in now. He may be dying out here. You have to turn this boat around."

Mark stared at me with hard, tough eyes.

"This is my boat. DON'T you dare tell me what to do. We are not turning around. This boat's destination is Beaufort."

Tom came over, standing between the captain and me.

"Linda, we have to go to Beaufort. We have to do what the Coast Guard has ordered or Mark will have a whole lot of trouble. Plus we need to get you to a doctor and offload the fish. The Coast Guard is searching for Joey."

"My ribs are fine—a doctor is not necessary. Please Tom. I can't give up on Joey."

"Linda, the Coast Guard is searching the area. We need to head to port. Arguing with Mark will only make the situation worse."

His look made it obvious he was siding with the captain. Frustration raged as I turned my attention to the waves outside the windshield. Where are you, Joey?

Not much time passed before the constant glare off the ocean had me rubbing my eyes. Eric caught this.

"Linda, you need to go below and rest. We will keep looking. Come on, I'll take you back to the cabin." His hand closed around my arm. He coaxed me back to the cabin, where my head barely hit the pillow before sleep and exhaustion won out again.

Later, a delicious smell awakened me. Beef stew? Maybe. Eric and Tom came into view. The elder fisherman was holding a steaming bowl of yum. "Rise and shine. Dinner is served."

My sore right arm struggled to prop me up. The ribs twinged. Eric helped me to sit up as Tom handed me the steaming bowl of stew. How could someone be delicate when she hadn't eaten in two days?

I wasn't. I tore into the stew like a hungry kitten.

"Easy," Tom advised me. "Don't eat too fast or you may get sick again."

Completely ignoring him while acting very unladylike, I devoured the stew. A bottle of water quenched my thirst. Sated, I reclined back against the pillow, soon drifting off to sleep.

Chapter 5. Beaufort, North Carolina

When my eyes opened, at first light, I finally felt somewhat refreshed. Eric was sitting in the chair to my right, dozing. He woke up when I struggled to sit up.

My ribs were really hurting. The pain reflected on my contorted face. While sitting on the side of the bunk, he reached out to touch my ribs.

"They really hurt this morning?" My hand brushed his away. "We can give you something for the pain."

"No thanks. It's not too bad."

"Are we back on that track this morning. You won't let me help you?"

"Eric, I just don't like taking drugs if I don't need to."

"OK. But if it becomes too painful will you tell me?"

"Yes," I lied.

"How about a cup of coffee." His offer was accompanied by a friendly smile.

"Great." Getting up this morning was a little easier as most of the dizziness was gone.

"I'll go get you some."

"Can I go with you? It would be great to stretch my legs."

"Sure. I'll go outside while you change." I struggled into the clothes worn yesterday.

We headed down a hallway lined with scarred, worn wood. At the end of a passageway, Eric swung open a door. Inside the room, stood a table large enough to seat six or eight. To the left was the stove and sink area. A full-sized, locking refrigerator sat next to a Formica countertop which was scratched and worn from years of hard use.

The smell of good coffee greeted me.

"Sit down next to Tom. I'll get you a mug."

The elder brother was flipping through a fishing magazine. He glanced up, then patted the seat next to him. His elbow bumped against my arm.

"How are you feeling today?"

"OK, I guess. Is there any news of Joey?"

"No, I'm sorry to say there's not."

Silence surrounded the table as I digested this news. We concentrated on our coffee.

Finally Tom broke the silence. "We should be in Beaufort late this afternoon. I guess the Coasties are sending someone over tomorrow morning to pick us up. They want to interview you about the sinking and us about your rescue."

It was a relief to not have to deal with the Coast Guard today.

"It would be a good idea to get those ribs x-rayed."

My return stare was less than happy. "Tom, forget the ribs. What I really need to do is look for Joey."

My mind wandered over the precarious situation. When we lost the boat, I was wearing only a T-shirt and shorts, no money, no credit cards, nothing in my pockets. I had no ID, no driver's license, really no way to get home to Naples. How the heck could I get on a plane with no ID? That assumed I could figure out a way to buy a plane ticket.

Eric stared intently at me. "You look like you're a thousand miles away."

"I was just thinking."

"About what?"

"Never mind."

"Linda, if you don't talk to us, we can't help you."

"You look like you lost your last friend," Tom said. He leaned his arm on the table so it barely touched mine.

"You guys have been great, but there are some things I need to figure out." Depression crept into my brain. A good cry would have been excellent right about then.

The elder brother elbowed me again. "Why don't you tell me what's bothering you? Maybe I can help."

"Oh you know the usual day-to-day problems." My voice cracked. Instead of crying, I steeled myself.

"Little things like losing my money, ID, credit cards and my partner when the boat went down. I have no idea what I'm going to do when we get to Beaufort. Look Tom, I appreciate your help. I'll figure something out." Shit. The last thing I wanted to do was dump on these men who saved my life.

The younger brother was blocking my path out of the dinette table. "Eric, could you please let me get up?"

Tom grabbed my wrist.

"Before you go, I have a question for you."

"What?"

"Do you really think we were going to just drop you on the dock when we arrived in Beaufort?"

"It's not your problem."

"Linda, you are right. It's not our problem. Let me make a deal with you. Why don't we take this one day at a time? Mark shouldn't have any problem with you staying on board in Beaufort. We'll figure the rest out as it comes. You need to worry about getting stronger and feeling better."

"What's my part of the deal?"

"Jesus," Eric said, getting up from the table. He turned back around then leaned toward me. "Here's what I want you to do. Sit there, relax, and tell me the breakfast I'm about to make for you is great."

The younger brother pulled out the fixings for pancakes. After refilling our coffee, he set a heaping plate of cakes in front of us. Syrup and butter were nearby.

"These are great." I tried not to wolf down the hot, fluffy flapjacks with warm butter melting down the sides.

"Good answer. When we are finished eating we can head to the pilothouse."

"That's great. Though I think we are beyond the area where Joey could be located," I said while quickly calculating the fishing boat's rough position in my head.

"We should be a few miles out of Beaufort," Tom said while studying me over his mug. "You obviously know a little about navigation."

"Yes. I've been offshore many times before."

"*Hmm*, you must feel pretty crappy about losing the boat."

"Tom, I feel completely overwhelmed."

"What happened to the boat?"

"We hit something. There was a hole in the bow. We couldn't keep her afloat."

"Was it your boat?"

"No. It was a delivery. That makes it twice as bad, losing a boat owned by someone else."

"It certainly explains the Coast Guard's response. It seems as though they want to talk to you pretty badly."

"Especially with Joey missing," Eric said.

"I don't have a whole lot to tell them."

"That seems to be the pattern with you." Tom turned his attention back to his coffee which he downed in one big gulp.

After breakfast, we went into the wheelhouse. "Good mornings" were passed around. Mark seemed irritable and short with me. Was it because of our exchange over Joey yesterday?

While sitting in the left-hand seat, I tried to figure out a way to make amends. The captain was sitting in his chair, looking straight ahead. The autopilot was steering.

"Mark, I'm sorry I upset you yesterday. I was out of line." Our captain turned to look at me for a few seconds. He returned his gaze to the sea in front of us.

"Apology accepted. You were emotional. This has to be tough for you."

A few minutes later, Tom left the wheelhouse. Eric relieved Mark on watch. We rounded the shoals, halfway to the Beaufort sea buoy. The ocean was calmer today, with the seas running about four feet. The wind was north at fifteen knots. Clear blue skies sparkled overhead.

Tom came back in. He sat in a chair behind Eric and me. There had not been much conversation until now.

"Where do you live?" Eric asked.

"Naples, Florida, is home now, but I used to live in Boston."

"Ah, the sunny, warm weather—better than the cold of the Bering Sea. What do you do in Naples?"

"I'm a sailing charter captain."

"Captain?" Eric asked, obviously surprised my rank.

"Yes, I have a thirty-four foot sailboat. We do day sailing charters and sunset sails."

The chitchat was interrupted by a call on the ship's radio.

"Pan, Pan, Pan. Hello all stations, this is the United States Coast Guard Morehead City Group, break. At 2330 local time on the 23rd of July 2009, the Coast Guard received a 406 megahertz distress signal from the sailing vessel *Wind Rose*. Break.

"The thirty-eight-foot white sailing vessel was reported sinking at thirty-four degrees twenty-six minutes north, seventy-six degrees twenty-three minutes west. Break.

"One crew member rescued, one crew member still missing. All vessels transiting the area are requested to keep a sharp lookout, assist if possible, and report all sightings to the U.S. Coast Guard. Break. This is the U.S. Coast Guard, Sector Morehead City, out."

My body stiffened. My guts wrenched hearing this message. Joey, where are you?

I rubbed my eyes, trying to stem the tears. I WILL NOT CRY. A few moments passed as the tension drained. I silently wept. Joey, I will find you.

Mark appeared in the wheelhouse as the Beaufort sea buoy came into view. We steamed up the channel by Radio Island and slid serenely past the beautiful white sand beaches.

As we passed the Beaufort Docks, tears welled up in my eyes. Joey and I had spent many fun days here, both aboard our own boat and during deliveries.

The fishermen tied up the boat farther down the channel. At that moment the reality hit me. Joey's loss came crashing down on me.

Trying not to cry in front of these fishermen, I headed for the dock. Mark stopped me as I was leaving the wheelhouse.

"Where are you going?"

"For a walk."

"Don't go far. I'm still responsible for you." As I neared the steel door leading to the dock, Tom stopped me.

"Going for a walk?" I nodded. "Wait a second." He returned a few minutes later carrying a pair of worn sneakers. "Can't have you going around barefoot." His kind smile almost made me cry.

"Thanks." I slipped on the shoes then leapt to the pier, scurrying away before the tears came. The sobs could no longer be controlled. Tears rolled down my face as I walked down the waterfront.

Mark had apparently instructed Eric to follow me, for I caught a glimpse of him a long distance behind me. He looked like he was trying to remain unnoticed.

Sitting on a rough wooden bench in front of the docks, I gazed at the yachts and thought of my lost mate. Suddenly there was a hand on my shoulder. Eric sat down next to me without a word. He stared out at the boats in front of us. We sat in silence for a few minutes.

He grabbed my hand. "Let's get back to the boat. Mark will be worried." We slowly walked back side by side.

Slipping past the fisherman in the galley, I made my way to the head. The cold water felt great splashed against my face. I frowned at my face that still showed some puffiness in the reflection in the mirror.

When I returned to the galley, Eric motioned for me to sit next to him. Mark was pouring Pusser's rum and Cokes for himself, Tom, and Eric. The elder brother grabbed a glass for me. We sipped the drinks as the guys discussed tomorrow's business.

"The crew can offload the catch while we deal with the Coast Guard," Mark said while looking at me.

"Before we do anything else, we ought to take you to the hospital to get your ribs checked out." Tom turned his attention to me.

"No, my ribs are fine. I don't need to go to a doctor."

"I think it's a good idea," Eric chimed in.

"No, Eric, I'm fine."

"Linda...."

"Eric, I'm fine, please stop."

He shook his head in resignation. "You are one tough, stubborn lady."

As we finished our second round of drinks, Mark began cooking dinner. Fried pork chops were accompanied by mashed potatoes and green beans. A plate was passed to me. My eyes locked on the pork chop. Déjà vu.

Of course there was no way Mark could have known pork chops were the last meal Joey and I ate together. My face must have had a strange look on it, because the captain sat down, staring at me.

"Don't you like pork chops?"

Snapping back to the present, I forced a smile.

"Even I know you shouldn't be critical of the captain's cooking. It's great, thanks." Mark returned to his dinner. Eric continued to stare at me.

He tried to catch my eye with a questioning look, but I averted my eyes. After dinner, Tom poured glasses of bourbon. We headed on deck to watch the sunset.

Mark brought out his guitar. He strummed out a couple of old Eagles songs. As the sun dropped below the horizon, he soulfully sang "Desperado" in the fading evening light.

Eric was sitting next to me, on the bait chest. His arm was pressed against mine. The alcohol numbed my brain, allowing me to relax.

The blond fisherman leaned close, whispering. "What was with the pork chops at dinner?"

"Pork chops were the last dinner Joey and I ate before we lost the boat." My eyes misted over. The blond fisherman slipped his arm around me.

"I'm sorry," he whispered.

My clouded brain told me to pull away, but my exhausted spirit was thankful for the companionship.

Eric drew me closer, pulling my head against his shoulder. My thoughts swam from the rum. Sleep crept up on me.

Someone shook me awake. "Linda, you need to get some sleep." My eyes opened to see Eric's face above me. I was lying across his lap with my head resting against his chest. He had both of his arms around me.

"I'm sorry." I tried to sit up, but he held on to me.

"Don't jump up. It's good to see you relax." he whispered.

We were alone on deck in the dark. The gleam from the Beaufort city lights cast a diffused glow on us.

"Let me get up." This time my struggle was not met with resistance.

"Take it easy. I'll help you. Let's get you back to your cabin." He eased me to a sitting position next to him. Shaking my head to clear some of the rum, I allowed the fisherman to help me back to my stateroom.

"Thanks."

"Are you going to be all right or do you need my help?"

"I'm fine. Good night."

Back in the cabin, I prepared for bed, my brain numb from the rum and exhaustion. Laying my head against the cool pillow, I listened to the stark silence.

Sleep overcame me as the only sound to break the utter, complete silence was the occasional creak of a dock line. My mind wandered through my first dream since the rescue.

I floated in the water. It was a bright, blue day. The warm water caressed me. Something grabbed my leg. I was pulled under. Get to the surface. Bubbles escaped from my throat.

They floated upward. The surface blurred. My vision darkened. Lungs were near bursting from the strain. In a desperate attempt to reach the surface, my arms lashed out. I was pulled further down. The pain. Oh God, it hurts.

A high-pitched, unearthly scream broke the profound silence on the fishing boat. The shriek reverberated through the pitch blackness. I fought to get to the surface, but the teeth grinding into my flesh hung on. My arms flailed uselessly. Something surrounded me, preventing me from swimming upward.

"Linda, wake up. It's just a nightmare." Eric's shout snapped me out of the dream. My lungs strained to gasp air despite a terrible pounding in my chest.

Arms were holding me tight. A hand rubbed the back of my neck, stroking my hair. My body shook.

"Easy, lady. It was a bad dream. You're safe."

"What the hell is going on?" I recognized Tom's voice.

Eric turned to him while still trying to calm me. "Linda had one helluva nightmare."

"The shriek scared the hell out of me," Mark said.

My body was shaking horribly. Eric held me against his chest.

"I'll stay with her. Why don't you guys get some sleep?" Satisfied, Mark and Tom left the cabin, switching off the light. Eric eased both of us down on the bunk.

My body quivered in fear as my breathing slowly returned to normal.

"Calm down." His voice soothed me. His hand slid under the back of my night shirt, massaging my tense back muscles. I tried to pull away.

"No."

"Linda, it's OK. Let me hold you. You had quite a fright. Do you want to talk about it?"

"No, I'm fine. You can go back to your cabin."

He stopped rubbing my back. His arms drew me tightly against him.

"I'll hold you. Get some sleep." His arms cuddled me tightly. I was too exhausted to argue with him. I drifted off to sleep.

Chapter 6. Coast Guard Sector Morehead City

Struggling to sit up, I slumped backward, my ribs in agony today. The T-shirt and sweatshirt were pulled on. My feet slipped into the navy blue shorts. What an exciting wardrobe.

Once inside the head, I let cold water douse the last bits of sleep from my brain. It was difficult to run the brush through my hair. Gee, I wished the pain would stop.

With my arm tucked against the aching ribs, I made my way to the galley. Tom was seated at the table, reading a newspaper.

"Can I refill your coffee?"

"Great, black will be fine." He returned his gaze to the paper. With coffee in hand, I sat across from him.

"You look really stiff this morning. Is it the ribs?"

"Yes."

"*Hmm*." Tom continued reading the paper.

"Where's Eric?"

"He went shopping."

How strange was that?

"You had a bad nightmare last night. I don't suppose you want to talk about it."

"Not really."

"That figures." He stared at me for a moment. "You really can't let anyone in, can you?"

"Tom, I don't know how to explain this. The whole thing is a huge shock. My head's really messed up right now. It's not...I really appreciate you guys for saving my life. I'm having trouble dealing with all that's happened. Does any of this make sense?"

He raised his eyes from the newspaper. "Yes, it makes sense. Something else makes sense also: letting us help you."

"Why would you do that?"

"Because it's the right thing to do. You seem like a nice lady." His eyes narrowed. "You also seem very frightened..." Our conversation was interrupted by Eric entering the galley.

"Good morning." His hand grazed my shoulder. He set down a bag then grabbed a cup of coffee. Settling next to his brother, he smiled at me. "Did you sleep well?"

"What is that supposed to mean?"

"We were just discussing the nightmare," Tom said.

"You were thrashing around the bunk. It must have been terrifying." Eric glanced at me.

I remained silent.

"OK, I get it. You don't want to talk about it. I bought you something." He reached over to hand the bag to me. I was taken aback. Why would he buy me something and what was it?

"Thanks." I chewed nervously on my lip. It was still weird to be rescued by two famous fishermen, especially when they were really nice guys.

"Aren't you going to look in the bag?" Eric grinned. Once the bag was opened, I found new clothes inside. My eyes rose to meet his. Don't cry, Linda, I thought to myself. How sweet was his gesture?

"We couldn't have you going to the Coast Guard wearing those old rags. I had to guess at the sizes."

"Thank you so much. Would you excuse me?"

Back in my cabin, I searched through the bag, finding a couple of pairs of new shorts, two nice tropical themed blouses, a pair of sandals, and a bra, size thirty-four C—perfect.

Struggling out of the sweatshirt and T-shirt, I looked at my current condition. The stress of the sinking had taken a toll on me, but overall my looks weren't too bad for a woman of forty-five. At five-feet-seven inches tall and 140 pounds, my body had never been termed voluptuous, but fit and trim. My strawberry blond hair was smooth but could use a trim.

As soon as I joined the guys back in the galley, Tom came over, looking at the new clothes. He whistled softly. "Don't you look great. Are you ready for the Coast Guard?"

"As long as you guys are there."

A few minutes later we were joined by Mark.

"The Coast Guard has a car waiting for us outside." We left to find a young Coast Guardsman waiting on the dock. He opened the door to the official looking car with the red and white emblem on its side. He drove us to the Morehead City base of operations, parking in front of a large white building.

Again opening the car door, he addressed us. "The commander is waiting for you." We walked into a small waiting room, where we were met by a pretty, young uniformed woman sitting behind a desk. A sign on the door to her right announced "Commander Francis Wentworth, Executive Officer."

"Linda Williams?" she asked, looking at me. I nodded. "You may go in." When she motioned me inside, I glanced back nervously at the fishermen. Eric gave me an encouraging smile.

Inside the room was a man of about fifty-five with dark hair graying around the edges. His posture was stiff behind a generic desk without any personal adornments. Stern eyes perused a pile of paperwork. After quite a few moments, he scrutinized me.

"Linda Williams?"

"Yes."

"Have a seat." He motioned to the two straight-backed office chairs facing his desk. I picked the one on the right.

He clasped his hands together then stared at me for a few moments, as if sizing me up.

"I am Commander Francis Wentworth, the executive officer of this Coast Guard sector. You are being interviewed about the sinking of the vessel *Wind Rose* off Cape Lookout Shoals, North Carolina. This interview will be recorded." Switching on the recorder, he added. "You are at this interview voluntarily and understand it's being recorded."

"Yes." I was not real happy with the situation.

"Tell me what happened."

I didn't like this guy's demeanor to start with. No hello, how are you?

Gathering my thoughts, I replied, "We were sailing southeast of Cape Lookout shoals heading to Beaufort. My watch was due to end at nine P.M. We were sailing a course of 250 degrees. The wind was out of the east at around fifteen knots." He nodded for me to continue.

"Everything was going well. At sunset I turned on the running lights. Joey was below, trying to rest. When he relieved me at nine, he checked our course and position. I went below to bed. Sometime later there was a loud crash with a huge bang on the boat near the bow. I ran up on deck."

"And how much alcohol had you two consumed?" Where did this question come from?

"Excuse me?"

"How much alcohol had you consumed prior to the collision?" He had a smug look on his face.

"What do you mean?" What the heck was this guy getting at?

"In my experience with you sailboat delivery people, whenever you hit something, alcohol is always involved. How much did you have to drink?"

Incensed, I yelled. "You son of a bitch. He may be dead out there and all you can do is ask if we were..." My voice cracked with rage. I was unable to say anything more. I bolted for the door, running straight into Tom.

"Linda, what's wrong?" the fisherman asked while grabbing me by the shoulders.

The commander stormed after me. A young Coast Guard ensign reached for his side arm but didn't remove it from the holster. Instead, he stepped between the commander and me.

"You will answer my questions," the commander's voice boomed.

"Screw you." Everyone in the room froze. No one spoke for a few moments.

The red-faced, furious commander looked first to the ensign, then at me.

"If you won't answer my questions, I'll have you detained." Looking back at the ensign he bellowed. "Take her into custody."

At this point Tom stepped between the ensign and me. He addressed the commander.

"Sir, may I have a moment of your time please." Tom looked at me, mouthing, "chill out."

The commander waved at the fisherman to follow him into his office, slamming the door shut. The young ensign stood near me but didn't attempt to arrest me.

Eric put his hand on my arm. "What the heck happened in there?" I was too distraught to speak.

The conversation from the inner office was loud enough for us to overhear.

"What do you want?" It sounded like the commander's voice.

"I'm Captain Thomas Iverson of the crab fishing vessel *Denali* from Dutch Harbor, Alaska." There was a pause. "Sir, I am one of the men who rescued Linda. She's had a tough few days. After spending twenty or so hours drifting alone in the Gulf Stream, well, sir, she's...emotional."

"She must answer all of my questions."

"Sir," Tom continued, "if you give me a few minutes with her to calm her down, I'll make sure she answers your questions."

"Do that." The commander ordered in a loud voice. The fisherman came back into the outer office to find Eric and Mark sitting next to me. The armed Coastie was nearby. He attempted to intercept Tom.

"Your boss gave me the OK to talk to her." The young ensign didn't seem to know what to do. Mark moved over one seat to allow Tom to sit next to me. When I opened my mouth to speak, he cut me off.

"You just pissed off the second in command of this Coast Guard station. Linda, that was not very smart."

"But..." Tom put his hand up silencing me.

"When we go in there, you are going to apologize." I tried to speak again, but the fisherman cut me off again. "I don't care what he said to you; we'll deal with that later. Right now we need to keep you out of trouble."

He leaned close, whispering. "Let's go talk real nice to this asshole. Answer his questions, then we're out of here."

The big fisherman pulled me to my feet, ushering me back inside the commander's office. The young armed ensign walked with us, looking unsure as to whether or not we should go in. As we passed the commander's secretary, she looked dumbfounded. Before she could intercept us, Tom opened the door.

"Sir, may we come in?"

"Come." The commander glared at me. We stood before him. There was no offer to sit down this time.

Tom nudged me. Clearing my throat, the words struggled out.

"Sir, I want to...apologize for my outburst." I almost choked on my words. He glared at me for a full minute. Anger smudged his face.

"That was not very ladylike and completely uncalled for," he admonished me. Oh you are wrong, and there's much more to say. I remained silent.

He stared at me with a self-satisfied look on his face. "Now are you ready to answer my questions? I am a busy man."

Well, you self-centered bastard. Tom sensed my hesitation. Could he read my thoughts? The fisherman nudged me again.

"Yes, sir."

"Good." The commander glared at me. "Now how much alcohol did you have to drink before the collision?"

My blood was boiling.

"None."

Tom stood rigid, with a poker face. He slowly clenched then opened his fists.

"What did you do after the collision?"

"I went on deck. Joey was standing behind the dodger looking out in front of us to see what we hit. I didn't see anything—no boat or anything. Joey went below to check the damage. The water was already over the cabin sole." I squirmed.

"He was in the V-berth, stuffing whatever he could find into the hole underneath the bunk, but the water was still pouring in. I grabbed my inflatable PFD then went back into the main cabin. I bailed out as much water as possible." I glanced at Tom who maintained his poker face.

"He pumped the manual bilge pump. We couldn't keep up with the rising water. Joey told me to call the Coast Guard and activate the EPIRB. He was trying to launch the liferaft when a big wave hit, swamping the boat. It washed me overboard with the EPIRB." I brushed an errant tear away.

"The emergency beacon was lost when a wave engulfed me. By now, the boat was too far away to swim back to. I yelled for Joey but never saw him again."

The commander stared at me for a few more seconds. Tears streamed down my face. His look softened. "I'm sorry you had such a bad experience. Are you OK now?" I shook my head no. "You can go into the waiting room. Send in the fishing boat's captain." He looked at Tom. "Tell my secretary to get her a glass of water."

After entering the waiting room, Tom signaled for Mark to go in. Though I tried to hide it, Eric saw me crying.

"What the heck happened in there?" He tried to put his arm around me, but I shrugged it off. Mark looked like he was ready to beat up the commander when he turned for the office.

Tom stopped him. "This guy may not be as bad as we think—go talk to him."

Mark closed the door behind him. We waited in the chairs for twenty minutes. Tom retold our encounter to Eric, who held my hand.

When the fishing captain came out of the office, he smiled. "We can go. The commander wants you stay in Beaufort for another day, then notify him where you will be."

"Is there any news of Joey? They are still searching, right?"

Mark sighed. "Yes, they still have aircraft searching. The commander gave me the name and phone number of the man in charge of the search. We'll go talk to him."

Exiting the building, we found our driver waiting. He drove us to another part of the base, stopping in front of another white building with a red roof on it.

Chapter 7. The Search and Rescue

The entrance to this building was similar to the other, with a reception area as you first walked in. Our driver announced our presence to another young Coastie on duty.

"You can go right in." He directed us into another room, full of computers, radar screens, radios, charts, and telephones.

A man of about thirty-five, fit looking in his white uniform, greeted us. Mark stepped up to shake hands with him.

"Hi, I'm Senior Chief Steve Miller. I assume you're the fishing crew." Introductions were made. After briefly clasping my hand, he stared for a moment before shaking his head.

"I'm sure you've already heard this, but I can't imagine floating in the Gulf Stream with only a life jacket on for so many hours.

"I'd rather not do it again."

"I guess not. Let me show you what we're doing." He led us to an ocean chart of the area. Our eyes followed his to a flashing board.

"These are the helicopters and ships that are active on your case. When the EPIRB went off, sector Norfolk, the rescue coordination center, immediately called the contact phone numbers for the emergency device to see if it was a false alarm." He paused.

"When we determined it wasn't, the location of the EPIRB—luckily you had the GPS version—was pinpointed. This is where the boat went down." He pointed to a red mark on the chart.

"We also received a weak mayday call from the vessel, but the coordinates couldn't be heard over the static."

"A Jayhawk helicopter was scrambled out of Elizabeth City. It flew to the last known location. As you know, the weather was awful. There were high winds and seas with terrible visibility. They made a sweep of the area but saw nothing. We recalled the chopper until the weather cleared the following day."

"Did you hear the helicopter fly over?" Eric asked.

"No. All I could hear was the howling wind."

The master chief leaned over the chart while scrutinizing me.

"Early the next morning, we dispatched an eighty-seven foot coastal patrol boat, the *Yellowfin*, which was in Morehead City on a training mission from Charleston. They steamed to the search area at eighteen knots, arriving at 1530 hours. They did an expanding-square search of the area."

The officer indicated the point on the chart where the boat sank, along with the progressively widening square area around it where the patrol boat searched.

"There were severe thunderstorms in the area, limiting visibility. We also sent out a Jayhawk first thing in the morning, but it had a mechanical issue, so it had to return to base. They didn't get airborne again until the afternoon.

"When they reached the search area, a line of severe thunderstorms was passing through, again limiting visibility. The Jayhawk did a vector search of the area, but they couldn't see much. By nightfall, when the storms had cleared, the helicopter had to return for fuel.

"It was dispatched again the next morning, performed a creeping-line search of the area, heading it in a more northeasterly direction. You were rescued by the time it reached the search area." Mark nodded his assent.

Chief Miller continued. "We did a plot to determine how far the vessel would have drifted, then sent the patrol boat on a search pattern in that direction. The Jayhawk has been flying everyday also." Senior Chief Miller looked at me.

"Do you know if Joey got into a liferaft?"

"I don't know for sure." I explained how he was attempting to launch the raft when the wave washed me overboard.

"We'll assume at this point he made it into the raft. The patrol boat is due back in Morehead City tomorrow for a quick turn around of fuel and provisions. We will send it back out to look for the liferaft.

"I am meeting with the lieutenants in charge of both the *Yellowfin* and the Jayhawks tomorrow morning to discuss the operational plan for the next phase of the search."

"I want to be at that meeting."

The senior chief looked at me with raised eyebrows. "I'm sorry. We cannot allow a civilian in a operational meeting due to added security measures from Homeland Security."

"That's not the right answer. I will be at that meeting."

The senior chief looked at Tom who had stepped next to me. The big fisherman put his hand on my shoulder.

"Linda, why don't we let them do their job? I'm sure Steve will call us as soon as the meeting is over."

Roughly pushing Tom's hand from my shoulder, my eyes bored into the senior chief.

"I will be at that meeting."

Senior Chief Miller sighed heavily. He looked at me for a long moment.

"Clearance would have to come from way up the chain of command to allow this."

Tom interceded before I had a chance to make things worse. "Senior chief, you would be doing us a great favor if you could try to make this happen. We were meeting with Commander Wentworth a few minutes ago. He is familiar with the sinking."

Senior Chief Miller looked surprised we knew his very senior boss. "Hang on a minute, I will see if he'll take my call."

He went over to his desk. After picking up the phone, Chief Miller spoke for a few moments before hanging up. A wry smile lit up his face when he returned.

"It seems you have friends in high places around here. Commander Wentworth has authorized me to allow two of you into the meeting. We will meet at eleven hundred tomorrow morning."

Thanking the chief, we went outside to find our driver waiting. While heading back to Beaufort, Tom studied me in the fading afternoon light.

"You don't know how to take "no" for an answer, do you?"

"My number one priority is finding Joey. I'll do whatever it takes."

Eric turned to me, looking concerned.

"Your number one priority should be getting better and recovering from the accident. You need to rest. I did like the way you handled the senior chief." He grinned. "Remind me not to get into a fight with you."

We were a couple of blocks from the dock when Mark chimed in.

"Linda, how about I take my favorite mermaid out to dinner—and maybe you two bozos also. A steak would do nicely tonight."

"Sounds good." We agreed.

After the Coastie dropped us at the waterfront, we walked to Ted's Steakout, a local restaurant near the docks. The restaurant was busy, so we spent our time waiting for a table at the cozy bar in the back.

Finally our table was ready. It felt weird having dinner in a nice steakhouse with these men. I could not help but feel a little guilty since Joey was not dining on the same perfectly grilled steaks as we were.

"Linda, you look a thousand miles away," Tom said while bumping my elbow with his.

"I was wondering if Joey was in the liferaft, starving, while we're eating dinner. Sorry guys."

Mark stared while finishing his glass of wine.

"Why don't we take a walk down the waterfront. It could help clear your head so you can sort this mess out," Eric said.

After the check was paid, we strolled through downtown Beaufort. It was a beautiful July evening, around eighty degrees with a light southwest breeze.

The downtown area was quaint, with old buildings interspersed with trendy shops. We strolled by Scuttlebutt, the nautical bookstore I spent so many hours in during past trips. My thoughts drifted to a book about old warships bought for Joey during our last stop here two years ago. Where are you, Joey?

My mind drifted, causing me to fall behind. While staring down at the sidewalk, I almost bumped into Eric, who waited for me.

"OK, I'll give you a nickel for your thoughts. They look too heavy to be worth only a penny."

Looking up at him, I noticed the kind smile on his face.

"I was thinking about Joey and all the good times spent here over the years. This is one of my favorite places."

"It's a neat town. How long have you known Joey?" Eric asked.

"About a thousand years, it seems. We've sailed and dived most of the oceans of the world, both on our boat and while doing deliveries."

"That's pretty special. It must really be hard, the waiting and not knowing."

We were far behind the others.

"We better catch up," I said, trying to lighten the situation. "Or they'll drink all of the rum."

Eric stopped. "Linda, wait a second."

"What's the matter?"

"Every time I try to talk to you, I get a flippant answer back. Why can't you talk to me?"

"I guess I don't know what to say."

"It's not good to keep it bottled up."

"I know. We should keep walking."

A short saunter brought us to the center of the boardwalk area. The walkway was made of rough-hewn planks of wood.

When we reached the square, the sun had begun its slide beyond the horizon. The afterglow painted the pretty pink and white flowers in the dark, rough wooden casks planted under the live oaks. The nautical code flags on the yardarm, spelling "Beaufort", flapped in the breeze.

Arriving back at the boat, we all piled into the galley. Tom mixed drinks.

"Here you go, Li'l Sis." Taken aback by this nickname, I widened my eyes and looked inquisitively to him.

"Well, after all we've been through together, I'm starting to think of you as my little sister. I always wanted a sister. Eric never quite fit the bill."

The elder brother laughed, playfully punching his younger sibling on the shoulder. We took our drinks to the wheelhouse, where Eric and I sat on the settee.

Capt. Marlena Brackebusch

Tom was on the left side watch seat as Mark received an update on their catch numbers from the mate. It seemed despite the detour to rescue me and search for Joey, they still had managed to haul in a great catch. The captain was pleased with the numbers.

"Who is going with you to the Coast Guard meeting tomorrow?"

I hadn't given it much thought, so my eyes looked from Tom to Eric.

"Maybe Eric should come with me?"

"All right," Mark said. "My wife, Michelle, can drive you there, then come back to the boat. She will give Tom and me a lift to the grocery store, so we can provision for the next trip.

"When do you head out again?" I dreaded the answer.

Mark's eyes narrowed. "The day after tomorrow we'll load bait and fuel. Our departure will be the following day, Thursday."

Two days, I decided, may not be enough to figure out my plan to find Joey. It looked to be an interesting day at the Coast Guard station tomorrow.

Mark and Tom left the wheelhouse. Eric and I were alone.

We sat in silence until Eric spoke in a soft voice. "You must be beat. Do you want to get some sleep?"

"I would love to grab a shower first."

He gave me a hand up then left me alone at the cabin door. My muscles ached from the long day.

The hot water felt great running down my face, but a strange feeling overwhelmed me. My body screamed to get out of the water. Breaths came out in shallow puffs, as my pulse raced. Panicking, I stumbled out of the shower and grabbed for a towel.

"That was weird." I shrugged off the feeling. After my hair was dry, I went to bed.

Despite the exhaustion, I slipped into sleep quite easily. A couple of hours passed before the dreams recurred.

I was floating in the ocean. The sky became black. Howling wind kicked up the waves. My arms thrashed. A wave crashed over my head. Salt water stung my eyes. A sailboat. Swim. Battered and abandoned.

The hulk was sinking. What just rammed me? I can't breath. A black fin. It's going under. No! Don't! My leg. Don't bite. I screamed and thrashed. Sharp teeth. My ankle. Punch. Something grabbed me. I can't move.

"Linda, wake up." Eric's voice seemed very distant. I woke with a start. My arms tried to lash out, but the fisherman had me wrapped in a bear hug.

"Let go!"

"Stop fighting me. It was only a dream."

"Let me go!" I pushed hard. He released me.

Breaths came out in pants. Tom sat on the bunk.

He grabbed my arm. I yanked it away. His hand settled on my shoulder.

"It's OK, Li'l Sis, just a bad dream." Tears flowed. What the heck is wrong with me? I wondered. I'm usually not such a wimp.

Mark stood in the doorway with his arms crossed.

"Why don't you go back to bed," Eric said, then turned to Tom. "I'll stay with her."

The fisherman attempted to pull me down on the bunk. I resisted.

"Lie down. Tell me about the dream."

"I'm fine. I don't want to talk about it. Please go."

"Linda, stop fighting me. Let me help you." I allowed the man to pull me against him. I was still shaking.

Tom replaced the blankets on me. The shaking slowly eased, but I was still breathing hard. Eric relaxed his grip while stroking my forehead.

"That was a bad nightmare. Do you want to tell me what happened?"

Shaking my head no, I tried to turn away to hide the tears and not be such a wimp in front of this tough fisherman. Eric put his hand on my cheek, gently wiping away the tears.

"It's OK to cry. You've been through hell the past few days."

"Eric, I'm usually not such a wimp."

"*Shh*, it's gonna be all right." He cuddled me. "Try to get some sleep."

As daylight streamed in the porthole, my eyes fluttered open. I reached across the bunk, but Eric was not there. My body stretched out. The ribs throbbed. Struggling to get up, my aching body felt exhausted. After dressing, I tried to fix my hair to look presentable.

Walking into the galley, the fishermen looked up at me. Tom waved me to the seat next to him.

"Coffee?" Eric asked.

"Great, thanks. Mark, I'm sorry I woke you up last night."

"I don't mind waking up, but you scared the bejesus out of me. And I don't scare easily." The smile, plastered on his face, let me know he was not too upset.

"Gee, how come I don't get an apology?" Tom elbowed me playfully.

"Sorry, Tom."

"I'll forgive you this time."

After Michelle cooked breakfast, she drove Eric and me to the Coast Guard station in their big black Chevy Blazer.

Once inside we were greeted by Senior Chief Miller. He introduced the patrol boat skipper, Larry Anderson, and the Jayhawk lieutenant, Mitch Connolly. The pilot looked at me.

"Are you the lady who was rescued from the sailboat?"

"Yes."

"I was the pilot who flew out to get you off the fishing boat. I have never had anyone refuse to get into my chopper before, especially when they are injured." He stared at me.

I certainly didn't want to antagonize this man who was searching for Joey, so I forced a smile to my face.

"I have a bad fear of heights. Riding in a helicopter would be terrifying. I didn't mean to offend you."

He stared at me until a smile formed on his face. "No offense taken. Maybe you'll change your mind sometime and give it a try. It's a lot of fun."

The senior chief leaned over the chart, pointing to the now expanded search area.

"We should concentrate this next search here." He indicated a large area of about a hundred square miles, marked in red, thirty miles northeast of Cape Lookout shoals.

"My guys have plotted the set and drift of the Gulf Stream in this area. If Joey made it into the liferaft, he should be there."

He glanced at the skipper of the patrol boat, who nodded in agreement.

"Mitch, we will have your guys fly sorties on the perimeter of this area. Make sure they look for a raft and possibly someone in a life jacket."

Eric was staring at the chart. "Chief Miller, how long will you search this area?"

"The patrol boat can stay out for three more days. Then it has to return for fuel and provisions. I can't say for sure at this point, but I doubt it would be sent out for this mission again. The area of uncertainty will be too large. We would continue the search with the Jayhawks, as they can cover much more area. Pan Pan calls will be broadcast for as long as it takes. Maybe another boat will find him."

"Please don't stop searching," I implored.

"Let's not get ahead of ourselves. If we have a little luck on our side, we'll find him on this mission." The senior chief ended the meeting.

Another young Coastie gave us a ride back to the fishing boat. We arrived to see Mark, Tom, and Michelle hauling groceries aboard the boat.

We grabbed bags, giving them a hand. I felt a pang of nostalgia, thinking back to all the times Joey and I provisioned here.

The afternoon was spent putting the foodstuffs away and cleaning up the boat. Michelle stayed to cook dinner as the rest of us chatted at the galley table.

"How did it go at the Coast Guard station?"

"It went OK." I recapped the meeting. "Where will you be fishing on your next trip?"

Mark looked at me suspiciously. "We will head northeast of the shoals. The tuna and swords are supposed to be running big there."

The chitchat continued through the dinner of spicy chili with big chunks of crusty, fresh-baked bread. The whole crew was in high spirits, anticipating the next trip with another big payday.

I was quiet throughout most of the meal. After dinner, we sat out on the back deck, on the bait cooler, with our legs dangling off. Tom sat in one of the deck chairs.

"You were pretty quiet during dinner. What were you thinking about?" Eric asked.

"Nothing."

"Do you want to head back to Naples? I can drive you there, if you like?"

"I need to stay here to find Joey. Thanks for the offer."

Mark and Michelle came out to join us for sunset. It was time to take my shot at the boat's captain.

"Mark, could I hire your boat to go out to search for Joey?"

He stared at me with surprise. It looked like he tried to suppress a grin.

"Linda, I would love to help you, but—no offense—you don't have enough money to keep me from fishing. One good tuna can bring me fifty thousand dollars in the Japanese Sushi markets."

Eric spoke up. "We'll figure something out. I'm sure all the guys will look for Joey when they are out fishing. I don't think mounting your own search would do any good. It might be better to go back to Naples. Take some time to recover from your injuries."

"Eric, you are very sweet, but I need to find Joey. Mark, would you consider letting me come along? We can search for him while you are fishing."

"Let me think about it." He and Michelle headed for the dock. "Guys, I'm going home tonight. I'll be back at nine A.M. to fuel and get the bait."

Chapter 8. The Search for Joey

Tom came over, sitting down on my other side. "Li'l Sis, I think Eric is right. There's not a whole lot more you can do here. Why not let him drive you to Naples? It's the best solution, considering you don't have a driver's license. It would be tough to get on a plane. Besides, we don't really need him on the boat."

"Thanks, brother." Eric looked at him, surprise lifting his eyebrows.

"Tom, would you talk to Mark? He'll listen to you. We can look for Joey while fishing. You guys are going to be in the right area. Please?"

The big fisherman stared at me for a long time.

"I really don't know if he'll go along with it. Is this really what you want to do?"

"Yes, Tom. I can't give up at this point."

"You must realize it would be a miracle to find him. The Coast Guard is searching with helicopters and ships and they've found nothing."

"Tom, if I give up now, I'll forever wonder if there was something more I could have done."

"If I do ask him, you need to make me a promise."

"What's that?"

"You need to do what he says. Don't give him a hard time. Do not argue with him."

"I promise."

A crafty smile formed on the elder fisherman's face. "Since I'm doing this big favor for you, I want you to do something for me."

"What's that?"

"It's simple. Answer a question for me."

"OK." There was something about his smile that raised red flags.

The elder brother settled next to me. The grin turned to mischievous.

"Remember when I was trying to put the intravenous line into your hand?"

"Yes."

"You recognized us as the fishing captains from the show. You're obviously a fan."

"I'll neither admit it nor deny it."

"Ha! What a cop out. My question is...is *Denali* your favorite boat on the show?"

His grin broadened. Was he teasing me or trying to embarrass me? When I attempted to climb off the bait box, Tom grabbed my arm.

"You have to answer. We made a deal."

"The answer is yes. Now let me go." Tom laughed. I scurried for the door to the cabin.

"Linda." Eric's voice stopped me. Both captains looked amused. "One more question. Who is your favorite captain?"

"That wasn't part of the deal." I murmured, rushing into the fishing boat.

Back at my cabin, a deep breath eased some of the tension from the guy's teasing. A knock on the door got my attention. Opening it a crack, I saw Eric's face.

"Linda, I hope your not upset with us. We were only teasing you."

"I know." A smile crept to my face. Eric pushed the door open a little more. "Did you want me to stay with you tonight, in case there are more nightmares?"

I considered this kind gesture. "No, I'll be fine."

He turned to head to his cabin. After settling into my bunk, I thought about this whole weird situation. No nightmares tonight was my final prayer before drifting off to sleep.

The sound of my own shriek woke me once again in the wee hours of the night. The now familiar scene included Eric waking me. I was shaking even more violently than before. Once again, he pulled me down on the bunk.

"Easy, lady." When my breathing returned to normal, he spoke again. "Linda, maybe you need to get off this boat. It may be the cause of these nightmares."

"Eric, I'm not ready to give up the search. We have to try to find Joey."

"We'll talk about it in the morning." Again, this kind fisherman cuddled me. I felt safe for the moment.

Early the next morning, I looked out the porthole to see the horizon shrouded in clouds. This natural phenomenon mirrored my state of mind. In the galley, Tom was pouring over the newspaper. Eric's attention was focused on something outside.

"Anything good in the news?" I asked.

Capt. Marlena Brackebusch

"Is there ever any good news in a newspaper?" Tom looked up at me. "Did you get any sleep with the nightmares?"

"There was only one. I slept OK afterward."

"Because your knight in shining armor was there to protect you?" The younger brother peered at me.

"Eric, I really appreciate what you are trying to do. It does help ease the terror of the dreams. But... I'm having a hard time being in the same bed with....a married man."

A painful expression crossed Eric's face. He rose to pour himself more coffee. Did I offend him? He stared out the galley port for a few seconds.

"Would you look at this? The Seattle Mariners beat the Yankees last night. They're really playing well this year." What the heck was Tom talking about? Baseball? When I looked at him, he gave me a fast shake of his head, no. Weird.

Mark walked in a moment later.

The conversation switched to fishing. Eric remained subdued.

After breakfast, Mark fired up the boat's engine. We went back down the channel by Radio Island, over to the fishing docks at Morehead City. First, the boat was fueled, which cost a pretty penny. The bait, including squid and fish, was loaded. Box after frozen box was passed aboard.

Back at their dock, the boat was washed and readied for tomorrow morning's trip.

While working on deck in the afternoon, Tom went over to Mark. They spoke earnestly, glancing at me a couple of times. Finally, the captain came over, wiping sweat from his forehead. He stared at me for a few seconds.

"We can search around between fishing sets. You can come along on one condition." He paused, scrutinizing me. "You need to promise me you'll do as I say. Make sure you wear a life jacket on deck."

"Mark, I promise...and thank you." Now there was even a better chance of finding Joey.

The following morning, we retraced our steps out the Beaufort channel. The course was southeast toward Cape Lookout Shoals. Our boat rode easily in the light chop. The wind was southwest at no more than five knots.

Eric was on watch with the autopilot steering. I sat in the left-hand watch chair. Mark and the crew were prepping their long line for the first set of the evening.

By late tonight, we should arrive in the area where *Wind Rose* went down. Flying fish darted across our path. The blue sky looked peaceful. The boat motored on.

The afternoon faded into evening as we rounded the red nun buoy which marked the end of the shoal. The course was changed more to the east.

Mark was at the helm studying water temperature gradients on a computer printout of the Gulf Stream. The edge was where the nutrients mix, creating food for the small bait fish and squid who became dinner for swordfish and tuna.

Sharks feed here, also. I shuddered at this thought. As we motored on in the rising swell, my thoughts turned to Joey. Was he looking at the same stars from the liferaft, hungry and thirsty from the past week's deprivations? Was he injured? Did this have anything to do with the recurrent nightmares?

At midnight, all the bright deck lights turned on. The fishing began. The first marker buoy was set out, with its radar reflector and blinking strobe light. As the miles of long line were reeled off the boat, the baited hooks were attached. Cyalume stick, like the toy lights kids play with at Halloween, created an eerie glow in the water. This glow would attract our quarry.

"Hustle up, guys. We need to finish this set," Mark called to the crew from the wheelhouse.

The line dangled below the surface of the water, hopefully snagging sword fish and tuna. The work went on past dawn, when the crew took a break to get some sleep.

Normally, the skipper would shut down the boat and drift, waiting for the fish to bite while conserving fuel. This morning Mark headed south, starting a search pattern he drew up on his chart. We motored slowly at five knots, scanning the horizon for Joey.

"The boat will continue on this course for four hours then move a couple of miles up the stream. We can look around while we steam back to pick up the long line." He rubbed his tired eyes, which squinted into the sun.

"Mark, I can't thank you enough for doing this."

"You can thank Tom. This is a favor to him." The curt tone of his voice lightened up. "Let's find Joey."

Tom came into the wheelhouse carrying two cups of coffee. "Would you like me to take over?"

"Sure." Mark updated the big fisherman on the search plan before heading off watch. I continued to stare out the windshield, hoping for some sign of my missing partner.

"Linda, I'm glad we're alone for a few minutes. I need to tell you something."

"What's up, Tom?"

"The other day, when we were in the galley, you made the comment about being in bed with a married man."

"Yes. Eric seemed really upset."

"There are two reasons he was so upset. The first is he didn't mean to make you uncomfortable by lying in bed next to you. His intentions were to make you feel safe."

"He did make me feel secure. It really helped. I don't think his wife would be too happy with him, even though there was nothing going on."

"Linda, Eric's not too great at discussing his feelings. He told me he was very upset to think his good intentions bothered you."

"I didn't mean to offend him."

"Listen. There's another reason he was so upset." Tom stared at me for a few seconds.

"Do not tell him I told you this. He recently went through a bad breakup with his wife. I'm not telling you any of the details, but it really messed him up. Broke his heart. That's the reason we are here." Tom tapped a pencil against the navigation chart.

"After the divorce, I thought it would be good for him to go to sea, away from Alaska. Clear his head. He's sworn off women. Then you drift up, literally." The fishing captain shook his head.

"I'm not sure the timing was good or bad. Listen Linda, why not let Eric be a friend? It would be good for both of you."

The younger brother walked in a moment later. He didn't realize Tom and I looked like two cats caught with a mouse.

At noon, a Coast Guard Jayhawk flew overhead. The pilot hailed us on the radio.

"Fishing Vessel Mary Louise, this is United States Coast Guard helicopter 6024, channel sixteen, over."

Tom picked up the microphone for the ship's radio. "Coast Guard, this is the Mary Louise."

After switching to a working channel, the Jayhawk pilot again called us.

"Mary Louise, CG helicopter 6024, is Linda on board? Over."

"CG helo, that's a roger. She's sitting right here, over"

"Mary Louise, CG helicopter 6024, Linda this is Mitch. Just wanted to let you know we are out here searching. Unfortunately, we haven't seen anything yet, over."

I reached for the microphone, which Tom handed to me. "CG helo, Mary Louise. Hi, Mitch, thanks a lot. We haven't seen anything either. I appreciate all of your help."

"Mary Louise, CG helicopter 6024, roger that, we'll be in touch. This is U.S. Coast Guard helicopter

6024 standing by on sixteen and twenty-two alpha." Mitch signed off, banking the helicopter away to resume his search.

The three of us sat in silence, staring out at the empty, endless swells rolling across the bow of the boat. After a few more minutes, Tom rubbed his eyes.

"Aren't you tired?"

"I'm exhausted, but I have to keep looking for Joey. He's got to be out here."

Eric came up behind me. "Linda, maybe you should get some rest. Have you eaten any lunch?"

"No, I'm not hungry." Realizing these guys might be, I figured a way to show some gratitude. "Are you guys hungry? I can make you a sandwich or something?"

"Why don't you get Tom something? I could use a cup of coffee."

The younger brother replaced his elder at the captain's seat, checking our position and course. Tom and I went to the galley, where we spent a few minutes making a new pot of coffee along with a couple of sandwiches.

It was back to the wheelhouse with a coffee and food for Eric. A glance at my watch showed three P.M. Only a few more hours of daylight left.

"Thanks." He took the food from me. "Are you doing OK? You look really tired."

"I'm fine. It's just so disheartening staring out across the water while not seeing anything. He's got to be here somewhere." A tear threatened to drip out of my eye.

"Linda, you are doing everything you can. I give you a lot of credit for coming back out here. It can't be easy heading back to sea after all you went through. You have to keep positive."

We neared the area where the long line began. Mark came back into the wheelhouse. He checked the coordinates of the first marker buoy.

"Eric, do you want to stay at the wheel? I'll pull the hooks."

"OK."

The blond fisherman slowed the boat, allowing the crew to grab the marker buoy. We watched the first ten hooks come back empty. Not a good start. The next hook had a small sword on it, still alive. Mark carefully removed the hook before tossing him back in.

The next line looked like it had tension on it. Our captain struggled to pull it to the surface.

"It feels like a tuna, a big one." The fish broke the surface of the water at the edge of the bright deck lights. It thrashed. The crew struggled to gaff it, dragging it through the same fish door I was dragged through only a few short days ago.

I shuddered at the sight. The hours dragged on as the long line was reeled in. Needing to stretch, I grabbed my life jacket.

"Eric, I'm going to get a little air."

"Make sure you stay out of the way."

Mark grabbed another hook with lots of tension on it. He strained to pull in the line. Suddenly, the water became frothy white.

A big shark cleared the surface. It took the entire crew to yank it aboard.

The denizen thrashed, only a few feet from me. It's huge teeth gnashed, grinding at the air. Falling backward while trying to stay clear of this predator, I nearly ran into Eric.

Having seen the dorsal fin of the shark, he grabbed the shotgun. As the shark thrashed, he took aim at its head. The loud blast signaled an end to the massive predator's life.

"A short-fin mako." Mark came over to me. "You OK?" A deep breath helped calm my very frayed nerves. The shark was easily twelve-feet-long. Could this be one of the denizens who harassed me?

Regardless, I couldn't help but be saddened by the death of such a beautiful animal.

"I'm fine."

"It's not the best fish to bring to market, but it should fetch us some decent money. Come on guys, we have more fish to board." Mark encouraged the crew.

Eric grabbed my arm, pulling me back into the wheelhouse. I sat for a long time in the other watch seat, shivering.

Another hour passed. The long line was reeled all the way in. Our captain came into the wheelhouse right at midnight. He sat in his chair, working on the catch numbers along with the estimated fish weights.

"I'm shutting the boat down for a few hours so everyone can sleep. We'll start rebaiting the hooks at 0500. I'll take watch. Go below and get some rest." He looked directly at me when he said this.

Opening my mouth to argue my need to look for Joey, Eric grabbed my arm and pulled me out the door. He silenced me with a look. Once out of earshot of Mark, he turned to me.

"You weren't going to argue with him, were you?"

"But, Eric."

"Did you forget your promise to Tom?" I shook my head no, realizing my mistake.

"I'm sorry, it must be the exhaustion." We turned for my cabin. I slipped inside to take a quick shower. While brushing my wet hair, I heard a knock on the door.

"Come in." Eric poked his head in.

"Are you OK after the shark thing?"

"Yes." He turned to leave. "Eric."

"Yeah."

"I'm sorry about the other morning. I didn't mean to offend you."

"Who says I was offended?"

"Tom told me you were upset. I didn't misread your intentions. I know you were trying to comfort me after the nightmares. Actually, it really did help. Sometimes I have a hard time...accepting help."

"That's the understatement of the week. Well, it looks like it doesn't matter anyway. You made it through last night with no nightmares. Let's hope the trend continues. Goodnight." He closed the door behind him.

Unfortunately, another peaceful night's sleep was not going to happen. Sharks were the theme of my dreams. After I shrieked myself awake, Eric was there. There was a moment's hesitation. He studied my frightened face before engulfing me in his arms.

"Are you good with this?"

I nodded yes.

He nestled against me before I drifted back to sleep.

When I awoke, Eric was gone. I assumed he must be on watch. It was four-thirty in the morning. I decided to rest a little more before heading back on deck.

It was still dark outside when I returned to the wheelhouse. Both Eric and Tom were there. The elder fisherman addressed me.

"Another nightmare last night?"

"Yes. It may have been caused by the shark we caught earlier."

"Linda, maybe coming on this trip wasn't such a good idea. When we get back to Beaufort, you need to get away from this boat."

"Tom, I need to find Joey."

"Jesus, Linda, look at yourself. You can't sleep and you're barely eating. Since we pulled you out of the water, you look like you've lost weight. This stress can't be good for you."

"But, Tom."

"It's my fault you are here. If I hadn't asked Mark, he would never have allowed you on board. I'm not going to make the same mistake again. When we get to Beaufort, you're off this boat."

"Don't I have any say in this?"

"No."

Maybe Tom was right, I thought. I should go back to Naples. After all, I have a business to run, though that's not a great excuse for giving up on Joey.

A Greyhound bus was my best option for the return trip, as I didn't see how I could get on an airplane without ID. Also, I needed to figure out a way to reimburse these guys for all their added expense, especially the extra fuel.

"You look like you're a thousand miles away." Eric looked at me.

"I was thinking of how to get home. A bus is the best option."

"I can drive you back. Make sure you get there safely."

"Eric, there is no way I would impose on you."

"We'll see." He turned his attention back to the sea.

The next day was spent baiting hooks and retrieving the long line, with some very spectacular fish attached to its hooks.

Mitch flew by this morning, reporting no sightings of Joey or any debris from the sunken sailboat. He also reported the *Yellowfin* was steaming back to Morehead City.

As darkness fell on our last night at sea, my eyes were straining, still holding out slim hope of finding my lost mate. My head drooped from exhaustion. Depression was sneaking in as the realization of our not finding Joey began registering in my brain.

Tom came up behind me. He rubbed my sore shoulders.

"Linda, go below and get something to eat. Eric is in the galley making dinner. You need to eat." There was no argument this time.

The younger brother smiled when I entered the galley. The cheeseburgers he whipped up smelled great. We enjoyed a good meal washed down with cool lemonade.

"Thanks, the burgers are great."

"You're very welcome. You look really beat."

"I'm going to try to sleep as soon as we clean up." Once the dishes were stowed, we headed for my cabin. Eric didn't even ask before cuddling me. It was only for a short time, before he left for watch. I rolled over, curled up, and went to sleep.

Soon, daylight was peeking in the porthole. The fishing boat bounced on the rising seas. Eric was back sleeping next to me, his arm draped across me. This handsome man was peacefully resting, his dirty blond hair slightly mussed.

I eased out of bed. My fatigued legs staggered to the head. Cold water was splashed on my face. Red, bloodshot eyes stared back at me from the mirror.

Returning to the cabin, I worked my way back to the bunk where the fisherman was still sleeping. After lying down next to him, he drew me close. The warmth of his body was comforting.

The rate of his breathing changed as he slowly woke up. He snuggled me closer. His warm breath tickled the back of my neck.

"Are you awake, Linda?"

"Yes."

He snuggled me even tighter. My back was against his chest. Both of his arms were wrapped tightly around me. There was silence for a few minutes.

"Linda," he whispered. "The boat will be back in Beaufort today. We need to figure out what happens from here."

"I would like to check with the Coast Guard, maybe tomorrow morning, then I guess I'll head back to Naples." Could he hear the sad pang in my voice? "I'll take the bus back to Florida."

"Not gonna happen," he whispered again. "I'll drive you back. I want to make sure you make it safely." His arms, wrapped tightly around me, tightened more.

"I can't ask you to do that. You have your work here."

"You didn't ask me. Where I come from, if you save someone's life you are responsible for them. I want to make sure you get home safely. Besides, I've always wanted to see Florida."

"Eric, you are a very sweet man, but I can get back to Naples on my own. You need to work on the boat. Maybe we can stay in touch, though." My voice broke. I wanted to climb off the bunk before I started crying.

The fisherman had a tight grip on me. He sighed heavily. "I'm not letting you off this bunk until you agree. They can do without me for a trip." Squirming, I understood there was no getting out of his grip until I acquiesced.

"OK, Eric, you can come to Naples—now let go of me." Turning my head, I saw the grin on his face.

"Linda, you are pretty stubborn, but you've met your match with me. I had a feeling with some gentle coaxing you would see things my way."

Eric left the cabin, allowing me a few moments to reflect on our conversation. Is this guy for real? He's such a different man from Joey. Being with him made me question my unflappable loyalty to Joey. Was the sheer number of years spent in a relationship sufficient reason to pursue this search at all cost?

I located the brothers on the back deck. They were mending a length of fishing line. I watched them skillfully tie a few knots. Eric broke the silence.

"Tom, Linda has agreed to let me drive her back to Naples at the end of this trip. I'll let Mark know I won't be on the next one."

Tom stopped his work for a moment to look at me. "Good, driving her back to Naples is the right things to do. Li'l Sis," he said with a gentle smile, "you need to get some rest. Get your head back on straight. We'll keep searching for Joey."

The remainder of the day was spent getting back to Beaufort and unloading the fish in Morehead City. One big tuna went right to a jet to be flown to Japan for sushi. It was a big payday for the guys.

After dinner, in the midst of the celebration, Mark pulled me aside. "Linda, I'm sorry we didn't find Joey."

Searching his dark brown eyes, I saw only kindness and compassion there. Knowing the huge debt of gratitude I owed this man, I forced a smile on my face. "Mark, thank you so much for everything."

Chapter 9. Naples

That night was more of the same, with little sleep and a couple of bad nightmares. The next morning, I rested in bed for a few extra moments, thinking something's got to give. These nightmares were really affecting me.

Looking at my watch, I saw it was the first of August. It would be steamy in Naples. After dressing and brushing the snarls out of my hair, I wandered down to the galley, finding Tom and Mark there.

"Where's Eric?"

"He went to get a rental car," Tom said. "Are you ready for a road trip?"

"I guess." These fishermen were turning the boat around quickly. They would head back to sea this afternoon for the next round with the tuna and swordfish.

While the men poured over paperwork, I took a minute to burn this scene into my memory. I realized I owed a great deal to the strangers who'd helped me so much.

"Mark, I can't thank you enough for everything you've done. When I get to Naples, I will send you a check for the extra fuel and expenses if you give me your address." A grin spread across his rugged features.

"Linda, don't worry about it. We didn't use much extra fuel. We will continue to look for Joey. You make sure to take care of yourself and get those ribs healed up."

Eric walked in. "Hey, good morning." His hand grazed my shoulder. "We're good to go when you're ready." As I gazed at the scene a moment longer, I noticed a slight frown on Tom's face.

"Let me get my stuff." Now that was an understatement. Back in the cabin, I straightened up the bunk. I did a quick check to ensure the head was tidy. My few meager possessions were stuffed into the borrowed duffel bag.

One last look around the cabin confirmed all was in order. It was sad to leave my home for the past couple of weeks. Gee, Linda, don't get sentimental and start crying over a stupid boat room. What the heck was wrong with me? The tears were rubbed away as I steeled myself.

As I turned to leave, Tom stood in the doorway. His hands were buried deep in the pockets of his jeans. He was in his tough-guy posture, but a gentle smile played around his rough features.

"I'll miss you, Li'l Sis."

There was no stopping the tears now. Tom hugged me tightly. "I'll miss you too." Before a total meltdown occurred, I pulled away, leaving the cabin for the final time. The elder brother stopped me.

"Here's my phone number. If you need anything, do not hesitate to call. Even if you simply want to talk."

"Thanks, Tom."

Outside, Eric gallantly opened the car door for me.

"Your chariot awaits." I looked back at the boat one last time.

We made the short drive to Morehead City. At the Coast Guard base, we checked in with Senior Chief Miller, who informed us the *Yellowfin* was headed back to Charleston. He promised to continue searching with the Jayhawks.

Leaving Morehead City behind, we wove our way through the back roads of North Carolina heading for I-95. There was not much talk as Eric concentrated on finding his way.

When the highway was reached, we turned south.

"Are you hungry?" Eric asked as lunchtime approached.

"Not really." Depression was creeping in, making this trip more difficult. By going back to Naples, I had to face the reality of losing Joey...forever.

"I think we should eat." There was a roadside sign ahead advertising restaurants. After exiting the highway, we stopped at a nondescript roadside restaurants. At least it wasn't a fast-food place.

"I'll have a Coke," he told the nondescript waitress while we settled into a large booth with high back benches and a red-checkered plastic table cloth.

As I sipped a Diet Coke, my eyes didn't really focus on the menu.

"Hey, cheer up. What's the matter?" Eric glanced up from his menu.

"I don't know, Eric. I have this really awful feeling. Not about this road trip...something else."

"Like what?" I shook my head as our food arrived. The fork only pushed the salad around the plate. Very little of it actually reached my mouth. Eric's eyes were on me as he wolfed down a cheeseburger and fries.

"Isn't your salad good?"

"I'm just not hungry, sorry."

We drove back onto the highway, making good time through North Carolina, South Carolina, and Georgia. As nighttime approached, the fisherman pulled off the road at a motel. He stopped the car in front of the office with a red vacancy sign flashing.

His eyes were on me in the dim light.

"Would you like your own room or should I get one with two double beds?" I hadn't really thought of this. Considering the added expense and my delicate financial situation, one room would be best. Also, with the nightmares, I was really afraid to be alone.

"I guess one is OK." Why was I so nervous? "I'll pay you back for this, I promise."

He chuckled, getting out of the car. "Don't worry about it."

The car door was closed before I could respond. He returned a few minutes later.

"We should get some dinner."

"OK."

It was only a short distance to a rib and steak joint. The cocktails and ribs made a pretty decent meal.

Once inside the room at the motel, Eric headed off for a shower. I slipped out of the room to fill the ice bucket. Sitting on one of the beds, I tried to occupy myself mixing two drinks. There were serious butter-flies in my stomach. Weird.

Eric came out of the bathroom wearing just shorts, his hair still dripping. The TV was turned on to the local news. I nervously handed him a drink.

"Thanks."

"I'm going to take a shower." I rushed off into the bathroom. Why the heck was I so nervous?

The steaming water ran down my back, easing some of the tension. Coming out of the bathroom wearing pajamas and feeling very awkward, I looked to Eric. He patted the side of the bed next to him.

"Come sit down." From the look of concern on his face, he must have picked up on my hesitation.

"What's wrong?"

"Nothing." I swallowed hard, sitting next to him. I stared blindly at the television.

"Why are you so tense?"

"I don't know. I just feel—awkward?"

He reached over, handing me a drink. His blue eyes searched mine.

I bit my lip nervously. "Maybe, it's because this is the first time we are completely alone together and not on the fishing boat."

"What do you think is going to happen?" He gave me a devilish grin, which greatly added to my discomfort.

"Do you take great pleasure in making me feel uncomfortable?"

He laughed. "You're too easy. Hell, why are you so tense? Are you afraid I'm going to jump on top of you and have my way with you?" He laughed again. My silence answered for me. He shook his head.

"If that was my intention, it would have happened the first night on the boat. Some hot sex with me is the perfect treatment for hypothermia. Talk about skyrocketing body temperatures."

"Eric, you're incorrigible." I couldn't help but join his laughter.

"Or maybe that's the fantasy, having sex with the famous crab-boat captain you dreamed about while watching him on TV." His grin was challenging. "Is that what you want, Linda?"

"Get a grip, Eric. What makes you think I fantasize about you?" I teased him back. "Now, I really want to change the subject. But before I do, I want you to know I've never met such a conceited, arrogant, egotistical man in my entire life." I smiled sweetly at him.

"Yeah, but I'm a nice guy, too. Remember that. Let's get some sleep. We have a long day tomorrow."

Later that night, the nightmares returned with a vengeance. Not only did I dream of sharks, but also of Joey adrift in the sea, sick and battered by the waves. He looked barely alive. His gaunt face stared back at me.

There was only fitful sleep until the dim rays of daylight streamed in the window. Eric was glancing out the window. He must have heard me stir. After turning around, he sat on the edge of the bed.

"Are you ready to head back on the road?" As I sat up, my ribs twinged again. Eric caught this. His hand gently touched my side. "They're hurting again. You really should get them x-rayed."

"I'm fine." I pushed his hand away. "I'll be ready to go in a few minutes."

Soon we pulled onto the southbound ramp of I-95. We headed for the Florida border.

"Do you mind some music?" I reached for the stereo.

"No, not at all. You seem better this morning."

The classic rock station was playing Boston's "Don't Look Back." The volume was low enough to allow conversation.

"Is rock all right with you?"

Eric glanced at me out of the corner of his eye, while concentrating on the road.

"It depends on the mood. If we are on *Denali,* in the middle of the night, pulling pots in a blizzard, then rock is perfect. If I'm at the ranch, relaxing by the fireplace, country or jazz works better."

"What about driving down the interstate at nearly ninety miles an hour?"

"Is that a crack about my driving?"

"No."

"Rock is fine." He backed off his speed.

We crossed the Florida border. After a quick lunch stop, we crossed the Sunshine State by Mickey's place. Turning south from I-4 onto I-75, we left Tampa behind. We cruised over the bridge spanning the Intracoastal Waterway at Beautiful Island. Joey and I had traversed this part of the ICW many times.

Naples' exits began to appear. Directing Eric to pull off at the Golden Gate exit, we cruised down the parkway to Goodlette-Frank Road as the scenery turned from highway blacktop to pretty manicured local roadways where palm trees and flowers abound.

A few minutes later, we pulled into the Cove Inn parking lot. We had arrived.

Eric appraised the pretty hotel from the car.

"This looks like a nice place. The tropical plants are gorgeous."

"Is this your first trip to Florida?" I asked, trying to keep the depression at bay.

"Yes, though I always wanted to see it. It's a heck of a long way from Alaska. Why don't you show me around?"

We walked up the three steps to the breezeway by the Chickee Bar and swimming pool area. As we turned right toward the boats, a couple of greetings were shouted by the usual cast of characters at the bar. I gave them a half-hearted wave.

"This is my boat." We stopped in front of a pretty emerald green sailboat. It was a huge battle to fight off the tears.

"She's a beauty." Eric took a moment to walk down the finger pier, admiring the stout and sturdy Westsail 32. She gleamed like a diamond in the hot Florida sunshine.

"This teak must be a bitch to maintain in this heat. I'm glad I own a crab boat. We don't worry too much about cosmetics because the pots are constantly slamming into her. This varnish would be gone in ten seconds." He turned back toward me.

"Linda, what's the matter?" He must have seen the look on my face.

"I feel like someone kicked me in the stomach, looking at her." The polished emerald green hull glistened along with her glowing varnished teak trim and handrails. "God only knows how many hours Joey and I spent spit-polishing this yacht every month."

The name on her sides, *Dark & Stormy*, reflected not only our favorite drink, but also, to some extent, Joey's and my relationship.

Eric walked back over to me. "I'm going to get a room in the hotel. Are you going to be OK?"

"Yes, I'm fine. I'll be along in a minute."

I stepped aboard my boat, removing the spare key hidden in the cockpit locker. The hatch slid open easily. A slight musty odor wafted out, as she had been closed up for several weeks.

The temperature down below resembled a blast furnace, but I hardly notice the heat as I sat on the starboard settee. There was a picture of Joey and me catching a fish offshore. We both wore huge grins on our faces. Numbness suffused my body and mind.

There were voices on the dock. I remained hidden while catching pieces of the conversation. Eric must have walked down the finger pier. He was accosted by a familiar voice.

"Hey, can I help you? That boat is private property." It was my good friend Shane. The five-foot-ten, wiry charter captain always looked out for everyone's boats. A stranger on the dock would arouse his suspicion.

"I'm Eric Iverson, a friend of Linda's."

"I'm Shane Wilson. I work for Linda and Joey. I run their charter boat over at the City Dock. Are they back?"

"I need to tell you something, but for now, please keep it quiet." Eric lowered his voice. Though I really didn't want him discussing the loss of *Wind* Rose, someone had to let Shane know about Joey. My ears strained to hear their words.

"Linda and Joey had an accident. They hit something off of Cape Hatteras then lost the boat they were delivering. The fishing boat I was manning rescued her. Joey is still missing."

"Damn, I didn't hear anything about this." Shane sounded very upset.

"She's pretty messed up right now. If you could continue running the business, I would appreciate it."

"Sure, of course. Is she on the boat?"

"Yes, but I don't know her state of mind right now. We just got here a few minutes ago."

"Tell her if she needs anything..."

"I will. Here's my cell phone number if you need to get in touch."

A moment later, the boat rocked. Eric poked his head through the hatch.

"It's me. Is it OK to come aboard?" I appreciated his etiquette.

"Sure." He walked down the companionway looking left and right, checking out the boat. He saw the sweat on my brow.

"It must be 110 degrees in here. Don't you have air conditioning?"

"I didn't open the sea cock."

"Let's get out of here. We can relax in the cool hotel room. I didn't expect Florida to be this hot." He reached out, taking my hand to lead me off the boat.

I walked like a zombie to the hotel room, not noticing its pretty tropical decor. Eric put his hand on my forehead, feeling my hot brow.

"Sit down in front of the fan. You're going to go from hypothermia to heat stroke if you don't watch it."

"I'm all right." Now in the cool air conditioning, I realized how hot my body felt.

"How about a cold drink?" Eric offered.

"As long as it has rum in it." At the sliding glass door, I looked out at the boats. We were in a room on the second floor, directly over my boat. Eric and I sipped our drinks in companionable silence for a few minutes.

"We should get dinner soon," Eric suggested. "Where would you like to go?"

Though I was not very hungry, neither one of us had eaten much today. I wanted to keep clear of the most popular haunts to avoid running into anyone I knew then having to give out long explanations.

We decided on the Crooked Palm Pub. Cool drinks were enjoyed in the tropical setting.

"Linda, why don't we take a ride around after dinner. Where's the beach?"

"It's that way." I motioned to the west.

"Do you want to go for a walk there after dinner?"

"OK," I said, trying to force a smile. After picking through my food, we hopped back in the car.

Capt. Marlena Brackebusch

I directed Eric down palm tree-lined Central Avenue past the public library. Like most Naples streets, Central Avenue was dotted with pretty pastel-colored houses and green manicured lawns. After four blocks, we stopped at the beach.

Quarters were dropped in the meter. We walked over the wooden walkway to the beach.

"Great beach. It seems to go on for miles." Silently, our bare feet meandered on the soft, sugar-white sand. It actually felt good to have the sand squish between my toes, relaxing me.

A gentle breeze flowed over us as we ambled down near the water. The warm, gentle waves washed over our feet. Suddenly, I tensed up. A strange feeling overwhelmed me. I swerved out of the water. Eric didn't miss this.

"Linda, why did you walk out of the water?"

"I don't know." I turned away from him. He grabbed my hand, spinning me around to face him.

"What's the matter?"

"I don't know. Since you rescued me, every time I get into the water, like in the shower, I get this strange feeling. Like I have to get out, get away from the water. The same thing just happened."

"*Hmm.*" He held my hands for a few moments while searching my eyes. "I guess it will take some time to get over the accident. We'll work on it."

After the short drive to the Cove Inn, we chatted at the kitchenette table.

"What's the game plan for tomorrow?" Eric asked.

"I would like to spend a few minutes, *um*, alone on the boat. My passport and money are there. That should be good enough to get a new driver's license. Then the credit card companies need to be called...." My voice trailed off as I quickly felt overwhelmed.

Eric must have sensed my distress. He reached over, placing his hand on top of mine.

"Let's take it one step at a time. I'll help you."

That night I slept uneasily. The dreams of the shark stormed back with a vengeance. The nightmare started off with me walking on the beach. A black night. I went swimming in the dark water.

Out of the corner of my eye, I sensed more than saw movement, a black triangular fin. The shark dragged me under. The water suffocated me. Joey's face circled my fading vision.

The cry woke me. Eric surrounded me with his arms. After not sleeping well the rest of the night, I was more tired when I arose early the next morning.

Forcing myself out of bed, I slipped down to the boat to pick up my passport and a couple of hundred dollars stashed away in a secret locker. A change of clothes was tossed into a bag.

Re-entering the room, I saw Eric making coffee.

"You got up before me today."

"I didn't sleep well." I joined him at the table.

"Everything OK on the boat?"

"Yeah. I put the air conditioner on so it won't be so hot. After we get the errands done today, I would like to check the batteries and some other stuff. It's been a while since we were on her."

"How about a little help with that?" Eric sat opposite me at the table. I fished a one-hundred-dollar bill out of my pocket, sliding it across the table.

"What's this?"

"It's a down payment on what I owe you. As soon as the bank opens, I'll have the rest." My eyes looked down at my coffee cup.

He pushed the money away.

"No way! You don't owe me anything."

"Eric. You have been amazing. Your incredible kindness can never be repaid. I have to at least repay the money you've spent."

He shrugged. "You forget I'm a dashing, wealthy television star. The money I've spent is a mere pittance." He teased me before becoming serious. "I know a way you can repay me. Take me sailing to the Keys. I've never been there."

"OK, you've got a deal, though I'm not sure I'm ready for a sailing trip right away."

The rest of the day was spent getting a new driver's license and trying to put my financial life back together. We ended the day sitting on the balcony, overlooking the bay and all the beautiful yachts, while watching the sunset.

"We should go to the Chickee Bar for a drink," Eric said, looking at me.

"Can we go another time? I don't have the strength for all the questions, which really don't have any answers at this time." My voice trailed off as I looked at *Dark & Stormy*.

Eric slid his folding beach chair closer to mine.

"Linda, take it slow. Maybe a change of scenery would be a good idea," Eric said but didn't elaborate.

Sitting there, staring at my beloved boat, I contemplated all that had gone on. I decided to make a phone call I'd been dreading.

"Eric, could I use your cell phone?"

"Sure." He gave me his phone with a puzzled look on his face.

The call was placed to the owner of *Wind Rose*. Stammering, I told my version of the sinking, though the Coast Guard had already called about the loss.

"I'm so sorry for the loss of your boat."

He expressed his concern for Joey, offering his assistance. This kind man also wished me well in my recovery. Hanging up, I pushed the phone back across the table.

Dreams and flashbacks intensely dominated my sleep later on. I was trapped inside the boat. The water crept to my ankles, then to my knees, then to the top of my thighs. My arms worked only in slow motion, dumping out the buckets of water.

A big wave hit, flipping the boat. The foaming cauldron engulfed me. I couldn't keep my head above water. Joey's deathly pale face floated in front of me. His eyes were closed. A voice was calling.

"Linda, wake up." Eric brought me back to reality. He held me as tears streamed down my face. Slowly, my heart stopped pounding.

"Linda," Eric whispered. "These nightmares are getting worse. Tell me what just happened."

My head rested on his outstretched arm.

"It was terrible. I dreamt Joey was dead, floating in front of me." My voice cracked. "I keep having this terrible feeling something is wrong."

"Let's call Senior Chief Miller in the morning to see if there's any news." I stayed awake for a long time.

Daylight streamed in the sliding door. My sore eyes located the fisherman sitting at the table, reading the newspaper. An overwhelming feeling of dread permeated my brain. I kept it to myself for now.

After finishing our coffee, we went to *Dark & Stormy*. Distilled water was added to the batteries. After carefully pulling out the dipstick, I checked the oil level. Next, I crawled into the narrow space behind the engine to check the transmission fluid.

Looking under a floorboard, I verified the bilges were dry. A bemused smile was on Eric's face. My eye caught him studying me.

"Why are you looking at me that way?"

He wiped a bead of sweat off his forehead.

"I'm not used to a woman knowing her way around an engine room. It's intriguing."

"Yeah, right," I said in disbelief, tossing a wadded up paper towel at him. It was a battle to return his smile.

Walking back to the hotel room, we ran into Shane. He hugged me, expressing his sorrow about the sinking. "Is there any word on Joey?"

"No, not yet. We're going to call the Coast Guard shortly."

"Linda, don't worry about the business. I have things under control. There's not much going on in August."

"I know, my friend. Thanks so much. Let's hope the hurricanes stay away."

After leaving Shane, we walked up the flight of stairs to the second floor. The cool air conditioning felt great.

"Linda, I'm going to call Chief Miller." Eric pulled out his phone, dialing the Morehead City number. After pleasantries were exchanged, the fisherman listened for a few minutes, wearing a poker face.

After he hung up, he turned to me. From his stiff posture, I could tell something was wrong.

"Linda, come sit down over here," he whispered, leading me to the couch.

"Eric, what's wrong?"

"Sit down. Linda, the Coast Guard has called off the search for Joey. They tried to reach you on the fishing boat. Chief Miller was just about to call my cell...."

"No!" I cried, lunging for Eric's cell phone. "We have to call them back. They have to keep searching. Eric, we have to...No!" My voice broke as the fisherman wrapped his arms around my quaking body. The sobs poured out of me. I tried to push him away, but he held on tight, allowing me to vent the hysteria.

Several tense moments passed. It took a long time before I was coherent again.

"Linda, listen to me. It's going to be all right. Calm down."

"Eric." I desperately tried to stem the tears. "We have to get on a plane to Morehead City. I have to persuade the Coast Guard to resume the search. Also, we have to get a hold of Mark. He'll help me search again. Joey has to be found."

"Linda. The Coast Guard has searched with ships and helicopters for almost two weeks. Do you really think going back while resuming your own search will do any good?"

"Maybe. If he was able to get into the liferaft."

"Linda, listen to me. I'm almost certain Mark would turn down your request. It doesn't make sense. What chance would we have finding him? The Coast Guard is going to continue to broadcast Pan Pan calls and look for him during routine missions."

My shoulder's drooped as my head was buried in my hands. All kinds of crazy thoughts swirled through my brain.

"Eric, I can take *Dark & Stormy* out to search for Joey."

"Linda, that's the craziest thing you've said so far. The Outer Banks is a week away by sailboat. Look, we need to come up with a plan to de-stress you. You need to forget about Joey and concentrate on your health."

"Forget about Joey? How can you say that?"

"Linda..." I knew he was being careful to choose the right words. "You need to face the facts. We don't know if he made it into the liferaft. If he did, surviving two weeks with no food or water is nearly impossible."

Eric sat next to me. Everything he said made sense.

After a few minutes, I looked out the sliding glass doors at *Dark & Stormy*. Reaching for the aching ribs, my right hand tried to rub away the pain. Joey, where are you? I knew deep in my heart he was still alive.

"Eric, I need to be alone." I dashed from the room, taking refuge on my boat. Hours passed as I blindly stared at the familiar surroundings. What the hell was I going to do?

There had to be a solution to my shattered future. A knock on the boat broke my reverie. Pushing the teak entry doors open, my eyes blinked in the bright sunlight. Eric was standing on the dock.

"I was worried about you. Can I come aboard?"

"Sure." We went below. Eric sat on the settee opposite me, quietly looking at me. Finally, he broke the silence.

"Linda, I'm worried about you. With the nightmares and the news today, I don't think sitting on this boat is good for you."

My gaze turned to him. While staring at him, I tried to toughen up my appearance.

"Eric, I'll be fine. I need to get back to my business and work through this. You have been great, but don't feel like you have to babysit me. You probably want to get back to fishing." My voice cracked at the end of this statement.

Eric rubbed his chin, frowning. "I hardly feel like I'm babysitting you. I'm here because I want to be here. Remember what I said about saving your life."

When I tried to interrupt him, he came over next to me. He put a finger to my lips, silencing me.

"Hear me out. You need a change of scenery. There is some work which needs my attention. How would you like to come to my ranch in Texas for a couple of weeks? You can de-stress and relax. Heal those ribs. You'll have plenty of room to roam around, with fresh clean air to clear your head."

"Eric, that's very sweet, but I don't think so. I need to stay here to get my business back together." Though my argument sounded somewhat persuasive, I actually liked the idea of getting away. The thought of being alone right now scared me.

"Linda, your excuse is not very convincing. Shane is running your business. I won't take no for an answer. Remember the last time we had a disagreement on the boat. I'm just as stubborn as you are, lady."

"OK." I was too exhausted to argue further.

We locked the boat then headed back to the hotel room. Eric made a few phone calls. When finished, he sat next to me with a smile.

"It's all set. Tomorrow, we have a one P.M. flight out of Ft. Myers for DFW Airport."

During the night, nightmares continued to plague me. Exhausted I dragged myself out of bed early to prep *Dark & Stormy* for an extended absence. I rechecked the dry bilge and shut off any seacocks not in use.

The position of the automatic bilge pump switch was double-checked. After packing my clothes like a zombie, I grabbed my checkbook.

Eric drove us north on U.S.-41. After a quick stop at the bank, we headed for the airport. Sitting in the departure lounge, Eric watched me fidget.

"You look very nervous."

"I'm not the biggest fan of flying."

"Oh, yeah, I remember the helicopter thing. We'll be fine. To be honest, I don't particularly like flying either, especially commercial airlines, but for a different reason. I hate crowds."

"What's the matter, did you leave the private jet at home?" I kidded him.

Eric studied me. "Actually, we fly on many charter flights, especially to Alaska and for the TV show. It's much more comfortable, especially when the network is paying for it." He winked.

We boarded the flight. My eyes checked the ticket stubs for the first time. We were seated in seats three A and B.

"Window or aisle?" Eric asked.

"Window," I mumbled. He guided me into the seat. I was taken aback by these First Class seats. Eric ordered drinks from the flight attendant as I looked at him.

"What?" he asked with upturned hands along with a shrug and a grin.

"First Class?"

"I told you, I hate crowds. I couldn't sit all squeezed up in the back. Plus, you get cocktails anytime you want." He handed me a drink. I tried to settle back in the seat. The jet taxied to the runway. Engines roared. My right hand gripped the armrest between our seats. Eric pried my hand off, holding it.

"You really don't like flying." He squeezed my hand comfortingly. Saying nothing, I braced my knees against the seat in front of me. My body stiffened in anticipation of takeoff.

"Relax, it's going to be fine."

Chapter 10. Texas

Once the jet was flying, I managed to simmer down. A couple of hours later, the plane circled DFW airport, landing easily. At the baggage claim, a tall man walked up to us. He shook hands warmly with Eric, who then introduced me.

"Linda, meet Ricardo, my ranch manager." Shaking hands with this man, I noticed he was at least six-feet tall and lanky. He wore a red plaid shirt and jeans. His jet-black hair was topped with a black cowboy hat. Thirty-five would be a reasonable guess for his age.

"Howdy, ma'am." He greeted me with a slight drawl. "Welcome to Texas." The three of us walked outside to a huge, forest-green Chevy Silverado four-door pickup truck.

Ricardo drove, discussing ranch business with Eric. From the back seat, I observed all the flat, dry scrub southeast of Dallas. We cruised through a small town adorned by more greenery then entered an area with small rolling hills.

Ricardo stopped in front of the entrance to a long dirt road. A tall gate blocked our path. He pushed a button on a remote control similar to a garage door opener. The gate swung open.

"Don't want the critters getting out," Eric said. I had pictured a little house with maybe a barn and a few cows. How wrong could I be?

Capt. Marlena Brackebusch

We drove down the dirt road for what seemed an eternity. Ricardo stopped in front of a big single-story ranch painted white with black shutters around the windows. The front porch was huge, with lounge chairs and a porch swing sporting comfortable brown cushions and pillows.

Eric led me into the living room. There was a sunken area off to the right with a fireplace. Wood was stacked nearby. A couple of very cozy-looking couches completed the seating area. This was definitely a masculine decor. Above the fireplace was a horn from a steer.

"Is this real?" I bent down to run my fingers through a soft animal-skin rug.

"Yes. It's from a big brown bear I shot a mile from here. He was taking some of my cattle."

The ceiling was accented with dark exposed wood beams. Windows lined the front wall with beige curtains drawn back, allowing sunlight to stream in.

On the other side of the sunken living room area a hallway connected to more rooms–bedrooms, perhaps. There were shelves on the left hand wall filled with books and nautical things, including a scale model of a sailing ship. Below the shelves was a small wet bar made of mahogany, lined with bar stools.

"Neat picture." Over the bar hung a picture of his crab boat, bashing through a storm. Eric came up behind me.

"Do you know what boat that is?"

"*Hmm*, is that the *Northern Belle?*"

"Cute, Linda. You damn well know what boat that is."

Yes, I did, but I did not give him the satisfaction.

He latched onto my arm, leading me down the hallway across from the entrance. The first door on the right was obviously his office—a computer sat on a wooden desk. There was a small TV on an end table. Most of the walls had book shelves, doubling the space as a library. A filing cabinet stood next to the desk, which had unopened mail stacked on it.

"My office." The next room was a bedroom decorated more femininely with bright yellows and greens on the two queen-size beds.

"Guest room number one." Adjacent to this room was a good-size Jack and Jill bathroom with walk-in shower. Doors led to the first guest room and a room to the left, which was the second guest bedroom.

Continuing on to the next bedroom, I discovered it was bright and airy with a more tropical theme. A fake bamboo plant stood in the corner with a stuffed parrot on it. A queen-size bed squeezed against the wall.

"My tropical guest room. I thought this would work for you, yes?"

"It's perfect, thanks."

"Ah and next is the master bedroom." He led me into an enormous master bedroom with a masculine flair. The décor was Western, with lots of dark wood and horse pictures. A picture of Eric roping a calf decorated the near wall. He rode a dapple gray, which looked like a quarter horse.

Taking my hand, he showed me the master bath, complete with twin sinks and a large jetted tub separate from the walk-in shower.

"What a lovely bathroom. It looks very comfortable."

"It does the job. Look at this." He pointed toward the drawn curtains on the other side of the king-size bed. We stepped over, looking out the sliding doors to a deck area complete with a large swimming pool. Nearby was a whirlpool spa. A grill stood next to the tropical wet bar with a thatched roof.

The view beyond stunned me. Rolling green pasture land flowed across the landscape. Off to the left, a good distance from the house, a huge barn overlooked a smaller building about halfway back to the house. Both were barn red with white accents.

"Eric, what is that corral over there?"

"It's a exercise area for the horses. Also, it is used to practice cattle roping. My guys and I enter rodeos as a calf roping team. It keeps my reflexes sharp."

Beyond the corral, a large group of cows munched on the verdant oasis beyond the picket fence. Sprawling shade trees dotted the property.

"What a superb backyard." I said appreciatively. "I guess the old saying is correct, 'everything is bigger in Texas.'"

"Come see the kitchen." We strolled into the room where a petite, Hispanic-looking lady fussed around the stove.

"Good afternoon, Maria."

"Eric." Her face lit up in a smile. Her small frame nearly disappeared in the big fisherman's hug.

"Linda, meet Maria, Ricardo's wife."

"Nice to meet you," we both said, clasping hands.

"I'm preparing dinner for seven. I hope that's OK?"

"Perfect, thanks," said Eric. I glanced around the kitchen with its center island, gray granite countertops, and brushed stainless appliances of every conceivable type.

Off to the left, a small dining room which could seat eight or ten included a glass-topped table. French doors divided the kitchen from the back deck and pool area.

"We have just enough time for a cocktail before dinner." With a glance at his watch, Eric routed us back to the living room.

"Rum?"

"Great."

The comfy sofa enveloped me in its silky embrace. The fisherman-turned-cowboy handed me a drink before squatting in front of the hearth. He hefted gnarled logs onto the black slate. Kindling hissed, crackling into a hearty blaze. Settling next to me, he asked. "What do you think of the place?"

"The ranch is spectacular. I particularly love the fireplace. What kind of rock is surrounding it?"

"It is river rock from the Alaska. Pretty exotic for Texas, but I love the texture." He glanced at me with a flash of uncertainty.

"Eric, I've been the one with all the tension and nervousness up until now. I can't help but get the feeling you are uncomfortable with me here."

"I wanted you to like this place. My wife hated it. You wouldn't believe my disappointment. This land was nothing but scrub when I bought it."

"Creating all of this must have been a whole lot of work. Did you always want to have a ranch?"

"When my family moved from Oregon to Alaska, it seemed like we moved to the wild west. The winters were terrible, all those hours of darkness. My mother was from Texas. We would get away for few weeks, every summer, at our aunt's house in Austin."

"Austin must be very different from Alaska."

"It is. The best part was the neighbors. They had several horses. I loved to watch their graceful movements. Also, they are very sensitive animals."

"Tell me how you came to buy this place."

"Linda, there was only so much cold and snow I could tolerate. When my dad passed away, Tom and I took over the business. My brother loves Alaska and all the snow and cold. When I finally grew up enough to realize what I wanted, I knew it was a ranch."

"So, you bought this place."

"Actually, it took quite a few years to find the right spot with an abundance of land. I spent two years and a ton of money building this place. I thought it would be a nice retirement home, which could support itself with the cattle business."

"Your wife had other ideas?"

"When she walked in, she almost turned around and left. Gee, you think you know someone."

"I'm sorry, Eric."

"You know we got a divorce." His voice was so quiet I barely heard what he said.

"I think I heard something about it on TV."

"More likely out of my brother's big mouth."

"He didn't...."

"Yes, he did. I noticed the change in you a couple of days after your comment about being in bed with a married man. Though still nervous, you allowed me to put my arms around you. Tom told you." He stared intently at me.

"Linda, I don't want to play games with you. If we are going to be friends, you have to be honest with me."

"Tom told me. He made me promise not to tell you."

Maria interrupted the conversation, announcing dinner. Ricardo stood as we entered the dining room.

The fisherman slid out a chair for me then sat to my left at the head of the table. He poured wine as Maria checked the serving dishes steaming away.

The meal of spicy stewed beef was quite a treat. I only allowed myself a little dessert. When finished, Eric led me toward the front door.

"Sunset is great from out front."

The porch swing swayed. Eric reappeared with two drinks. He settled next to me.

"Brandy? I hope that's OK"

"Great." The porch swing creaked, slowly swinging back and forth as the sun set. Brilliant red streaks reflected off the clouds. Cicadas chirped, breaking the silence.

"Tomorrow morning, we can check out the animals. Do you like horses?"

"I love horses. How many do you have?"

"Oh, a few. Do you ride?"

"It's been a while."

"Riding on horseback is the best way to see the ranch. We'll take a little time to go exploring tomorrow."

Now this idea made me nervous. From the picture in the bedroom, this cowboy was obviously an expert rider. My rusty, self-taught skills hadn't been used in years. Was there any hope of not making a fool of myself?

Once the darkness descended, a chill nipped the air. Eric caught me rubbing my arms. "Are you cold?"

"It's a little chilly out here."

"Let's go sit by the fire."

Back in the living room, he cast another log to the hearth. Ricardo poked his head in.

"Do you need anything else from me tonight, boss?"

"No thanks, Ricardo. Why don't we meet after lunch tomorrow? You can bring me up to speed on the ranch. I'm taking Linda riding in the morning."

"No problem. I have work to do in the garage. Would you like Maria to cook breakfast before your ride?"

"No, we'll be fine. I'll rustle something up." They exchanged good nights.

"Where do Ricardo and Maria live?"

"They live in a house on the other side of this one," Eric said. "Sometimes they eat here and sometimes not. Since the break up..." he paused obviously in pain.

We sat in silence. The mesmerizing sound of the crackling fire along with all the stress soon had my head drooping.

"You look exhausted. How about some sleep?"

My head leaned against his soft denim shirt.

"Sorry, I dosed off for a second."

"Ricardo put your bags in the guest room."

"I would love a shower first."

"There are clean towels in the guest bath. You should find everything you need in there—holler if you need anything else. I'll take a shower too." He gazed at me with a strange look on his face.

My nightgown was covered by the fluffy robe hanging in the bathroom. The fleecy material warded off the evening chill.

The velvet black night sky suspended flecks of stars out the back window. The stress of the sinking boat and the traumatic aftermath trickled from my brain. Guilt, for coming here to Texas instead of going back to look for Joey, seeped in.

There was movement behind me. A hand grazed my neck.

"Linda. Do you want me to stay with you, in case the nightmares return?" His voice was a low whisper. My eyes rose to meet the uncertainty in his.

"Please stay."

He drew back the covers. My body was tense next to his. Eric held me close. The uncomfortable feeling lessened as sleep inundated me.

Capt. Marlena Brackebusch

More nightmares plagued my dreams. Dark, sinister shapes became the vicious teeth of a man-eating shark. Cold water, along with Joey's gaunt face, woke me with a shriek. Strong arms comforted me.

When was this going to end?

I stared at the ceiling until daybreak.

Chapter 11. The Ranch

A few moments later, I pulled the bathrobe around me.

Wandering to the kitchen, I found our daily coffee routine comforting.

With mug in hand, I stared out the window. A man saddling a horse caught my eye. Eric came over, following my gaze.

"That's Daniel, my horse trainer. He's young but really good with the horses.

"How many horses do you have?"

"You'll see," he said evasively. "How about some breakfast?" Eric pulled bagels from the fridge. We lingered over the food, enjoying the quiet time after the craziness of the past couple of weeks.

After breakfast, I returned to the bedroom to change. "Wear some long pants."

I found him waiting for me in the living room wearing a blue denim shirt, jeans, and a black cowboy hat. He handed me a similar black cowboy hat with some studs on it. I felt silly putting it on.

We strolled across the soft green grass to the barn. Daniel exercised a horse in the corral. He rode over.

"Good morning, Mr. Eric." He greeted his boss politely.

"Morning, Daniel. This is Linda."

"Morning, ma'am." The young man tipped his cowboy hat.

"Linda and I are taking Sonny and Outlaw for a ride this morning."

"Shall I saddle them for you?" Daniel asked.

"No, we'll get it."

My nervousness escalated. Not only had I not ridden in a long time, but I doubted I remembered how to saddle a horse. I feared I'd look like a nitwit.

"I'm going to show her the other horses first." He motioned toward the horse Daniel was riding, a beautiful bay. "That's Chico, one of my roping horses. He's also good around the barrels."

A short walk brought us to the barn, if you could call it that. It was more like a resort for horses, with two opposing rows of large stalls. Everything was spotless. The sweet smell of fresh cut hay permeated the air.

In the first stall stood an older-looking palomino with a white mane. He sauntered over, poking his head out, looking at us with calm eyes. The big horse nuzzled Eric's hand. He, in turn, stroked the steed's forehead.

"This is Sonny." Eric scratched him behind the ears. "You'll ride him. He's a nice, easygoing middle-aged fellow."

Inside the next stall was a big dapple gray, probably the one pictured in the master bedroom.

"This is Outlaw. I'll ride him. He's quite spirited." The following stall contained a bay mare.

"Ah, our beautiful mare Daisy. She's an ex-thoroughbred racehorse and Blackjack's mom."

Continuing down the line, he introduced me to a few more horses. Finally, we arrived at the end stall. As I approached, Eric cautioned me.

"That's Blackjack's stall. He's the most ornery thoroughbred I've ever met. He likes to bite, especially if he doesn't know you. He's a two-year-old descendant of Secretariat. We hope to start racing him soon."

Nearing the stall, I was surprised by the jet black horse who charged at the gate, whinnying. He kicked the stall door, but I didn't back away.

"Careful," Eric warned. Blackjack stared at me with a wild look in his eyes, then lunged. He tried to bite me, but I jerked my hand away in time. I pushed his head away while not backing down.

"That's not very nice," I said softly. He backed off a step as I reached into my pocket. A carrot, procured from the fridge and concealed until the right moment, was produced.

"You have to be nice." My eyes didn't leave the black horse as he dropped his head, extending his muzzle. Fuzzy lips gently took the carrot. He nuzzled my hand for a second before flipping up his head then stomping around his stall like a naughty child.

"You're great with horses." Eric looked amazed. "Or do you just know the way to their heart?"

"Just like a man—through his stomach." I chuckled as Eric reached for me playfully. I ducked out of his grasp. "Seriously, though, I think I understand them. You have to promise not to laugh at me." I stopped.

Eric looked inquisitively at me.

"I haven't ridden in a long time and never had any formal training."

"It's OK. I'll teach you. I promise not to laugh." He led me into the tack room. The walls were lined with many different types of saddles and bridles. The air was scented with the rich aroma of leather.

"English or Western?" he asked. Thankfully I knew the answer to this.

"Western." He grabbed a saddle with a bridle. I reached for them, but he carried them into the barn. We walked over to Sonny's stall.

"Can you open the gate?" Walking into the stall, he plopped the saddle on Sonny's back.

"Linda, grab his halter." While I held the horse's head, Eric slipped the bit into his mouth.

"Loop the bridle over his ears. Always be careful, because they are very sensitive about their ears." He buckled the leather behind the palomino's head.

"Make the saddle snug, but not too tight. You'll get a feel for it after a few times." He straightened up, turning back to me. "We'll adjust the stirrups later."

We returned to the tack room to repeat the process with Outlaw. He guided the gray out of the stall, tying him to a post outside. Then we brought Sonny out, to a position near Outlaw.

Eric guessed at the stirrup adjustment before turning to me.

"Rider up. Just put your foot in the stirrup and swing your leg over," he said when I hesitated for a moment.

"I know." I answered him with irritation in my voice. He gave me a hand up, adjusting the other stirrup. The reins felt foreign in my hands.

He hopped onto Outlaw, moving his horse close to mine until our legs touched.

"You ready?" I nodded. "Squeeze with your legs. We'll go slowly. Sonny will follow Outlaw." Giving his horse a nearly imperceptible kick, he walked off with my horse following.

I was not too pleased with the horse walking off on his own, but I decided to go with it.

Eric looked back with a smile. We walked over to a fence with a gate in it. The fisherman jumped off his horse, handing me the reins.

"Take them through."

Great, I now had both horses under my control. Hoping they didn't bolt, I kicked Sonny lightly. The two horses walked through the gate, stopping when I eased back on the reins. The gate closed behind us.

"Good job." I was amazed by how effortlessly he jumped back on his mount.

The man was an enigma: a fisherman in the freezing cold Bering Sea, but also a cattleman and horseman.

We walked the horses down the trail with Eric giving me some riding pointers.

"Ready to go faster?" I nodded. He kicked his horse into a trot then a canter. We rode though a field of bright green grass, laden with wild flowers, until I suddenly pulled back on Sonny. Eric circled around. He must have noticed my wincing.

"Oh shit, your ribs, I forgot about them. I'm sorry." He looked concerned.

"It's OK. They're a little painful when the horses run." It took a few moments, but I regained my breath.

"Why don't we head back? That's enough for today." Side by side, we walked the horses back to the barn. As we rode, I took a moment to enjoy the warm sun on my face. Butterflies cruised from one wildflower to another. Back at the barn, we dismounted. Daniel appeared from inside the barn.

"I'll take them from you if you like, Mr. Eric?"

"Thanks, Daniel. How's Blackjack doing today?"

"He's being himself. I had him in the corral on a lunge line earlier. Blackjack is behaving himself—sort of." Daniel grinned. "I thought I would give him a ride later this afternoon."

"Call me when you do. I'd like to see his progress." We walked back to the house in comfortable silence. When we neared it, Eric turned to me.

"Did you have fun?"

"Yes, it was great, though I think I have a long way to go."

"Just seeing you smile after all you've been through makes it worth-while." We neared the pool area. "How about a swim in the pool to cool off?"

His eyes narrowed as a look of panic passed quickly over my face. I tried to regain my happy look.

"Sure, why not?"

Walking to the guest bedroom to change, I formulated my plan. Sitting next to the pool was fine, but getting in, well, that could be another story. Silently chastising myself because I was afraid to get into the water—after all the scuba diving I've done in the past—I grabbed a towel.

Eric and I almost bumped into each other coming out of the bedrooms. He took my arm, leading me to the pool area. Dropping his towel on a lounge chair, he dove into the pool like a schoolboy.

"Come on in, it's great."

Beads of perspiration collected on my forehead, both from the warm day and the rising panic of getting in the water. What the heck was wrong with me? I used to think nothing of diving off the boat thirty miles offshore to check out a sunken wreck. Now I wouldn't get into a clean, clear eight-foot-deep swimming pool?

Determined to conquer my fear, I sat on the side of the pool, dangling my feet into the water. A cold shiver passed through me.

Eric swam over. "Too cold for your Florida blood?" After studying the look on my face, he hoisted himself out of the pool, settling next to me.

"Linda, what's wrong?"

My vision blurred as I pictured myself drifting alone in the Gulf Stream on that hot, sunny day. Shaking my head to clear it, my voice quivered.

"I don't know...the water."

"Easy." His cold hand touched my shoulder. I'm sure he could feel the tension. "We'll have to take it slow."

Maria walked up to the pool deck carrying a tray of drinks. "I thought you could use cold lemonade."

Setting the tray on a table, she added. "I also made my famous Southwest chicken salad, if you like."

"That's something I don't wanna miss. Thanks Maria," Eric said.

After the excellent food, Eric turned to me.

"Linda, do you mind if Ricado and I take a few minutes to go over the ranch business?"

"No problem, Eric. I'll be in the living room."

Sitting on the couch alone allowed me time to reflect on the past couple of weeks' events. The cool, dark interior provided a great refuge for my contemplation.

My mind wandered to Joey. Even though my heart hoped he was somehow still alive, my head knew every day that passed decreased his chance for survival. Again I felt guilty for coming out here to Dallas, but the change of scenery had helped clear my head.

My mind wandered over the prospects for my future, possibly without Joey. The thought of living on the boat alone depressed me. My thoughts turned to Eric. He had been so sweet and kind.

First he saved my life, pulling me out of the water. Now he was becoming a great friend, helping me deal with the possible loss of Joey and the torment of the nightmares. This friendship would be great to cultivate.

A hand on my shoulder broke my reverie. Looking up, I saw Eric standing above me.

"You look like you were a thousand miles away." He sat down next to me.

"I was just thinking."

"About what?"

"About what a nice guy you are." I avoided disclosing the contents of my musings.

"You don't know me that well yet." He laughed, heading for the stereo.

"Music?"

"Great."

Country music played, not my favorite, but I appreciated the Dierks Bentley song playing. Eric went to the kitchen, returning with two iced teas. We sat in silence, listening to the music. What a great way to spend a hot, August Texas afternoon.

"What were you really thinking about earlier?"

Glancing up at him, I was not sure how to respond.

"I was thinking about everything that's gone on the past couple of weeks. It's more than most people have to deal with their entire lives."

"That's why I'm glad you agreed to come here. You can relax and sort it all out."

Before we could discuss this further, Eric's cell phone rang. He listened for a moment.

"Great we'll be right there." He turned to me. "Daniel is ready to ride Blackjack. Would you like to come and see?"

"You bet," I said, not knowing what to expect. I didn't know if this was going to be like a wild west movie, busting broncos, getting knocked around but ultimately winning the battle.

We donned black cowboy hats before walking to the corral. The Texas sun was brutal. The first corral was more of a ring, with jumps and barrels, and rodeo outfitting. This ring led to another corral which was a huge oblong.

Daniel met us outside without Blackjack.

"I thought I would take him slowly around the ring a few times, then if he behaves, and you can open the other gate, I'll let him rip out in the oval."

"Great plan. If he's unruly you should take him straight back to the barn with no play time," Eric told the younger man.

"Got it, boss." Daniel strode to the barn. He returned leading Blackjack. For the first time, I got a good look at this magnificent horse. Though only a couple of years old, he was already all of sixteen hands. The horse sported a shiny, jet-black coat and perfectly groomed mane and tail. I could see his attitude right away as he strutted into the ring.

"He's gorgeous." I looked to Eric. "Why no 'playtime' if he's bad?"

"Thoroughbreds are born to run. That's all he wants to do. He has to learn to behave before he gets to do what he wants."

After keeping the horse in one spot for a few moments, Daniel mounted up, walking Blackjack around the ring a couple of times, fighting to keep control of the horse.

He spoke softly while controlling him with a gentle hand. No riding crop at all. He stopped Blackjack then dismounted, making the big horse stand still. With a quick motion, he remounted him.

"He's being a pretty good boy today, boss. Will you open the gate?"

Eric motioned for me to follow him. We went over to the fence.

"Watch this," Eric whispered to me. He opened the gate. Blackjack fidgeted as Daniel kept a firm hand on him. Then he let the horse rip. Blackjack galloped off in a blur.

I never saw a horse run so fast. Daniel expertly guided him around the big oval for a couple of laps. When they returned to us, Blackjack was breathing hard but looked ready for more. Daniel struggled to get him back into the smaller ring then to the barn.

"I've never seen a horse run so fast, Eric. Have you ridden him?"

"No. We are training him to run races. It takes a special hand. I don't do that kind of riding, plus I'm too heavy for him. It would ruin him. I'd sure like to go that fast." Contemplating this, we walked back to the house, arriving in time for another great dinner.

The porch swing was again our nightly sunset haunt. We swung slowly, enjoying the view.

"Would you like to go riding again tomorrow? There's a place I would like to show you. It's a fairly long ride, but we can take it slow."

Thinking for a moment, I already felt the stiffness in my legs, but how could I refuse?

"Are you sure?" I asked him. "You don't have to babysit me. There must be business you need to conduct."

Eric stared at me for quite a few moments.

"I didn't realize how bad my marriage was until it was over. I would have given anything for my wife to go riding with me. She hated horses. The world would end if she got dirty. Our riding together helps me as much, if not more, than it helps you."

I had not considered this. "I'd love to go."

"Great." Eric took our empty glasses into the house for refills. When he returned, we sat for a long time in the growing darkness, listening to the crickets.

Exhausted, I looked to Eric. "Either I go to bed or fall asleep here."

He smiled. "There's paper work that needs my attention. You go ahead."

My head barely hit the pillow before I was sound asleep. Later, I barely realized Eric had slipped into the bed. The nightmares surged over me again, but they seemed less intense, allowing a half-decent night's sleep.

The next morning sunlight woke me. Maria puttered around the kitchen making breakfast. She set steaming bowls of food on the table. Eric was intent on an article in the newspaper.

"Anything good?" I asked.

"There's a discussion of cattle prices. This year's calves are going to bring in good money."

"It must be tricky running two businesses."

"Well, yes and no. Tom and I share the responsibility of the boat, when and where to fish. Fred, our cousin, takes care of the maintenance.

"Here at the ranch, I am lucky enough to have Ricardo and Maria." He nodded at them. A faint smile played on the ranch manger's face. "I only worry about the big things."

After breakfast, we changed into riding clothes. Outside, we walked toward a two-seater ATV parked near the back door.

"This is the way to get to the barn." Eric grinned. In his right hand was a picnic basket, in his left a soft-sided cooler. I looked inquiringly at him.

"Our picnic." He motioned me onto the ATV next to him. He drove off, careering the vehicle toward the barn. When he stopped, I caught my breath.

"Wow, that's fast"

"You ain't seen nothing yet."

"I think I'll stick to the horses."

Daniel led Sonny and Outlaw, fully saddled, to us. Eric attached the picnic basket and cooler to Outlaw then gave me a hand up on Sonny.

We rode for a long time. As the sun rose higher in the sky, the day became quite hot. We cantered over a small hill opening up to a long, grassy slope leading down to a large pond.

Several fences terminating at the water's edge. On this side of the pond stood a dock with both a rowboat and a kayak. A couple of huge shade trees dangled over the water.

A tire swing was tied to one of the lower branches of the tree. A few ducks paddled around, their webbed feet easily visible in the clear water.

"This pond is very pretty." I broke the silence.

"It lies on the junction of four farms. Rather than fight over ownership, we decided all four farms have use of it. The water is spring fed and crystal clear. Several different kinds of fish are in there. Let's go down."

He kicked Outlaw lightly. We rode down to a grassy area under the shade trees.

"This is one of my favorite places," Eric said, leaning his left arm against the horn of his saddle. "We have a huge Fourth of July party here every year. All the folks from the surrounding farms come. There is a big cookout with games for the kids and adults. The highlight is a bareback horse race across the pond followed by a fireworks celebration."

Eric swung his right leg over Outlaw's back, dropping to the ground. After removing the cooler and picnic basket, he walked his horse to the pond for a drink.

"Bring Sonny down." After dismounting, I led the golden horse alongside Outlaw. He bent his head down to drink with Outlaw. We tied the horses to a low branch of the shade tree. Eric pulled out a black and white checkered blanket from his saddle bag, spreading it on the grass.

"Come with me." We meandered down to the dock. After removing his riding boots, he dangling his feet in the water. Sitting next to him, I did the same.

"This isn't going to do." He walked back to his horse. Swim trunks came out of his saddle bag. Behind the monstrous tree trunk, he changed. Then like a little kid, he ran the full length of the dock, leaping into the pond with a big splash. Surfacing, he grinned like a little boy.

"Put your bathing suit on and come in—it's great!"

"I didn't bring it." I hoped he didn't hear the relief in my voice.

"It's in my saddle bag." He smiled mischievously.

Reluctantly, I changed behind the same big tree. Returning to the dock, I again dangled my feet over the side. Eric swam over, grabbing me by the ankle. I freaked out, trying to pull away. He stared at me with a look of irritation.

"I wasn't going to pull you in the water." He held my foot until I stopped struggling. With a quick heave on his arms, he hoisted himself out of the lake and sat next to me. "What was that all about?"

"I'm sorry, it's the water. I used to love going into water, but now...I don't know." My explanation sounded lame even to me.

"You need to go back in. Come on." Eric pulled me to my feet. I followed him to the beach adjacent to the dock.

"Come into the water." When I hesitated, he reached back to pull me into the ankle deep water.

"Eric, this is stupid."

"What's stupid?"

"Not being able to jump into the water. It's not like there are sharks in here. I know that."

"Linda, you've been through a terrible trauma, one most people wouldn't be able to comprehend. I can't imagine how terrifying it was to float for untold hours around the ocean with no boat around."

He guided me a few steps further until I stopped again. "Sit down here. I'll be right back. Don't move."

He returned with two glasses of wine. We sipped them in silence for a few minutes.

"Linda, it seems as though you have two choices."

I turned my head to look at him.

"You can work on getting over this fear of the water. I'm here to help you. In order to have a really awesome friendship, you have to work beyond this. Both of our lives are built around the ocean." He paused then gave me a crooked grin.

"Your other choice is to move to Iowa."

"Iowa?"

He laughed softly. "Yes, Iowa. That's about as far away from the ocean as you can get. There's not much water in the cornfields."

"I guess the decision is made. I really don't want to move to Iowa."

Eric grinned, pulling me to my feet. "Hungry?"

"Yes."

"Now there's a change for the better. You're finally eating something."

As we walked out of the pond, I stopped Eric with a little hug.

"Thanks."

We stretched out on the blanket, enjoying the yummy feast. Watermelon made a refreshing dessert. Staring up at the sky, I relaxed for a few minutes in the cool shade. The cowboy lay down on the blanket a few feet away, hands clasped behind his head.

Around three o'clock, we packed everything up. Before we mounted, I grabbed his hand.

"Thanks for sharing this spot with me. I really like it here." He grinned, motioning me up on Sonny. We rode back to the ranch in companionable silence.

Chapter 12. A Visitor at the Ranch.

Later in the evening, we enjoyed the porch swing again. Sunset didn't disappoint us as we swayed. There wasn't much conversation. The quiet time was OK with me. Eric's cell phone rang.

"Hello, brother...I'm at the ranch. I have our mermaid with me." He smiled. "It's a long story. What's that? Great, I'll tell her."

He hung up the phone, turning to me with a grin on his face. "That was Tom. They finished with the third trip and caught a couple of huge tuna. They had a great haul. Unfortunately, there's no news on Joey." He paused for a moment. "Are you interested in having company?"

"Tom?"

"Yep. He's coming out the day after tomorrow for a couple of days before heading up to Alaska."

"That's great." We sat in silence for a long time as I thought about Joey and where he could be or if he was still alive.

Later, in bed, the nightmares still plagued me.

The next day was filled with ranch dealings for Eric, so I occupied myself wandering around the land, trying to gather my thoughts about plans for the future.

Capt. Marlena Brackebusch

Some time was spent in the shade of a big red oak tree. As I leaned against the rough bark between two massive roots, my fingers doodled in the loose dirt. I let my mind wander over the events of the past few weeks.

If Joey were found, I promised myself things would be different. I was tired of all the years spent living my life in his shadow. For the past fifteen years, Joey's dreams were followed. He wanted to sail to the Pacific, so we did. He had the vision to start a boat delivery business. The next thing I knew, we were traipsing all around the Atlantic.

He didn't want anymore kids. At forty-five, it could be too late for me. Hell, he didn't even want a damn dog.

I didn't even know what my dreams were anymore. Maybe his disappearance would allow me to find out who I really was.

If he isn't found, should I continue with the charter business? I love the customers, but the work was often backbreaking. Maybe Eric was right. I could move to Iowa and settle down with a nice guy.

Eric? My mother would love that, though a fisherman was not exactly the professional she hoped for. She always wanted me to marry a doctor or lawyer.

Marry? I shuddered at the thought.

As the afternoon wound down, I rambled back to the house. Even though the afternoon was dwindling, the heat and humidity sweltered. Finding Eric in his swim trunks, reading paperwork by the pool, I greeted him with a smile.

"Hi."

"Hi, yourself. Where have you been all day? I'm sorry I've been preoccupied."

"I wandered around trying to figure things out and clear my head. How about a swim in the pool? I'll go change."

Without waiting for a reply, I hurried to the guest bedroom to put on my bathing suit. Grabbing a towel, I returned poolside in no time.

Eric set down his paperwork. He accepted my outstretched hand. Gritting my teeth, I led him to the pool. When I hesitated, he nudged me.

"Linda, I don't have all day."

Was he irritated or simply being supportive? We took the final step into the pool.

"Well?"

"I feel like bolting out of this water."

"You won't. Why the change?"

"I've decided I can't let this thing beat me. These nightmares are not going to control my life. They can't keep me away from snorkeling and scuba diving." I sprinkled water on my arms.

"That's awesome," Eric said while floating on his back. "Before long, you'll be back to those deep-sea pastimes. Without being petrified."

After showering off and changing, I looked for the cowboy in the living room.

He was ensconced on the couch listening to classic rock. "Lady," by Styx, played. He motioned for me to sit next to him.

"I thought you didn't listen to rock here at the ranch."

"What can I say? It fit my mood."

"I love this song."

He moved across the room to the wet bar. Two glasses were filled with ice. Lime garnished the cocktails.

"My special mojito recipe. They're perfect for a hot August afternoon with rock and roll playing."

After dinner we enjoyed the nightly ritual of sunset on the porch swing. Swaying slowly back and forth, we discussed Tom's arrival tomorrow.

"He arrives at one P.M. Would you like to drive to the airport with me to pick him up?"

"I'd love to, unless you guys have things you need to discuss."

Eric twirled an ice cube in his glass. "Nothing too important. We'll leave here at noon, pick him up then grab some lunch." We spent more time enjoying the sunset before heading off to bed.

The nightmares recurred but were definitely lessening their grip, leaving me refreshed in the morning.

As our noon departure approached, Eric grabbed his black cowboy hat, as usual. We headed for the building between the house and the barn. The front of this building was painted red like the barn and was dominated by three large doors. Bypassing these, we entered through a smaller, locked side door.

Not having been in this building before, I gazed at all the mechanical items and machines stored there. The first vehicle encountered was the huge, green Chevy truck. Next to it sat a spotless bright red convertible.

"My one mechanical indulgence, a '67' Mustang convertible," Eric explained. Also in the garage were several four-wheeled ATVs along with other assorted machinery.

We climbed in the truck, heading for the airport. After parking, we found the arrival area for Tom's flight. He appeared among the throng of passengers. He indulged me with a big hug.

"How's my Li'l Sis?" he asked, looking intently at me.

"I'm doing great, for the most part." He and Eric shook hands, embracing briefly as guys do. Good conversation flowed over lunch before we cruised back to the ranch.

Eric settled Tom in the other guest bedroom before we gathered in the living room. The younger brother made cocktails as we caught up on things.

"Tell me what's going on with you two. I was a little surprised to hear you were in Texas." Tom grabbed my hand. Looking at Eric, I was not sure how to answer this.

"Linda was having a tough time with the nightmares and, of course, with the Coast Guard calling off the search. I thought it would be better for her to get away to clear her head."

"This is certainly a nice quiet place to do that." Tom agreed, turning to me. "How do you like it here, Linda?"

"The horses, the open spaces, this house...it's all very relaxing. I'm enjoying everything."

"Did you forget to mention Eric?" Eric teased me, looking at Tom. "What about him?"

"Oh, he's OK."

"Just OK, huh. How would you like to get your own drink?" He swaggered toward me with a drink in hand and a false frown on his brow.

"OK, OK, he's pretty good too." I attempted to take the drink from his hand.

"Pretty good?" He pulled the drink away from me. "What does a guy have to do to get a compliment around here?" The two brothers exchanged a knowing glance.

We chatted until dinner. Maria made her specialty, barbecue ribs, in Tom's honor. We devoured ribs dripping in the best barbecue sauce I've ever tasted, with the meat falling off the bone.

The recent fishing trip was discussed. Tom described the huge tuna and swordfish they caught, two of which were immediately flown out to the Japanese markets. All the talk of fishing brought back the horrors of the sinking, so I sat quietly, trying to smile and not think of Joey.

After dinner, we lounged on the front porch. The brothers smoked cigars. Eric and I reclined in our usual spots on the swing.

Tom relaxed in one of the recliners. "Linda, I stopped by to see Chief Miller before coming out here. He felt really bad about having to cancel the search for Joey." He paused, letting this sink in. "He promised to try to route as many training missions to the area as possible. He also said Mitch is going to fly that way whenever he can."

"Thanks, Tom." No more words would come without the tears flowing. Not wanting to cry in front of these men, I excused myself.

Eric stood up to follow, but Tom stopped him. Through the open window, I picked up bits and pieces of the brothers' conversation.

"Give her a few minutes, bro." There was silence for a few moments until Tom spoke again. "I'm a little surprised you brought her here."

"She was completely devastated, sitting in her boat like she was lost. I couldn't leave her like that."

"And, maybe, just maybe, you like her, too," Tom said.

"Maybe."

Chapter 13. Back to Naples

After spending another day with Tom working around the ranch, we spent the afternoon chatting with him about an upcoming salmon trip on their boat. The elder brother would skipper the trip.

I was quiet, for the most part, until an idea popped into my head. "Eric, do you remember when we were in Beaufort talking to Mitch at the Coast Guard Station? He said he'd take me flying in a helicopter, if I wanted to go."

"I'm not sure he meant it that way. It seemed as though he suggested you should try it. Why are you thinking about this?"

"If Mitch could take me, we could do one last look around for Joey."

"Linda," Eric sighed. "Do you really think it would do any good?"

"Think about it. We could plot the drift of the Gulf Stream. If Joey did make it into the raft, he may be out there, just hanging on, waiting for me to find him. Eric, I have to do this, search one more time."

Tom drummed his fingers on the table. "It may give her some closure, bro."

"OK, we'll call Mitch." Eric dialed the number then passed his cell phone to me.

Capt. Marlena Brackebusch

"Hello, is Lieutenant Mitch Connolly there please?" I held for a few minutes before a familiar voice came on the phone.

"Hi, Mitch, it's Linda Williams." I listened for a moment to the pilot's strong but friendly voice.

"I hope I'm not bothering you, but I wanted to check to see if there's any news." The Coast Guard officer recapped the recent efforts to find Joey, which all came up blank. He told me he flew all around the offshore waters of Hatteras, much farther than any of the official search areas.

"Mitch, I wanted to ask you if I could take you up on the offer you made while I was there. I want to hire you to fly me out to have one more look around, please." My voice trailed off at the end of this request. There was silence on the other end of the line.

"Linda," Mitch said, loud enough for Eric and Tom to hear too. "You realize I can't fly you in a Coast Guard helicopter. That would never be approved." He paused. "I do have a friend who has a big bird he uses for surveying and photo shoots. I can call him to see if we can borrow it." The tone of his voice brightened. "So you're ready to fly in a helicopter now?"

"Mitch, I need to do something. I can't just give up." My voice dropped at the end of this statement.

"Linda, give me your cell number. I'll call him to see if we can work something out. I have a couple of days off this weekend. I hope you realize I'm willing to do this because I love to fly. There's no real chance of finding Joey after all this time."

"I know, Mitch. I have to try one more time."

After giving him my number, he hung up. I relayed the conversation to the guys.

"Linda, I have to agree with Mitch. There's not much chance Joey is still alive."

"Eric, there are many documented cases of sailors surviving weeks in a liferaft."

"True. But look at it this way, we don't even know whether or not he made it into the liferaft."

"Eric, why the hell are you so against this?"

"I'm against this because it is a waste of time."

"A waste of time in your opinion. Why do all men have to be so stubborn? Is it only your opinion which counts? Fine. Stay here. I'll go to Beaufort on my own."

"Linda, calm down." Tom stood up, grabbing my arm as I tried to leave. "Don't be so emotional."

"I'm not being emotional." I lowered my voice a few octaves.

"Call it what you want. Instead of yelling and storming out of here like an emotional, oops, I mean irrational, oops, I mean temperamental..." A broad grin radiated around the elder brother's face. "Why don't you sit down. I'm sure you and Eric can come up with a plan."

The younger brother took a deep breath. "Since the work here at the ranch is under control, maybe you'd like to head back to Naples. We can see how your business is doing. Then we can go to Beaufort."

"I should try to catch up on the paperwork, at the very least."

Tom left the next morning. Eric and I returned to Naples the following day. Right before we left, Eric hired a jockey to start seriously training Blackjack for his first race, a stakes race a month from now in Dallas.

Arriving back in Naples, we clambered aboard *Dark & Stormy*, to put on the air conditioner. Climbing under the quarter berth cushion in the stifling heat, I opened the sea cock, the valve which allows salt water into the air conditioner to cool it.

Eric flipped the circuit breaker while wiping a bead of sweat off his forehead. Early September was a hot, steamy time in Naples. It would take a long while to cool the boat down in this heat.

"Why don't we treat ourselves to a night in the hotel?" Eric suggested. Secretly I was relieved. It would be very awkward spending the night on *Dark & Stormy* without Joey, especially because Eric would be there. Even though there was nothing physical going on between us, I was still uncomfortable. This was Joey's home and it was difficult bringing another man into it.

After dinner we strolled along the dazzling white sand beach which lined the Naples shoreline.

"Eric, look at the storm clouds forming offshore."

"It looks like we are in for serious rain."

"It's odd, having this much rain so late in the season."

"What's our plan for tomorrow?" Eric asked as we sloshed our feet through the rippling waves on the shore.

"I want to check out *Flipper*. Shane said he would be available to go over the businesses' books."

Flipper was my thirty-four foot sloop. The name fit nicely with my company's name–Blue Dolphin

Sailing Charters. The boat was docked directly across from *Dark & Stormy* on the Naples City Dock.

Thunder boomed closer, so we decided to make a sprint for the car. We jogged across the soft sand.

As soon as we ducked into the car, the rain exploded in torrents. Wind blasted the car as we huddled together watching the maelstrom outside the rain-streaked windshield. Water poured down in buckets. Lightning slashed across the black sky.

Like most summer squalls in Naples, it was over quickly. That night the nightmares came back with a vengeance. Was it our presence on *Dark & Stormy* or the afternoon squalls that had triggered their re-emergence.

After drifting, tumbling, and fighting to stay afloat during a severe thunderstorm, all was suddenly still. The night was pitch black. A blaze of light. A triangular fin. Blurry images taunted me. Teeth sliced my thigh. The predator dragged me under. My fists swung wildly, missing the beast. Joey's face floated in the distance. Something gripped both my wrists.

Eric straddled me, restraining my wrists.

"Take it easy. You had a bad dream." I didn't understand what was going on. Why was he holding me down?

"Eric, what's wrong?"

"You almost beat the stuffing out of me." He grinned, released me, then rolled onto the bed. "Remind me never to get into a fist fight with you!"

My face flushed with embarrassment.

"Eric, I'm so sorry...the shark."

"It's OK." He chuckled, drawing me close. Sleep only came in small bits the rest of the night as I tossed and turned uneasily.

The next morning, the smell of freshly brewed coffee swirled around the room. Eric was ensconced at the small dinette table with the local news rag in hand.

I settled across the table from him. "Good morning, cowboy. I'm sorry about last night."

He put down the newspaper, giving me his full attention.

"The dream was about a shark biting me in the thigh and dragging me underwater. I guess I was trying to hit it with my fists. I hope I didn't hit you too hard."

Eric was silent until my gaze went back to him. A smile played around the corners of his lips.

"You're the first girl who has beat me up since kindergarten." He laughed. "I'm lucky I don't have a black eye. Explaining that would be an obvious knock to my manhood."

"I didn't realize you were such a wimp."

"A wimp. Did you just call me a wimp?"

"Cowboy, I call it like I see it."

"Lady, you better watch yourself."

I called Shane to set up a meeting with him for eleven A.M. on *Dark & Stormy.*

As we munched on breakfast, Eric's cell phone rang. "Hi, Mitch. Yes, I'll tell her. Thanks. We'll see you then." Eric stared at me. "Obviously, that was Mitch. His friend can fly us over the Outer Banks on Sunday. I'll make plane reservations."

He spent a few minutes on his lap top. "I also E-mailed Mark to let him know we are coming."

After breakfast we went over to the City Dock to check on *Flipper*. After unlocking the boat and stowing the hatch boards we slipped below.

The spotless galley, on the port side, was equipped with a fridge containing soft drinks and bottled water all organized by type.

Dark blue cushions, dotted with accent pillows, lined the main salon. Everything was in its place, exactly what I would have expected from Shane.

"Would you like the ten-cent tour?"

"Absolutely."

"Here's the V-berth. I had a special inner spring mattress made for her." We looked at the custom-fitted bedspread depicting a beach scene with Cape Hatteras lighthouse on it. An involuntary shiver tingled my spine.

The neat and tidy head was next. It was adorned with embroidered dolphin towels. A quick peek in the aft cabin finished the tour.

"Neat boat, Linda. What do you have in her for power?"

"A three cylinder, thirty horsepower Yanmar diesel." Grabbing a paper towel, I reached in the engine room to check both the engine oil and transmission fluid. Eric observed my work with a bemused smile. Satisfied, we climbed on deck.

"Here are the control lines for the roller furling mainsail."

"The sail unwinds from here. That's pretty neat. It seems much simpler than having to haul the sail up each time."

"It is. I didn't realize you sail."

His face wore a sly smile. "I've been out a few times. I wouldn't put myself in your category, though it's a lot of fun."

"It's almost eleven. We have to meet Shane."

A brisk jog brought us back to the Cove. We took refuge in the cool interior with Shane. We studied the sheets of paper placed on top of the varnished teak dining table. The overhead brass lamp glowed.

"Things have been slow, as you would expect this time of year." Shane seemed to struggle with his words as he recapped the recent charter activity. I stopped him, putting my hand over his on the table.

"I really appreciate everything you're doing. I'm not sure I could cope very well without friends like you."

"Linda, I'm so sorry. I wish there was more we could do."

Steeling myself, I forced a smile. "Just keep doing what you're doing. It's been a huge help not having to worry about the business or the boat. We were on her earlier—she looks great."

Shane beamed at the compliment. "After I take care of a few things this week, I can take over again if you like."

"That would be great. Eric and I are flying back to Beaufort to take one last look for Joey." Silence dominated the cabin for a few seconds.

Shane nodded his head in sympathy as he climbed the cabin steps to the deck. "There is a charter tomorrow at eleven A.M."

"I'll take care of it."

Eric leaned back on the settee. "That will be a good time to break me in. See if I'll make adequate crew."

My eyes focused on him. How things were turning out seemed weird. Then I caught sight of a picture of Joey, hanging on the port bulkhead between the bronze barometer and clock.

"Eric, you're such a sweetie, but you don't have to go to work with me." Secretly, I was pleased to have the extra help aboard.

"I'd like to see what goes on."

Shrugging my shoulders, I agreed. "Would you like to go to the Dock restaurant for lunch? It's one of my favorite spots. There's one condition. Lunch is on me."

"OK. I'll let you get away with this one."

We strolled to this historic restaurant on the other side of the Cove Inn. Once inside the rustic bar, we found seats at the local's end of the bar. Ceiling fans swirled overhead pushing the tropical heat from the cozy dining room. Iced teas and grilled tuna sandwiches tasted awesome.

"What would you like to do this afternoon?" Eric asked.

"I don't know. It might be nice to chill out."

After lunch, we checked out of the hotel then returned to *Dark & Stormy* to relax for the afternoon.

Eric thumbed through a sailing magazine on the starboard settee cushion. I puttered around nervously. Rain pelted the deck with thunder booming in the distance.

After dinner, we watched the local news as I mulled over the sleeping arrangements. It would be too unsettling having Eric sleep in the V-berth after Joey and I shared it for so many years. In the future, that arrangement could turn out to be acceptable, but I was not ready to make the jump now.

"Eric."

"Yes."

"*Um,* would you mind sleeping in the quarter berth tonight?

"You'll be OK if the nightmares recur?"

"I don't know." An awkward silence hung between us.

"The quaterberth is fine."

The nightmares attacked viciously. I woke to Eric sitting on the edge of the V-berth. The following morning dawned early.

"Your nightmares were pretty intense last night. I can't imagine you slept very well." Eric glanced up from an article in the local news rag.

"I didn't. My body feels like it was dragged beneath an old clipper ship full of barnacles. Silly me thinking it would help to sleep on this boat. All the reminders of Joey dredged up this image of the sinking. I can't get it out of my head."

Eric's brow furrowed. "The nightmare you had last night occurred previously?"

"Yes, though a new pattern of terror is emerging. The dreams I had aboard Mark's boat were brief flashes of blurry scenes. I remembered bailing out the boat in slow motion. After the wave knocked me overboard, I could anticipate a shark attacking, but could do nothing to prevent it. Last night's version was different. It was like watching a movie."

"A movie starring Joey."

"How did you know I dreamt about him?"

"You shouted his name several times."

"Joey was attacked by a shark in last night's vision. It bit him in the left thigh, when he was only a few feet away from the liferaft. Why would I have such a specific dream?"

"I don't know."

"This may sound crazy, but I think he made it to the liferaft. Joey may be asking me for help."

"Linda, that does sound crazy. When we discussed going to Beaufort while in Texas, I was against the whole idea. If you actually see the vast search area for yourself maybe the nightmares will end."

"I hope so. Eric, let's put this whole subject to rest for now. I need to get my head together for the charter today."

After breakfast, we prepped *Flipper* for the afternoon sail. Hearing voices on the dock, Eric stepped up, gallantly helping our guests aboard.

As they settled in the cockpit, I introduced myself. They were Joe and Mandy from Chicago with their two tween children.

Capt. Marlena Brackebusch

A quick safety briefing was given as we cruised down the bay. "The life jackets are in the locker there on the right hand side. Enough of the technical stuff, let the fun begin."

Eric handed out sodas and waters as we settled into the tour of Naples Bay and the mansions of Port Royal. The cowboy and the kids scampered to the bow to watch dolphins cruise alongside. Even though Cindy was hesitant, the two kids soon posed like young pirates.

The parents cameras' snapped away. As we approached Gordon Pass, I was thankful for the light east wind. The gentle breeze allowed us a nice sail up the beach with no wave action.

It was a beautiful day, with temperatures in the low eighties and not a cloud in the deep blue sky. The kids came back to the cockpit to help Eric roll out the mainsail. Our guests' young son put his back into pulling out the jib under the fisherman's watchful eye.

I steered the boat off the wind. "You'll make sailors out of them before the day is out."

Both parents stretched out on the raised cockpit seats, very relaxed. The wheel was handed over to their son, Jason. He steered aggressively (another NASCAR driver perhaps), so I nudged Eric to give him a hand. In my years of chartering experience, I'd learned that young men listen to male sailors better than female.

The fisherman squatted next to him. "Jason, ease the wheel over. Give the boat a second to respond. Do you feel the tug on the wheel when the wind gusts?"

"Yes, sir." The young man's face was blistered with concentration.

"Don't let the wind pull you around."

The front edge of the jib thundered as it luffed.

"Ease her to port, Jason."

The young man tugged the wheel to the left. When the wind caught in the sail, *Flipper* heeled over, accelerating nicely, skimming across the aquamarine water of the Gulf.

A huge grin plastered the boy's face.

We turned the boat around by the Naples Beach Club. When the conversation lagged, I brought up a new subject.

"What do you guys like to watch on TV? Do you ever watch the Exploration Channel?" Eric looked at me warily. Up until this point, I had not revealed his identity. He caught my eye, shaking his head no. I grinned at him.

"I love that channel and also all the animal channels," Cindy said.

"Have you ever seen the show, 'Crabs from the Deep'?" I asked as Eric gave me a stern look.

"We have," the father said. "It's amazing how they go out to catch all those crabs in all kinds of weather. Those guys are a little crazy, if you ask me. It must take a lot of guts."

Jason stared at the fisherman. "Can I ask you something, Eric?"

The crab fisherman gave me a withering look. "Sure, what would you like to know?"

"How come you aren't the captain? I mean, isn't the man usually the captain?" Jason innocently asked.

His mother rebuked him. "Jason, a woman can be a captain as well as a man can. I don't think that was a very polite question. I haven't raised my son to be sexist. You should apologize to Captain Linda."

Eric raised his hand to intercede. "It's OK, Jason, I understand where you're coming from, but this boat and business belong to Captain Linda. I'm here to help out."

The young man cautiously glanced at his mother then apologized to me. "Sorry, Captain Linda." I smiled my acceptance as he continued. "Wouldn't you want your own boat, instead of just helping out?"

Eric considered this when Jason's mom interceded again. "If this is too personal, you don't have to answer."

The fisherman's face burgeoned into a wide smile. "No, it's OK. I actually do own a business, but it's not sailing related." His eyes narrowed at me. "I own a cattle ranch in Texas."

"Way cool," Cindy said.

As we approached Gordon Pass to return to our dock, I decided to change the subject.

"Eric, do you mind rolling up the jib please? I'm going to start the engine."

With the engine engaged, Eric and Jason rolled up the jib. We puttered back down Naples Bay, centering our conversation on the enormous houses. A big black and white osprey soared by with a fish gripped in its talons.

Back at the dock, we bid goodbye to our guests who chatted excitedly as they strolled away from the boat.

Down below, I stowed the cushions in the V-berth. "More happy customers." When I turned around, Eric stood directly in front of me. I tried to step around him, but he blocked my path.

His big hands closed around my wrists as his body pinned me against the bunk. His serious stare was offset by the gleam in his eye.

"Eric, what's up?"

"First you called me a wimp yesterday. Today, you tried to throw me to the sharks during a charter... What was all that about 'Crabs from the Deep'? Trying to put me on the spot?" I squirmed as his grip on my wrists tightened.

"Eric, I was just having fun with you..." The words barely left my mouth, when he released my left wrist. His hand grabbed the back of my neck. His lips brushed mine. I was shocked but secretly pleased. Eric stepped back, grinning.

He turned for the companionway. "Would you like me to rinse the deck?"

I attempted to catch my breath. What the heck was that?

Once water splashed on the deck, I felt it was safe to close up the boat. The lock clicked in place. Eric was coiling the hose when he turned to see the look on my face. "I guess that will teach you to mess with me." He extended his hand, helping me onto the dock.

Walking quickly down the dock, I made my way back to *Dark & Stormy* without making eye contact with the cowboy. Swinging open the cockpit doors, I dashed below.

Capt. Marlena Brackebusch

Refuge was taken behind my laptop computer, entering the details of today's charter with my head swimming. Eric's eyes bored into me as he reclined on the port settee, very quiet. Chancing a peek at him over the top of the computer, I noted his huge grin.

"You can't hide behind the computer all day."

My face flushed scarlet. Focus on the computer, Linda, I told myself. The words on the charter information page blurred as Eric slid across the settee. Without a word, he perched next to me. The computer was pulled from my hands. His arm slipped around me. My whole body stiffened as my face again flushed.

"I do believe I embarrassed you."

Blinking, I responded sharply. "No, you didn't embarrass me, just caught me off guard."

He leaned close, whispering in my ear. "If I didn't embarrass you, why is your face all red?"

"Leave me alone." I pushed him away.

His grin didn't fade as he made us a couple of iced teas. My lungs drew in a deep breath then let it out slowly. What was I to make of this man?

Eric busied himself preparing a couple of steaks for dinner. I was completely ignored, which allowed me a reprieve from his teasing. We savored the nice meal before enjoying a lovely sunset from the cockpit. Before the end of the evening, we strolled around Crayton Cove.

The bay waters were still as dusk descended. On our way back, we stopped by the Chickee Bar. Several good friends of mine were enjoying drinks. Deciding it was time to introduce Eric, I took his hand.

Jan, a longtime bartender at the Cove, worked behind the bar. My good friend Captain George was chatting with Toby and Marlena, our neighbors who live aboard their sailboat *Rum & Tonic*. They greeted us. With a chickee punch in hand, I mustered up the strength to explain Joey's absence.

They all looked at me expectantly. Eric broke the silence while shaking hands with the group.

"Eric Iverson..., a friend of Linda's." He recapped the basic story of the sinking and Joey's disappearance.

Standing there awkwardly, I finally joined the conversation.

"We are heading back to Beaufort tomorrow to search for Joey again. I was wondering if you guys could look after *Dark & Stormy*."

"Linda, of course, we'll look after the boat. If there's anything else we can do...." Marlena said, giving me a slight hug.

A tear threatened, thinking of all the evenings Joey and I'd spent with them having drinks on one boat or the other.

"No, keeping an eye on her would be great."

Chapter 14. Beaufort and the New Search for Joey

The next morning, we woke in anticipation of flying to Beaufort. Eric arranged for us to stay with Mark and Michelle. The tuna captain was picking us up at the New Bern Airport.

"Good morning." I sat across the table from Eric.

"Last night set a new world record for consecutive days without a nightmare." He set down the newspaper. "Maybe we're heading in the right direction."

Not feeling as though any reply was necessary, I sipped my coffee silence. Butterflies danced in my stomach while showering. After drying my hair, I hauled clothes out of the drawers and stuffed them into my suitcase.

As I leaned against the bunk, the realization hit me. This might be the last search for Joey. I silently prayed we find him...one way or another.

Eric packed his stuff in his duffel bag. We locked the boat then drove for the airport, grabbing lunch before boarding our flight.

Sitting next to me on the jet, he automatically grabbed my hand before the death grip went on the armrest. His smile reassured me. Soon after circling the New Bern Airport, the jet made a perfect landing.

Mark waited by the baggage claim. He shook Eric's hand then hugged me.

"Was your flight OK?" He took one of our bags from Eric.

"Yeah, it was great. Thanks for letting us stay with you." Eric grabbed another bag.

The two men chatted about fishing as we drove the short distance to Beaufort. Michelle and I exchanged hugs back at their house. The four of us settled on the front porch for cocktails before dinner. They had a great view of Taylor Creek. Swirls of tide rushed by, while ducks paddled around.

The guys grilled chicken. Michelle and I caught up on things while putting together a salad in the kitchen.

"How are things with you and Eric?" she asked with a sly smile on her face.

"Great." We chitchatted more before enjoying the food. The sun dipped into the river. After dinner, the rocking chairs on the cool back porch was the place to relax. A few stars peeked through the leaves of the live oaks.

Around ten P.M., Eric pulled me to my feet.

"We better get some sleep, lady. Mitch is picking us up early."

He gently shook me awake right before dawn. We tiptoed down the stairs trying not to wake our hosts. Like all good fishermen, Mark was up early, sitting in the kitchen, drinking coffee. Typically, he was reading the Sunday paper.

The guys chatted while I sipped coffee, deep in thought. I was trying to fight off a panicky feeling.

The image in my mind of flying around in a helicopter was not high on my list of fun things to do in Beaufort. The need to find Joey had to overcome the fear of flying.

The doorbell rang. Mitch followed Mark into the kitchen. His six-foot-two lean frame was wearing jeans, a blue work shirt, and a leather flight jacket. A U.S. Coast Guard ball cap covered his short, dark crew cut.

After accepting a cup of black coffee from Mark, the Coast Guard officer shook our hands before sitting down in a chair across the table from me.

"Mitch, I can't thank you enough for setting this up today."

"Are you ready to fly in the bird, Linda?" He smiled reassuringly.

"About as ready as I'll ever be."

"What kind of helicopter are we flying in?" Eric asked.

"We'll be flying a Sikorsky S-76A with added fuel tanks for additional range. My buddy Jake should have her all ready by the time we get there."

The three of us piled into his red pickup truck, driving the short distance to the general aviation center. We were met by a six-foot-tall stocky, shaggy-haired man of about forty-five wearing a flight jumpsuit. The guy had a tough scarred face, but beneath his rough exterior sparkled kind, gentle eyes.

"Linda and Eric, meet our pilot and chopper owner, Jake Hammond." We exchanged hellos as the guys shook hands. Jake grasped my hand while staring hard at me. It was pretty obvious that Mitch had explained my situation.

"I'm sorry to hear about Joey. Let's see if we can find something today. We've set up a search grid." He led us over to a map on the table. Coordinates were pointed out.

"We'll head for Cape Lookout Shoals first. Then I'll take us east to Diamond Shoals Light. After searching this area, I've plotted a course northeast for 100 miles out to sea. On the way back, we'll zigzag across the Gulf Stream to Cape Lookout. If the liferaft drifted any farther away, it would be difficult to find. The current fans out too much, creating an impossibly large search area."

My stomach did a flip as we looked over this plan, but I had to be strong.

"I've already pre-flighted the bird, so we'll get you inside before Mitch does a quick walk around with me."

The Coastie and I fell a few steps behind the other guys as we walked toward the parked aircraft.

"Jake was an ace pilot in the Marines. He flew a Blackhawk, which is similar to the bird we'll be flying in today. I'm not sure he kept count of the endless missions over Saudi Arabia and the Red Sea. We'll be in the hands of an expert pilot today."

"I wasn't aware of his background. His experience makes me feel a little better, though I'm still not comfortable with flying."

"It will be great. You'll see."

Eric and Jake walked side-by-side ahead of us. As we rounded a small airplane, there was the helicopter. My stomach dropped while my eyes took in the black chopper with dark blue stripes on it. It appeared tiny. Mitch stopped beside me, watching my reaction. I swallowed hard, trying to ease my bone-dry mouth.

"Linda, I'm not sure I like the look on your face."

"I don't think I can get in there."

"It's a little late to back out now. Jake has gone through a lot of trouble setting this up." The Coastie clutched my arm. The other guys stopped to look back at us. Seeing the look on my face, Eric stepped toward me, but the Coast Guardsman waved him back.

"Mitch, I can't."

"Linda, get your butt in the chopper. You can't refuse to fly with me twice." The Coast Guard officer had a firm grip on my arm, pulling me to the helicopter. Jake opened the back door as Mitch motioned Eric inside.

"Hop on in, Eric. Linda will be right beside you." The two men firmly guided me into the bird, not allowing me to back out.

"Sit." The Coastie guided me into the seat next to Eric. He buckled the shoulder and waist harnesses around me.

"Don't even think about getting out. Jake and I are going to give this bird a once over, then we're out of here." He took a second to stare at me before closing the door to my right.

Eric reached over. "What?"

"I'm scared to death. I really want to get out of here." Tears were forced back. "Dammit, Linda, be strong." The impulse to jump out of the chopper was fought off.

"Take it easy. There's no reason to be afraid. These guys have gone through a ton of trouble to set this up. Have some faith, Linda."

Jake opened the left hand door. He climbed in, glancing in my direction. He must have seen the look of mortal fear on my face.

"Linda, this bird is really safe. Relax." The chopper's owner closed his door then buckled up his harness.

Mitch climbed in a moment later. He turned around, patting my knee.

"Hey, we'll have none of those tears. Trust me— everything's going to be fine." He reached over to hand me a headset, which he plugged in next to me. The process was repeated with Eric. After buckling his own harness, he made a radio check of our headsets.

"You two ready to go?"

"Yes," I said through gritted teeth.

"Everyone keep your eyes open. Let us know if you see anything. If there is no immediate reply, we may be on the radio with air traffic control, so repeat yourself until we answer you." Mitch instructed us as Jake fired up the engine.

The helicopter vibrated as the pilot revved up the motor. The main and tail rotors turned. Eric squeezed my hand. Jake turned to me with a grin.

"Here we go." His gruff voice filled our head sets as the bird lifted off. Squeezing my eyes shut, I felt a hand on my knee.

"Linda, you can't see anything with your eyes closed," Mitch said in a playful voice.

"Just fly this thing please."

Laughing, Mitch replied. "I'm not doing anything, it's all Jake."

My stomach rolled as our pilot banked the chopper sharply. For a moment, it was nearly on its side. The shoulder harnesses strained to keep me in the seat. I must have let out a squeak, because Mitch's hand was again on my knee.

"Linda, take some deep breaths and relax. Don't try to hold yourself so stiffly. Go with the flow. Let your muscles relax. If you feel sick there are bags in the pocket behind my seat."

"I'm not feeling sick, only scared to death."

"Linda, look out the window on Eric's side, there's Cape Lookout Lighthouse." Jake pointed out the window on the left side.

My eyes opened to a slit. A tall, black and white diamond-patterned lighthouse was not very far below us. A long elbow of land, lined with gorgeous sand dunes, enclosed the bay at Cape Lookout. Joey and I anchored here many times.

"We are at Checkpoint Charley," Mitch said as his eyes scanned the navigation chart.

"Roger that. I'm going to turn to the northeast. We'll slow down, flying at 150 feet over the water toward Diamond Shoals. Everyone keep a sharp lookout." These words were barely out of Jake' mouth when he eased the stick to the left, banking the chopper sharply to the northeast, causing my stomach to do another flip.

He straightened out. It felt as though we were flying just inches above the wave tops. As the chopper slowed to a crawl, I had the sensation we were going to fall into the sea.

Mitch again grabbed my knee. "Linda it's OK, look outside. That's what we're here for. Jake, can I take a minute to go in back?"

"Sure, man, I think I can handle it." The ex-Marine quipped into the mic as our other pilot unbuckled himself. The tall man wedged himself between Eric's seat and mine.

"How can I make this flight easier for you?" He squatted next to me.

"Shit, Mitch, you should be up in the front. What if something happens?"

The Coast Guard man squeezed close to me. When he spoke, he had to shout over all the noise in the cabin.

"Linda, Jake flies this bird everyday by himself. He doesn't need me. Now you need to calm down and trust us. We're not going to find Joey if you're back here panicking."

He tapped our pilot on the shoulder.

"Hey buddy, can you hover for a minute?" Our pilot stopped the helicopter in place. The chopper was hovering with the cabin calm and upright. "Do you see how easy this is? Why don't you sit up front? Jake can show you how to fly this."

"Hell, no."

Mitch grinned at me. "I don't know how you can sail across oceans but don't like flying in a helicopter.

Listen, we're going to keep straight and level until we reach Diamond Shoals. Try to relax and look for Joey, OK?"

I nodded my head. The tall man returned to his seat, strapping back in. Jake eased the helicopter forward, skimming the waves tops as we all stared out at the empty water.

Despite the sea being a beautiful blue with calm waves, thinking of floating out there made me shudder. Looking off to our left, we could hardly see the coastline. Ocracoke must be nearby.

The flight continued on a straight line until two small objects appeared on the horizon. Jake guided the helo into a slight climb. A moment later, he slowed down, then hovered over Cape Hatteras Lighthouse.

The black-and-white candy striping was a stark contrast to the white sand beach below. It looked very pretty in the late morning sunlight. Little waves splashed on the beach only a few hundred yards away.

"Do you know why Hatteras Light is black-and-white striped and Lookout has the diamonds on it?" Jake asked no one in particular.

"No, why?" Eric asked him.

Pulling the helicopter away from the lighthouse slightly, he hovered again, giving us a great view.

"You know Hatteras overlooks Diamond Shoals. It was supposed to have the diamond pattern on it. This is how the legend goes.

"The Coast Guard dropped the painter off at Cape Lookout to put the striped design on the newly built lighthouse. He started painting, but soon took a break. As luck would have it, the guy walked down the beach. Guess what he found?"

"I'll bite. What did he find, Jake?" I asked.

"He found a cask of rum washed up on the beach. The guy had a dandy time with the booze. When he returned to the painting, he was confused or drunk. He screwed up, painting the diamonds on Cape Lookout Light." He paused.

"You can imagine the heap of trouble he was in. The lighthouse service didn't want to spend the extra time or money so they left it that way. Hatteras was next in line for a paint job. It was finished with the black stripes."

"You are messing with us buddy." Mitch said. "I'm in the Coast Guard. I never heard that story."

"Mitch, I swear every word is true. You know the old saying, 'wine, women, and song'—or in this case rum—are all trouble. No offense, Linda." He turned around with a sly grin on his face.

Without warning, he sped up, banking the helicopter to the right. We flew over to the second object–Diamond Shoals Light, which marked the dangerous sand bars extending twenty miles off of Cape Hatteras. This was the same light Joey and I had sailed by only a couple of weeks ago.

Multitudes of ships had sunk here. Wicked storms formed between the cold air from the north, mixing with the warm waters of the Gulf Stream. That's why Cape Hatteras was known as the graveyard of the Atlantic.

"Mitch, what's that?" I pointed toward the dilapidated light tower to my right. Something below caught my attention.

Our co-pilot craned his neck. "I don't see anything. What are you looking at?"

"Down near the bottom of the right hand leg of the tower. There's something yellow." I strained to see what it was.

The Coastie grabbed his binoculars while Jake banked the chopper around. He zoomed the bird toward the structure, nearly at water level.

"There is something there. It looks like it might be a yellow horseshoe buoy. Did you have one on the sailboat?"

"Yes, there was one on the back rail. I'm sure it had *Wind Rose* painted on it."

"I don't see any way we can get down there to have a look at it, as this structure is in the way." Our pilot pulled back from the abandoned light tower. "Do you think you can get your buddies to come out in a boat and grab it?" Jake asked Mitch.

"There's one way to find out. Eric and Linda, switch your channel on the armrest to number one. I'm going to call in the cavalry."

We switched, hearing the Coast Guard man's voice on the marine VHF channel sixteen.

"U.S. Coast Guard Cape Hatteras Group, this is helo November twenty-four romeo delta, over."

"Helo romeo delta, this is the U.S. Coast Guard Station Cape Hatteras Group. Switch and answer twenty-two alpha."

"Coast Guard, romeo delta, roger, switching to twenty-two alpha,"

"Romeo delta, Hatteras group. What can we do for you?"

"Hatteras group, this is Lieutenant Mitch Connolly from Morehead City group. Are you the duty officer in charge?"

"Roger that, I'm Ensign Morelli."

"Roger that Ensign. I am on a private recon mission looking for the sailor lost off the *Wind Rose.* I'm at Diamond Shoals light. There is what looks to be a Type IV personal flotation device caught on one of the legs of the tower. It sure would be nice to know if it belonged to the sailboat."

"Are you requesting our assistance to check out the object?"

"Roger, if you have any assets in the vicinity."

"We have a patrol boat ten miles to your northeast. I'll vector it to your location. Stand by."

We hovered for a few minutes seaward of the tower. Soon a voice crackled over the radio.

"Helo romeo delta, Station Hatteras. The patrol boat will be at your location in ten minutes."

"Roger, we'll stand by." Mitch called into his radio. "It's great to have friends when you need them."

Jake adjusted his sunglasses. "I'm gonna back off so we don't hit the boat with all my rotor wash. Mitch, do you want to take her for a few minutes?"

The Marine handed the controls off to the Coastie.

"It's amazing how you can keep a helo stationary like this, with the wind and all." I was impressed with the handling of the chopper along with the skill of both pilots.

Jake looked at me as if surprised by my relative calm. "Each bird is a little different. I fly this one everyday so I know all its nuances...to be able to predict what she will do. Mitch is actually doing a pretty good job keeping her still, seeing as he hasn't flown this one before."

"Jake, I think that was more information then I needed."

Mitch reached back, tapping my knee once again.

"Hey, how about a little moral support for me, lady."

"Get your hand off my knee and fly this damn thing." My request made both pilots laugh.

Looking below, we saw the familiar red of the Coast Guard boat as it sped up to the light tower. The crew expertly maneuvered close to the right hand leg, not an easy task in the chop beneath the structure.

"They sent a thirty-six-foot Long Range Interceptor, rigid inflatable boat. It should be able to get close enough to grab the horseshoe buoy. Switch back to the VHF, then we'll make contact," Mitch said.

"Coast Guard Interceptor, this is helo romeo delta at your six, Lieutenant Mitch Connolly, Morehead City Group."

"Helo, Interceptor six. Stand by one. We are retrieving the PFD."

The helmsman of the Coast Guard vessel maneuvered close to the tower. The big inflatable boat was nearly swept into the jagged steel girder. Wash poured out of its outboard as the coxswain gunned the engines.

One of the crew snagged the horseshoe buoy with a long pole. The man carried the PFD to the cockpit of the boat. The radio squawked again.

"Helo romeo delta, this is U.S. Coast Guard Interceptor six. The buoy definitely says *Wind Rose* on it. We'll take it in with us."

"Roger, Coast Guard. This is Helo romeo delta; we'll proceed with our flight plan. Thanks for your help."

Our co-pilot turned the controls over to Jake, who flew us back over the light tower. We switched to the on-board communications channel.

"Mitch." I leaned forward, putting my hand on his shoulder. "Do you think Joey climbed into the tower?"

The Coast Guard man turned around to look at me. "I doubt it. From the look of those ladders, it would be nearly impossible to reach them from the water's surface."

He consulted a book in front of him. "We're near high tide. The bottom rungs of the ladders are rusted away. Look how high they are above the water."

Jake circled the tower at the level of the old living quarters. I strained to look inside.

"Maybe we should take a peek inside, just to be sure." The Marine looked to Mitch. "Crazier things have happened before."

"It might be a little dangerous, buddy. We don't know what kind of shape the structure is in."

"That's why you need a Marine to do it." Jake grinned at Mitch. "I'll take a hand-held radio and flashlight with me. You see the hatch over there?"

We all looked at the square door near the left hand side of the roof.

"It must be the access hatch. Drop me off there. Be careful not to touch down. We don't know how stable the roof is. I'll try to climb inside to take a look around."

Eric grabbed the Marine's shoulder. "Jake, we don't want you getting hurt. Are you sure you want to do this?"

"I live for adventure." Our pilot answered then became serious. "If I see anything unsafe, I'll come back out."

Mitch eased the helicopter over the light tower, hovering twenty feet above the roof. Jake unbuckled his harness then opened the door. The bird dropped down until the Marine jumped off the skids only a few feet from the access hatch. Our Coastie yanked the helo back up, hovering a short distance away.

We watched Jake struggle to open the access hatch. A few seconds later his voice boomed over the radio.

"Mitch, this lid is stuck. There is a crowbar in the very back of the cabin. Can you grab it and toss it down?"

Our co-pilot turned to Eric. "I'm gonna hold her steady for a couple of minutes. See if you can find the crowbar." The fisherman unbuckled his harness, stooping as he made his way into the back of the fuselage. He returned a few minutes later with the crowbar in hand.

Mitch's voice again filled our ears. "Great. Buckle back in. Open the door next to you with the red latch. I'm going to hover very close to Jake. Toss the bar near him."

Eric opened the door. The Coastie eased the chopper closer to Jake. The crowbar fell a few feet away. The Marine retrieved it, then muscled open the hatch. A moment later, he disappeared from view.

"OK, I'm in," Jake said. "It looks as though no one's been in here for a long time. I'm going to do a recon anyway."

We waited patiently, hovering above the structure for ten minutes. All of a sudden, Jake reemerged from the access hatch. He waved for the chopper to return. "Come pick me up."

It took very skillful flying from Mitch as he pushed the bird closer to the crouching man. Jake reached for the door with his left hand, yanking it open. Wind flooded the chopper, pushing it a few inches away, but our co-pilot anticipated this. He steered a fraction toward Jake, who threw the crowbar and flashlight inside.

With a big tug, he vaulted himself in. After the door was closed and the harnesses put on, the Marine turned to us as Mitch zoomed the bird skyward.

"There was nothing in there but a mass of cobwebs with no sign of human habitation for a long time." He turned toward Mitch, lightly punching him on the shoulder while grinning. "Great flying, buddy, I taught you well. Now give me back my bird."

"You got it, Jake." The Coast Guard man removed his hands from the controls then turned to me.

"Sorry about that, Linda, but we'll keep looking. Jake, we burned a lot of fuel there, maybe we better top up before heading offshore."

Our pilot's eyes settled on the fuel gauges. "Right, buddy, we'll make a pit stop at Hatteras. Can you call air traffic then give me a vector?" He banked the chopper sharply to the right.

I was suddenly looking straight down at the water. My breath caught in my throat as Jake spun the bird on a sharp 180 degree turn. "Oh shit."

Jake quickly pulled the chopper level. "Sorry Linda, I forgot I have Chicken Little in the back seat." He turned around, grinning at me.

Recovering slightly, I tried to smile at Jake. "Maybe I'll just get off in Hatteras."

"Suit yourself, but it's a long walk back to Beaufort."

After a short flight into the Outer Banks, we set down at Cape Hatteras airport. I breathed a sigh of relief as the chopper touched down. Jake shut off the engine.

"I'm going to fuel up our bird. Why don't you guys take a break and stretch your legs?"

He didn't have to ask me twice. I already had the harnesses off when Mitch opened the door.

"Stick by me walking to the building, I don't want to lose track of you." He took my arm, helping me out of the chopper.

"Do you think I'm going to run away?"

"I wouldn't put it past you." He laughed. "What did you think of the flight?" The three of us walked to the aviation building.

"I was really freaked out at first, but after a while it was really interesting. It's amazing how much control you have over the movement. You guys are great pilots."

"It's all the military training. You do the same thing hundreds of times. It's like sailing a boat—it becomes routine after a while. Though I have to say, we usually winch people in and out of the Jayhawks I fly. It was challenging picking up Jake in the doorway without touching down."

After using the restrooms and grabbing cold sodas, the three of us strolled back to the chopper.

Jake pre-flighted the bird again, checking everything.

Mitch turned to me as we approached the chopper. "It's nice not having to drag you this time." He teased me. "We brought you a Coke, buddy."

"Thanks." Our pilot looked at me. "So you decided to come back. Can't get enough of my flying, can you?"

"It's too long a walk. Can you do me a favor this time? Fly straight and level with no more acrobatics?"

"You ain't seen nothing yet." He laughed, turning to Mitch. "I'm gonna hit the head. I'll be right back."

Eric and I settled back in the chopper. Mitch gave the outside a once over. These guys might be nonchalant about flying, I thought, but they were actually very safety conscious.

Jake rejoined us, powering up the bird. I braced myself as we soared skyward. Banking sharply left, we cruised over Hatteras Light then headed for the open sea. Once clear of the shoals, Jake again skimmed the wave tops, which were now building. The wash of the rotor churned the water below us.

Behind us, the coastline faded away. My apprehension built. It didn't help when Mitch turned around, tapping me on the knee.

"Linda, don't freak out on me. There are life jackets under your seats, just in case."

"Is there something wrong you're not telling me?"

"No, everything's cool. We always need to be prepared." He turned his attention to the sea out the front windshield.

We followed the axis of the Gulf Stream, which the guys downloaded from a U.S. Navy website.

"We're now one hundred miles out. We'll backtrack from here. If Joey made it any farther, it would be a miracle to find him." Jake said, spinning the chopper in a sharp turn to the southwest. Nothing was out here except for a large container ship steaming northward. Two fishing boats cruised off to our right. No orange liferaft, nor any other debris was spotted.

The black helicopter crisscrossed the Gulf Stream for the remainder of the afternoon. Our last stop was the red nun buoy off of Cape Lookout. Around four P.M., we crossed our original departure point as the sun dropped toward the horizon.

Jake hovered over the nun buoy for a minute or so while turning to me. "Linda, unfortunately I think that does it. We have covered a heck of a lot of area today and didn't see anything...I'm sorry."

"Jake, we appreciate everything. You did a great job," Eric said.

"OK, we'll head back to the barn," Mitch called over the radio.

Our pilot banked the chopper, flying back over Cape Lookout. We touched down a few moments later, at the airport. I was stiff and tired after the long day of flying. Eric and I stood aside as the pilots tied down the rotor blades, securing the helicopter for the night.

As the two military guys rejoined us, Eric extended his hand to the former Marine.

"Jake, thanks for today. Can we buy you guys dinner to show our appreciation?"

"I'd never pass up a free meal. How about you, Mitch?"

"Sounds good. You did all right today, Linda. Sorry we didn't find anything."

"Thanks, Mitch. I'm disappointed but really glad we tried."

The three of us piled into the red truck, with Jake following behind. After finding parking in downtown Beaufort, we strolled to Clawson's Restaurant.

Eric called Mark and Michelle, who agreed to meet us there.

As we awaited our meals, Mitch turned to me. "Overall, what did you think of flying in a chopper?"

"It was exciting. After about the first twenty minutes, I felt pretty comfortable, except when Jake kept making those sharp turns." It was tough to keep a straight face when Jake grinned.

"Unfortunately, Linda, if you fly in a straight line all the time, you'll never get to come home. You just keep going and going until you plop into the sea." After dinner, we enjoyed a short walk on the Beaufort boardwalk. Eric, Mitch, and I stopped to look at a sailboat coming into the dock. My heart wrenched.

"I guess this is really the end of the search." I stated the obvious.

"Unless something solid pops up, yes. The horseshoe buoy isn't enough to restart a search."

The Coast Guard man leaned against the rail by the water.

"Mitch, it was really great of you guys to give us your time today. I hope we can stay in touch. Oh, by the way, I have to pay Jake for the fuel." I turned in the Marine's direction. He was chatting with Mark and Michelle.

"Already taken care of." Eric slipped his arm around me.

"Eric, you can't pay for that." I pulled away from him. "That was my responsibility."

"We'll work it out later. Let's catch up with Mark, Michelle, and Jake."

"Why don't we head back to the house for a nightcap?" Mark suggested. One last drink in Beaufort was enjoyed on Mark and Michelle's front porch overlooking the river.

Chapter 15. Sailing to Key West

The following morning we were back in Naples. As I opened the hatch to *Dark & Stormy,* depression settled over me. My bag was dumped on the V-berth.

"Eric, I'm going to sit on deck." He headed below, while I settled into a shady spot in the cockpit. Across the bay, local kids were out sailing dinghies.

A nice breeze blew out of the east. Young sailors whipped across the bay, with their little prams healing far over. A slight shift in their body weights caused the mainsails to flip over in very sharp tacks.

"Are you doing all right, Linda?"

"Yes. I was watching the kids sail. They really know how to maneuver those little boats." A dolphin cruised behind my boat, in search of fish. A couple of gulls sat on the piling. squawking for food.

"I'm real sorry Joey wasn't found."

"I know, Eric." He reclined on the starboard cockpit cushion, looking at me. "My sister and her husband should be told about this."

"Your sister in Key West?"

"Yes. We should sail down there. I promised you a trip to the Keys."

"Are you sure you're up for a sail?"

"A promise is a promise, Eric."

"What does your sister do in Key West for work?"

"She's a tarot card reader." The thought brought a smile to my face.

"She's a what?"

"A tarot card reader, like a fortune teller."

"You're kidding me, Linda."

"No, really. The funniest thing is she actually seems to believe it. Considering her background, it's hysterical."

"I'm completely lost. You'd better explain."

"Eva and her husband Merlin used to live in New York City. She was an accountant and chief financial officer for a fortune 500 company. Mom always thought of her as little miss perfect."

"Do I get the feeling you were little miss... trouble?"

"Where did you ever get that idea? I can't say I was trouble, more like a non-conformist. The other teen girls would be sunning themselves on blankets at the beach, looking at the boys. I'd spend my time exploring tidal pools, examining crabs and snails."

"I see, a tomboy."

"Don't get me wrong, Eric, I've always liked boys just fine." I gave him a cagey smile. "I was never the cliquey type. There were more important things to see in the world than shopping malls.

"Eva was the complete opposite. A five hundred dollar handbag was necessary attire. When I was working on a whale research vessel right out of college, she told me to get a real job. Find a nice guy. Settle down and have two point five kids."

"Two point five kids? That would be difficult." Eric laughed.

"You know what I mean. Be one of the sheep."

"I guess I'm one of the sheep." He smiled. "I have two kids. Maybe you could consider it two point five if you include their little dog."

"With your daredevil fishing career, I would hardly call you a sheep. Anyway, she married the perfect guy, Merlin. He was a stockbroker making way more than five figures. They had a chic apartment in the Upper East Side of New York overlooking Central Park."

"I've heard it's an expensive neighborhood."

"Yes. They had the perfect life. They worked twelve-hour days while I lazed around the boat anchored off one Caribbean island or another, with an older man. My mother was horrified."

"Eva called me on the phone one day. Don't get me wrong, I love my sister, though sometimes I would cringe when her number showed up on the Caller ID. 'Linda, you need to get your life together. Linda, you need to find a nice guy with a real job. Linda...' You get the picture."

"Yes, I do."

"This particular day, about a year ago, I answered the phone cautiously, waiting for the imminent lecture. Do you know what she told me?"

"No, what?"

"She told me I was right all along. Eva and Merlin were chucking all the corporate crap and the rat race. They were moving to Key West to live on a boat. I thought she had gone mad."

"That's certainly a life style change."

"I'm telling you all of this so you don't think my sister is a complete wacko when you meet her."

"Now, Linda. Why would I think that?" He grinned again.

"Eric," I said taking his hand, "you haven't heard the best part. You didn't ask me what Merlin does in Key West."

"Are you going to keep me in suspense, woman?"

"Only for a second. Merlin is a street performer. He does a show at Mallory Square with his dancing poodles." I tried to hold back the laughter.

"What?" Eric laughed. "You're not serious."

"It's absolutely hysterical, considering his background. You better prepare yourself for Key West. It's a strange place."

"When do you want to leave?"

"Well, Eric, it's an overnight sail. How about tomorrow afternoon? I want to check in with Shane first. We also need to provision the boat."

A pang of fear crept into my brain. This would be my first overnight sail since losing *Wind Rose.*

The rest of the day was spent prepping the boat for the offshore sail. We filled the water tanks, checked the engine fluids and belts, all the necessary equipment to ensure the boat would operate flawlessly. The safety gear was surveyed.

When my hands gripped the inflatable life jackets, fear ripped through me. A flashback to the night when Eric rescued me invaded my brain.

"What's the matter, Linda?"

"I was thinking about the night you rescued me. It's all kind of hazy. I don't think my brain was working very well. The water was so cold." Despite the warm afternoon, I hugged my shivering body. Eric put his hand on my shoulder.

"It's OK. Recovering from such a traumatic incident is not going to be overnight. We'll work through it." I attempted to muster the best smile possible.

After a quick run to Publix for food, I stowed the groceries aboard.

"What do you feel like doing for dinner, Linda?" I brushed a few strands of hair away from my forehead. With a tired sigh, I glanced at Eric.

"How about I throw chicken on the grill?"

"I've got a better idea. You look really tired. Why don't you sit down in the cockpit? I'll get you a glass of wine, then I'll put the chicken on the grill."

"Eric?"

"Yes?"

"What did I do to deserve you?"

He looked serious. "Nothing, yet."

We enjoyed a glass of wine while the chicken smoked away on the grill. After dinner, the stars burst from the sky. Lightning flashed off to the east. Mullet jumped all around the boat. Peace and quiet abounded until bedtime.

The nightmares were only a series of flashes. Cold water. A dark night. A streak lit up the black water. The life jacket chafed my neck. Wind and blinding rain.

My eyes stared at the headliner in the dim light for only a second before Eric turned on the light. He leaned against the V-berth with a frown.

"It wasn't a bad one. Sorry to wake you."

After checking in with Shane the following day, we left for the Keys. There was a great forecast, northeast to easterly winds at ten knots. A couple of hours later the boat was ready. Eric's enthusiasm was infectious. I found myself actually looking forward to the trip.

We puttered down Naples Bay. As we neared the pass, I stepped up to main sail.

"What do you need, Captain?" Eric grinned as I pulled off a couple of sail ties while giving him a stern look.

"Knock off the 'Captain' stuff. We need to get the mainsail up."

"Shall I hoist her, Captain?"

With a nod, I spun the boat into the wind.

Eric didn't strain much as his strong shoulder muscles yanked on the halyard, pulling the mainsail skyward. The canvas flapped in the afternoon breeze. The sail filled with a whoosh. "Stormy" leaned to starboard as I steered her off the wind.

"The sandbars are very tight coming out this pass. How often do they dredge this?"

"Not often enough. It's only six feet deep at the outer marker."

Beautiful Key Island passed by our left. White sand beaches stretched for miles. With the wind blowing off the beach, the Gulf was flat calm. Our course was set at 190 degrees magnetic. The lovely Gulf stretched for ninety miles, separating us from Margaritaville. Wonderful silence surrounded the sloop when the engine was turned off.

With a team effort, the jib rolled out. Once the autopilot was set, we settled down in the cockpit for a splendid afternoon sail in the warm, gentle breeze.

"How about a cold drink?" Eric went below soon returning with a couple of iced teas. The bimini gave us good shade from the sun. The conditions were idyllic.

"Tell me about this boat. When did you buy her?"

"A few years ago, in Boston. It was about a year after Joey and I started dating. We were making plans to sail around the world."

"Did you do that?"

"No. We started delivering boats for other folks to build up the cruising kitty. When Joey's wife divorced him, she ended up with most of the money."

"I was lucky my ex was more reasonable. We split everything fifty-fifty." Eric's eyes stared out of his dark glasses. "Linda, let me ask you something. Why didn't Joey marry you? It seemed as though you were together a long time."

"I'm not sure I have a good answer for that question. Despite our close relationship, he had a hang up about our age difference. Also, he was very self-centered. Marriage didn't advance his cause."

"Hmm." The boat continued to slide through the calm seas with the sails billowing out to starboard. The warm sun shining on the water made the Gulf a beautiful emerald green.

Eric pulled his shirt off, stretching out on the starboard settee.

"I could get used to this sailing thing. It sure beats fishing in the freezing cold of the Bering Sea."

"Yeah, but the crab fishing sounds exciting. I'd love to see it for myself."

"Maybe you will someday." The afternoon slid into evening. The sun dropped toward the horizon.

After slipping below, I handed Eric a glass of Pinot Grigio. Pots banged, causing delicious smells to waft into the cockpit.

"What the heck smells so good?"

"I'm throwing a little food together."

The yummy dinner of sautéed shrimp and rice topped off a nearly perfect afternoon. Dishes were washed, dried, then stowed. The sloop continued south in the gentle roll of the evening swell.

Darkness descended, sparking my apprehension. Eric sensed my nervousness. When I went on deck, to check the running lights for the second time, he grabbed my hand, pulling me to the seat next to him.

"You just checked the lights for the hundredth time. Why don't you relax?"

"The conditions tonight are very similar to the way they were on the night of the sinking. I'm a little edgy."

"Take it easy. If I thought you would be this upset, I wouldn't have suggested coming out here."

"Eric, I need to do this."

"Yes you do. You need to get beyond the fear. Why not concentrate on the beautiful evening? We're sailing along just fine." With a huge sigh, I tried to relax while watching the stars. We sailed on into the night with a half moon lighting up our path.

"What kind of a watch schedule would you like to do tonight, Linda?"

"It is a rather short trip, but we should keep to regular watches. How about four hours on and four off? I'm pretty wired, so why don't I stay up for the first watch?

"OK. I'll grab a pillow and stretch out over here."

"Eric, you can sleep down below. I'm fine."

"I know. It's such a beautiful night. Plus, the temperature's cooler out here." Was he trying to make me feel better by staying nearby or did he really want to sleep on deck? I settled down near the chartplotter.

The red line down the center of the screen delineated our course for Key West. I'd made this trip countless times before. In a couple of hours, the offshore tower would blink its white strobe light off our port side.

A few shrimp boats might pass us, all lit up with bright white lights pointed toward the water to attract shrimp. On the horizon, they often looked like a string of white pearls.

With another huge sigh, I listened to the outhaul on the mainsail groaning where it passed through a block. The sloop swayed off course to port as a little puff drove her upwind. The autopilot hissed, steering us back on course. The boat could sail on and on forever as long as the wind stayed steady.

Lightning flashed across the sky to the east. It could be heat lightning over the Everglades. A glance to my right saw Eric sleeping peacefully.

Capt. Marlena Brackebusch

Questions about my future swirled around my head. Does Eric consider me a friend or does he simply feel responsibility toward me? The next few days should be real interesting.

My reverie was interrupted by a luffing sail. The wind shifted abruptly to the southeast. Reaching across the big fisherman sleeping on the the starboard side, I deposited the winch handle into the top gear. With a few loud cranks, the jib tightened.

The big fisherman stirred. "What's wrong?" He sat up, bumping into me.

"Nothing. The wind's shifted. There is weather to the east, headed our way. Looks like a little squall."

"What would you like to do, Skipper?"

"I'm going to reef the mainsail, just to be safe."

"Do you need help?"

"No, I have it." After I first clipped my safety harness to a line on the cabin top, my toe kicked off the rope clutch holding the main halyard. The line wrapped around the winch on the cabin top would control the speed of descent of the main. At the mast, I tugged at the heavy cloth, working the sail down the mast. The big steel ring hooked on the boom.

A line through the back of the sail, about a third of the way up, held the main to the boom, creating a smaller, more manageable triangle of cloth.

The time was very near to the hour when Joey and I hit the object—whatever it was–off Cape Lookout and lost the sailing yacht. My body shuddered as the wind picked up. Lightning streaked closer. A raucous crack of thunder boomed nearby. The boat heeled way over in a huge gust.

The jib flapped as I rolled it up. Eric leaned over to give me a hand. The wind blasted to twenty-five knots. The staysail and main were drawing fine. My sturdy sloop easily handled the twenty-five knot gusts.

Waves built, rocking the boat hard. A huge gust hit, slamming her way over on her side. Water gushed over the rail. Grabbing the wheel, I flipped off the autopilot. The wind escalated past forty. I struggled to muscle the wheel around, fighting hard to keep her to weather.

The canvass flailed, cracking against the rigging. Wind and rain buffeted the little sloop...and us.

"Eric, we need to get the main down." My shout was nearly lost in the cacophony. A bolt of lightning exploded twenty feet from the bow.

The fisherman nodded. With sea legs gained from a thousand days on the brutal Bering Sea, Eric climbed on the cabin top, wrestling down the unruly sail. The boat bucked like a bronco while heeling way over.

Waves crashed over the bow. Rain pelted us so hard, I could barely see. Instinct kicked in, allowing me to hold the bow into the weather. The forward third of the staysail was full of wind. How did I ever make it through the squall in the Gulf Stream adrift, cold, and exhausted?

A few tense moments passed. The sail was lashed to the boom. I eased the bow off the wind, allowing the staysail to steady us.

"Now this is some weather." Eric grinned at me through his rain-stained face. I quivered but also felt the great adrenaline rush.

"Would you like me to take her?" Eric's hand was alongside mine on the cold wheel. "You're soaking wet. Why don't you go below to dry off?"

Experience told me the storm was easing. Bright areas peeked through the dark clouds to the east. Not realizing how badly I was shivering, I looked to Eric.

"OK, I'll just be a minute." Going below, dripping wet, I searched for a towel to wipe the cold rain from my face. With dry clothes covered by a rain jacket, I popped back into the cockpit.

"I put the autopilot back on. Do you want me to put the jib back up?"

"I'll get it. Why don't you dry off?"

The wind died off...as it so often does after a severe squall. I flipped the switch for the engine. *Dark & Stormy* puttered south. Eric reappeared on deck, drying his head with a towel. After shaking out his hair, he sopped the water off the cushion.

"What an intense squall. It's amazing how quickly the weather springs up here in Florida."

"It's the heat building up over the Everglades. All the moisture makes the atmosphere unstable. This squall reminded me of the one I was in while adrift in the Gulf Stream. It was tough keeping my head above water. Getting over the sinking is going to take a long time."

"Yes. Though, I'd have to say, you seemed to handle this squall great. The boat was under control.

I don't think I've ever seen rain come down so hard. *Stormy* handled the squall great, too."

"She's tough." The weather moved off to the west. Stars twinkled overhead.

"What a beautiful night it is now." I was grateful for the warmth of his body next to mine. My tired head leaned against his shoulder.

"I love being out at sea," Eric whispered. "It's real special to be able to venture out here. We see the stars as most people never see them. It's like our own theater.

"Here we are sailing in a gentle wind. The beauty is amazing. Even in a storm, you feel so alive. My ex-wife never understood my love for the sea. To her all that mattered was her own loneliness when I was away."

He turned to me with a serious stare in the dim, red light of the cockpit. "I'm glad you and I met, even if it was under such strange circumstances."

Not sure how to reply to this, I remained quiet. He tightened his arm around my shoulder. Thinking of Joey and where he was, I also thought about this man sitting next to me. Where was all of this going? Thankfully, Eric saved me from further discussion.

"Why don't you get some sleep?"

"Yeah, I am tired. Good night." After heading below, I double checked the bilge and bilge pump. All was well. Though I was exhausted, sleep didn't come easily. The adrenaline hadn't worn off yet. I reflected on Joey and the collision.

Capt. Marlena Brackebusch

What did we hit that night? Staring into the darkness, I thought about being adrift for all of those hours.

My brain finally dosed off. It seemed as though only a few minutes passed before Eric gently shook me awake.

"It's your watch. I can stay up if you like, but you were pretty adamant about keeping watches."

"No, the watch is mine. Thanks for waking me." With a shake of my head, the cobwebs cleared. On deck, the night was black. The stars twinkled, but no moon lit the dusky sea.

The chart plotter cast a soft glow around the cockpit. A small triangle in the middle of the screen confirmed our position. We were sailing at four and a half knots about fifty miles west of Marathon and twenty miles north of green buoy number one. This marker was our target for the entrance to the Northwest Channel into Key West.

Eric must have raised the main while I was sleeping. I never even heard him. With the wind abeam and the seas light, the only sound was the whoosh of water passing under the hull. The bow rose, taking on each little wave. The autopilot steered slowly back and forth, keeping us on course.

The light at the top of the mast glowed brightly enough to allow my eyes to scan the sails. The steady wind kept them full; no adjustment was necessary.

My ears picked up the creaks and groans of the rigging. Most of my watch passed before pink streaks of light gathered in the eastern sky. Smith Shoal light blinked ahead, slightly to starboard.

"How about a cup of coffee?" Eric popped his head up from down below.

"I'll get it." I busied myself making coffee. Soon the boat went from a musty, post-rain smell to the wonderful aroma of fresh java.

We spent a few minutes enjoying sunrise before prepping the boat for the trip down the Northwest Channel to Key West. A few hours passed as we cruised at a comfortable three knots fighting an outgoing tide. The water was smooth as we approached the capital of the Conch Republic.

At a couple minutes past noon, we stashed the sails, motoring by Tank Island.

"See the big plaza where the cruise ship is docked, Eric?"

"Yes." He shielded his eyes from the sun with his hand.

"That's Mallory Square."

"Oh, the place where Merlin performs with the dogs?"

"Yes. We'll head over there one night for the sunset celebration. It's a crazy event."

"Great. You'll have to show me all the sights. We can even go out to the reef to do a little snorkeling." He stared at me with a look of encouragement. Did he realize what a huge undertaking it would be to get me back into the ocean? I suspected he did.

"I'm going to call Eva." The subject was changed before he could pursue the snorkeling idea. My sister had no idea Joey was missing. I couldn't figure a way to tell her about the accident.

"Linda, you're here in Key West?"

"Yes, we are docking at the Bight, Sis."

"I'll be over to catch your lines. Will you be at "D" dock?"

"Yes. Thanks sis. See you in a few minutes."

My nervousness showed. As I steered my yacht toward the marina. Eric stood next to me, watching the chart plotter.

"Hey, why are you so tense?" He bumped my arm with his elbow.

"I'm nervous about seeing Eva and Merlin. I don't have any idea how I'm going to explain..."

"Oh, I get it. It will be difficult to explain the handsome, dashing fisherman you are with." He grinned. This man had an uncanny knack for finding ways to relieve my tension. I returned the smile.

"Knock off the egotistical bull and get the dock lines ready."

"Aye, aye, Captain." We both laughed at his mock salute. Pointing out the slip reserved alongside D dock, I also pointed out Eva and Merlin's boat, *Done Trading,* one dock over.

The fisherman stood ready with the lines. With a quick flip of the wheel, the boat spun alongside D dock. Eric stepped off, securing our bow line. As I hopped off with the stern line, Eva took it from me. Instead of securing it, she hugged me.

"I missed you, little sis. I was worried when I didn't hear from you." Eric walked back taking the stern line from Eva.

"Do you think we can tie up the boat, ladies?" He feigned annoyance. Eva glanced at the big fisherman before looking to me with raised eyebrows.

"It's a very long story. I'll tell you later." I answered her questioning look before taking the spring lines from the fisherman's outstretched hand. A moment later, he jumped off the boat again.

"Hi, I'm Eric." He shook my sister's hand with his best boyish smile.

"Eva."

We appraised my sister. She was a good inch taller than I and skinny as a reed. Her pretty face was adorned with dark green eyes. Long blond hair framed the tanned complexion. The flowing dress patterned in tropical flowers, fit in nicely with the "tarot card reader" persona.

When Eric stepped back aboard to get the power cord, my sister asked. "What gives...where's Joey?"

"That's the hundred thousand dollar question. I'll tell you over cocktails. Can I invite us over to your boat? It will take the air conditioner on *Dark & Stormy* a long time to cool her down."

"Sure, come on. Merlin should be home soon." Eva turned for her boat.

"We'll be there in a couple of minutes. I have a few things to tidy up first." I went below to clean up the boat. After she was locked, we rinsed off the salt.

Chapter 16. Key West

A short while later, we strolled over to Eva's boat. "What did she say about me?"

"Nothing really. She was shocked because Joey wasn't here. I couldn't tell her the story over the phone. I didn't know how." We knocked, then stepped aboard the trawler. Eric checked the boat out.

"Very nice. I can see you both are really into varnish." Eric was referring to the perfectly varnished handrails capping the stanchions along the foredeck. The polished cabin top extended nearly to the bow, providing a large area for lounging or sun tanning.

Aft of the pilothouse was a covered deck complete with comfortable, folding deck chairs. We slipped through the sliding teak door into the cool, dark interior.

"Working on the boat keeps me out of trouble." I gave him a crafty smile. "Hello, we're here."

The air conditioning felt great after another steamy day. Two little dogs, barking for attention, jumped on me while eying Eric.

"Flotsam, Jetsam, knock it off." The sharp rebuke came from my brother-in-law Merlin, coming up the steps from below.

"Linda, it's great to see you. Who's your friend?"

"Eric Iverson." The two men shook hands. Merlin, a five-foot-eleven lanky guy with dark hair graying around his ears, sported a mostly black goatee and mustache. The hippy, college-professor look was topped off with cut-off shorts, sandals and a "Jimmy Buffet" T-shirt.

"Please, sit down, make yourselves at home. Eva is mixing cocktails." Merlin motioned toward an unoccupied settee. "It's been a long time since we've seen you, Linda, what's been going on?"

The former stock broker stared hard at Eric questioningly. Eva appeared from below, bearing a tray of cocktails with appetizers.

"My famous rum punch. It's a special mixture of orange, pineapple, and lime with a couple of secret ingredients. Captain Morgan's is the floater." She winked at us while setting down the tray of appetizers. Eric helped himself to a couple of chips with salsa. All eyes were on me.

"I don't know where to start. You know Joey and I where delivering the sailing yacht to Lauderdale...." My eyes swiveled to Eric for support then returned to Merlin. The big fisherman squeezed my hand.

"The boat was sailing off Cape Lookout in the Gulf Stream. It was nine-thirty P.M. We hit something, I don't know what. It put a hole in the boat. Water poured in. We tried to stop the leak and bail the boat for a couple of hours. Then I grabbed the EPIRB and my inflatable life vest. Joey was trying to put the liferaft into the water when a wave knocked me overboard." A couple of tears were pushed back.

"That's the last time I saw Joey."

"Oh my God," Eva gasped. She squeezed next to me.

"Then what happened?" Merlin asked.

"I was adrift in the Gulf Stream for a long time until Eric and his brother, along with the other fishermen, rescued me."

"We owe you a huge debt of gratitude." Eva looked at Eric who sipped his drink quietly.

"She's the best fish I've ever pulled out of the sea." His attempt to lighten the situation caused a frown to form on Merlin's face.

"Seriously, she's had a tough time with this. I'm just trying to be supportive. Be a good friend."

Merlin rubbed his goatee while staring at Eric.

"So you come back to Naples and decide to sail to the Keys—seems pretty soon after to me." Merlin looked skeptically at Eric. "What kind of fisherman are you?"

Eric returned Merlin's stare. There was a sense of hostility from my brother-in-law.

"My brother and I own a crab fishing boat in Alaska. We were helping a friend catch tuna off the Carolinas when we found Linda."

"Are you the guy on that TV show?" Eva interrupted. "On the boat *Denali*. Oh my God!" My sister looked at me wide-eyed. I gave her a don't-go-there look.

"There's a nice fresh mahi mahi in my fridge," I told them. "Should we cook up it for dinner?" It was a feeble attempt to change the subject, but somehow it worked.

"I'll be happy to grill it." Merlin was a great chef in addition to being a street performer.

Eric and I strolled back to *Dark & Stormy* to retrieve the fish.

"Your sister seemed nice, but I'm not sure Merlin likes me. I don't know why."

"He used to be a stock trader in New York, as I told you. He's skeptical about everyone. Give him time."

After bringing the fish back to the trawler, the two men went to the galley to marinate it, leaving Eva and me alone.

"Linda, I can't believe he's the guy from the TV show. The one you always liked. It has to be a billion-to-one chance he would be the one to rescue you from the sea." She gripped my hands, wide-eyed. One thing could always be said for my sister. She was very direct. "He seems very nice."

"Eva, I know, it's really weird. I don't know if I could have coped with this if he wasn't so sweet and supportive. The first couple of days I was like a zombie. And now with Joey missing...it's really hard." My throat clogged with emotion.

As the guys reappeared with a fresh set of drinks, Eric caught the look between Eva and me.

"Were you two talking about me?" He grinned an adorable grin.

"As a matter of fact, we were." Eva left it at that. "So how long are you staying in Key West?"

"I don't know. A few days, I would guess. Depends on what Linda wants to do. There's more sorting out to do on her business. At some point, we should head back to Texas. There are several head of new calves that need to be vaccinated. Also, one of my horses is running in a thoroughbred race in Dallas."

"That's quite a schedule. I hope we get to spend a lot of time with you two while you're here." Eva smiled at Eric. My mind pondered all the "we's" in his statement.

Merlin announced dinner was ready. Their galley was bright and airy with mahogany-trimmed white walls.

"The mahi is great," Eric said between mouthfuls.

"It's a key lime recipe with fresh basil."

"And this cool salad with fresh papaya chunks really tops off a great meal," I added.

After dinner, we retreated to the pilot house for more wine. Eva left for a moment, returning with her tarot cards.

"Oh no, please. No tarot readings." I protested.

"I have to, Linda. I need to get a better feel for the spirit of this man you brought into our presence." She lit incense.

"It would be great to have Eva read my cards." Eric grinned. "It would be a new experience."

"Really!" I gave up my protest as my sister retrieved her tarot cards from their special wooden box. They were wrapped in a dark purple scarf. One can never tell if she actually believed all this hocu-pocus, or was simply having fun.

The cards were unwrapped. The scarf was carefully refolded. A glance at Eric showed a bemused but serious look on his face.

Eva closed her eyes then shuffled the cards. Handing them to Eric, she held her hands over his on the deck.

"I would like you to cut the cards." Without a word he did as told. "Now remove the top four cards. Place them in a diamond pattern on the table." He did this while watching Eva.

"Interesting," she said. "They are all upright. Do you see the orientation?" We nodded. All of the cards were in an upright position.

"Hmm. See this one?" She pointed to the top card in the diamond pattern.

"That is the Lover's cards. It indicates harmony and union. Some form of test and consideration."

"Your next card is the Star." Her finger tapped a bright, colorful tarot. "It foretells fresh hope and renewal, a healing of old wounds."

"This lower card is the Judgment. It describes change and improvement.

My sister paused a few moments before revealing the final card reading.

"Ah, your last card is the Fool. It foretells beginnings with a new journey in life. Very interesting." She stopped talking and gazed first at the cards then at Eric, then at me.

"What does it all mean?" Eric's eyes filled with curiosity.

"I can't tell for sure until I read Linda's cards," Eva said mysteriously.

"This is ridiculous. I'm not playing this game." My irritation showed. I couldn't believe Eric was buying this.

"Oh, come on. What are you afraid of?" the fisherman asked. Eva stared at me with a hurt look on her face. It was obvious she did believe this stuff.

"OK." My sister reshuffled the cards then gave them to me, placing her hands over mine on the cards. As she removed her hands, I cut the deck. The top four cards were arranged in the same diamond pattern. One of my cards, the lower one, was upside down.

"Oh my," Eva exclaimed. Eric leaned close to have a better look at the tarots. "Your top card is the Tower. It tells a story of disruption, sudden dramatic upheaval, and loss.

"*Hmm*. The right hand one is also the Fool. In this placement it means important decisions need to be made. The Moon is at the bottom spot in the pyramid. That's bad. It means bad news is coming." She tapped her fingers restlessly on the table.

"With the Judgment card to the left, good times are due. It may take a while, but good health, vitality and love–maybe even marriage–are on your horizon." Everyone in the pilot house grew silent. Eva finished in a whisper.

"The only conclusion from this reading is—I must tell you–Joey is not coming back. Linda, you will need to make hard decisions. The fact you both received the Judgment card is very unusual. It indicates you're going to spend a whole lot of time together. Who knows where this may lead?"

You could cut the silence with a knife. My face flushed as I avoided the fisherman's stare.

Capt. Marlena Brackebusch

"I need to get some air." With one fluid move, I leapt out the trawler door. After a jump to the dock, I scurried along the boardwalk not really noticing the stifling heat and humidity. Beads of perspiration dotted my forehead while making my way along the Key West waterfront.

As usual, many tourists and locals made the most of the waterfront bars. Schooner Wharf was packed. A Jimmy Buffet wannabe sang, strumming his guitar. Someone grabbed my arm.

"Linda, wait up." Eric fell into step with me.

"I can't talk right now." When I tried to turn away, he tightened his grip on my arm.

"Hey, come on. Let's get a drink." We waded into the crowd at Schooner Wharf beneath the sheet-metal roof overhanging bright red bougainvillea in the entrance.

Luckily, there was an open table. The makeshift stage housed the performer. A scrawny-looking dog reclined on the dusty floor a few feet away. The air was filled with the aroma of stale beer and wafts of cigarette smoke.

The singer was dressed in a torn leather jacket with faded blue jeans. He looked like he sampled the ganja he sang about and had not showered for a week. A nearly empty bottle of Bud, along with his tip jar sat atop the worn, scuffed amp.

A heavy-set waitress with jet black hair and a gay pride T-shirt walked up to us. "What'll it be?"

"Two dark and stormy's," Eric ordered. She shuffled off. His eyes seared into me. Pretending to be interested in the singing, I stared at the makeshift stage.

My face still burned red.

"Linda, talk to me. What's wrong?"

"Did you hear what she said? About Joey...about you and...me." I averted my eyes. He reached over, but I pulled away.

"Listen, Linda. I heard what she said. It was all in good fun. I'm not taking any of the reading seriously. Anyway, the you-and-me part wasn't totally bad, was it?" I tried to figure out if his boyish grin was serious or not. The cold alcohol slipped down my throat while I contemplated the situation.

"What you don't get is Eva is usually very accurate with her premonitions or card reads, or whatever you want to call them." We drank in silence as the singer crooned "Margaritaville," banging away on his old Gibson guitar.

"Let's go back to the boat. It's been a long day," I said as the singer switched to Johnny Cash. After paying the tab, we strolled back to the boat...in silence.

It was a beautiful evening albeit a little hot with not much breeze. We stopped on our dock as Eva approached. Eric excused himself, heading aboard *Dark & Stormy*.

"Linda, I'm sorry. I didn't mean to upset you so."

"Forget it." I cut her off, turning toward my boat.

"Linda, you know he's awfully sweet and what a looker. He's hot!"

Looking back at my sister, I couldn't help but laugh. She always figured a way to make the best out of a bad situation. I turned back, embracing her in a big hug.

Once back aboard my boat, Eric was reading a magazine. He glanced up.

"Linda, why don't you sit down with me?"

"Eric, I don't want to talk about it."

"Let me talk for just a minute." He pulled me to the seat next to him. "Linda. You need to figure out what you're going to do if Joey doesn't come back. I know this is tough, but the chances of his still being alive are slim, at best." Tears welled in my eyes. Dammit, I didn't want this man to see me cry.

"Eric, I know." Without another word, I took refuge in the V-berth. Nightmares plagued me continuously throughout the night. After the shriek woke me, Eric leaned on the V-berth cushion. I pushed him away.

The next morning, I gazed out the door to the V-berth to see the fisherman sitting on the port settee with his feet up near the nav station. The local rag, the Citizen, was in his hands. I poured myself a cup of coffee.

"Good morning. Did you get a chance to sort things out since last night?" He glanced up from the paper.

"I'm not sure. It's too early."

"You're definitely not a morning person." Sitting across from him, I watched him read the paper while thinking about what Eva said—he is a looker and a great guy. I needed to reconcile all this in my head.

"Saving the world again?"

"No, *um*, I was thinking about our plans for today."

"You promised to take me snorkeling, so how about we do that?"

"OK, I guess we could go out to Sand Key. It's supposed to be a hot day."

"The hotter the better when we're snorkeling. Do you want to invite Eva and Merlin?"

"Sure." I dialed my sister's number. Unfortunately, they had a bunch of things which needed attention, so they could not break away. We agreed to meet for supper at the Turtle Kraals after we returned.

With coffee finished, we fired up the motor, heading down the channel toward Sand Key. This route brought us between the eastern ship channel and the Lakes, a shallow area between small mangrove islands to the southwest of Key West.

It was a lovely day with a faint easterly breeze. The clear water allowed us to watch a dolphin scoot by. Due to the light wind, the sails weren't raised for the five-mile trek to the metal tower guarding the reef.

A turtle raised his neck above the water's surface for a gulp of air. After seeing us, he dove. His four little legs working furiously propelling him to safety. Tiny fish darted back into the Sargasso weed floating by.

"This ride out makes it worth the trip. There is so much wildlife here. The clear water makes everything so vibrant." Eric stood by the dodger, staring into the water like a little kid.

"Tourist," I kidded him.

An hour later, we swung around the southeast side of Sand Key to pick up a white mooring buoy.

"Eric, could you slip the dock line through the eye in the buoy line, please?"

"Sure." With a quick flip of his wrist, we were secured to the mooring.

While walking back to the cockpit, Eric leaned over the side, gazing at all the brightly colored fish under the boat.

"Linda, come here." When I joined him, he pointed to a big blue fish beneath us. "What's that?"

"It's a parrot fish. They're reef grazers who eat the coral, grinding it up to produce fine sand."

"This should be a great snorkel with a marine biologist." He eyed me.

I picked a spot that required only a short swim to the reef, which protruded from the little island with the rusting skeletal light structure built upon it.

"Eric, I'm not sure I'm ready to get into the water."

He shook his head at me. "We came all the way down here, so you can't back out now."

"You just don't get it, do you?" The irritation in his voice made me edgy. "I wasn't taking a pleasure swim out in the Gulf Stream when you found me. You have no idea how close I came to giving up...to dying. It's not so easy to jump in again." I immediately felt bad for snapping at the fisherman.

"I'm sorry."

"No apology is necessary. It's better to see you get angry, than being depressed all the time. My lady, you need to trust your knight in shining armor. This big, strong fisherman will protect you from the denizens of the deep."

"Give me a break. If you wear your shining armor in the ocean, you'll sink like a rock."

"Why don't we get into the water near the boat? We'll be within a few feet of the ladder if you get uncomfortable. I won't let anything happen to you."

"OK." After we changed into swimsuits, Eric donned his mask and snorkel, jumping off at the boarding gate on the starboard side. He disappeared in a cloud of bubbles. I shuddered.

"The water's bathtub temperature. Come on in."

"I'm going down the boarding ladder." My foot felt for the first rung. In my left hand were my fins. The dive mask covered my face.

"I feel like an idiot climbing down the ladder after all the diving I've done." When I hesitated, he climbed up behind me.

"Only a couple more steps."

Fear gripped me. My mind flashed back to floating in the Gulf Stream all alone.

"I can't do this." I whispered. Eric stood behind me on the ladder, holding on to me.

"You can't go back now. Take another step down."

"Eric, let go of me."

"Linda, I'm not going to force you. It's your decision, but think about it. If you quit now, the fear wins. You may never get back into the water again."

He stepped back down the ladder. I followed, shaking.

"I'm going to ease into the water. I'll keep my hands on the ladder. Come down in front of me. I'll keep you close to the boat."

"Damn it, Eric."

"Come on." One more step took me into the sea. The cool surrounded me. I immediately stuck my mask into the water. Only bright reef fish cruised beneath us.

"I can't help thinking about the Gulf Stream. About being all alone."

"You're not alone." He dipped his mask in the water. "Linda, there's a little coral head only a few yards away. Let's go check it out."

My hand released the ladder. With a couple of kicks of our fins, we drifted over a patch of coral.

"Is that brain coral?" Eric asked.

"Yes, it's surrounded by staghorn coral. See the pink anemone over there?" My finger pointed to a clump of arms waving in the current. "See the little orange and white fish? It's a clown fish."

"Like Nemo." My mask came out of the water to look at this man treading water next to me.

"I never would guess you watched cartoons."

"My daughter made me take her to see it. It was a cute movie."

We spent a few more minutes enjoying the reef. When the turn for the boat was made, a silver torpedo with sharp, pointed teeth stopped us in our tracks. He was all of five feet long.

"What's that?" Eric asked, his voice edgy.

"A barracuda. They're pretty territorial, but not usually aggressive. Hang here for a moment. I bet he'll leave." We hovered for a couple of minutes. With a flick of his pectoral fins, the barry was gone.

Two kicks of my fins brought me back to the ladder. Just before climbing out, I saw one more special sight.

"Eric, look! A spotted eagle ray."

"What a graceful fish. Look at the way his wings flap so slowly, like he's soaring over the reef."

After climbing out of the sea, we showered off with the warm cockpit shower.

"You did great, lady."

"Once again, a thank you is order."

"Why are you thanking me?" He shrugged his shoulders. "You took me snorkeling. It was awesome."

"You know, for getting me back into the water."

"You are welcome. How about getting me lunch woman? I'm hungry." He grinned at me.

"Coming right up." The big fisherman stretched out in the sunshine with a beer. I busied myself making sandwiches.

We hung out for about an hour before firing up the engine for the ride back to Key West Bight. After casting off the mooring, Eric traversed his way back to the cockpit.

"What do you think of sailing back outside the reef? We can do some fishing, then reenter Key West by going down the ship channel."

Not realizing he'd looked at the navigation chart, I glanced at him with surprise. A gentle sea breeze stirred out of the southeast. It would make for a relaxing sail back. The only trouble was, *Dark & Stormy* would be in the Gulf Stream.

"Sure, why not?"

"Why don't we do a little fishing? What's good to catch around here?" Eric asked after setting the sails. He grabbed the fishing pole.

"Mahi mahi would be perfect, you know, what we had for dinner last night. Actually I have a really good mahi lure." In the tackle box, I found a blue feather lure with a huge hook. I carefully placed it on his out-stretched palm.

"Now that's a fish hook." Eric added it to the steel leader. Soon the lure skipped off the second wave in our wake.

"This water is getting prettier by the minute."

"Yeah, Gulf Stream blue." I felt a chill surge down my spine. From my refuge in the shade, I watched him sit with his back to the sun. His eyes scanned our fishing lure along with the pretty scene astern of us. After thirty minutes of easy sailing in the light southeast wind, the fisherman's skin looked red from the sun.

"If you're not careful, you'll look like a Maine Lobsta," I scolded him in my best fake New England accent.

"Well, why don't you do something about it, woman. Put some sunscreen on my back?"

Somewhat taken aback by the tone of his voice, I grabbed a can of spray sunscreen. Creeping up behind him, I sprayed the cold aerosol on his hot back. With a yelp he leapt a good foot off the seat.

"There's your sunscreen, sir."

He reached over to grab me, but I ducked out of his grip. Down below, I turned on the music. *Dark &*

Stormy continued sailing lazily toward the entrance buoy for the ship channel.

Staccato clicks rang out from the fishing reel. *Zing!* The fishing line flew out. Eric and I both lunged for the rod almost running into each other.

"You get it, Eric."

Spinning around, I flicked my wrist to release the jib sheet. The now flapping sail slowed us down.

The fish danced on the surface of the water as Eric fought him. It must be a big one, I figured, because he sure gave the fisherman quite a battle. Line went out, then line was reeled in. The pole bent in a crazy arch.

"Come on. Give up already." Eric sweated furiously as a flash of green broke the water only yards astern of us. The net was ready.

"Linda, I'm going to bring him alongside. Take the rod." I was forward of the boarding gate when Eric gave me the rod. As I held the splashing fish near the surface, the fisherman netted his prize.

"What a beauty." He grunted, straining to lift the large bull mahi out of the water. It landed with a splat then thrashed around the gunnel.

"Linda, do you have a club or a fillet knife."

"I have something better." After dashing below, I returned on deck with a bottle of rum.

"Rum? This is no time for a drink."

"It's not for us, it's for him. Hold his head steady." Eric looked skeptical.

"That may be easier said than done."

"I thought you were a big, strong fisherman." With another grunt, he grabbed the fish by its gills. I poured a healthy shot of rum down his throat. With a mighty shiver, the fish died.

"What a magnificent fish. Look at the colors. I never caught one of these before." The crab fisherman examined his catch with wonder in his eyes. We watched as the colors slowly drained from the dorado. "That's a neat trick with the rum. I've never heard of it."

"At least he died with a smile on his face. It's a little sad, taking a life, but he'll make a great supper. That's a big bull mahi." I patted Eric's arm.

"Nice catch. Let's E-mail a picture to Tom and the guys from the boat." After pictures, Eric filleted the fish. The fillets were rinsed in salt water before being packed away in the fridge.

"The wind is dying."

"Why don't you start the engine?" I called out from below. The red and white harbor entrance buoy bobbed directly ahead. After rounding the mark, he steered the boat down the channel past a massive departing cruise ship. The happy ship's passengers partied at the rails while waving.

Mallory Square was empty at this time of day. Ten minutes later, we slipped back into our designated boat slip. After securing the lines, we hosed off the boat. A cool shower washed away the heat and grime of the day.

A pretty white sundress with a bird-of-paradise pattern dressed up my mood for the evening. After a dash of makeup and my colorful parrot earrings, I was ready for an evening out in the capital of the Conch Republic.

Eric wore white jeans and a tropical print dress shirt...and his ever-present black cowboy hat. Looking at him, I couldn't help but laugh.

"We look like a couple of tourists!"

"And what's wrong with that, lady? We are tourists." Eric grinned at me, gallantly helping me off the boat. We strolled to the Turtle Kraals Restaurant which overlooked the pens where sea turtles were once kept until harvested for meat.

The view from the fun restaurant took in all the pretty yachts in the harbor. As Merlin and Eva arrived, we all enjoyed a margarita at the Tower Bar on top of the restaurant.

Pelicans dove into the sea in search of fish. A few white sails drifted in the fading afternoon breeze. After drinks, we went below, sitting on the rustic wooden benches.

"This is excellent fried shrimp." Eric washed his dinner down with a beer. "What's the plan for the rest of the evening?"

"Eric, you are in for a real treat. We'll pick up the pooches then head for Mallory Square. The dogs and I have a performance tonight." Merlin grinned.

Back at the trawler, the poodles were all excited. They knew it was nearly showtime. With their leashes attached, our foursome strolled down Greene Street toward the famed sunset locale.

Several locals greeted us as we approach Mallory Square. Merlin set up a couple of hoops and a boom box. With a pirate bandanna on Jetsam and a pink tutu on Flotsam, the dogs began dancing before Merlin had a chance to direct them. They jumped through hoops and paraded around Merlin in circles to the delight of the tourists.

Their grand finale featured a series of choreographed jumps to the *Pirates of the Caribbean* music. The crowd went wild. We laughed almost uncontrollably as the sun sank into the water over Key West Harbor.

Eric slipped his arm around me.

"Watch for the green flash."

"What's that, Linda?"

"It's an atmospheric phenomenon. When the top of the sun sinks below the horizon, sometimes you see a bright green flash."

"Does this have anything to do with the tequila we drank?"

"No, silly. It only occurs in the tropics. It's doubtful you would see it in Alaska."

The sun set to the right of Tank Island—this time without the green flash–but a spectacle of colors rewarded us nonetheless.

Merlin picked up his tip jar, chuckling over the twenty-five dollars in it. "I'm glad we don't have to survive on this."

Arriving back at the boats, we could feel a slight evening breeze blowing across the docks. We took refuge on the flybridge, watching the stars while enjoying a beautiful Key West evening.

"What are you two up to tomorrow?" Eva asked.

"We'll play tourist. Eric has never been on the Conch Train. We can stop by the Hemingway house and do all the sights. Would you guys like to come over tomorrow night for dinner? There a fresh caught mahi in the fridge."

"That sounds great." Merlin said. "I can never get enough mahi."

Realizing how tired I was, we returned to *Dark & Stormy*.

"What a great evening." Eric said once aboard.

"It was fun."

Despite a relaxing day, the nightmares gave me no reprieve. I drifted on my back on a bright sunny day. Looking around for the boat, I could see nothing but water on the horizon.

Panicking, I started swimming but didn't know which way to go. A black wall of clouds engulfed me. Waves crashed against my face. Between drenching rains, my eyes picked up something in the distance. It looked like a boat.

The deck was awash. Stroke after exhausting stroke brought me only a little closer. A black fin sliced the rough water. It submerged. My left thigh exploded in pain. Sharp daggers sank in. The monster shook me like a rag doll.

My fists punched and punched as I was dragged under. Extreme pressure agonized my ears. Joey's face floated before me.

"Linda, wake up. I'm here. You're safe." Eric's voice roused me from the nightmare. His arm wrapped tightly around me. My lungs strained to draw in breaths. Tears streamed down my face. He was holding me so tight, I couldn't wipe them away.

The fisherman eased us down on the V-berth.

"*Shh.*" He gently brushed the hot droplets of water away from my eyes.

When he drew me against his chest, I tried to push him away.

"Why are you trying to push me away?" It took quite a few seconds for me to calm down.

"I'm so sick and tired of these nightmares, aren't you?"

"I have to admit a full night's sleep would be nice. Tell what this dream was about."

"Eric, it was so real. I felt the shark biting my leg."

"Do you think the snorkeling brought it on? It's been a few days since you've had such a bad one."

"It must have been. When we swam to the reef, I had a flashback to the night I was thrown off the boat.

Without another word he cuddled me. The very faint hint of dawn crept through the cabin's porthole. There would be no more sleep this morning, because I was too wired. I allowed myself another ten minutes of dozing, slowly mulling over the nightmare. If Joey could only be found....

Moments later, Eric climbed off the bunk. I watched him rummage about the galley.

He slipped into the aft cabin, re-emerging dressed in a pair of beige shorts with a white-horse-scene T-shirt. On his head went the black cowboy hat. The fisherman slipped out the companionway.

The boat rocked gently as he stepped onto the dock. I had a pretty good idea where he was headed–the Waterfront Market–for the morning newspaper.

As I struggled to get out of bed, my feet grazed the cool fiberglass floor. In the galley, I set out two big coffee mugs.

The wonderful aroma swirled around the cabin. A gentle rock of the boat announced the man's return. He came below with a wax paper bag and the newspaper.

"You're up. I was going to let you sleep in while I read the paper."

"After the nightmare last night I'm not sure I'll ever sleep again. Sit down and read your paper. The coffee's ready."

"Why did you tense up when I hugged you just now?" He asked before releasing me.

"I don't know," I lied, trying to pull away from him.

"You don't lie very well. What's wrong?"

"Nothing. If you let me go, I'll get you a cup of coffee." He released me with a shake of his head.

"Sometime this century you are going to have to talk about your feelings. I can't go on wondering if every move I make is going to upset you."

Mugs of steaming coffee sat between us on the table. Two warm fluffy croissants were found inside the wax bag.

"Thanks for the croissants."

"You're welcome. That was a nice attempt to change the subject." He mumbled while studying the newspaper in front of him. His brow was furrowed with irritation.

My brain tried to reconcile this man with the loss of Joey. If Joey was really gone, what should I do about

Eric? Did he want some kind of future with me or was he simply being nice because he felt responsibility for saving my life?

What if we found Joey? Then what would I do about Eric? The past few weeks, I'd grown close to him. I would hate to abandon this budding relationship. Could we continue on as friends?

"Linda." I had the feeling he was calling my name repeatedly. He slid around the galley table, slipping his arm around my waist.

"Didn't you hear me call you?"

"No, sorry." Blinking back to the present, I looked up at him.

"Linda, you were a thousand miles away. What were you thinking about?"

"Oh, nothing."

He tightened his grip. His hand gently cradled my chin as he lifted my face to look at him.

"Whenever you look serious, I ask you what you are thinking. You always say 'nothing.' I'm not accepting your answer this time. You were too deep in thought. Tell me what you were thinking."

Squirming, I tried to break free of his grasp. For a moment, it felt as though I was talking to Joey. A flash of intimidation seared through me. A couple of deep breaths came out as a sigh. Maybe this was a good time to talk to him.

"I was thinking about you, us...and Joey." He backed off, giving me his full attention.

"I was trying to figure out where we go from here if we don't find Joey. I wasn't sure if you were doing all of this because you felt responsibility toward me for saving my life, or..."

"Linda, you need to understand a couple of things about me. First, I have a pretty long fuse when I comes to getting angry. You keep giving me all these mixed signals and I'm getting pretty frustrated. I have no idea where we go from here." His eyes bored into mine.

"You need to reconcile this Joey thing before we can discuss any kind of future." He ran his hand through his hair then turned his attention back to me.

"When my wife filed for divorce, I was completely destroyed. She gave me no warning. There was an envelope from her lawyer on the table when I came back from fishing. All her stuff was gone. At that very moment, I promised myself to never, ever get emotionally involved with another woman."

Eric stood, walking over to the chart table. It appeared as though he was having a difficult time with this discussion. His fingers trailed along the chart of Key West. Then he turned back to me. Pain lit up his eyes.

"Then you floated up, literally. You are a completely different woman from her, so adventurous. She would never go snorkeling because her precious hair might get wet." A faint smile played around his lips. He sat down next to me once again.

"I would like to see where this relationship goes. We both have baggage. Joey may be alive and maybe not." He paused.

"Listen, there are a few jobs at the ranch that need my attention in the near future. Blackjack is entered in his first race in two weeks. Why don't you come with me? You seemed much more relaxed in Dallas."

"The ranch was good for me. Are you sure you can put up with me and the nightmares?" I attempted a smile.

"We can keep this thing a friendship for now, with no pressure. I'll put up with your nightmares if you'll come to Seattle with me when we're finished with the ranch work. Another crew member is needed to bring *Denali* to Alaska."

I looked at him with complete surprise. How cool would it be to go on their crab boat?

"That is, if you want to go. I know you said *Denali* was your favorite boat on the show, though you didn't recognize the picture at my house."

"Eric, I don't want to go through that again. Of course, I want to go on *Denali*. Would it be all right with Tom?"

"Tom thinks the world of you. I'm sure it would be fine. But I'll call and ask him...to be sure."

"OK, then, why don't we see Key West?"

After changing and tidying up, we locked the boat then walked into the bright Key West sunshine.

Chapter 17. The Sail Back to Naples

Heading over to the other side of the Waterfront Market, Eric and I strolled down Caroline Street, making a right onto Simonton and then a left onto Front Street. We stopped now and again to look into the windows of shops before ending up at the Conch Train Depot.

Settling into seats near the front, we listened to the narration of the history of Key West as the train cruised around Old Town. Stopping at Whitehead Street, the Hemingway Home stood before us. We roamed around the lush tropical garden, watching the sixty odd cats living there.

"Linda, look at this cat. It has six toes."

"Actually, the first six-toed cat was given to Hemingway by a ship's captain. They've had quite a few descend from that kitty."

"Weird. I wouldn't mind bringing one home to breed with our barnyard mousers at the ranch."

"Then you would have very literary kitties. Why don't we take the train to Sloppy Joe's bar for lunch. It's an neat, famous old bar."

"Neat? I don't believe I've ever seen a 'neat' bar. All the ones I go to are cluttered, mostly with sots."

I grinned. "You can be really goofy, but I love it. You really know how to make me laugh."

Eric and I disembarked the tram again in front of the red brick building.

"They've really modernized the front of this place. It used to be an old brick building. Let's go inside." I led Eric into the dark, cool interior.

"This is a nice change from all the heat outside. What's good to eat here?"

"I've had the conch fritters before. They're really good." We enjoyed Cuba Libres with spicy fish tacos and conch fritters in this landmark bar of Key West.

"What do you think of Key West?" I asked him as we strolled out of the dark recesses of the bar.

"It's great. I'd love to come back here again to see more." He grabbed my hand for the stroll back to *Dark & Stormy*.

As we planned to leave early the next day, I took a few minutes to check the engine oil and other essential motor stuff.

The afternoon was enjoyed in the cool air conditioning while listening to tropical music on a local radio station. Around four P.M., Eric pulled the mahi fillets out of the fridge. He trimmed the fish putting them in a plastic container with lime juice.

He searched through the spices on the boat, finding just what he was looking for. The herb was sprinkled generously on the marinating fish. I tried to see what he was adding to the fish, but he playfully pushed me away with his shoulder.

"It's a secret."

248

Rebuked, I settled back on the settee with my lemonade. "I didn't know you liked to cook."

After setting the marinating fish in the fridge, he sat down on the opposite settee. "I love to cook—when I have the time. Especially grilling." He leaned back against a throw pillow.

There was a knock on the boat, so I popped up to see who it was. Eva and Merlin stood on the dock. My sister was carrying a key lime pie from Kermit's. Seeing the box, I knew dessert would be delicious.

"I hope we're not too early," Eva called out as she stepped aboard the boat.

"Not at all. Come on down below." Eric, the Southern gentleman, stood up as the couple entered the salon. He shook hands with Merlin. Once they were comfortably seated on the port settee, Eric offered drinks.

"I don't think I can compete with your rum punch from yesterday, but I can make a mean drink myself."

"You are quite the charmer, aren't you?" Eva scrutinized the cowboy.

"I have my moments." It was interesting how Eric puttered around the galley, playing the perfect host aboard my boat. It made me feel a little self-conscious. The contrast to Joey was immense as he would sit around expecting me to do everything.

The scrumptious marinated fish dinner was sauteed to perfection.

"Cilantro." I fixed my eyes on the fisherman between bites of the delicious, steaming fish.

"I'll never tell." His droll expression told me I nailed his secret spice. The rest of the evening sped by. We were sad to see Eva and Merlin depart, but they needed to walk the dogs. Tomorrow morning would dawn early for our sail back to Naples, so we decided to call it an early evening.

Alone, Eric sat with his back against the bulkhead. He patted the seat next to his leg, inviting me to sit down. As I did, he wrapped his arms around me. We sipped our cocktails in silence for a few minutes as I enjoyed his embrace.

"We better get some sleep. Tomorrow will be a long day." I attempted to pull out of his embrace. He held on to me a little longer. A long sigh escaped him.

"It was fun having Eva and Merlin over tonight. I appreciate all of your efforts."

"I enjoyed them. I enjoy holding you even more."

"Yes, this is nice, but we need to rest."

"Linda, sleep is overrated."

"Maybe so, but do you want me to be a zombie tomorrow?"

"No, go on to bed. I'm glad you had a good evening." I detected a pang of disappointment in his voice.

After crawling into the V-berth, I prayed there were no nightmares tonight.

Eric shook me awake early the next morning. A good night's sleep had left me refreshed...for a change.

"I'm going to check the marine forecast." I flipped on the VHF radio.

"The offshore marine forecast, west of eighty-one degrees west. Southeast winds, ten to fifteen knots with two to four foot seas." The computerized voice continued. "Ten percent chance of rain."

"A perfect forecast." Eric slid the hatch open. "I'll grab the sail cover." After twenty minutes of prep, we motored back out the Northwest Channel. We both coiled lines then stowed them with the fenders in the starboard cockpit locker. The main went up easily. Once the sail was set, the autopilot went on.

The sun poked over the horizon in a blaze of golden beams as my little yacht reached off on the aquamarine Gulf. The temperature was warm but not stifling yet.

"What a perfect breeze." Eric watched the jib luff occasionally as the sail lost wind when dropping off the small rolling seas. Nodding, I consulted the chart plotter.

"We'll keep our course slightly east of north. The next land sighted will be Marco Island," I said as the little mangrove dots disappeared astern of us.

Suddenly, a cold shiver rushed through me. I glanced at Eric, stretched out on the starboard cockpit cushion, perusing a sailing magazine in the early morning sunshine.

"I could get used to this sailing thing. It's almost too relaxing, though." He glanced in my direction, catching the look on my face. "Linda, what's wrong?"

"Nothing. I just had a weird feeling. Like something is not right." I gently "knocked on wood"—there was no point in tempting fate.

The gentle beam reach continued, rolling the sloop northward. A small pod of dolphins darted by, soon leaving the sea around us deserted once again.

Around noon, I consulted the chart plotter. "We are making good time. At this speed we should be at the pass right after sunset." *Dark & Stormy* sliced away at a comfortable six point two knots.

A few minutes later, I went below for a couple of cold sodas. The red light on the nav station circuit board caught my attention. The bilge pump was running. No big deal—the bilge pump often ran for a short time to clear the air conditioner condensate water or perhaps to remove the little water we took in while motoring out today.

The light stayed on. A knot formed in my stomach.

"Eric, we may have a problem." I called to him on deck. He was at my side in an instant, having picked up on the tone of my voice. His eyes followed mine to the bilge pump indicator light. Dropping down on my hands and knees, I yanked up the bilge boards.

"Maybe the pump is stuck." Eric leaned over my shoulder. Looking into the bilge, we saw a steady stream of water flowing in from the back of the boat.

"Oh, God." Almost immediately, I started shaking.

"I'll check it." Eric went to the engine room.

"I'll close all of the sea cocks." I scurried around, pulling up floorboards and digging into lockers, closing all the valves that allowed salt water into the boat.

My glance rested on the EPIRB for a second. My cool was difficult to maintain.

"Linda, get me a screwdriver." Eric called from the engine room, interrupting the building panic in my brain.

"Slotted or Phillips?" I grabbed the tool kit, fumbling with the latch.

"Slotted." The muffled reply came from the engine room.

"What is it?" My shaky, three-octave-higher voice asked as I peered over his shoulder.

"Engine hose. The hose clamp came loose. The hose worked itself off. I've almost got it." Eric grunted as he tightened the clamp while leaning over the engine.

Backing off to give him room to get out, I checked the bilge to see most of the water was already gone. Eric looked at me. I'm sure he saw the angst on my face.

"Linda, it's all right." He guided me to the settee. "Sit here, I'm going to check on deck." He checked our course then scanned the horizon for dangers. I felt like puking, as all the feelings and memories from the night of the sinking rushed back.

"Shit." I brushed off the feeling then joined him on deck. "A stupid hose clamp. I nearly flipped out over a stupid hose clamp. Damn."

"Yeah, but you didn't. You did fine."

Perched behind the wheel, I rested my forehead on the cool steel. I closed my eyes, breathing deeply. How devastating would it be if something happened to *Dark & Stormy?*

"You know, when I looked at the red light on the bilge pump, the memories of that night flooded back. I have to get beyond this. It really makes me mad."

Capt. Marlena Brackebusch

Staring out at the sea, I wondered if I would ever be rid of these demons.

"Linda, you know, it's going to be a while until you can get beyond that night. You've got to give yourself time. Every wave, every squall, every mile you sail brings your recovery a little closer."

"You're right, Eric. I just wish we'd found Joey. Not knowing what happened to him is eating me up. If the wave hadn't washed me overboard, I might have been able to help him."

"Maybe you could have and maybe not. The timing of finding you that night was a miracle. If you were in a different spot, we may not have seen you."

"How did you spot me?"

"You have Tom to thank for that one. He was up on the bow, looking for the long-line marker buoy. The light on it had stopped working. He was scanning the water with the binoculars, when he saw the faint blink from the strobe on your life jacket." He'd never told me this part of the story before.

"While he kept an eye on you, I put on a survival suit. When we came alongside, I jumped into the water."

"That was incredibly brave. It was pitch black out. There was a chance they wouldn't find you again in the darkness." Eric stared off the bow of my little sloop.

"Little lady, many years ago, we were fishing off Alaska. It was right after Tom and I took over the boat. Hell, we were just kids ourselves." The big fisherman looked at me with a haunted look on his face.

"It happened during opilio crab season. The weather was brutal. Waves peaked at twenty-five feet. There was blowing snow. The wind chill was fifteen below zero." He returned his stare to the sea.

"I was at the helm, of course. I'd been there for thirty hours. The weather and ice were so bad, I should have shut down the boat. We all thought we were invincible back then." His eyes looked very tired as he glanced at me.

"Something drew my attention away for a mere second. The wave hit. It smashed over the boat. Equipment and crew went flying across the deck." Eric's voice dropped off to a whisper. "When the green water finally drained from the deck, he was gone. Jeremy. My green horn deckhand."

The fishing captain rubbed his rough hands over his eyes as if trying to blot out the memory. "I spun the boat around. Half a dozen other boats joined the search. The Coast Guard sent out two choppers along with a cutter. We scoured a fifty mile search area for the next twelve hours."

Eric stood up, gripping the boom with his hand. He spun around to face me. His eyes exposed his agony. "We never found anything. The Coast Guard finally called off the search. Jeremy was only twenty years old. I'll never forgive myself."

"Eric, it was an accident."

"If I had exercised better judgment, it never would have happened. Linda, you have no idea how horrible if was to have to tell his mom."

Capt. Marlena Brackebusch

The fisherman collapsed onto the cushion next to me. "Her husband had died a few months earlier. That's why Jeremy went fishing...to support the family. His mom leaned against me, sobbing for a few seconds. Then she dried her eyes and told me the same thing. It was an accident. It wasn't my fault."

Eric stared at me. "I promised myself two things that day. One, to never needlessly endanger anyone ever again. And two, if I could, I would try to make amends for that terrible mistake. Jumping into the water to rescue you was never in question. There was no hesitation. You needed to be rescued." He looked away.

"Geez, Eric. I'm sorry. Rescuing me may bring you good karma."

He shrugged his shoulders then turned back to me.

"It has taken a lifetime to get beyond that night. That's why I keep telling you, it will take a long time to get over your trauma. Meanwhile, I'm here to rescue you...again." Eric tried hard to bring a smile to his face.

"I thought this trip was to pay you back for rescuing me the first time. What's the payback going to be now?"

"I'll think of something." We fell back into a silent reverie as *Dark & Stormy* continued to glide toward Naples.

By mid-afternoon, we were abeam of Cape Sable, thirty miles offshore. The water became the more emerald color of the southwest Florida Gulf of Mexico. Bait fish spit out of the water. Smooth-gray torpedoes erupted around the boat as bottlenose dolphins jumped out of our wake.

The chase was on. The sleek mammals used our vessel to help corral the silver delicacies attempting to hide in our slipstream.

Eric and I sat on the bow with our legs dangling over the side, watching as the smooth gray bodies rode our bow wave. One of them turned on its side. He looked at us with a dolphin smile.

"It's amazing how they swim so fast but don't even look like it's an effort, Linda."

"I see them everyday and never get tired of the show." After twenty minutes, the dolphins disappeared into the sea. We retreated to the cool shade of the cockpit. The wind was dying. I fired up the motor while Eric yanked in the jib.

"Other than the loose engine hose, which gave you the willies, this has been a perfect day." He closed his eyes for a nap.

The mainsail was left up to steady us in the gentle roll. I went below to organize supper. We had chicken breasts marinating in white wine. Along with a cold salad, it should make a nice easy meal for a hot evening.

I settled in by the helm to keep watch. A few puffy white clouds drifted by on the light breeze. While watching Eric nap, I thought about his story earlier. I came to a new understanding: He knew what I was going through.

How was it possible, in all the thousands of miles of ocean, that the fishermen could find me drifting out in the Gulf Stream? Thoughts turned to

Joey. It was incredibly sad losing my partner of many years. He would have loved this sail. Could he still be alive, maybe adrift in the liferaft that was never found?

Thinking about what Eva predicted during the tarot card reading, I wondered if there was a future for Eric and me.

The fisherman stirred, going below to the head. Sneaking down behind him, I mixed a couple of cocktails. As he came back on deck, his hair was mussed from sleep.

"I made you a drink."

"Thanks. Twenty miles to go." He watched the numbers click down on the chart plotter. "I'm going to be sad to see this trip end. It was too short. We could have used a couple of weeks in the Keys." He looked to me. "You'll have to take me again."

"Absolutely." The sun sank toward the western horizon. With about an hour or so before sunset, I sautéed the marinating chicken. When it was done to perfection, I passed up two glasses of wine along with two plates of food. We munched on dinner while watching the sun set. As the top dipped below the horizon, we witnessed the green flash.

"Did you see that?" Eric exclaimed. "A green flash...I didn't think it really existed!"

"I told you I've seen it before. Did you think I lied to you?" I pretended to be offended.

"No, but it was amazing." He sat back down next to me. "I didn't think you lied, maybe exaggerated a little."

"You'll have to listen to me from now on." I let him off the hook.

To the west, the purple-magenta afterglow of sunset lingered in the sky. Looking to the east, we sighted the first land since Key West. The lights of Marco Island blinked on, one by one. A star's dim glow peeked out from the charcoal gray sky above us.

"Star light, star bright first star I see tonight," I said, looking overhead. Eric followed my gaze.

"What are you wishing for on the first star, Linda?"

"Nothing."

"Liar."

Chapter 18. Back to Dallas

We arrive back at my dock space adjacent to the Cove Inn at midnight. After a quick cocktail, both of us went to bed, hoping for a good night's sleep. During the night, one particularly bad nightmare ripped through my dreams.

Dark & Stormy was sinking. Waves crashed. The deck submerged beneath my feet. As the yacht plunged to the depths, I was dragged under. Joey's face grimaced.

Eric's arms surrounded me. We'd been through this routine so many times, nothing needed to be said. He pulled me down on the V-berth. I still wasn't comfortable with him in Joey's bed, but the nightmare was too unsettling to push him away.

Dawn crept in the portholes. I crawled out of the bunk, heading into the galley. The only sound was the hiss of the air conditioning. With coffee in hand, I curled up on the port settee, leaning against the galley table. There must be a way to rid my subconscious of these nightmares.

"Morning." The cowboy brushed by my shoulder as he headed for the coffee maker. He settled down on the same bunk as me.

"The nightmare seemed like a bad one."

"It was. I dreamed this boat sank. Every time I see Joey face, he is grimacing."

"It's a good thing we are headed back to Dallas. You seem to do better at the ranch."

"The engine hose didn't help yesterday." I shuddered.

Later, I met with Shane about the business then prepped my boat for an extended absence. I fidgeted, again, once aboard the plane. Eric's hand covered mine.

Ricardo met us at the airport. The guys caught up on business on the way back to the ranch. Eric had a busy week ahead of him vaccinating the new calves before Blackjack would run his first race the following weekend in Dallas.

Arriving back at his house, I wandered into the kitchen to say hello to Maria. Eric and I chilled out for the afternoon, on the big living room couch in front of the fire.

"It's been quite a hectic few days," I said. "It's amazing how chilly the weather has become here in such a short time. The fire feels great."

Eric remained quiet for a few minutes as he rested his hand on my shoulder. Absently, he twirled a few strands of my long hair in his fingers.

"We are going to have a busy week, lady. Are you going to help us round up the calves and vaccinate them?"

"Do you want me to help? I won't be in the way?" I was unsure of what my job would be.

"I think you'll do just fine. We could use the extra help."

Maria called us in for dinner. Eric and Ricardo discussed tomorrow morning's plans. A friend and fellow rancher, Gene, would be over at first light to take a four-wheeler out to the far pasture loaded with the necessary gear for tagging the calves.

Eric, Daniel, Ricardo, and I would ride out on horseback. Once there, we were going to separate the calves from the herd, moving them into a pen in small groups.

Our plan was to tag, vaccinate, and de-worm them, leaving pellets containing medicine to kill worms in the feed troughs for the older cows to eat. It sounded like an interesting endeavor.

"The cows bulk up their weight much quicker when they don't have any worms," Eric said.

After supper, we decided to sit by the fire for it was chilly on the front porch. Around ten P.M., Eric stood up, pulling me to my feet.

"We have an early morning tomorrow. Let's get some sleep."

During the night only one nightmare occurred—nothing too scary, but still unsettling. I dreamt Joey was attacked by a shark. Though it brutally attacked him, he still managed to make it to the liferaft. He was lying in a pool of blood, griping his left thigh.

As I tossed and turned from the dream, Eric pulled me against him until I settled down.

Sometime later, he slipped out of bed. Looking out the window, I saw it was pitch black outside. Faint moonlight glowed through the pane. Eric pulled on his jeans and boots. It was four-fifteen.

"Eric, where are you going?"

Capt. Marlena Brackebusch

"We need to get an early start today. Gene will be here at four thirty." Eric buttoned his blue work shirt. "Make sure you dress warmly—the ride out will be cold. I'll meet Gene then come back in for breakfast."

After he left the room, I dragged myself out of bed thinking I much preferred sailors' hours to ranchers'. Jeans with boots were slid on, as well as the old "North Carolina" sweatshirt. A windbreaker and the black cowboy hat topped off my gear.

Maria was in the kitchen, making sandwiches for everyone. Bacon sizzled away on the stove. The guys filed in a few moments later.

Eric introduced a big, burly man. "Linda, this is Gene. He owns the ranch to the west of us."

The rancher tipped his hat to me as I poured java for the three men. "This may be a silly question, but how do you guys like your coffee?"

"Black." They answered in unison, as expected. Handing them cups of coffee, I sat next to Eric.

"Everything is loaded on the ATV. Daniel is saddling the horses. Are you ready to become a real cowgirl?" Eric grinned at me. I nodded with a nervous smile. My riding was nowhere near the level of these men.

After breakfast, we gathered up a couple of soft-sided coolers with the sandwiches and drinks from Maria. The air outside was chilly. Wet grass squeaked underfoot. Our boots swished through the morning dew. It felt as though there was frost in the air. The smell of burning wood permeated the predawn air, no doubt coming from a distant fireplace.

Ricardo beat us to the barn. He helped Daniel saddle the horses. As I clutched Sonny's reins, my leg easily swung over his back as I mounted up. Eric noticed the ease with which I did this.

"All right cowgirl, good job." My smile was hidden by coaxing Sonny out of the barn. Eric rode right behind me on Outlaw. The four of us trotted to the far pasture to begin our work.

The boss explained each of the new calves needed to be "caught" in a temporary wooden pen, which Gene was setting up.

"This is the part of cattle ranching when your riding is put to the test. The little calves can be real difficult. They don't like to be separated from their moms," Eric explained as we rode in the early dawn light.

"The pen is shaped like a triangle, so we can funnel the calves into it. Once they are in the tight holding gate, each calf gets an ear tag, vaccination, and deworming medicine. It's going to take a coordinated riding effort between the four of us and Gene's two Border Collies to separate the calves from the herd." Eric paused thinking about something, then continued.

"Once we get a good group in the pen, we all dismount and start tagging. One thing you want to watch out for is the momma cows," Eric warned me. "They can get pretty upset and aggressive when you take their babies away."

"How long do you think this whole process will take?" I asked him.

"Well, it depends on how good you are at rounding up cattle, cowgirl." He frowned at me. "Generally, it takes two to three days." The conversation stopped as we broke into a canter, quickly crossing the inner pasture.

We rode for another forty-five minutes to an outer pasture. Once there, Ricardo opened the gate. Our foursome trotted up to Gene who had already set up the pen.

Before Eric dismounted, I edged Sonny next to him, whispering. "What do you want me to do so I don't get in the way and look like a fool?"

"I would never let you look like a fool. Stick close to me. You'll get the hang of it."

The four of us rode toward the herd of cows with the two dogs close behind. Ricardo circled to the left with Daniel breaking off to the right. The dogs ran straight in, helping to separate the calves from the cows.

The pups really knew what they were doing, nipping at the heels of the calves while barking. As the calves separated, the cows became agitated and tried to follow. Eric and I intercepted them, driving them back away from the calves. It was total melee. Soon we had twenty calves milling around, kept together by the dogs.

We worked them into the pen, where Gene closed the gate behind them. Daniel stayed atop Diablo, keeping any stray mother cows away. Ricardo, Eric, and I dismounted to help Gene, who climbed into the pen. One by one we funneled the calves into a chute. Eric slipped a temporary rope around one's head to steady it.

Ricardo handed me a clipboard. "Linda, can you log the information?"

"Sure."

"Number 1064. Male. Red Braham."

Ricardo slipped the deworming pill to the back of the calves throat. The ear tag was clipped on, followed by a quick shot in the rump. In a matter of a couple of minutes, the calf was released. He looked back at us with a defiant moo, before rejoining the herd in search of his mom.

Eric came up behind me. "See how it's done? Easy." After a couple of rounds, I was able to jot down the info then help Ricardo with the injections.

"I didn't know you knew how to give vaccines."

"Yes, Eric. I used to work at a vet's office...a long time ago." He shook his head with surprise then continued working.

This process went on throughout the day until four P.M. By then we were all dirty, sweaty, and exhausted. Tiredly, we climbed back on the horses, who were equally exhausted.

"I'm surprised the horses can even walk after all of that, Eric." I patted Sonny on the neck.

"They're pretty tired, but after good food, water, and a little rest, they will be ready to go again tomorrow." We took it easy, riding the horses back to the barn. When we arrived, the tack was removed. The horses were fed and watered.

"I can do the rest if you like, Mr. Eric," Daniel offered.

"Thanks, Daniel. Linda and I will wipe down our tack then call it a day." After cleaning up the saddles and bridles, Eric and I trudged slowly back to the house in the fading light.

"I think I'm ready for a shower and a cocktail. How about you, Linda?"

"That sounds good. I'm almost too tired to move. Today was a lot of work and you guys were doing most of it."

Eric stopped, looking at me. He wiped something from my cheek. "You were great today. I was especially happy to see the way you rode Sonny. You're getting good."

After refreshing showers, we relaxed with cocktails in the living room. Dinner soon followed, then we returned to the couch. My head drooped as we snuggled by the fire. Eric's phone rang.

"Well, hello, brother. What's going on?" He looked at me then mouthed "Tom." I nodded.

"We are doing great. I'm at the ranch in Texas. Blackjack is racing...his first...this weekend in Dallas." He listened more then replied. "Let me check with the lady of the house."

He put his hand over the receiver, turning to me. "Would you like company this weekend? Tom wants to fly out to watch the race."

My eyes brightened at the prospect. I took the phone from Eric's hands.

"Hi, Tom, I would love to see you this weekend."

His deep voice boomed through the receiver. "Hey, Li'l Sis, that's great. How are you? What's this about Eric calling you the 'lady of the house' and checking with you...hmm?" he teased me. I hadn't really caught his brother's statement until Tom mentioned it.

"I don't know."

Eric took the phone back, chatting with his brother a few minutes longer as I contemplated the "lady of the house" statement. After hanging up, Eric must have seen the deep look of contemplation on my face.

"Uh oh." He grabbed my hand while staring intently at me. "Whenever you have that look on your face, it means trouble. What were you thinking?"

"Oh, nothing." I wasn't sure I wanted to discuss this with him.

"Oh no, you're not getting out of it so easily. Every time you have a serious look on your face you don't want to talk about it. You're not dodging me this time. What did Tom say?"

I paused for a second then thought, what the heck. After all, he made the comment. Let's see what this cowboy meant by it.

"Tom was teasing me about your 'lady of the house' comment. What did you mean by it?"

He was silent as a faint smile played around his face. The man fidgeted, seemingly at a loss for words. "I don't know—it just came out." He paused, looking me in the eye.

"Well, you are the lady of the house, sort of." He grinned, continuing. "At least a guy can be hopeful."

This totally floored me. I hadn't realized Eric's feelings for me had reached this level.

"Are you messing with me?" I asked him suspiciously. He didn't answer. Instead he slid his hand behind my neck, leaning over me. Instead of the light kiss he'd surprised me with a couple of times in the past, he took his time. It sounds corny to say it, but the kiss did take my breath away. Leaning back only slightly, he stared into my eyes.

"There are things I don't kid about." His voice was husky. I tried to pull away, but he held me by the arm.

"What's the matter, Linda?"

"I don't know Eric. I really like you, geez you're a really wonderful man...."

But?"

"But I haven't totally gotten my head around this thing with Joey. We don't really know what happened to him. It's so unfinished. I haven't been able to let go yet. Do you understand?"

He paused for a few moments to gather his response. "I completely understand what you're saying. When my wife filed for divorce, I had no warning. I guess there were plenty of warning signs, but I chose to ignore them.

"At least there was the closure of the divorce. You don't even have that." He paused again.

"Let me warn you right now. I am very attracted to you. You make me happy." Eric's voice trailed off as he finished his last sentence. He wrapped his arms around me. I allowed my head to relax against his shoulder. His lips were very close to my ear as he whispered.

"Linda, I'll wait as long as it takes for you to sort this out. And I'll do anything I can to help you."

Wow. I'd never met a man who was so sweet, yet such a tough guy. I had a lot to think about.

After a few minutes, I pulled away.

"Eric, thanks." We sat in silence for a little longer, enjoying the crackle of the fire. It had been a long day. We soon retired for much needed sleep.

Chapter 19. Blackjack's First Race

The next two days were repeats of day one, lots of calves and lots of vaccinations. On the third day, we finished early. Daniel planned for Eric's new jockey, Manuel, to give Blackjack his last practice ride in the oval before Sunday's race.

"On Saturday, we'll take Blackjack out to the track to get him used to it. There will be many sights and sounds he's not seen before. Also, all the different horses will throw him off his game.

"The race officials promised Manuel could ride him on the actual track, for a couple of practice sessions. The footing will be different from our oval. This will allow Blackjack to feel comfortable on Sunday."

"Will it be all right for me to come with you on Saturday, Eric?"

"Absolutely. On Saturday night, we'll stay in a hotel. There are many sights in the area around the track to enjoy."

We were leaning against the oval fence when Manuel rode into the smaller corral atop Blackjack, led by Ricardo riding Chico. Daniel opened the gate to the oval. Blackjack tried to bolt. It took all of Ricardo's and Manuel's strength to hold him back.

Daniel patiently grabbed Blackjack's halter from the ranch manager. He waited for the signal. Blackjack charged off in a blur of speed. Eric timed his sprint over the eight furlong distance. The black steed finished the distance in 115 seconds, an excellent time.

Manual slowed him down, walking him near us. "He runs pretty good. We should do OK this weekend." The jockey cantered Blackjack around the oval a couple more times.

Daniel strode over. "Mr. Eric, I just want to make sure I've got this right. You want Ricardo and me to drive your truck to Dallas Saturday with Blackjack and Chico to get them settled in." He consulted his notes. "We are doing a practice session at one P.M. with Manuel. After settling Blackjack in his stall for the night, Ricardo and I come back here. Is that right, sir?" The shy young man looked down at the ground now and again.

Eric tipped back his black cowboy hat while studying the younger man. "It sounds like you have the plan right son, but you need to realize you are Blackjack's trainer now. If he performs well, we will race him all over. I would appreciate it if you would drop the mister stuff and just call me 'Eric.'"

Daniel's face reddened and contorted, showing many different emotions. He stared at the ground, which he kicked with the toe of his boot. Then he looked his boss in the eye.

"Well, sir, I don't mean to disagree with you, but my daddy always told me to respect my boss," he whispered, looking almost fearfully at Eric, then casting his eyes back to the ground. I wanted to go over and hug him because he was such a cutie.

Eric clapped Daniel on his back "You show me plenty of respect, son, but we're partners in training Blackjack. 'Eric' will do just fine."

The young man fidgeted for a second, then said, "Yes, sir." He turned back toward Blackjack and Manuel.

Eric chuckled, taking my hand. We walked toward the house. "What a great find Daniel is. I think he'd lay his life down for me."

Back at the house it was nearly dinnertime. After a quick shower, I joined the guys and Maria for another wonderful meal.

Afterward, Eric and I retreat to the living room and another great fire before heading to bed. A really bad nightmare tormented me during the night. The rest of the night was spent in an unsettled sleep.

Saturday morning finally arrived. Eric gently shook me awake. "Hey, Sleeping Beauty, we have to get to Dallas today." I looked up at him in the dim morning light. He sat on the bed with a cup of coffee in his hand. A white, dressy shirt and blues jeans were topped off with his typical black cowboy hat.

"Thanks." The coffee was hot and strong.

"How are you feeling today after last night's traumas?"

"I feel great. Ready to go watch Blackjack get ready for his big race." He saw through the lie, knowing I didn't sleep well. I made an effort to be cheerful.

"Let me get up and get dressed. I'll be ready in a minute." For the first time in a couple of weeks, my sore ribs ached. Heading into the bathroom, I put on a new denim blouse, bought in Naples, with a cowgirl outlined in rhinestones on the back. A pair of gold horse earrings and a dash of makeup and I was good to go.

The cowgirl garb should surprise the cowboy, I thought. Back in the guest room, I grabbed a light jacket and, of course, my black cowgirl hat. I felt a little silly wearing it, but it did keep the sun off my face. When in Rome....

Eric was in the kitchen munching on a bagel while reading the paper, as usual. I smiled to myself at this routine. He glanced up, putting the paper down. When my back was turned to him while not-so-innocently filling a coffee mug, I felt his stare.

"Well, look at you. You look like a regular cowgirl."

I ignored him. "Would you like a refill on your coffee?" As I turned around, my coffee almost dumped on his white shirt. The cowboy snuck up behind me, silently.

He touched my wrist, feeling the denim material of the blouse around the cuff.

"Where did you get this shirt?"

"Do you like it?" I asked innocently. "I found it in Naples, of all places."

"I like it a lot." He slid his hand around my waist to my back. His fingers played with the rhinestones, causing chills to shoot up my spine.

"Easy, cowboy. Or you'll be wearing my coffee."

"Sit down, I'll make you breakfast."

"Just a bagel is fine, thanks." I took refuge behind a section of the newspaper. When Eric delivered the bagel, his finger lightly touched the horse earring on my right ear.

"I like the earrings, too. I'd say you are ready for a weekend of horse racing in Dallas.

"Eric, if Daniel is driving to Dallas in the truck, how are we getting there?"

"We are taking the Mustang—we are going to Dallas in style."

We finished eating in silence then packed our bags. I was glad I shopped while in Naples. A couple of new dresses would look...surprising...this weekend.

When Eric finished packing in the master bedroom, he stopped by the guest room.

"You all packed?" He eyed my suitcase and garment bag.

"Yep." When I attempted to lift the suitcase, my ribs twinged. He easily took the luggage from me.

"I got it."

"Thanks."

"If you wait here at the house, I'll bring the car up."

He strode for the garage, soon returning in the gorgeous Mustang convertible with the top down.

I ran my hand along the sleek frame. "This is beautiful."

"It's my one big indulgence." He stashed our suitcases in the trunk then gallantly opened the door for me. The big engine rumbled as we cruised down the street.

"Listen to the hum. Tell me about your car."

"Let me see. As you know, she's a Mustang, fully restored, 1967 with all original parts. The body color is candy apple red. The interior leather is dark saddle. Her engine is a 390 cubic inch, six point four liter V8. She really flies." He added with a grin.

"This car is absolutely beautiful. You're right, we are going to Dallas in style." When we arrived at the interstate, Eric showed me what he meant by "flying." We tooled along the highway at eight-five miles per hour on the exhilarating ride to the airport. My hair would pay for it later.

DFW was reached in record time. Tom's familiar face popped out of the crowd. The big crab fisherman swooped me off my feet in a bear hug.

"Hey, Li'l Sis, what a nice welcoming committee."

"Hi, Tom, we're glad you're here." He and Eric shook hands, embracing briefly. After collecting his bags, we made our way back to the Mustang. When Tom saw it, he rubbed his hands together.

"You brought the 'Stang. Now I'm a happy man." We piled into the car with me sharing the back seat with the elder brother's luggage. It was a better ride in the back because my hair wasn't blown quite so much.

We cruised toward Grand Prairie, just south of Dallas where the racetrack was located. Tom kept egging on his brother to drive faster. The car's speedometer topped ninety. I silently prayed no state troopers lurked nearby.

At last we arrived, a little windblown but in one piece. Eric booked us a couple of rooms in the Hyatt.

After checking in, we went to the track to see if Daniel and Ricardo had arrived.

We parked in the lot by the stables. Our threesome wandered by the endless row of stalls. Several beautiful horses poked their heads out as we passed by. Daniel was found walking Blackjack around.

"How's he doing, son?" Eric asked his trainer.

"Fine, sir. I just unloaded him." Blackjack had a wild look in his eyes. He stomped around like a naughty child. Ricardo walked Chico over. This easy going horse had a calming influence over the thoroughbred.

Eric stroked Blackjack's neck. "How was the ride, son?"

"It was fine, sir. Blackjack's a little uneasy in the new surroundings. I'm going to walk him around and get him used to things." Daniel looked very proud of his role as trainer.

"Great. We're going to register, to see what we need to do." Eric grabbed Tom and me.

We walked over to the race officials' office. All the information seemed in order for the big race tomorrow.

"There is a special area of the stands near the finish line set aside for the owners and trainers. Here are the passes to get in." The lady behind the desk handed plastic ID cards to us.

"Thank you." Eric turned to Tom and me. "Let's go check it out." We wandered over to a nicely enclosed, air-conditioned area with comfortable tables and chairs. There was a nice bar and restaurant with a privileged view of the track. Eric glanced at his watch. "It's almost lunch time. Are you two hungry?"

"Now that's a silly question," Tom said with a smirk. Drinks were sipped as we watched a couple of horses canter around the dirt track. After lunch, we located Daniel and company. They were preparing for Blackjack's practice session. Our trainer spoke with a track official as we walked up.

Turning to us, Daniel filled us in. "He said we can bring Blackjack over to run him around the track a few times. I especially want him to get used to the gate." Ricardo trotted over atop Chico. Manuel mounted Blackjack. We followed to the racecourse.

The black stallion's agitation was palpable. He knew something was going on as he pranced alongside Chico. When they neared the post, Blackjack shied away, because he'd never been in a starting gate before.

Ricardo led him around again. The track officials must be used to this. The second time around they grabbed Blackjack, forcing him into the gate. The bell rang. Eric's horse bolted out in a blur, running the eight furlongs in 110 seconds.

"Will you look at that! Eric, this was his best time yet."

"Yes, he should be very competitive this weekend."

As Manuel cantered the big horse around to get him used to the track, I grabbed Eric's hand.

"This is so exciting." He returned my smile with a nervous one.

Blackjack went through the gate routine a couple more times. He appeared to be adapting to this new routine.

Back near the stables, Ricardo walked the big horse around, cooling him off. Daniel approached us cautiously. "Um, Mr. Eric, can I speak with you for a minute, sir."

Eric stepped toward Daniel, putting his hand on the younger man's shoulder. "What is it, son? Did you forget what I said about the "mister" part?"

"Um, no sir, I'm just not used to it. Eric." He corrected himself. "I don't mean to change your plans, but I don't feel good leaving Blackjack here all afternoon and tonight by himself." He paused, staring at the ground.

"I hope you're not upset, but I asked Ricardo if he could feed and water the horses at the ranch so I can keep an eye on Blackjack." He shifted uncomfortably from one foot to the other, waiting for his boss' response.

There was a bemused smile on Eric's face, but Daniel missed it by looking at the ground, like he was about to be cussed out.

"Son, I really appreciate your concern for Blackjack. It would be a good idea to walk him around again late this afternoon when things settle down."

Eric grinned again. "Where do you intend to sleep tonight?" He teased his young horse trainer.

I so wanted to rescue Daniel. The young man looked bewildered as he picked his head up, looking around the track. Eric managed a serious look on his face.

"There's probably a bunk house here somewhere; if not, I'll just sleep in Chico's stall. That way if Blackjack gets upset, I'll be nearby," Daniel mumbled, unsure of how to answer Eric.

His boss chuckled softly. "I'll make you a deal. You can stay here. Take care of Blackjack until six-thirty. Then you are going out to dinner with Tom, Linda, and me. You'll stay at the hotel with us. Blackjack will be fine overnight. The track officials have my cell number if there is a problem. Do you have a change of clothes with you?"

Daniel straightened up. He looked at his boss with awe. "Sir, oh my gosh, sir, you want me to have dinner with you? But, sir, I didn't mean to change everything." He babbled on. "I do have some clothes."

Eric must have decided to take it easy on the addled young man. "We'll pick you up at six-thirty."

The cowboy turned, grabbing my hand. Our threesome headed for the parking lot. When out of earshot of Daniel, I scolded Eric. "You didn't have to be so hard on him. I wanted to go over and give him a big hug."

"Hard on him? Me?" Eric said, grinning. Back at the hotel, he arranged a room for Daniel near ours. Entering our room for the first time, we found our bags were put there by the bellman.

While we inspected the room, there was a knock on the door. Tom poked his head in. "You two want to get a cocktail down in the lobby bar?"

"Why don't you guys go ahead? I want to hang up a few things." I pushed Eric toward the door. "Get a little man time in."

Eric smiled his thanks. "Linda, could you hang up my shirts, too, please?"

Tom mimicked his brother while shaking his head. "Linda, could you hang up my shirts? Now he's having her doing all his domestic tasks. What's next?" The elder brother playfully punched his sibling on the shoulder. They were such little boys when they were together.

It was nice to have a little alone time. The clothes were hung up and my toiletries went into the bathroom. Satisfied, I locked up the room. The two guys were found in the bar having a drink at a small, round leather-topped table.

"May I join you guys?" They both stood at my approach.

"Absolutely—but only if you're a cowgirl." Eric pulled out a chair for me.

"Oh my dear, sir." I said in a fake Southern accent. "I don't think I can join you then as I'm a sailor, not a cowgirl."

"Close enough," Tom laughed, guiding me into a chair. His brother ordered me a drink. We chatted happily for a while.

"Tom, what have you been up to?"

"Well, Linda, I've been working on the boat, supervising the yard work. The new paint job looks great."

"What...what's that smile for?" Eric caught the look on my face.

"I can't wait to see her. You did repaint her dark blue again, didn't you Tom?"

"Oh, yes. And we had an outline of Mt. Denali painted on her bow, with a crab outline inside. It looks pretty neat. That's painted in white."

"Let me get this straight. You really want to go out on a smelly fishing boat on the cold, rough waters of the Pacific Northwest, when you could be sailing on the nice warm waters of the Gulf of Mexico?" Eric asked.

"Try and keep me away." Both brothers shook their heads. I knew they had no idea what to make of me.

The afternoon waned.

"Linda, I'm going to head to the track to check on Daniel. Would you like to come?" He grabbed his cowboy hat, plopping it on his head.

"If it's all right with you, I would prefer to relax in the room. A hot shower would freshen me up for the evening."

While Eric and I discussed our plans, Tom's eyes scanned the crowd in the bar.

"I think I'll use this time to allow these Dallas ladies the opportunity to have a cocktail with a handsome Bering Sea fisherman." Tom's sly smile announced his agenda. His brother chuckled then escorted me to the elevator.

"I'll be back soon."

Back in our room, the hot water washed away the dust and grime from the track. The dress I'd selected for the evening had a tropical theme. Gold sailboat earrings topped off the outfit nicely. After I heard the door to our room close, Eric walked up behind me. He stopped, watching me in the mirror. A soft whistle emerged from him.

"Don't you look pretty." He ran his fingers along the top of the back of my dress, just below the neck line. Goosebumps awakened along the trail of his finger. The cowboy's grin acknowledged the subconscious reaction. No comment was necessary.

Instead, he turned for the bathroom. The shower was heard a moment later. Reclining on the couch, I scanned the view of the pool from the large bay window. Eric came out of the bedroom a few minutes later, his hair still damp. He wore black jeans, a nice white dress shirt, and a bolo necktie.

With black cowboy hat in hand, he grabbed my hand.

"Tom said he'd wait for us in the bar downstairs."

"Is he having any luck?" My shrewd smile brought a grin to his face.

"With Tom you never know. He was engaged in conversation with a couple of pretty ladies."

Down in the bar, we joined Tom for a drink. There was no sign of any imminent conquest for the elder brother.

To our surprise, Daniel appeared a moment later, with a nice suit on. He looked freshly scrubbed. Eric did a double take on him.

"Nice suit, son."

"I thought I should dress up for Blackjack's first race, being his trainer and all. I wanted to look respectable." Daniel blushed then stared at his feet.

The four of us piled into the Mustang for the short drive to the steak house. The food was delicious.

Capt. Marlena Brackebusch

The rib-eye steaks definitely lived up to the Texas reputation.

After his initial shyness wore off, Daniel joined the conversation and appeared to be enjoying himself. After the short drive back to the hotel, Eric, Tom, and I decided to have a drink in our room. Daniel declined, wanting to keep a clear head for tomorrow.

"You two go ahead, I want to talk to Daniel for a moment." Eric pulled Daniel aside.

Tom and I hopped into the elevator. He turned to me. "How's everything going with you and Eric?" I paused for a moment before responding.

"He's really amazing. I'm having a wonderful time with him. The only problem is, I haven't totally figured out the Joey thing, yet." My voice trailed off.

"I'm glad we have a few moments alone because I wanted to talk to you about that. Now's a good time, since Eric is distracted." The elevator stopped at our floor. Tom led me from the elevator, pausing in front of my room. He seemed to be on edge.

"Let's see what they have in that minibar." Tom pried the room key from my hand then fumbled with the door. His actions seemed odd. The elder brother headed directly for the minibar. Ice was scooped out of the bucket on the counter top.

"How about a bourbon?" Not my favorite drink, but I nodded in agreement, perplexed by his demeanor. He poured a nip over ice in each glass, adding a dash of water. I stood by the window looking at the view of the pool. Tom handed me a drink while taking me by the hand.

"Linda, come over here and sit with me. I want to talk to you about something."

I was mystified as to what was going on. Once I was comfortably seated next to the big fisherman, my eyes looked at the serious, almost painful expression on his rugged face. He slipped his arm around me.

"Li'l Sis, do you remember when Eric and I pulled you out of the water?"

"I could never forget that night."

"Do you remember how sick, cold and dehydrated you were? I was really worried about you for a few hours." His black eyes bore into mine.

"You were in the water for what, twenty hours or so?" I nodded again. He paused, tightening his grip on my hand.

"Li'l Sis, I know Eric would never say this to you. He's too sensitive and all that." He paused once again. It seemed as though this man was struggling to find the right words.

When Tom was about to speak again, Eric opened the door. The elder brother released me then sat back on the couch.

Eric must have seen the serious look on both of our faces. "What's up with you two?"

"Nothing." Tom forced a smile to his face. "We were having a chat. Let me get you a drink, bro."

Eric sat next to me. His eyes looked questioningly into mine. A moment later, his brother handed him a cocktail. We made small talk until Tom left a short time later.

Capt. Marlena Brackebusch

As Eric and I were getting ready for bed, he asked, "What was up with you and Tom earlier? I got the feeling I was disturbing a serious conversation."

"He was talking about the night you two pulled me out of the water. Tom said he was very concerned with my physical condition. He was about to say something else, when you came in. I don't quite know what he was getting at."

"*Hmm.*" Eric looked at me. "I'll have to talk with him about this."

"Eric, please, let me handle this."

Only one nightmare plagued me during the night, but it was a bad one. I dreamt about a horrific storm. Waves blasted me. Salt-choking mist made breathing nearly impossible. A shark seized Joey. Slashed his leg. The predator dragged him under. Waking from the dream, I felt Eric pull me closer.

A glance at my watch showed five A.M. A few moments later, the cowboy climber out of bed. When I tried to get up, he gently pushed me back down.

"Stay in bed. I'm going to drive Daniel to the track to check on the horses. I promised him we'd head over early. I'll be back for breakfast."

Dozing a while longer, I woke up to the smell of coffee. Struggling out of bed, my feet toddled into the sitting room where Eric was reclined on the small couch, perusing the USA Today.

My hand brushed against his shoulder in greeting. He continued reading for another minute before putting down the paper. His full attention was turned to me. My legs were tucked under me while seated on an armchair near the window. The warm sun streamed in, removing the morning chill. His deep voice caught my attention.

"Good morning. How are you feeling after round one thousand with the nightmares?"

"I feel OK, just a little tired. How are you?"

"Great. Excited about the race today. I drove Daniel to the track. Blackjack and Chico are fine."

We soon met Tom for a quick breakfast before heading for the track. Once there, one felt the rampant energy exuded by the mighty black stallion as we approached Blackjack's stall. He was busting to break free of the wooden enclosure. There was a wild, almost feral flash in his charcoal eyes.

At the officials' office, Eric finalized the paperwork before we strolled to the stands to watch the race. In the owners' area, there were a couple of ranchers who owned the property to the east of Eric's. Homer, a stately gentleman with graying hair, was escorted by a matronly woman introduced as his wife, Barbara. A cute, smartly dressed young lady had her arm linked through the elderly man's.

"This is my granddaughter, Tina." After introductions, Eric turned his attention toward the track. Touching his arm lightly, my fingers stroked his arm in an attempt to relieve his rising tension.

Ten minutes before the race, Daniel appeared in the same suit and tie from last night. He greeted everyone then turned his attention to Tina, who he was obviously acquainted with. As the official trainer of Blackjack, he was watching the race with us.

Capt. Marlena Brackebusch

All nine horses cantered around before the starting gate. Blackjack drew the number five post position, not really what we wanted. Daniel preferred an outside spot to allow him room to run.

The track officials started loading the horses into the gate. As Blackjack approached, he tried to shy away, but Ricardo had a firm grip on him. The track hands managed to get him into the gate. The rest of the horses were loaded.

The bell rang. All horses made a clean break. Blackjack galloped in fourth, sandwiched between a couple of steeds. He was squeezed back to fifth. You could tell Manuel was holding him back. Around the first turn, our horse ran in fifth place. Manuel tried to edge him outside.

At the halfway point, our big black blur was still fifth, but a little running room opened in front of him. Manuel encouraged him by tapping him lightly with the riding crop. Blackjack didn't need much egging on. His legs pounded on the dirt, leaving a trail of dust in his wake. Our boy slipped past the number four horse.

The colts along with a lone filly thundered around the final turn. Blackjack struggled ahead of the number three horse, who was a large brown block of heaving muscle. All the horses strained when they entered the home stretch. Three massive equines were abreast for the final sprint home. Our stallion galloped smack in the middle of the melee.

"Look at Blackjack." Eric yelled, his body tense with excitement. "He's pulling ahead."

With a mere furlong to go, Blackjack magically rocketed ahead, as if he'd just started running. He streaked ahead of the competition. With nostrils flared, our horse dug in.

"Go, Blackjack, go!" We all hollered, jumping up and down. His lead widened as he streaked for the finish line. Our stallion blazed across the finish line two lengths in front of the other horses. He won! We erupted in a cheer.

Eric and Daniel jogged to the winner's circle to meet Manuel and Blackjack. Lots of pictures were taken as they accepted their prize. When Eric rejoined us in the owners' area, I surprised him with a kiss. He grinned, returning to the celebration.

After a half hour of partying, we decided to take the bash back to the ranch. Outside in the parking lot, Tom grabbed the car keys from Eric, who'd had a few drinks. "My turn to drive, bro."

The evening was filled with good food, wine, and stories of the race. Finally Eric, Tom, and I retired to the front porch.

"When do you think you two will get to Seattle?" Tom asked.

"I haven't booked the flight. Next weekend wouldn't be unreasonable." Eric looked to me for approval.

"Fine with me."

"We'll spend Sunday with my daughters. Why don't we meet you at the boat on Monday?" Eric asked Tom. This plan of meeting up with his daughters was news to me.

"Yeah, that sounds good. We can take a couple of days to clean up, provision, and fuel. Then we're off. Are you sure you are up for this?" Tom directed this question to me. "It can get really rough on the trip to Alaska."

"I'll be fine." Eric went inside to refill our drinks. While he was gone, Tom moved over next to me.

"Linda, do you remember what we were discussing the other night?" Tom asked seriously.

"Yes, you were talking about rescuing me."

"Right. You were very cold and sick. If I'm not mistaken, you were adrift in the ocean for twenty hours or so, right?"

"Yes, Tom."

"Well, this is what I wanted to tell you. What Eric would never say." His voice trailed off. "Linda, you have to understand Joey is gone. There is no way he could have survived out there this long, even in a liferaft. You need to accept it and come to grips with it. You need to get on with your life." His voice was just above a whisper.

Tom paused, letting this sink in. He slipped his arm around me in a brotherly way.

"I'm sorry to be the one to tell you this, but it had to be said." I sighed deeply, looking at the big crab fisherman. A tear formed in my eye.

"Tom, I know you are right. I think about this every day, but it's really hard to completely give up hope. I guess that's dumb."

"No, it's not dumb. But look at the situation this way. You have a real chance to have a great life with

Eric. I've watched the two of you together. You're perfect for each other.

"Linda, you need to decide between Eric and the slim chance that Joey is still alive. Very slim chance." When Tom said this, his brother walked back in with our drinks. He caught the end of Tom's statement. He must have seen the look on my face.

"Tom, what's up?" Eric asked.

"We were discussing Joey and you." Tom explained to his brother.

"Eric?" I rose out of Tom's grasp, then looked the younger brother in the eye. "Do you believe Joey is dead?"

The younger crab man stood very still for a moment. It almost looked like he was unsure of what to say. A flash of compassion was quickly replaced by a firm set to his jaw. "Yes, yes I do."

Sighing heavily, I turned away. "Well, I guess that's it then." I walked into the house.

From the living room, I heard the brothers continue the discussion.

"Tom, I better make sure she's all right."

"Bro, why don't you give her a few minutes?"

"I think what you said just devastated her."

"No, no way, Eric. She knew it deep down. Linda just didn't want to admit it. She'll fight through this."

The front door creaked open. Eric found me sitting on the couch in the darkness, just staring at the empty fireplace.

"Linda, honey, do you want to talk about this?" He must have seen my eyes were red from crying.

"No. Not really. I need time to think this through. It not as if anything Tom said wasn't already known."

The younger brother sat down next to me.

"Tom pretty much nailed it. Joey's gone. I guess I've known it for a while. I didn't want to admit it. Some days it feels as thought I'm just operating on automatic pilot. As if I'm watching my life go by. This entire past few months is simply one big nightmare."

"Linda, I hope you don't consider all of this a nightmare." Eric allowed a small smile to creep around his face.

"No, the time spent with my knight in shining armor has been great. But it seems as though Tom is pushing me into a relationship I'm not ready for. He doesn't realize the baggage I still need to shed from my past with Joey."

"Why do I get the feeling that relationship wasn't so rosy? If my inklings are correct, I'm surprised you spent so much time even worrying if he was alive."

"It's complicated, Eric."

"It always is."

We sat in the silent living room for another ten minutes or so until one of us spoke again.

"I'll give you a nickel for your thoughts." I said to Eric, using his line.

"I don't know what to say. Other than I'm sorry for your loss."

"I'm sorry about the timing of this discussion. It's supposed to be a celebration of Blackjack's success."

"Linda, I've had a nearly perfect weekend. Maybe this was a good time for this to come up. Tom has a knack for timing things."

The next morning, I woke up to sunshine peeking through the slats in the mini-blinds. Both my mind and soul felt more refreshed than they had in months. After dressing, I located Tom and Eric in the kitchen.

"Just call me Miss Sleepyhead. It's almost eight o'clock. Why did you let me sleep so late?"

"You needed your rest. We're having a lazy morning. Tom doesn't have to be at the airport until noon."

Leaning over the elder brother, I widened my arms to surround his big chest. He stood up, embracing me in another of his bear hugs.

"Are you OK, Li'l Sis, after our talk last night?"

"Tom, you know you were right. I actually think I feel better because of it. Thanks. But I'm still not one hundred percent over it. There's still this block of doubt in my mind."

"Despite the overwhelming evidence, you still feel as though Joey is alive?" The elder brother looked at me with raised eyebrows.

"It's something in my gut."

"Woman's intuition?" Tom smirked. "Give me a break."

"Tom, that's not really fair."

"Linda, remember what I told you."

"Maybe we should head for the airport. I don't want to hear anymore of this." Anger smeared Eric's face.

After seeing Tom off on the plane, we headed back to the ranch to formulate the week's activities.

We planned on doing a bunch of riding. Also, Eric had a few head of calves to deliver to a nearby rancher.

That evening, we sat by the hearth with a fire blazing away. It seemed like a good time to ask Eric about his daughters.

"Eric."

"*Hmm*." He moved closer to me.

"When we get to Seattle this weekend, do you want to spend Sunday alone with your daughters? If you do, it would be fine with me."

He turned to me with a puzzled expression on his face. "Why would I want you to do that? You should meet them. They're great young ladies."

"All right," I said, biting my lip nervously. "You know, Joey never wanted me to interact with his kids. He acted like he was ashamed of our relationship."

Eric must have seen what I was getting at.

"Linda, don't take this the wrong way, but I'm not Joey. I want you to be a part of my life. My whole life."

"OK, then I would love to meet your daughters. Tell me about them."

"Caroline is the older one. She's five-foot-eight, with short dark brown hair and pretty green eyes. She is my smart, quiet one."

"At twenty-one years old, she is about to graduate from college with a business degree. Her minor is in foreign languages. She wants to continue school for her MBA." Eric paused, a far-away look in his eyes.

"Kristen is my younger daughter. She is the spitfire. Her red curly hair is only a little shorter than her sister's. My younger girl is very assertive. Like me, she is a very "hands on" type of person."

"At eighteen years of age, she needs to get serious about her life. I hope...but can't count on it...she'll be starting college in the fall." Eric looked wistful. "I say this because if I let her, she would like to run the crab boat instead of going to school. You always know where you stand with Kristen." Eric's eyes gleamed as he talked about his girls.

"They sound great. I can't wait to meet them. If you need time alone with them to discuss personal things, let me know."

Eric took my hand. "That's very sweet. Actually, Kristen has had a really hard time with the divorce. Even though she and I are very much alike, I still think she blames me for being away so much."

We stared at the flames, in silence, for a long time.

The next morning my eyes fluttered open. It was seven-thirty already. I wandered to the kitchen to find Eric at the stove cooking eggs.

"Ah, you are just in time, my lady. I'm making heuvos rancheros. There's fresh salsa in the fridge which Maria made yesterday."

"Good morning. You let me sleep late, again."

"It's great you were able to sleep so well with no nightmares. You looked so peaceful when I got up, I didn't want to wake you."

"What's the plan for today?"

"Breakfast first, then we'll go to the stable. I want to give the horses a once over. Next, Daniel, you, and

Capt. Marlena Brackebusch

I will ride out to the south pasture. We need to drive a few head of calves back to the small pen by the oval.

After lunch, we need to load the calves into the trailer. We'll run them down the road to another ranch. Later this afternoon, Manuel is coming over to work with Blackjack."

"*Phew*! I'm exhausted just listening to this plan," I laughed. "Are you always so detailed about everything?"

Eric stopped cooking the eggs. He looked at me with a puzzled expression. "What, am I too organized for you?"

"You're much too organized for me. No time for spontaneity in any of that plan." I loved to teased him.

He set down the pot holder and spatula, turning off the gas to the burner. He came over to me with a mischievous grin on his face. Sitting down next to me, he leaned over, slipping his hands around the back of my head and neck.

I tried to escape but wasn't quick enough. The cowboy kissed me. It wasn't the quick peck on the cheek type kiss. It was more like the 'bigger in Texas" type kiss. My eyes blinked rapidly as he released me only enough to look me in the eye.

A huge grin formed on his face. Was it in response to my gasp for breath? Or the hot rush of red flooding my checks?

"*Ha*. Got you. Tell me, Linda, was that spontaneous enough for you or would you like me to show you more?" He stared at me, not letting go. A laugh emerged when I tried to escape his grasp.

"I think that's good for now," I mumbled, completely caught off guard.

He released me. "Let this be a lesson to you woman. Don't challenge me unless you're up for it."

It took a few moments to regain my composure. A steaming bowl of eggs was set down on the table along with warm corn meal tortillas fresh out of the oven. The table already had the rest of the fixings on it.

The cowboy sat next to me. He glanced over as I leaned away from him slightly. "You're safe until after breakfast." I didn't know whether I was relieved or disappointed.

After breakfast, I stood at the sink, looking out the window. The cowboy slipped up behind me. His arms encompassed me. My body tensed. My exhale was prolonged.

"I'm not sure I like the sound of your sigh. Why are you so tense?"

I wriggled around to face him.

"Eric, I can't do this. Not yet."

Frustration traversed his brow.

"Linda, there is a limit to my patience. I'm getting pretty close to that limit. I told you I have a long fuse, but it's nearing the end."

"I'm sorry."

"Linda, I've invested too much of my soul for this to continue as a mere friendship much longer. You need to decide pretty damn quickly what you want."

He turned away in disgust and strode from the room.

The rest of the week was spent dealing with ranch work. I tiptoed around the cowboy trying hard to avoid any more unhappy encounters. My brain swirled while grappling with decisions I wasn't prepared to make.

Eric and I rode on horseback for many hours around the pastures. This daily routine of a morning ride not only vastly improved my horsemanship, but also proved very therapeutic. After each session, I spent a considerable about of time simply brushing Sonny's coat or combing his mane.

Friday arrived. The cowboy and I spent our final day at the ranch working on a few miscellaneous tasks. It was an unusually hot day. In Boston, we called these hot spells Indian summer. Sweat dotted our brows as we cleared brush that had overgrown near the gate to the south pasture. The big crab man hacked away at the tangle with a machete. I raked up the loose overgrowth, tossing it into the trailer.

"It's a hot day." Eric paused to wipe his forehead. "Why don't we break for lunch?"

"Great. Eric, I have an idea. Why don't we go for a swim in the pool then sit in the hot tub for a few minutes? It would be good for my aching muscles."

"Linda, every once in a while you do have a great idea."

After a quick shower to remove the ranch grime, I slipped on my swimsuit. Eric was already floating around the pool.

He only opened one eye as he floated around on his back. In a flash, I was standing in the waist deep water next to him.

"Well look what you just did. You came in with no hesitation."

"Swimming is one area of my psyche which seems to be healing."

"Excellent. Let's get in the hot tub." Moments later, the warm water massaged away the aches from the strenuous activity.

We spent the remainder of the afternoon between the pool, hot tub, and the lounge chairs soaking up a few more rays of sun before heading north.

After dinner, our last evening at the ranch found us in the living room, beside a newly stoked fire. The warm glow chased away the nip in the air during the cool Dallas evening. Eric sat against the arm rest of the big leather couch. I was curled up against his side with my feet tucked underneath me. His arm was around me. We sat in companionable silence while watching the roaring flames.

"You haven't said much about your ribs lately. How are they feeling?" Eric's fingers gently grazed my ribs.

Tensing, I looked up at him. "They feel much better. There are only a few twinges when I'm doing something strenuous, like when we were cleaning up all the brush."

"I'm glad you're better. It seems as though you are relaxing much more, too. The nightmares are diminishing."

"It would be great to be able to put all this behind me. If only my mind would stop wondering about Joey. I'd like to concentrate more on you." I gave him a devlish smile.

"I would like that, too."

Chapter 20. Seattle

The next morning, we were up early to begin our journey north. Ricardo drove us to DFW Airport. After shaking his hand, Eric led me to the flight bound for Seattle.

"For somebody who hates heights, I sure am flying a lot lately," I said to Eric as the jet engines roared.

He grabbed my hand. "You're definitely handling it much better."

The jet taxied to the runway. I always hated the initial roll down the runway. A pilot friend once told me the first one thousand feet of takeoff are the most critical. My hand was intercepted before the death grip on the armrest was completed.

"Easy, cowgirl," Eric whispered in my ear. The big jet took off easily and climbed to cruising altitude, 34,500 feet. Once the flight leveled off, I relaxed.

"Linda, look out the window." Eric leaned over me, gazing out the small port. White, snow-capped pinnacles ascended from the black rock below. Each peak looked as though a dollop of whip cream was plastered upon it. Dashes of green valleys were interspersed among the giant boulders of the Rockies.

"They're beautiful." My pleasant reverie was disrupted when the jet bounced sharply.

"Shit," slipped out in a whisper.

"Relax. It's only turbulence. *Denali* will be bouncing much more on the passage to Alaska."

"Yes, I know, Eric. Keep in mind, I can swim. If this jet takes a dive, flapping my arms won't do much good." My wicked smile lightened the tense mood.

"Agreed. But if you spend much time in the water of the Bering Sea, you'll come out as an ice cube."

"I guess I'll need to find a big, strong crab fisherman to warm me up again. Do you know someone who might be available?"

"Let me check around to see if I can come up with one."

His sly grin was answered by a fake punch to his shoulder. The rest of the flight wasn't too bad. At two-thirty, we landed at Sea Tac airport. Inside a sporty rental car, we cruised to the downtown Seattle Marriott hotel.

Once settled, he called his daughters to let them know we'd arrived.

"We'll meet them for breakfast tomorrow. They both have dates tonight," Eric explained. "There's a interesting little bar nearby. We can stretch our legs on the way."

"Great idea."

A heavy mist hung in the air. Gray stratus clouds mottled the sky, obliterating the sun as they often did in the Pacific northwest. The wind whipped around the corners of the buildings.

The Lazy Salmon was tucked between two small guest houses. The warm air swirled around us, chasing the chill away. We found a rickety table for two near the blazing wood-burning stove.

"*Brrrr*, it's a chilly day."

"A nice glass of brandy should warm us up."

I nodded in agreement while looking around this cozy establishment. The entrance stood beneath the black awning, surrounded by tall, red-bricked walls. The traditional exterior didn't divulge the contemporary interior. The long, black bar was lit with modern pendant lights. Walls were adorned by big slate panels.

"This is an interesting place."

"It's pretty modern for a simple fishing captain, though it's a nice comfortable spot in this part of town."

"Have you spent much time in Seattle, Eric?"

"Every few years we would sail the boat down when she needed a major overhaul. Though it is a couple of thousand miles, the yards here are more competitively priced than the ones in Alaska."

"Tom told me about the paint job. What other work did you have done?"

"The port engine gave us fits last year. We spent most of the season running on one engine. If you watched the show, you would know this." His ice-blue eyes stared at me as if he was trying to figure out whether or not I did know this. My smile was carefully hidden.

"We used to come here every few seasons when Tom and I fished with our dad. It was always a great time. Can you imagine two teenage boys, with a pile of money in their pockets, released in the vast city of

Seattle? Remember, we came here after spending two months cooped up on the boat, working our butts off, catching crabs. Those were some wild times."

"I bet the young ladies of Seattle were thrilled to have you guys here." A dark look came over his face.

"Yeah, well whatever. We should see the sights tomorrow."

"Eric, why did you change the subject?"

He stared at me for a few moments before answering.

"Linda, I met my ex-wife here, after a fishing trip. It's still difficult to talk about." He gazed out the mist-stained front window.

"The rain's let up. Why don't we find a spot for dinner?" After bundling up once again, we strolled down the damp streets. A cute seafood restaurant caught our attention. Delicious halibut steaks were washed down with a local Riesling. The food kept the conversation at bay.

The mist could almost be called rain again, as we hustled back to the hotel. Since the murky darkness of night descended, the temperature plummeted a few more degrees.

Back at the hotel, cocktails were enjoyed on the room's balcony. Though the air was cold, the views of Lake Union and the surrounding skyline were stunning.

The misty rain continued to drip out of the sky, sending us back to the warm refuge of the hotel room. After helping me remove my jacket, Eric surrounded me with his warm arms. I shivered from both the chill and his tenacious embrace.

"Are you having fun?" He asked while holding me at arm's length.

"Yes," I smiled at him. "I always have fun with you." He pulled me close for a few minutes longer. After breaking free of his grasp, I took refuge in the bathroom. This relationship was definitely heating up. After our argument in Dallas, I had to be careful how to proceed since I wasn't at all sure I was ready to make the leap so soon after loosing Joey.

Fortunately, the remainder of the night was spent in the same comfortable snuggle which I'd grown used to as my mind tried to bury the thoughts of my lost relationship. Remorse and anguish drifted around my subconscious. Was it reasonable to allow this incredibly strange twist of fate to guide me into a more serious relationship with this fisherman?

Vivid dreams of Joey, sharks, storms, and towering mountains of water swirled around my brain all night. Despite all the evidence to the contrary, I still believed Joey was alive, somewhere. Faint light, from a gray morning, seeped through the fog in my head. The husky fisherman was up early as usual. He leaned over a table while making coffee. His eyes were on a copy of the USA Today.

"Eric," I called to him.

"Morning," he smiled at me.

"Come here, please." He sat on the bed next to me.

"You had another tough night."

"The nightmares won't leave me alone." I grabbed his hand, holding it close to my heart.

"It seemed as though you tossed and turned all night."

"Linda, it was difficult coming back to Seattle. My ex and I spent so much time here. Also, it is getting more and more difficult just lying next to you."

"I disappointed you."

Pulling his hand free, he brushed the hair out of my eyes.

"I would be lying if I said I wasn't a little disappointed. After all, I am a hot-blooded American man." He laughed, then became serious again. "I'm willing to wait until you are ready."

"Eric, don't think I'm not wildly attracted to you, because I am. But even though my head knows Joey is gone, my heart hasn't totally caught up yet." My explanation seemed lame even to me.

Eric grinned at me. "You're wildly attracted to me?"

Sitting up, I leaned in and my lips brushed his ear as I whispered, "You are a very sexy man."

He leaned over, his hands on either side of my waist. The kiss barely brushed my lips.

"You better watch it, cowgirl. Don't tease me too much." A moment later, he handed me a cup of coffee. Sighing deeply, I climbed out of bed, wondering why life had to be so complicated.

Eric's phone rang.

"Hi Caroline. Yes, we'll meet you here for breakfast in an hour."

Nervous energy had me scurrying around the room trying to make my appearance just right for the big meeting with his daughters.

Eric chuckled. "What are you so nervous about?"

"I want to make a good impression on your daughters. I want them to like me."

He laughed, pulling me into his lap. "They will like you just fine."

We headed down in the elevator to meet the girls. The pretty young lady admiring the art on the wall of the lobby had to be Caroline. She looked like her father, only with darker hair.

She greeted her dad with a huge smile along with a big hug. Eric introduced me.

"It's a pleasure to meet you." I gave her a slight embrace.

"You too, Linda. My dad's told me a lot about you." Now that surprised me, as we hadn't really discussed this.

A few seconds later, Kristen showed up. Eric embraced his younger daughter also, though her greeting wasn't as enthusiastic as her sister's. The younger sister barely shook hands with me. Her attention turned to her father, who guided the three of us to the restaurant in the lobby. I sat between Eric and Caroline.

"It's great to see you girls. What have you been up to?"

"The new semester at school is intense," Caroline said while beaming. "I met a new guy." She studied her coffee while her dad digested this news.

"OK, what is his deal?" There was caution in Eric's voice.

"Dad, don't worry, he's a nice guy. He's in law school. Kristen has a new boyfriend, too."

"I'm almost afraid to ask." Eric chuckled, looking to his younger daughter. She gave him a sullen gaze.

"Are you going to tell me, or do I have to drag it out of you?"

"Not in front of her," Kristen mumbled, inclining her head in my direction.

Her father ignored this while repeatedly attempting to engage the younger daughter in conversation. She only gave him short, curt answers.

Halfway through breakfast, Kristen turned her attention to me. "Where did you meet my father?" The way she said this was almost challenging.

Hesitating a second, I did not want to lie to her. "We met in North Carolina, when he was fishing there in July."

Eric joined the conversation. "Linda is a sailor, a charter sailing captain. She was delivering a boat. Didn't you do some sailing in high school?"

She rolled her eyes. "You know I did, Dad."

"Would you would like to come to Florida to go sailing with me sometime? Caroline you are welcome also." My offer was greeted by a cold stare from the younger sibling.

"Not likely." Kristen gave me piercing look.

Caroline glared at her sister. "You don't have to be rude to Linda. You could say 'no thank you.'" The elder sister turned her attention to me. "I would love to come to Florida but more for the beach. I'm not much of a boat person."

Kristen held her tongue as Eric gave her a stern look. The rest of the breakfast was more of the same. Eric was right. I knew where I stood with Kristen.

After breakfast, we headed back into the lobby. Caroline grabbed my arm, leading me over to a sculpture on the other side of the room. This gave Eric and Kristen a moment alone.

"Sorry about my sister. She's having a hard time with the divorce. I am too, but there is no reason to take it out on you."

"You are very perceptive for someone so young."

"I could see Dad squirming like he wanted to scold her, but he didn't want to make a scene. I'm sure he's having a few choice words with her now." Caroline smiled.

"I haven't known your Dad for a long time, but this has been really hard on him, too."

A moment later, we were rejoined by the other two. Kristen looked very upset. Eric tried to lighten the situation.

"Ladies, why don't we do a little sightseeing? Since you two live here, you'd be perfect to show us around."

"Dad, you act like you've never been here before," Kirsten said snidely.

Caroline grabbed her father's arm and mine, leading us to the hotel entrance, while ignoring her sister.

"Why don't we walk around the city center? There are nice parks with great views of the Space Needle and Mount Rainier. Did you know that this area, along with the Space Needle, were built for the 1962 World's Fair?"

Capt. Marlena Brackebusch

Our foursome spent the morning wandering around, enjoying unusually good weather for Seattle. Kristen was still very quiet, but Caroline made up for it by keeping the conversation flowing.

Suddenly Kristen piped up. "Why don't we go up the Space Needle?" Everyone seemed surprised by this. "We can have lunch up there."

Eric glanced at me for confirmation, knowing my fear of heights. Kristen caught the look. Her eyes rolled but she remained silent.

Not wanting to upset her further, I said, "That sounds like fun, Kristen. I bet the views are great up there." Eric squeezed my hand. We all boarded the monorail for the two-minute ride to "The Needle." At the bottom of the structure, looking up, I could immediately appreciate the enormity of the immense structure towering in front of us. Though a chill crept into me, I wasn't about to let Eric down.

Kristen must have sensed my hesitation. "Did you know the Space Needle is 605 feet high?" She looked at me with a defiant smile as she said this. After purchasing tickets, the elevator on the exterior of the building whisked us up all 605 feet at blazing speed. My concentration was on Eric, not the height.

At the observation deck, we wandered toward the huge glass windows. The views of snowcapped Mt. Rainier were breathtaking.

"Kristen, this is really spectacular," I said. She looked surprised by the compliment, accepting the praise quietly. After being seated in the restaurant, the girls headed off to the ladies room. Eric pulled me aside. It was the first time we'd had a private moment all morning.

"I'm sorry about Kristen. I spoke with her at the hotel."

Holding up my hand, I stopped his apology. "Eric, let things take their course. It's normal for her to be unhappy. She thinks I'm taking the place of her mom with you. She probably feels threatened."

"The divorce was well before I met you."

"We'll talk about this later," I promised as the girls walked up.

We chatted about the scenery passing before us as the restaurant slowly rotated. Kristen was quiet, but seemed to be loosening up a little.

Finally she addressed me again. "So you are going up to Alaska on the boat with Dad?" She didn't appear too happy.

"Yes, it's a trade off for your Dad helping me with my business in Naples," I replied. She looked at her father but didn't go any further with this. With a sigh, she turned her attention out the window. After lunch, both daughters bid us goodbye, saying they needed to get ready for their dates. After a hug, they promised to see their father over Christmas break.

Eric and I went back to the hotel, a little exhausted from the day's activities. We plopped down on the comfy balcony chairs for sunset.

"Thanks," Eric said.

"For what?"

"For being so nice to Kristen. She isn't normally that way. Also I'm proud of you for going up the Space Needle. I know it was hard."

I returned his smile. "OK, I will accept the praise, but don't be so hard on Kristen. She's trying to deal with the break up. Since you told me how close you two are, it's that much harder on her. I assume she still lives with her mom?"

"Yes, we had—she still has—the condo here in Seattle. She always wanted to live here. I thought it would be less disruptive to have Kristen finish high school here, though she knows she has an open invitation to stay with me anytime I'm in Texas."

"Now for Caroline, she is a wonderful, smart, very perceptive young lady. She's going to do well."

He had the smile of a proud father.

"Yes, she's a great kid. She's never been any trouble." We enjoyed the pretty evening, with a full spectrum of colors reflecting off the waters of the lake. A light dinner was enjoyed in a nearby restaurant before retiring to our room. A long hot shower soothed away all of the day's stresses. When I came out of the bathroom, Eric was stretched out on the bed, watching the news.

"Today is our last day of comfort before the fishing boat." He took my place in the bathroom. When he came out, we held hands while watching TV. Exhaustion finally won out. A quiet, no nightmare sleep was much needed.

The next morning, we puttered around, packing our bags for the trip to the fishing boat.

"There's the famous market and the aquarium." The fisherman pointed out the sights we didn't have time to enjoy before heading for the commercial part of the harbor. "Are you ready to head offshore in a couple of days?"

"Eric, you act like I have never been out in the ocean before. I have been offshore hundreds of times."

"Yes, but in light of what happened a couple months ago, I want to be sure we are not making a mistake."

I reached over to squeeze his hand. "Eric, I'm fine. I trust you and Tom."

He turned the car into the shipyard. Tom was standing by the entrance to a run-down warehouse, speaking with a man who looked to be the yard manager. He hustled over to us.

"We're just about to splash her." Tom leaned in the car window. There was none of his normal exuberant greeting. He seemed to be all business today. "Why don't you park over there?"

We drove the short distance to the marine railway. There in front of us towered the 103-foot fishing vessel, *Denali*. She looked huge out of the water. Gleaming dark blue paint shined on her hull. Her bulbous bow was bright with red anti-fouling paint. The dry dock began to flood. Soon the huge fishing boat was home again in the water.

Once she was afloat, Eric guided me to the gangway between the dry dock and the boat. As we stepped aboard, I took a moment to look around the deck. Tom grabbed my hand.

"This way," he ordered, pulling me toward the wheelhouse. Eric tossed our bags on deck before helping two other guys scramble to untie the mooring warps.

The engines roared to life when Tom pressed the ignition switches. "We have to get her out of dry dock. These guys don't fool around," he explained. The twin throttles were eased forward. On the intercom, he said, "OK guys, cast off the bow first."

The bowline was disengaged by the dry dock crew. As more lines were released, Tom eased the throttles forward. *Denali* responded, making way into the river for the short run to the commercial fishing docks.

Our captain eased the boat alongside a huge stone pier where several other vessels were secured. A couple of rough-looking characters grabbed the monkey fist at the end of the heaving line. Soon the heavy warps were looped over rusting steel bollards on the pier. Tom let out a sigh of relief. He turned to me with a smile.

"Welcome aboard, Li'l Sis. Sorry we were so rushed, but they like to get the boat out of dry dock as soon as it's finished to allow another boat in. Time is money."

"No problem." I gawked around the pilothouse. Having been a big fan of their boat on the fishing show, it was strange to stand here in the wheelhouse gazing around at the familiar scenes previously seen only on television. Somehow it was bigger in real life.

Eric climbed through the door. He followed my gaze around the wheelhouse.

"Well, what do you think?" he asked. I looked up at him, trying to remain cool.

"I'm not sure I can find the right words to describe this. It's so much more massive than it looks on TV."

He took my hand. "Let me show you around."

After descending down a couple of steps in the back of the pilothouse, we came upon a small room.

"That's the captain's quarters." I glanced in at the neatly made double bunk, the mahogany desk to the right, along with a small wardrobe for clothes. Above the desk were repeaters for the depth and speed. A separate chart plotter was off to the right.

"This other door leads to the captain's head with shower." We peeked in at the compact facilities.

Back in the hallway, we descended a few more steps to the galley. Cream-colored Formica counter tops lined one side along with a full-sized refrigerator freezer. On the countertop stood a microwave and coffee maker. Like the other fishing boat, this one also had a four burner stove and oven.

To our left was a dinette area where I spied a flat screen TV with DVD player. Somehow from watching the show, I didn't get the idea these guys had time to watch many movies.

The other side of the galley led to the crew's quarters.

"Here's the ready room." Eric led me through a door, to a room lined with lockers and fishing gear. Suits of foul-weather clothes hung off the locker doors. "This is where we suit up before heading on deck."

Capt. Marlena Brackebusch

After leaving the ready room, we peeked into the crew's quarters. Another door was off to the right of the hallway. "Engine room. I'll show you it later."

Another large hatch led to the outside deck. A long expanse of steel extended forward of the superstructure, all the way to the small enclosure on the bow.

"This is where we stack all of the pots," Eric explained.

I smiled to myself. This was way too cool—seeing in person what I'd watched so often on TV.

A little farther up the deck the crane, pot launcher, and bait station stood ready for action.

"We bait and retrieve the pots here, but you already knew that." He grinned while pointing out a couple of open holes around the deck.

"See those holes? You want to watch those. They lead to the tanks. When we're fishing we leave a couple of them open to be able to put crabs in the tanks. You don't want to fall into one," he warned, "or you'll owe us a case of beer." His grin broadened.

After returning inside, the fisherman led me down the stairs to the engine room.

"This is much bigger than my engine room." Eric showed me the two monstrous engines that propelled the boat. There was also a huge generator, far larger than the engine on my sailboat.

"This is the main electrical panel. You should know where that is in case of an electrical fire. Also, the engine room manual release for the fire suppression system is right next to it. Of course, there is an automatic, too. This is just in case."

Next to all of this was a big, red fire extinguisher. Leaving the engine room, we went back to the wheelhouse. Starting at the captain's chair with *Denali* embroidered on it, Eric pointed out all of the navigation equipment and ship's monitors.

"These monitor the bilges, engine room, and all of the crab storage tanks."

"This is pretty overwhelming, Eric."

Tom poked his head in. "Bro, I'm having a crew meeting in the galley in five minutes."

"We'll be right there."

Seated at the galley table was Fred, their cousin. He was joined by another man who was all of six-foot-two with dark hair. I guessed his age as late twenties.

"All right, we have a huge list of stuff to get done with only a couple of days to do it. Let's get to work. Fred, you take all the engine stuff and hydraulics. Brett, make sure the tanks are cleaned and flushed out."

The captain turned to us. "Eric and Linda, make sure the galley is clean and everything works. Fill the water tanks. I'll work on the wheelhouse, checking all the navigation gear. At three P.M. we'll have a safety drill on deck. I want to see life jackets and survival suits. Eric, make sure Linda knows where all the safety equipment is.

"Tomorrow morning we'll provision then go to the fuel dock to top up the tanks. Our departure for Alaska will be first thing Wednesday morning. That's all."

It was a surprised to see Tom so businesslike.

Eric and I looked around the galley. He explained where the supplies were kept, including the first-aid kit for superficial problems. A more serious trauma kit complete with drugs was locked up in the captain's quarters. There were two fire extinguishers in the galley.

"Does the fire equipment reflect the bad cooking around here?" I asked.

Eric answered me with a smile and a *tssh* sound. We wiped down everything. All the equipment seemed to work. The whole process took a couple of hours. The final touch was a clean, mopped floor.

"I want to check the level of the propane tanks for the stove," Eric said. Inside the large vented locker were the twin propane tanks. Eric lifted up the one in use. "Pretty heavy, it should be OK."

He glanced at his watch. "Hungry?"

"I could go for some lunch."

"Let's round up the boys." In the pilot house, Tom and Fred were conferring about engine stuff.

"Both engines are running fine," Fred said to our captain. They turned around when we entered.

"You guys want to go to lunch?" Eric asked.

Tom considered this. "Yeah, why not, I could use a break." Fred nodded in agreement. Back outside, Brett was climbing into one of the tanks.

"No, you guys go ahead. I still have two more tanks to survey."

Only a block away sat a small restaurant. It was dimly lit, with plumes of cigarette smoke swirling around. Rough-looking characters hunched over the bar. They stared at the blond woman walking in with a group of their cronies.

We slid into a booth on the far side. The table's surface was scarred from what looked like knife gouges. As we chatted, a heavyset woman wrote down our orders. When she departed, Tom took the lead in the conversation.

"It looks like we are making good progress."

"I want to change one of the hydraulic lines on the crane. Eric, would you give me a hand after the safety drill?"

"Sure, Fred." There were more discussions throughout lunch about mechanical and navigation issues. I sat quietly, taking it all in. It was obvious the trio had gone through this routine many times.

After lunch, we went back to the boat. Eric gave me a tour of the safety gear. In the ready room, there was a big red locker with survival suits for the crew. Each name was written on the bag in bold letters. There were several extras.

"Where's Tom's suit?" I asked Eric, not seeing one for him.

"We don't let him have one," he laughed. "No, I'm kidding. Because he is technically the captain for this trip, his suit is in the wheelhouse. It's the most likely place he would be during an emergency."

"Why is Tom the captain on this trip?"

"Well, as you may know, during king crab season he is the captain. Finding them is his specialty." Eric paused. "During opilio crab season, I'm the captain. That's my specialty. We usually keep the boat in Alaska during the off-season, fishing halibut or salmon. Tom skippers most of these trips.

"Since we brought the boat to Seattle for work to be done on her, I deferred to Tom, as he is older."

Eric returned his attention to the survival suits. He picked one of the spares. Shaking the bag, he nodded as the orange suit fell to the deck. "Let me show you how to put it on." He guided me into the suit feet first. I pulled it up to my waist. Eric stopped. He stared at me with a strange look on his face. I think we had a simultaneous déjà vu.

"This isn't the easiest thing to get on, is it?" My smile eased the look of concern on his face.

"If this boat were sinking, you'd get it on pretty fast." Eric zipped up the front then yanked the hood on. The flaps covered most of my face. I could barely breathe as the memories from the night of my rescue came flooding back.

"You have to be able to put it on in sixty seconds, according to Coast Guard regulations," Eric explained, breaking my reverie. "They will be here tomorrow afternoon to give us our safety clearance to steam for Dutch Harbor."

"I'll be ready." After struggling out of the survival suit, we stuffed it back into the bag. Eric affixed duck tape with my name on it to the suit before replacing it in the locker. The next locker over housed the life jackets. Eric made sure I knew how to put on a PFD.

Because of my past experience, I chuckled at this. I did give him credit for thoroughness.

Another locker contained flares: hand-held, flare gun, and parachute flares. The use of each was explained.

"The expiration dates look good." The dry box was replaced in its home.

On the aft deck sat the twin six-man liferafts.

"These are to be released only on Tom's command."

Hydrostatically released emergency beacons, or EPIRBs, like the one we had on the sailboat sat nearby.

"There are additional EPIRBs in the wheelhouse."

Back at the pilothouse, Tom was poring over nautical charts.

"These indicator lights are for the engine fire suppression system. There are remote releases here."

A multitude of additional safety equipment soon had my head spinning. VHF radios, single side band radios, fire extinguisher, man overboard alarms with remote switches for everything was nearly overwhelming.

Tom must have seen the bewildered look on my face. "I'll make it very easy for you. If you hear any alarms on the boat, come straight to the wheelhouse. We all have our areas to cover when an emergency arises. You come here and help me with whatever I am doing. Got it?"

"All right, Tom."

"If you see something wrong, just scream loudly." The elder brother grinned at me.

"Oh yes. I'll become the hysterical female."

"I doubt it."

Tom grabbed his survival suit and life jacket from the wheelhouse for the safety drill.

Back on deck, our leader organized the drill. "Let's put on the life jackets first." Everyone complied. Tom walked around, checking them.

"Now the survival suits," he commanded, getting his watch ready. "Go." The stopwatch was started. Eric donned his suit quickly. When he turned to help me, we barely beat the sixty-second time limit.

Tom repeated the drill alone, perfectly. While we packed up the suits, our captain asked about the progress of the work.

"I only have the hydraulic line left," Fred said.

"Why don't we all pitch in on the repair?"

Fred donned a climbing harness. Hand over hand, he inched his way up the crane. Fifty feet over the deck, the engineer turned the wrench on the faulty hose. Drips of red hydraulic fluid were toweled from the deck.

"This fluid is very slippery. We don't want to ice skate later," Tom explained.

"Heads up." A big steel wrench clattered to the deck nearby. It just missed Eric's head.

"That's why you never stand under the crane."

The new hose was passed up to the man dangling above.

"I'm sure glad you didn't ask me to do this repair," I said at Eric.

"No, we are saving your crane repairs for under-way, when we have thirty-foot seas. It's more fun when the boat is rolling." Tom grinned at me.

"I don't think so."

Moments later, Fred's feet touched solid steel again.

"That wraps up today, ladies and gentlemen," our captain announced.

"I'll see you guys tomorrow." Brett headed for the pier.

"I'm going to finish tidying up the engine room." Fred carried his tools in the direction of the ready room.

Tom, Eric, and I went to the wheelhouse.

Standing by the captain's chair, I mentally reviewed the switches and lights.

"Crab tanks, engine alarms, man-overboard alarm." I was interrupted by a hand on my shoulder. Both bothers looked amused.

"Do you have it all down pat?" Tom tried to look serious.

"No, but I'll get it." The two brothers chuckled over this.

"Bro, why don't you two take the captain's quarters on this trip? It will give you a little privacy."

"Tom, that's very sweet of you, thanks." I answered for both of us. Eric shrugged his shoulders.

After settling in the captain's quarters then showering, we joined Tom. The three of us went ashore for cocktails and dinner. Fred declined to join us because he had a date for the evening.

Dinner was at a nice downtown Seattle restaurant. It was fun listening to the two brothers try to out-do each other at story telling. I couldn't help wondering how much was true.

"Do you remember the time we welded the *Arctic Fox's* trap door shut? We stole their crabs, replacing them with plastic ones. I would have loved to see their faces." Tom laughed.

"Yeah, but payback was a bitch," Eric said.

"What did they do?" I asked

"They tied paint balls to our shot. When the rope came through the block, we were doused in red. It took several hours to clean it up."

After a couple more drinks and stories, we stumbled back to the boat. Though I was exhausted, my ears listened to the sounds of the boat which was new to me.

The next morning, we piled into a beat-up truck for the provisioning run. The guys were like little kids, piling the shopping carts high with food and paper goods. Four stuffed carts were finally rung up to a hefty total.

Everything from steaks to frozen peas to ice cream were shoved in the rear of our vehicle. Back at *Denali,* the five of us carried load after load aboard. Eric and I stayed in the galley after the third load. Piles of stuff were stowed.

"I've never seen so many rolls of paper towels and toilet paper in one place...ever."

"Everything costs three times as much in Dutch Harbor. We wanted to take advantage of the lower prices here," Eric said.

It took a couple of hours to find room for everything. As we neared the finish, I felt the engines rumble to life.

"Come on, we'll go to the wheelhouse." Eric grabbed my hand.

Over at the fueling pier, diesel was endlessly pumped into the massive tanks. The fuel bill topped the grocery bill.

Once back at the fishing dock, everyone headed to the galley for lunch. It was amusing to watch the fisherman make sandwiches. Everything was tossed on the galley table followed by a sort of feeding frenzy.

After lunch, the Coasties showed up to check the whole boat over. This brought back a few bad memories for me. They were very professional. After the safety drills, Tom received our clearance to leave for Dutch Harbor.

Everyone was in a celebratory mood that night. We had one more dinner ashore followed by a couple too many drinks. Later, Eric and I were alone in the wheelhouse. He made a last-minute check of the weather faxes.

"Are you ready for tomorrow?" He asked me quietly.

"Absolutely. How does the weather look?" I leaned over his shoulder to see the swirls of wind depicted there.

He pointed to a circular whirl between the mainland and the Aleutian Islands.

"There's a low out here. It should be out of our way by the time we get there. We should have smooth sailing."

Chapter 21. North to Alaska

The next morning, Tom rallied everyone at the crack of dawn to ready the boat for sea. The big ship steamed up Puget Sound. After a left turn, we cruised out the Strait of Juan de Fuca. Long Pacific Ocean rollers greeted us, lifting the bow of the fishing boat. White spray flew over the forward superstructure as she crashed off the peaks of the swells.

"The course is 303 magnetic." Tom turned to Eric and me. The younger brother had just come in from the back deck. "Ten knots should get us there in six days."

"How many miles do we have, Tom?" I asked.

He stooped over the chart plotter. "It looks like just under 1600 nautical miles."

Snow-topped mountains lined the passageway to the mighty Pacific Ocean. Tall pine trees clung precipitously to the rocky landscape. I reveled in the wild, natural beauty of this waterway.

"Linda, look...a grizzly." A huge brown bear stalked the boulder-strewn beach. "We see tons of them in Alaska."

"Are they after salmon?" I asked.

Tom rubbed his black beard. "It's pretty late in the season. I would bet she is a pregnant female bulking up on whatever she can find. It will be time for her winter beddy bye soon."

The autopilot was set, allowing our captain to recline back in his seat. He turned to me a moment later. "Linda, I don't want you to take this the wrong way, but I haven't had you on this boat before. I don't want you going out on deck alone this trip."

I glanced at the elder brother. He was staring straight ahead. I was a little baffled by his order, but he was the captain, so I felt compelled to comply.

Tom fidgeted when I didn't answer him right away. "I know you have a ton of sailing experience, but it's different on a fishing boat. If you slipped overboard, the hypothermia could kill you in seconds."

Was our captain being chivalrous, overly protective, or both? He glanced at me out of the corner of his eye, like he was expecting me to erupt. I decided to let him off the hook.

"No problem. I guess Eric will have to escort me everywhere. What a shame." The two brothers looked surprised at my sweet smile of acquiescence.

Tom appeared to sigh with relief. "Can you take over, bro, while I grab a coffee and something to eat?"

"Sure." Eric replaced his brother in the captain's chair.

"You two want anything?" We both responded no.

After a few minutes of silence, I initiated a conversation. "Eric, it's a beautiful trip out through the Strait. *Denali* rides really nice."

He looked at me with a surprised look on his face. "You're not upset with Tom? I thought you would be."

"No, I'm not. He is a little overprotective, but he's the captain. And after everything with the rescue, I'm not totally surprised. I guess you will have to chaperone me." I smiled sideways at Eric. "What's happening with the watch schedule?"

"When we are fishing, the captain usually stays on watch until he can no longer stay awake, sometimes forty-eight hours or longer. Since this is only a delivery, Tom, Fred, and I will alternate four-hour watches. Our captain set it up so he has the midnight to four watch," Eric answered, glancing at me again.

"You can do watch with me, if you like." I was a little disappointed, but also not surprised to be excluded from the watch routine.

I didn't know how to run this boat, but I was determined to learn. Tom came back in to resume his watch. Eric grabbed my hand. "Let's go up to the bow. The breeze will be nice there."

The sights were magnificent along the rocky shoreline. The chilly breeze whipped our hair. Cold spray dashed over the boat, spritzing us with salty brine. It was not long before we headed inside to the warmth of the galley for lunch.

Later I grabbed a paperback novel that was high on my reading list. After knocking on the wheelhouse door, I checked to see if it was OK to read there.

"Of course, Li'l Sis." Tom smiled. I leaned over his shoulder. A quick glance at the chart plotter showed us leaving the Strait and Seattle behind. The large crab boat lumbered over the rising swells.

Immersed in my novel, I lost track of time until Eric came on watch, replacing his brother in the captain's chair. His feet were propped up in front of him.

Catching me looking at him, he grinned. "What?"

"I didn't say anything."

"What were you thinking?" he asked.

"I can't say, because I don't want to swell your head any bigger because you won't be able to fit it through the doorways."

He slipped up behind me. His arms slid around me. A string of light kisses paraded down my neck, sending shivers down my spine.

"I asked you what you were thinking." His voice was husky.

"Aren't you on watch? Shouldn't you be watching all those dials and things?"

"You better watch yourself, lady, or there may be trouble." He planted one more kiss on my neck before retuning to the helm. I buried my nose in the book while trying to hide another shiver.

Fred came in to relieve Eric near the end of his watch. "How would you like to give me a hand making dinner?" Eric asked me.

"Oh may I? That would be lovely," I said in a fake Southern-belle accent. We both laughed then left for the galley, where we found Tom drinking coffee. A day-old newspaper had his attention.

Eric and I gathered the ingredients to make baked chicken, *Denali* style. Once the bird was in the oven, we sat with Tom, who eyed me with a cautious look.

"How's it going?"

"Everything's great." Eric flipped on the TV with DVD player. We watched *Indiana Jones* in companionable silence complete with microwaved popcorn. When dinner finished cooking, I made stove-top stuffing with steamed frozen veggies. After dinner, Tom relieved Fred so he could eat. This left Eric and I with a little quiet time.

"Would you like to go out to the back deck? The stars should be nice."

I nodded. "Let me get my jacket." Before heading out, Eric called to Tom to let him know we'd be out back.

"Do you guys always let each other know when you are going on deck?"

We climbed out the back hatch and into the chilly air before he answered me. "Yes, for a couple of reasons. One, when you are on the aft deck, the person in the wheelhouse can't see you. If you fell overboard, it could be hours until someone knew. The other reason is when we are fishing, there are all kinds of activities going on. Pots swing, bait is made, crab sorted while waves crash over the deck."

He leaned against the rail while finishing his explanation. "The captain expects "x" number of people on deck. He's constantly counting and accounting for everyone. If someone goes in, say, to go to the bathroom when a wave hits, they wouldn't be accounted for. Immediately, you assume they went overboard.

"The boat has to be swung around right away, because the water is so cold a crew member wouldn't last long. That wastes precious time if someone is on board and doing fine...just in the bathroom. So you let the skipper know where you are when you are going on or off the deck."

We stood on the aft deck, which was quite dark except for the white glow of the stern light. The stars were big and beautiful on this clear night.

We gazed off the starboard side at strange-colored swirls, which appeared to be moving to the north.

"What's that?" I asked Eric.

"That's the Aurora Borealis, the Northern Lights." We watched in awe as yellow waves undulated across the sky. Flashes of purple streaked toward the heavens. Blue-white light blasted down like powerful streaks of lightning.

"It's amazing, Eric."

"You've never seen it before?"

"No."

"We hope to see much more on this trip. You look cold. Why don't we head in?"

Eric called Tom on the intercom, once we were safely inside.

"I'm going to check the weather." He headed for the wheelhouse. I made my way to a hot shower to chase the chills away.

Eric came back to the cabin as I was brushing out my wet hair.

"Everything OK?" I asked.

"Yes, everything's fine." He took the brush from my hand, gently brushing out a few snarls.

"You were so funny on Mark's boat, Linda."

"Funny?"

"After I pulled you out of the water, you didn't want anyone's help. Do you remember when I had to force the brush out of your hand?" He laughed softly at the memory. "You were in so much pain, you couldn't lift the brush over your head, but you were determined to try."

"Eric, I'm a pretty independent person. I always have been. Joey wanted to be waited on. He would never lift a finger to help me. What a jerk." The last words came out in a whisper.

"Why did you stay with him if he was such a jerk?"

"I'm sorry. With him missing and all, I shouldn't have said that."

"Linda, I don't think I'll ever figure you out."

"That's just the way I want it."

He didn't miss my wicked smile as we headed to bed.

Sometime during the night, Eric's wristwatch beeped.

"What's the matter?" I asked, barely on the edge of consciousness.

"Nothing, I need to go on watch. Would you like to join me?"

"Yes, I'll do watch with you." After he left the cabin, I pulled on the old "North Carolina" sweatshirt. Water and coffee grounds were poured into the pot. As I waited for the brew, Tom came in.

"Are you looking for coffee?"

"Yeah, Li'l Sis. Did you get some sleep?"

"Yes, but I don't know how you will, with all the coffee you drink."

"I'll put my head down. When I'm captain, I don't sleep much."

"What's the matter? Don't you trust your baby brother?" Eric called from the wheelhouse steps. Tom rolled his eyes, then grinned.

"Get back on watch before I beat your ass."

"Aye, aye, captain."

After handing the younger brother a cup of joe, I had to ask him about the recent exchange of words.

"Isn't it weird being captain on some trips and crew on others? Do you guys every have any problems or get into arguments?"

"Not really. Tom and I grew up as very close brothers. We were pretty much inseparable. Don't get me wrong; he would usually beat the heck out of me when we fought. Tom has a very short temper. You really have to wind me up to make me snap." He checked something on the radar. "We have mutual respect for each other. Every once in a while he tells me where to fish or how to fish."

"How do you respond?"

"I tell him to shut up. Or I say, 'Don't you tell me what to do.' It usually works."

He stared at the radar again. I looked over his shoulder.

"A commercial ship?" I asked.

"Yes. It's an oil tanker, probably headed for Valdez. We should be able to see the range lights." Both of us squinted out the windscreen.

"With all the lights on this boat it's difficult to pick them up, Eric."

"There they are, at eleven o'clock. He should pass in front of us with no problem."

The blip on the green radar screen quickly closed with us. His starboard green light slipped ahead of us a mile or so away. A few moments later, the screen was blank again. The rest of the watch passed by quickly. Fred and Tom were heard conversing in the galley around seven thirty. Heading that way, I found Tom making a new pot of coffee.

"Would you guys like breakfast?"

"Some bacon and eggs would be great, Li'l Sis. Can I help you?" Tom asked me.

"No, sit down, I have it." I pulled out the staples for breakfast. Soon Eric poked his head below for a second.

"Something smells good."

"Get back on watch, you." I pretended to scold him. "You'll get some." He turned back into the wheelhouse.

A few minutes later, I went to the wheelhouse armed with a fresh cup of coffee for our relief captain. After handing it to him, I gazed out the windshield. My fingers gently massaged the back of his neck.

"I could get used to you being on board." After the cousin relieved Eric, he and Tom discussed the night's events between mouthfuls of breakfast.

There was more of the same throughout the second day. *Denali* steamed ahead at ten knots on the same course of 303. Around two P.M., Tom called on the intercom.

"Eric and Linda, come to the wheelhouse." We were down in the galley talking with Fred as he gathered up the fixings for dinner. At the sound of Tom's voice, Eric and I scrambled to join him.

"What's up, brother?" The younger man asked as we entered the wheelhouse. Tom pointed off the port bow. Making a bee line for our fishing boat was a pod of orcas, killer whales. There were at least thirty of them.

I was beside myself, acting like a little kid.

"Grab your jacket. We'll go watch them."

Eric and I scrambled down the steps, sprinting for the bow. We climbed a ladder to a little platform by the forward range light. This gave us a great view of the frolicking mammals. The majestic whales cavorted around and under our boat. They were truly amazing. Thirty feet of slick black and white torpedoes surfing along our bow wave like dolphins. One big male with a very tall dorsal fin leapt out of the water, landing with a huge splash.

Then they were gone.

"That was incredible. Thanks, Tom." Our captain eased the throttles forward as Eric and I warmed up in the wheelhouse.

"It's awfully cold for my Florida blood," I laughed.

"It will be warmer in the galley." We took refuge there until the chill went away.

The next day, the skies filled with angry gray clouds. The wind increased to twenty knots, whipping the sea into white caps. *Denali* started bouncing around. Eric and Tom were looking at the weather fax when I came into the wheelhouse.

"Some weather picking up?" I asked.

Tom stared at me for a moment. "A little. Nothing we can't handle."

I peeked over their shoulders. There was a low-pressure system forming to our west. The projected track intersected with our heading. A big pressure drop was forecast, down to 971mb. With that low pressure and the very steep drop, I knew the wind and seas were going to increase fast, maybe to hurricane force.

As the day progressed, the wind built to fifty knots. Walls of breaking black seas increased to eighteen feet. *Denali* rode well up the steep face of the waves. *Bang!* The huge steel bulb on the bow crashed down the back side, jarring our teeth. Then the mighty steel ship would roll sharply from side to side.

By nightfall the wind increased again to sixty knots. Breaking towers of water rose to twenty-five feet. Snow streaked across our field of vision in a mini-blizzard. An hour later, it was a complete whiteout. It appeared as though Eric was closely watching my reaction to all the terrible weather.

"Linda, are you comfortable with this weather?"

"It's pretty cool. I've never been at sea in a blizzard before. You need to have faith in the radar, because I can't even see the bow. If it was only snow on the deck and not sea water, I would talk you into building a snowman." My devilish grin brought a smile to the tough fisherman's face.

"I didn't expect you to take the storm in stride."

"I'm not about to wimp out in front of you guys. You'll never ask me back."

Tom entered the wheelhouse. "Hey, kids. Building a snow man would be fun, but I don't want anyone one deck unless it's absolutely necessary."

By four A.M. there was blowing snow across the deck, but the wind seemed to ease.

Eric and I spent most of our watch with our eyes glued to the radar, since visibility was still poor. When the sun finally rose, the blow was by us. The seas moderated.

The remainder of the ride to Unalaska was an easy run. On the evening of the sixth day, we rounded Priest Rock. Dutch Harbor was a mere cobweb of lights before us in a lonely black sea.

Chapter 22. Dutch Harbor

"Grab a warm jacket; it's always cold here," Eric warned, as we joined Tom and Fred climbing off *Denali*. We were greeted by a couple of other fishermen from the television show, as we walked toward the bars and restaurants. From what I could see of Dutch Harbor, it was basically a big harbor with lots of fishing boats in it, though it seemed like a nice little town.

On Main Street, we went into a bar named the Watering Hole.

"Hey, it's about time you guys got here." Shouts from other fishing crews were heard above the raucous din drifting around the crowded bar.

The crew of *Denali* shook many hands. Eric introduced me to as many people as possible in the packed bar. A couple of seats opened up at the far end.

"A Jack Daniels on the rocks. What would you like Linda?" Eric asked me.

"Rum and Coke." I thought a Dark & Stormy would be too complicated for this working man's pub. Eric headed for the restroom.

I sipped my drink while taking it all in. A hand grazed my elbow. After spinning around, I recognized the narrator of the fishing show. He was five-feet-ten inches tall, trim but muscular. His handsome face showed some of his Asian heritage. A thin mustache and beard surrounded his lips.

"Jonathan Steele." He smiled, extending his hand. I don't know why, but alarm bells rang in my head.

"Who are you with?" He was very direct. I knew from the show he was a math professor at a Boston college before chucking it all for journalism and television. He had quite a reputation for doggedly pursuing stories.

"I'm with *Denali*," I said evasively.

He grinned at me. "I figured that out. I mean WHO are you with?" Eric had already warned me about Jonathan. He would pry into every aspect of my life. I was not sure I wanted the story of the yacht sinking plastered all over television. Tom walked up behind me. His arm draped around my shoulders.

"She's with me." He extended his hand to the TV man. Eric walked up a moment later. He did not miss the exchange.

"Now, that's not what my sources tell me, Tom." He threw a sideways glance at Eric, who maintained a poker face.

"Then why the hell did you ask?" Tom stared defiantly at the reporter.

"I was just trying to have a conversation with the lady. Don't get all huffy," Jonathan replied. One could tell by his demeanor he was trying to get at something. "Did you come up on the boat?"

"Yes," I answered.

"How did it feel being out in the middle of the ocean?"

"I felt perfectly safe on *Denali*. She's a great boat. I had a lot of fun." I forced a smile.

"Are you going out crab fishing with these guys?" he asked. I didn't know how to answer this, as we hadn't discussed the possibility. Secretly, I knew I'd love to.

"I don't know." Eric looked like he was getting uncomfortable.

"If you do, you'll have to sign a contract with the producers. I'd like to get a little background information. Like how you and Eric met."

"Back off, Jonathan," Tom said. He stood up, towering over the reporter.

"Gee, Tom. Don't get all upset." He turned to me. "We'll chat later."

"I can hardly wait." I gave him a sickeningly sweet smile.

Jonathan moved off to chat with another fisherman.

Eric sighed with relief.

"Usually Jonathan isn't too bad a guy. But he obviously smelled a story. I wonder if he knows about the rescue," Tom said.

"I haven't told many people about it. Somehow these things get out," Eric replied.

"Do you want to go out for king crabs with us?" Tom asked, to my surprise. I looked at him then at Eric.

"I'd love to. Is that an offer?"

"I don't see why not, if Eric agrees." There was doubt in the younger brother's eyes.

"I can do the cooking and make sure you guys always have fresh coffee. I'm sure I can help out with other things."

"Not on deck," Eric said gruffly. "It's too dangerous."

"She can stay in the wheelhouse with me, to keep me awake." Tom laughed.

"We'll talk about it later." Eric ended the conversation abruptly. We had a couple of more drinks before heading off for dinner. After dinner, back at the Watering Hole, the conversation around the bar centered on the upcoming season. Weather predictions and crab stocks were tossed about.

At eleven, Eric and I left the bar for the walk back to *Denali*. We walked briskly in the night chill to keep warm. Back at the boat, we went to the captain's stateroom.

"Eric, why don't you want me to come king crab fishing?"

He put his arms around me. "I never said I didn't want you to come. It would have been nice to discuss it first."

"I didn't bring it up, Tom did. I answered his question honestly."

"That's true." He paused. "Do you really want to go? How about your business?"

"November and early December are usually slow. I can call Shane to see if he's OK with it."

"If that's what you want to do then it's fine with me. After king crab season, we can fly to Seattle to see my daughters for Christmas Eve. Then we'll fly back to Naples to see your family on Christmas Day.

"You know we are going to have cameras on the boat for the show. Be ready to be filmed at any time.

Watch out for Jonathan Steele. He won't stop until he has the whole story."

The next morning, when I woke up the guys were already in the galley.

"We need to wash off the deck then load the traps today." Tom nodded when I sat down.

"I can wash the deck, if you like," I offered.

Tom grinned. "That's fine. When we load the pots, make sure you don't get under any. This afternoon the guys are coming to install the cameras for the show. Eric, do you and Linda want to make a provisioning run this afternoon?"

"Sure. It will keep her away from Jonathan," Eric said.

Tom continued. "Tomorrow we will load bait. The fuel needs to be topped off, also. The Coast Guard is scheduled to give us our clearance."

The rest of the morning was spent cleaning up the boat and loading the pots. Brett and another crew member joined us to help tie down the traps. Eric showed me how it was done. Fred operated the crane, loading the pots at blinding speed.

Once the traps were aboard, each was checked and rechecked for holes or other faults. At lunchtime, we squeezed into the galley for another feeding frenzy.

"I'm Malu. We weren't properly introduced." The huge man looked to be Polynesian. He was six-foot-three and full of muscle with a friendly smile.

Then there was Zack, a big blond-haired guy who looked like he just flew in from the corn fields of

Iowa. Both of these guys had fished on the boat for years.

After lunch, the camera guys showed up with the show's producer. Jonathan Steele strolled aboard a moment later. When he approached me, Tom slipped between us.

"Jonathan, I want to discuss the camera placements." This allowed me to slip away to the galley.

Eric walked in a few minutes later. "They want you to sign a contract. It will pay pretty well." In the wheelhouse, I looked over the long page of legaleses then signed the contract. I was not really thrilled about this aspect of the trip, but I guessed there was no choice.

Jonathan smiled at me. "How about we do an interview later on this afternoon. I need background info on you."

"OK."

Tom must have noticed the look of anguish on my face. "You'll get used to the cameras."

Eric and I ducked out of the conversation, grabbing an old pickup truck on the quay for the ride to the supermarket. We only needed to top up the fresh stuff, like bread and veggies. I didn't realize "topping up" to a fisherman meant two cart loads. Arriving back at the boat, we grabbed all available hands to load the groceries aboard.

As we stored them, Jonathan Steele poked his head in. "I can get the background info on you now, if you like." I looked uncertainly at Eric. He shrugged his shoulders.

"OK, I guess."

"Where are you from?"

"I was born in Massachusetts. School was at Woods Hole Oceanographic Institute. I moved to Naples, Florida, where I own a sailing charter business."

Jonathan turned on a voice recorder. "What's your degree in?"

"My undergraduate degree is in biology and business. My master's is in marine mammal sciences. I am a certified dive master and a U.S. Coast Guard Master Mariner." The questioning went on while Eric and I put away all the food.

"How about we get this on film, say in twenty minutes in the wheelhouse?"

"OK," I said nervously. After going back to the captain's stateroom, I changed into nicer clothes, fixed my hair then slapped on makeup.

Eric grinned at my fussing. "Easy, cowgirl. You look great. Wait until three in the morning, when they catch you at a bad time."

"I can hardly wait." We went up to the wheelhouse. The film crew had me sit in the captain's chair. Tom was there with Jonathan, the producer, and a cameraman. Jonathan leaned against the navigation equipment.

"It's just like we're having a conversation. Don't look at the camera," he instructed. The producer said, "Go." Jonathan repeated the questions he asked earlier.

When that line of grilling was over, he dropped the bombshell.

"How did you and Eric meet?" I instantly went on alert. He looked like he picked up on this hesitation.

"We met in Beaufort, North Carolina. He was on a fishing trip."

"And what were you doing there?"

"I was delivering a sailboat to Florida."

"Is it true that he pulled you out of the water in the middle of the night?"

Tom stepped in front of the camera. "That's enough Jonathan. You're way out of line."

"It is true?" Jonathan rubbed his goatee. "What's the matter, Tom? It would make a great story. We could do a whole special on this. Also, I may have some information about Joey."

"This interview is over." Tom grabbed my arm to lead me away, but I turned back to Jonathan.

"What information do you have about Joey?"

"There's a rumor going around about a man who was rescued from a liferaft a few days after your sailboat went down. Right in the same area."

"How come the Coast Guard knows nothing of this?" Eric asked

"My sources tell me these rescuers may have unscrupulous ties, maybe drugs, maybe piracy. Those types wouldn't exactly report a rescue to the Coast Guard. Keep in mind the network has deep pockets. We might be willing to look into this if we can get an exclusive on the story."

Eric and Tom wore stunned looks on their faces.

"I'll do anything to find Joey," I said.

The younger brother interrupted me. "Jonathan, if this is a ploy to get her to talk to you..."

Jonathan raised his hand to stop Eric. "There is no ploy. You don't need to say anything more now. Just sign an agreement giving us an exclusive. I'll put the wheels in motion."

After I signed the agreement, Jonathan added, "You guys go fishing. I'll start looking into this Joey thing. We'll touch base with you when you get back."

It was late in the afternoon, when the cameramen left the boat for the evening.

"Let's get off this boat. I could use a cocktail," Tom said. We went back to the Watering Hole. The captains gathered for a final toast. A couple of boats were heading out tomorrow morning. All the crews toasted good fishing and the safe return of all boats. Of course, the cameramen caught all of this for TV.

Eric and I managed a few minutes alone.

"What do you make of Jonathan's statement about Joey?"

The big fisherman's eyes were filled with compassion. "It seems farfetched to me, but Jonathan usually doesn't waste time. It may be a ploy to get you to talk about it."

The next morning, we organized a bucket brigade to load the bait on board. The crew wore heavy gloves. Box after box of frozen cod and herring were passed along the line from the dock to the bait freezer. Brett and Zack were in the freezer, stacking the bait.

"I've never seen so much damn bait. We better catch a pile of crabs," Brett said while wiping a bead of sweat from his head.

This went on for a good part of the morning. Later, we topped up the fuel. At three in the afternoon, the Coast Guard arrived to do the last minute safety inspection. We were all set to leave. A final jaunt to the Watering Hole provided farewell camaraderie.

The next morning, the fishing boat was a frenzy of activity. The lines were cast off as we steamed to the Bering Sea.

After twenty-four hours of motoring, Tom slowed the boat. One by one, the pots were baited and set.

Lines of traps were set out like strings of pearls. Tom diligently logged the number and position of each pot. It took the better part of a day and a half to set everything. Tom spread them out over a wide area, to find out where the crabs were hiding.

I spent most of this time in the wheelhouse or galley helping with what I could. There was always fresh coffee along with good comfort food for the hungry guys. The crew rotated on deck.

When the pots were finally set, Eric took the helm to steam back toward the first pot. Our captain went below for a nap. Eric looked exhausted from the lack of sleep. We had a four-hour steam back to the first pot.

"Aren't you going to get any sleep before we start picking up the pots?" I asked him.

"It's more important for Tom to sleep so he can stay sharp. If he wakes up early, I may catch a few minutes."

He rubbed his tired eyes. These guys were professional, dedicated fishermen. Eric was running the boat after being on deck for thirty-six hours with no sleep. Their hard work made me feel useless.

It was dark outside when we approached the first pot. Tom mysteriously reappeared in the wheelhouse to take the helm.

Now began the grueling job of pulling up the pots. Eric went to the galley to eat dinner before heading on deck. Moments later, the first pot came into view. There were a few king crabs in it. Bait was replaced. The pot went back into the water. This process was repeated countless times.

The number of crabs in each pot steadily grew. This cycle went on for days. The tanks slowly filled. Once they reached their first quota, we went back to Dutch for an offload. The crab removal took several hours to complete.

"Hey guys, why don't you get a good night's sleep. We'll head out again in the morning." Tom announced to the delight of the crew. At six A.M. the next morning, we departed. Up until then the weather was good, but a low-pressure system was building.

"I hope we beat the weather to the strings." Tom confided to Eric. The pots soaked while we went back to Dutch. We all hoped they would have lots of crabs in them. On the way out to the fishing grounds, I decided to have a talk with our captain.

"Tom."

"Yeah, Li'l Sis'." The nickname always brought a smile to my face.

"There must be something more I can do to help out on the boat."

"You're doing fine."

"I noticed when you guys are resetting the pots, there is no one to get the bait ready. It slows you down." Tom looked at me.

"I can help get bait together."

"NO WAY," said a voice behind me. It was Eric. "There is no way you are going on deck. Period. If you fell overboard, it would be a death sentence because the water temperature is close to freezing. I couldn't handle that."

Tom shrugged, deferring to his brother. "The decision is made."

I had to drop it for now. The weather worsened the nearer we crept to the fishing grounds. Despite the building seas, pots came on the boat, pots left the boat. The crabs started to fill the tanks again.

When we were three-quarters full, the weather subsided, leaving behind a nasty swell. *Bang*! An eight hundred pound pot slipped out of the launcher, pinning Brett's arm to the table. He never even yelped in pain. After a few tense moments, Fred managed to lift the pot off with the crane.

Tom turned to me. "Get the trauma kit. Meet them in the ready room." Eric helped Brett off deck. The fishing ceased for now.

I made it there at the same time as the guys came off deck. Brett grimaced in pain. Eric worked his jacket off then checked his arm. It was bruising up already. Brett tried to move the arm.

"I don't think it's broken, just badly bruised," the deck boss said.

"Why don't you take a break for a while. Ice it down." Eric put the deck boss' arm in a sling. He laid his lanky body down on the seat at the galley table. I rushed to the freezer for a bag of frozen vegetables to put on the bruise.

"Thanks, Linda." He grimaced again. Tom came down from the wheelhouse to look at it.

"Dumb ass," the captain yelled at his old friend. "After all these years you are not smart enough to stay out from behind the sorting table." He punched Brett lightly on the shoulder before heading back to the helm.

The fishing resumed a man short. The time it took to cycle the pots increased dramatically. It was also the middle of the night. Tom drummed his fingers on the throttles. It was taking twice as long to haul the pots.

Going below to check on Brett, I discovered he was sound asleep, sitting at the galley table. I found a warm blanket to slip around him. On deck, the guys once again fell behind making bait.

It was three A.M. The guys moved around like zombies.

"Tom?"

"Yeah."

"There may be a way to speed up the deck. We can get this thing done." The big fisherman turned to look at me. We were only a few thousand pounds away from filling the boat for this last trip.

"I'll be right back." Going to the captain's stateroom, I returned with my iPod. There was nothing like a little rock and roll to liven things up. I turned on the stereo, set the iPod, then looked at our captain.

"Tom, hear me out before you say no. I can go on deck to make bait. This will speed up the process. I promise to stay in the bait corner and not move. One of the guys can come over to get it. They are obviously struggling without Brett." Tom slowed the boat down. He confronted me.

"Eric is going to kill me for agreeing with you. Listen and listen good. Put a life jacket on. DO NOT get behind the sorting table. Don't chop your hands off in the bait grinder. Make sure you keep both feet on the boat. Go straight to Eric. Tell him I said it was OK."

"Tom, thanks. Start the iPod when I get out there." Zipping down to the ready room, I donned a life jacket with foul weather gear. When I carefully opened the door, a cold blast of wind greeted me. I hustled over to the bait station. As I turned to look at the guys on deck, Eric pinned me to the wall of the forward superstructure.

"What the hell are you doing out here?"

"Tom told me to come out to help with the bait. He said to tell you he said it was OK."

"I don't give a damn what Tom said. Get the hell inside, now." He grabbed my arm, viciously thrusting me back toward the ready room.

"Eric, knock it off. Leave her alone. I told her to go on deck." Tom yelled at his brother over the loud hailer.

The younger brother's gesture to the captain was not well received. He pushed me a second time toward the ready room.

"I told you to get inside." Eric growled.

"Bro, don't make me go captain on you. I'll come down there and beat your ass. Then we'll be down two men. Let Linda prep the bait." Tom glared out the windscreen at his younger brother.

"Shit. Get over to the bait station. Grind the bait. I'll show you how to thread the fish on the hangers. We'll come to get it. I don't want you anywhere near the sorting table."

"OK." When I started grinding up bait, music streamed out of the iPod. The guys looked up at Tom in surprise.

"A little motivation, courtesy of Linda," Tom said over the intercom. The song "Rock and Roll Band" by Boston started playing. All the guys picked up their pace.

Eric showed me how to thread the cod on the hangers. Soon there were an abundance of bait setups ready. The speed on deck picked up as we rocked to "Come Sail Away" by Styx.

Even the younger brother seemed to relax. He came over to get a few bait setups as "Lady" by Styx began to play. He stopped for a moment. A slight smile crept around his lips.

An hour later, we finished resetting the pots. Eric sent me back inside.

"Go to the wheelhouse. Let Tom know you are off deck." Heading into the ready room, I stripped off the foulies and life jacket then went directly to the wheelhouse.

Our captain high-fived me as I walked in. "Great job, Li'l Sis. I'm sorry Eric was so pissed."

"Yeah, but he was better when I came in."

"*Ugh*," Tom teased me, holding his nose. "You smell like fish. You better do something about that."

We both laughed before I checked on Brett, who was awake but in pain. He looked at me. "Were you out on deck taking my place?"

"To say I was taking your place would be a huge compliment. No, I was just helping with bait."

"Thanks."

"No problem. We have to help each other out." I smiled, patting his good arm. After setting up a new pot of coffee, I went to the captain's stateroom for a shower. When I returned, Brett was getting ready to head back on deck. Dawn was breaking outside. The deck boss went out to relieve Eric. I greeted him with a cup of coffee.

"I thought I made it clear that I didn't want you on the deck." He was obviously still aggravated.

"I'm sorry if I upset you. I was just trying to help."

He looked at me for a minute before a smile broke out on his face. "The music was a good call." I breathed a sigh of relief.

Several hours later, the last trap came aboard. All the guys were jubilant as they came off deck. Tom set a course back to Dutch.

Eric joined Tom and me in the wheelhouse.

"Another successful king crab season, brother," Eric exclaimed happily. He turned to me. "What did you think of the trip?"

"It was great, but you guys work way too hard."

The crew took turns at the wheel for the twenty-four hour run back to Dutch. The next morning, Eric and I were having coffee in the galley when Tom came down from the wheelhouse.

"Linda, do you mind taking watch for a few minutes? I need to talk to Eric." He grabbed a coffee cup. Startled by this request, I glanced at our captain before heading upstairs.

It was way too cool sitting in the captain's chair. The autopilot steered back and forth. Ten minutes later, Tom relieved me.

"Thanks." I said.

"For what?" Tom gave me his tough-guy look.

"For trusting me on watch for a few minutes."

"You earned it." He turned back to chartplotter. I thought I saw a crinkle of a smile radiating to his eyes.

Later on that afternoon, we pulled into Dutch Harbor for the last offload of the season, a task that lasted well into the next morning. All hands pitched in to clean the boat before heading home for the Christmas holidays.

A preholiday party took place that evening at the Watering Hole. All the fishing crews were celebrating. There was a lot of talk about the upcoming opilio crab season. Eric and I finally went back to *Denali* about midnight.

Chapter 23. Back to Naples

The next morning Eric, Tom, and I bid goodbye to the crew as they caught an early flight out of Dutch Harbor. After lunch, we went to the airport for our flight. We were due to fly on a small, chartered turbo prop plane back to Seattle. The only problem was, I didn't realize how small.

As we walked onto the tarmac, I looked at the plane. Small was a huge understatement. When I stopped in my tracks, Eric must have sensed why I was uneasy.

"Linda, we're not going through this again, are we?" The tone of his voice was less than supportive.

"Eric, I'm not sure I can do this."

Tom took my hand, pulling me to the plane's steps. "It's OK, Li'l Sis. We fly these planes all the time. They're fun."

The copilot was doing his preflight check on the outside of the plane. He must have seen my reluctance.

"Hi, I'm Ed Peterson, the copilot. Is everything OK?" These pilots consider all the fishermen VIPs, due to the harshness of their work.

"Yeah, we're fine," Tom said. "We have a first time flier on these little planes. She's not fond of flying to begin with."

"You don't like my plane?" Ed asked me with a smile.

"No, its fine." I swallowed hard.

The copilot looked up at the sky. "The weather is good. It should be a pretty smooth flight."

Tom, Eric, and I climbed the steps into the plane. Eric and I sat together. Tom sat directly behind me. It felt as though I was in a coffin. I was not particularly claustrophobic, but I could feel panic coming on.

The flight attendant offered us a drink. She too must have heard the exchange with the copilot. Eric held my hand. The cocktail tasted great, but didn't calm me very much.

Eric turned to me, squeezing my hand. "You know, we can't stay in Dutch Harbor forever."

The plane taxied down the runway, taking off on the steepest climb out I'd ever experienced. Soon it leveled off. Ed came out of the cockpit to sit in the seat across from Eric.

"I just wanted to check on you guys. Are you OK?"

"I'm great." I tried to return his smile, but it was not very convincing. He eyed my death grip on Eric's hand.

"You guys have lots of opportunities to break your hands when fishing. I bet you don't expect to break one on the flight home."

Eric nodded at the copilot. "She's fine."

"OK. I wanted to let you know we're going to have turbulence when we fly over the mountains. Don't let it bother you." He turned for the cockpit.

"I'm sorry, Eric. I can't help it."

"In every other aspect you are one tough lady. Your fear of flying is kind of funny," he laughed. The turbulence over the mountains turned out not to be too bad. Soon we circled SeaTac Airport. As we deplaned, Eric shook the copilot's hand.

Tom rented a car then dropped us at the downtown Marriott. He was heading to Portland to meet up with a lady friend.

When we entered our room, I collapsed on the bed. Eric lay down next to me. Between the lack of sleep on the boat and the flying ordeal, I was exhausted.

He put his arms around me, pulling me close. For the first time that day, I felt relaxed.

Later at dinner, Eric's cell phone rang. I overheard part of the conversation. It sounded like Caroline. They spoke for a few minutes until he handed the phone to me.

"Hi, Caroline, Merry Christmas."

"Merry Christmas to you, Linda. Dad tells me you'll be here for Christmas Eve. I hope you'll come over to my place. I'm cooking dinner." Looking to Eric, I raised my eyebrows. He nodded his approval.

"We'd love to. What can we bring?"

"Just yourselves." I gave the phone back to Eric. He chatted for a few more moments before hanging up.

"Tom's going to be there," Eric said.

"That's wonderful. I was hoping to see him again before the holidays."

We spent the next couple of days enjoying Seattle with all its Christmas decorations. The raw, rainy weather didn't dampen our spirits. We window shopped for Christmas gifts for the girls.

Christmas Eve arrived. It was very cold and wet. We spent the early morning drinking coffee in bed while watching TV. My head rested against Eric's shoulder as he held me close.

I looked up at him. "Eric?"

"Yeah."

"I don't think I've had a happier Christmas Eve in a long time." He didn't reply. Instead he took my coffee cup from me, placing it on the night stand. He pulled me close. A long, hard kiss followed.

"Me neither." His voice was husky. For a moment my thoughts drifted to Joey and Jonathan Steele. We'd heard nothing from him since we came back from the fishing trip. I struggled to put them out of my thoughts. Instead, I concentrated on this man in bed with me.

We spent a nice day relaxing together. Around five in the evening, Kristen came by in her car to pick us up. She greeted her dad with a big hug, then smiled at me. The younger daughter even attempted a cursory hug.

As we drove to Caroline's place, Kristen and her dad caught up on news. Her job was going well. She'd even decided on a college, which would start next summer. Eric was very pleased.

We arrived at Caroline's apartment. It was beautifully decked out for the holidays. When we paused by her tree, I took her arm. "Caroline, it's lovely."

"Do you really think so, Linda?"

"Yes, I really think so, don't you Eric?" He put his arm around his daughter.

Being a man, he probably didn't care one way or another, but he answered correctly. "Not nearly as lovely as my daughter."

Caroline laughed as the doorbell rang. Eric and I took the bottle of wine we brought to the kitchen. Tom's voice boomed into the apartment. He hugged his two nieces while dropping gifts under the tree. The elder brother found his way into the kitchen, where hugs and greetings were exchanged.

The evening went well, but ended too soon. The elder brother offered to drive us to the airport for our red-eye flight to Naples. It was a good thing we'd had lots of practice not sleeping recently. We were due to meet Eva and Merlin in Naples for Christmas morning.

They were bringing their trawler up from Key West to stay at the Naples City Dock. As we arrived at the airport, Tom hugged me for a long time.

"I'm gonna miss you, Li'l Sis." Tears welled up in my eyes.

"Merry Christmas, Tom." Eric and I boarded the flight to Ft. Myers. He was soon sound asleep. Even I manage to catch a few zzz's.

We landed at Southwest International at five-thirty A.M. The warm Florida air was a welcome relief from the cold dampness of Seattle.

Eric drove to Naples. We stepped aboard *Dark & Stormy*. It was a bright, sunny Christmas Day. As we brought our stuff aboard, Eric took a moment to pull me close. "Merry Christmas, Linda."

"Merry Christmas, Eric."

Capt. Marlena Brackebusch

"It's nice to be in the warm weather again." We were in the middle of unpacking when my cell phone rang. Eva's number flashed on the Caller ID screen.

"Merry Christmas, Linda. Merlin and I were walking the dogs when we saw you two get on the boat."

"Merry Christmas, Eva. Where are you?"

"We are at the beginning of the City Dock."

"We'll be right there," I replied, hanging up the phone. "No rest for the wicked," I said to Eric.

We met my sister and her husband where the dock started. Hugs were exchanged.

The two poodles jumped and barked excitedly. They wore Christmas bandanas. On the way to their trawler, we waved to Captain Marlene, the assistant dock master. We exchanged a hug with a "Merry Christmas." Arriving at Eva and Merlin's trawler, we admired all their decorations, including a big snowman on the flybridge.

We put the dogs back aboard then went to the Cove Inn coffee shop for breakfast. We enjoyed their famous pancakes and fabulous hot coffee while catching up on events.

"How was your weather up in the Bering Sea?" Merlin asked. Eric deferred to me.

"We had one low pressure system come through when we were fishing, but it wasn't too bad."

"How big were the waves?" Eva asked.

Eric answered. "The worst ones were about thirty foot. No big deal."

There was a couple at the adjoining table. The man turned toward Eric. He tapped the fishing captain on the arm.

"I'm sorry to interrupt you. I don't normally eavesdrop, but did you say you were in thirty-foot waves and they were no big deal?"

"Yes. That's about normal where we fish." The man shook his head, turning back to his breakfast.

We spent the remainder of the day relaxing with Eva and Merlin. Our host grilled nice rib-eye steaks for Christmas dinner. We spent the rest of the evening on the flybridge.

"What are your plans from here?" Eva asked after dinner.

"We are going to relax a few days here. I really need to soak up the sunshine. Opie season starts in a week's time. How about you two? How long will you be in town?" Eric asked

"A couple of days," said Merlin. "Then I have to get back to work at Mallory Square."

The evening grew late. Eric and I headed back to *Dark & Stormy*. As we stepped aboard, Eric's cell phone rang.

"Hold on a second Jonathan, I want to put you on speaker phone." Eric switched the phone over. "Go ahead."

"Merry Christmas, you two. I wanted to let you know I am investigating this Joey thing. Though I don't have any firm leads, there are plenty of rumors drifting around. My team is checking further."

We both slept pretty well, but I tossed and turned thinking about Joey. Where the heck was he?

A beautiful dawn greeted us. I leaned out of the companionway to admire the beautiful morning. A light east wind ruffled the water behind my boat.

"Why don't we take a stroll to the beach, Linda."

"Great idea." Once at the pier, we watched pelicans dive on a school of bait fish.

"They're so prehistoric." Eric grinned as a pair of dolphins cruised by, much to the delight of the tourists. An old man helped his grandson put a wiggling shrimp on a small hook. We held hands, simply enjoying the peaceful morning.

Back at the Cove Inn, we ran into Shane.

"This week looks real busy," he began. "I divvied up most of the charters among the other guys. Here's a list for you two to cover."

"We'll take care of it," I assured him.

Back at *Dark & Stormy*, I turned to Eric. "You don't have to come with me on the charters if you don't want to."

"I would like to help you. You helped with the ranch and fishing, didn't you?" I nodded.

Where did I find this man? Over the next few days many charters were completed. The rest of the time was spent on the beach.

On New Years Eve, we decided to join the festivities at the Cove Inn. Cocktails, music, and great conversation flowed around us.

Jan, one of the bartenders, grabbed Eric's arm. "Now I know who you are. I've been trying to figure it out since the first time you were here. You're the fishing captain from the TV Show. On *Denali*."

"Busted," Eric grinned.

"I didn't know we had a celebrity at our bar."

Captain George shook hands with Eric. "It must be amazing fishing up there, but way too cold."

"Ask Linda. We just finished fishing for king crab." Trying to deflect attention away from Eric, I tried to change the subject.

Midnight arrived. We were hanging out at the railing, overlooking the bay. Horns sounded from the yachts nearby. Stars twinkled overhead. Eric embraced me. After a prolonged kiss he wished me a Happy New Year.

"Happy New Year to you, Eric." I smiled happily. A strange feeling washed over me. I had the feeling it would not be such a happy New Year.

Shaking off the bad vibes, I led Eric back to the boat.

The next morning he was up early, as usual. After dragging myself out of bed, I joined him for a cup of hot joe at the galley table.

"Too much partying last night?" Eric asked.

"No, it's too early this morning." I tried to gather up a smile.

"What shall we do today, my lady?" Fortunately, Shane was running the charter boat.

"It's supposed to be a nice warm day. Why don't we take this boat out for a spin, Eric?"

"You know, Linda, every once in a while you have a really great idea. I would love to go sailing."

Capt. Marlena Brackebusch

My cell phone rang. "It's Mitch."

"Hi, Linda." His voice came through the speaker phone. "Happy New Year. I wanted to let you know I was speaking with Senior Chief Miller yesterday."

My hopes rose. "What did he say?"

"He told me a TV producer you know, Jonathan Steele, was looking into a rumor. There is a story going around saying someone was rescued from a life raft close to the time when you lost *Wind Rose*. Chief Miller did an investigation and believes the rumor to be false."

"I see."

"Linda, the Coast Guard has no knowledge of any drug boats or pirates in the area." He laughed softly. "I think it was someone with a good imagination. I'm sorry."

"Thanks, Mitch. I appreciate the call."

Eric reached out to me. "It seemed pretty farfetched to begin with."

"Yes it did." I chewed on my lip, deep in thought. Then my eyes brightened. "Come on Eric, let's go sailing."

After breakfast we checked the engine fluids, fired up the engine, then puttered down Naples Bay. We left the sand bars of Gordon Pass behind.

The Gulf was a gorgeous aquamarine. After Eric pulled off his shirt, I enjoyed the view as he hauled the sparkling white mainsail skyward. Ten knots of southerly wind filled the canvass, driving my little sloop into the vast Gulf.

"Do you want me to get the jib, Linda?"

"Thanks. It will give me another opportunity to enjoy the view of your muscles." Eric stared back at my innocent smile.

Light chop lulled the yacht into an easy sway. Bright, sunny skies were much appreciated after the gray dampness of Seattle and Alaska. The autopilot whirred away as we crept out of sight of land.

We could have been the only boat on the vast sea. There was no traffic offshore, despite the large number of boats I knew were out here. Only a cursory glance around us disturbed the quiet enjoyment of the day.

"This sure beats the Bering Sea." I watched him relax. I was so happy he'd come into my life. Thoughts of Joey popped up for a second, but his memory was thrust a little further back in my subconscious. The relationship with Joey seemed so long ago. Decisions about the fisherman and my future needed to be made very soon.

After a couple of hours, we enjoyed lunch in the sunshine. I slipped below to add music to the mix. Back on deck, I intentionally sat close to the fisherman.

"What?" He shifted slightly to pull his arm around me.

"I didn't say anything."

"Are we going through that again?"

"Going through what?" I made a poor attempt to hide my cagey smile.

"You couldn't sit much closer unless you were in my lap." His face broke into a grin.

"An interesting proposition." My smile went from cagey to enticing.

"Really. Are you ready to find out what a hot lover I am?"

"Get a grip, Eric." I reached up, dragging his head close so I could whisper in his ear. "I'm getting close."

"You're such a tease," he laughed, pushing me away. The previous song faded away. "Lady" by Styx replaced it.

"Our song." He smiled before dragging me back against him. His kiss nearly knocked me out. Damn. It still felt too weird on this boat, where so many memories of Joey haunted me.

As our favorite song played, Eric's hands began a journey of exploration. He eased me onto the cockpit cushion. I eagerly responded to his touch until a vision of Joey's grimacing face floated up from my subconscious.

"Eric, I can't." I pushed the fisherman away. "Not on this boat."

He opened his eyes, which flashed with frustration. A moment later, he hoisted himself off me. After glancing at the sea astern of us, he turned on me.

"You can't do it on this boat. You can't do it in the hotel. You can't do it at the ranch. Linda, where the hell can you have sex with me?" Anger crossed his face. I felt some of the old intimidation often felt with Joey.

"Do you want to tell me why you came on to me? Now, you push me away. I thought I told you in Dallas how frustrated I was. You keep sending me mixed signals. I'm almost beginning to feel a little used."

"Eric, I'm sorry. I really want you. It's just this boat..."

"Linda." He cut me off. "I really don't want to hear any more excuses. Since I'm flying back to Dutch tomorrow, I thought we could advance our relationship before I leave. Give me something to look forward to when I return."

"Wait a minute, Eric. You're leaving tomorrow? Since when? You never told me this before."

"Opilio crab season starts in a week's time. I need time to get the boat ready."

"You're leaving just like that? You didn't even ask me whether or not I wanted to go."

"That's because you are not going."

"We didn't even discuss this."

"There is nothing to discuss. It's too dangerous. You're not going."

Memories of Joey's domineering attitude drifted into my psyche. Eric was beginning to sound just like him.

"I can't believe you made this decision without consulting me. I don't give a damn about going fishing aboard your stupid boat, but I'm not about to allow you to make an important decision about our relationship without first consulting me."

"Seems like you've made many important decisions about...our so called relationship...without me. For instance, maybe I should turn Eric on again then slam the door in his face."

"Eric, this isn't all about sex."

"Linda, you are absolutely correct. But sex is a big part of it. We've been in the same bed for months. I think I've been incredibly patient with you."

"I'm so sorry I've disappointed you, captain crab man. Maybe it would be better for you to leave. I don't want to talk about this anymore."

"Fine. I'll sit on the bow." The ride back to port was shrouded in tension. Only a few words were said as we tied the boat back up in her slip.

"Maybe it would best if I got a room in the hotel."

"Eric."

"Linda, I need some time to think. Being near you is too much of a temptation. I don't want to be disappointed again. Why don't we chat tomorrow morning."

After a sleepless night, a knock on the boat roused me from bed. Eric poked his head in.

"Can I come aboard?"

"Yes."

"I have a couple of hours until my flight leaves. I thought we could talk."

"I don't get it, Eric."

"Do you remember the story I told you? When I lost my greenhorn over the side?"

"Yes."

"I can't take that chance with you."

"But, Eric, you didn't even discuss this with me."

"I didn't want you to try to talk me out of my decision."

"Eric, I know it's dangerous, but you guys are very careful. I promise to stay inside if that's what you want."

"Linda, I don't want to talk about this anymore. That's the end of the discussion."

"I didn't realize we discussed this at all."

"Linda, it's too dangerous. Every year we lose a boat or two out there. Some of the guys don't come back. You're not going. I've made my decision." The tone of his voice grew louder.

I looked at him in disbelief and shock. He'd never acted this way before. It was definitely out of character for him.

"Eric, does this have to do with my going on deck to help with the bait?"

He eyes narrowed. "No. Risking my life for crabs is an acceptable risk. Risking your life is not. Remember, after saving your life, I'm responsible for you. It's my decision."

It took a tremendous effort to not scream at this man. "Eric, my understanding of a relationship is two people make decisions together after discussing things. No one person makes a mandate. I went through that with Joey. I can't go through that with you."

"Linda, I've made my decision. You are NOT going, period. We could discuss this all day, but it's not going to change my mind." Red flared on his cheeks. He was obviously getting upset.

"Look, I don't want you to question my judgment on this. I am not going to put you in a position where you can get hurt. I don't want any further discussion."

"YOU don't want to discuss this so you just book a flight out and not even tell me. What the hell, Eric?"

"Linda, I didn't want to get you upset."

"Well, I'm upset now."

He paused a moment before speaking in a quiet voice. "I'll see you when I get back."

I clamped my mouth shut while trying to figure out what the hell to do. I really didn't care about going on the boat during the severe weather of opie fishing season. I would worry like hell about him, but I could deal with that.

What I couldn't and wouldn't deal with was him ordering me around. I was not getting into another relationship with a domineering man. He seemed so different. Now he was acting just like Joey.

"I don't think so," I whispered.

"What do you mean?" Eric asked warily.

"I can't have a relationship with a man who won't consider my opinion. Damn, Eric, you're not even listening to me now. If you leave like this, don't bother coming back."

"Is that how you really feel?"

I nodded my head yes. He looked at me for a long moment.

"I need to pack the rest of my stuff." With a shake of his head, he went to the V-berth.

While watching him stuff his clothes in his duffel bag, I thought back on all the things we'd been through together, from the rescue to his gentle care as I struggled with the pain of the recovery. There were endless days of searching for Joey. A wistful smile swirled through my brain as I remembered the fun we'd had riding around the ranch.

I recalled how cute he was when wiping the sweat off his brow after vaccinating the calves. The horse race in Dallas was an awesome weekend. Even meeting his daughters turned out fine.

Then there was our time spent bringing *Denali* to Dutch Harbor, not to mention the exciting crab fishing. It had all culminated in our last wonderful week here in Naples. I was falling in love with this man. Until Joey's specter destroyed the moment. Could it really be over?

As I finished these thoughts, Eric walked to the companionway. He stood frozen for a moment.

"Linda, I'm sorry you don't understand."

One last look was cast in my direction. His head shook. His face was a sea of pain.

Very slowly he pushed the companionway doors open then stepped onto the deck. I couldn't even look at him.

Through the porthole, I watched him jump to the finger pier then slowly walk up the dock.

I had a piercing desire to run to him. Throw my arms around him. Then everything would be fine.

I rushed on deck. My eyes followed his stride toward the breezeway. He didn't even look back. Tears streamed down my face as I watched him disappear from my life.

Capt. Marlena Brackebusch

Scenes from *Treacherous Voyage*

My feet were propped up on the port settee, in the cabin of *Dark & Stormy*. A nearly empty coffee cup sat next to my elbow. The grinning smiley face on the yellow mug made me want to pitch it overboard, or maybe chuck it at Eric.

Nearly a month had past since he stormed off this boat, ending out growing friendship. I was two for two with men last year. First, I lost Joey when the yacht sank. Then I lost Eric to a stupid fight.

It's so damn hard, but I'll fight through this mess like I've fought through all the other hard times in my forty-five years of life, I thought.

To take my mind off men, I've spent the last month working on my boat, varnishing the wood and polishing the fiberglass. During a short lunch break, I was sitting below. A fluffy pillow was propped behind my back, but I was still uncomfortable.

My eyes scanned the bank statement. Two stupid little pennies evaded my perfect checking account balance. The phone rang. I recognized the Alaskan area code, but not the phone number. It wasn't Eric's. This didn't surprise me. He had no reason to call.

The voice mail beeped. The heck with it, I was not interested in talking with anyone from Alaska. Not five minutes later the phone rang again. The same phone number, followed by another voice mail, which I ignored a second time. Then I thought, what if something happened to Eric? "Give it up, Linda. It's not your concern anymore."

Several days ago, there was another tough day aboard *Denali*. Eric sat in the captain's chair in a dreadful funk. It was three A.M. A blizzard caused a near white out as the wind peaked at sixty knots.

"Watch it, big wave, Eric said to the crew over the loud hailer. He watched a huge roller crash across the deck, washing the fisherman around like toys in a bath tub.

"Damn," he muttered under his breath. The fishing captain kneaded his brow with his fist in an attempt to scrub her image from his exhausted brain.

Every cell of his gray matter was required to focus completely since he had been at the helm for forty hours in this miserable tempest.

After the nasty confrontation aboard the crab boat, Tom glared at his younger brother.

"Eric, we need to talk." Tom tested Eric's mood. "You need to come to grips with this Linda thing. If it's over, you need to put her behind you. If it's not, you need to talk to her, bro." The elder brother gripped his sibling's shoulder.

"Tell me what happened, maybe I can help."

Sitting in the dusty Barracuda Bar, Jonathan Steele wiped a bead of sweat from his brow. The steamy, tropical heat was nearly unbearable. The TV man tried hard not to look like the gringo he was. Worn, wrinkled blue jeans and an old T-shirt still made him look out-of-place.

A black ball cap sat askew on his head, covering his uncombed hair. He sipped his Carib beer slowly.

The guy with the scratchy, menacing voice should meet him at any moment. He was the same guy who Jonathan spoke with on the motel's phone a mere hour ago.

"I know what happened to the gringo you look for."

Jonathan shifted his position on the bar stool. He tried to look tough, but not too tough. He wasn't looking for a fight. The ace reporter was digging for information.

On the other side of the bar sat two other gringos. They surrounded a filthy, scratched table. The former Marine, Jake Hammond, doodled a carving on the marred table top with his pocket knife.

"I hope this wasn't a friggin' waste of time, coming down to this steamy hell hole."

His attention was focused on all the seedy characters inside the bar.

A week ago, Jonathan had organized this expedition to Port of Spain, Trinidad. The trio flew on a private jet to this southern Caribbean locale.

"We'll head down to follow up on a rumor I heard. A drug smuggling boat picked up a guy out of a liferaft, off the Carolinas. This happened shortly after the sinking of *Wind Rose*," Jonathan told Jake over the phone last week. "The boat might be docked in Trinidad."

Author Biography

Capt. Marlena Brackebusch grew up in New Jersey and started sailing small dinghy sailboats at the age of seven. After being away from the sea for several years, she resumed sailing in Boston during college. She taught sailing for U-Mass-Boston, as well as several renowned sailing schools around the East Coast of the U.S. and the Caribbean. During the late 1980s and early '90s, she and a friend completed a four-year world circumnavigation aboard their thirty-one-foot sailing yacht. Since then, she has been teaching sailing for the American Sailing Association, delivering yachts all over the world, and chartering boats in Naples, Florida. She now resides in Naples, where she is owner of Island Sailing, a company dedicated to providing fun sailing adventures. She is a U.S. Coast Guard Licensed Master Mariner, an American Sailing Association Sailing Instructor, and a PADI Certified Scuba Diver.

Made in the USA
Charleston, SC
04 April 2014